ON THE OFFENSIVE

A RYAN KAINE NOVEL

KERRY J DONOVAN

The right of Kerry J Donovan to be identified as the Author of this work has been asserted in accordance with the Copyright, Designs, and Patents Act, 1988.

©Kerry J Donovan, July 2023

All rights reserved. No part of this novel may be reproduced or transmitted in any form or by any means, electronic or mechanical, including photocopying, recording, or any information storage and retrieval system without prior written permission of the Author and without similar conditions including this condition being imposed on any subsequent purchaser. Your support for the Author's rights is appreciated.

All major characters in this work are fictitious. Any resemblance to actual persons, living or dead, is purely coincidental.

Edited by Nicole O'Brien
This book uses UK English, grammar, and punctuation.

My heartfelt thanks go to Ed Van Den Berg for all his help and encouragement. Thanks, mate.

ON THE OFFENSIVE
"BY STRENGTH AND GUILE"

1

Tuesday 30th May – Micah Williams

Toulouse-Matabiau Station, Toulouse, France

Don't look back.

Micah repeated the same three words in his head, over and over. His mantra. For Molly. He could do this for Molly. He had to.

Body drenched in sweat, stomach clenching, he'd already puked into a gutter once since leaving the German's grubby apartment. It hadn't helped. Left a bitter taste in his mouth. He needed water, but couldn't spare the time to buy one. The scorching sun beat down on his head and shoulders, merciless. The head insufferable.

Don't look back.

No point in looking back. How could he spot them even if they *were* following him. What would the evil bastards look like, anyway? So many people. All total strangers. They could be anywhere. Everywhere.

Don't look back.

Despite the words and the intention, Micah glanced over his shoulder. Couldn't help himself. The pull was too strong. Dozens, no, hundreds of people thronged the station's concourse. Any one of them could be watching him drag his wheeled suitcase over the shiny tiles and into the station. Any one of them.

Oh God.

The elderly Frenchman leaning against the support column, sucking on the roll-up cigarette. Did he just sneer at Micah through half-closed eyes? No. The smoke had stung his eyes. The stinging blue smoke. Nothing more.

The station announcer's garbled message boomed through the station, the echo and language making it unintelligible.

The woman in the headscarf. Did they call it a hijab? A burqa? Was she looking at him through those dark eyes? With most of her face hidden by the headgear, he couldn't tell what she saw, what she thought, what she looked like. Couldn't tell her intentions. Which was the whole point of the hijab-burqa. The woman bent, picked up a small child from a bench, and balanced him on her hip. Pulling her own wheeled case behind her like a small animal on a lead, she manoeuvred her way through the crowd, heading towards the platforms.

Micah swallowed. Definitely not. She wasn't one of *them*.

What about the middle-aged couple in the loud clothes surrounded by suitcases? Were they paying him undue attention?

Stop it, Micah.

That's what paranoia led to. Everyone became the enemy even if they were innocent.

Another passenger—a middle-aged man in a flowery shirt and blue, knee-length shorts—glanced away as Micah caught his eye. Suspicious or shy?

Pack it in. You'll never know. You'll never see them watching.

A family—father, mother, and two blonde-haired girls—bustled past on their way from the platforms towards the taxi rank he'd left behind him. The smaller of the girls dropped her doll and bawled as the family continued on their way, oblivious to the disaster. Mother turned, stopped the troop, picked up doll and daughter, and they continued on their way, catastrophe averted.

Micah gritted his teeth. Molly needed him to follow the instructions to the letter.

Don't look back.

The handle of his case slipped in his sweaty fist. Could he go through with it? What had they slipped into his case? The sealed tin of talcum powder tucked in the toiletry bag amongst his T-shirts and his underwear looked innocuous enough, inconspicuous, but Micah knew better. Why go to all the trouble of coercing him into taking it for a simple tin of talc? No, it had to be more sinister than talc. In his fist, it seemed to weigh far more than the 500 grams the label claimed. Far more.

Drugs probably. Not that Micah would ever open it to find out. That much curiosity would lead to disaster. He had to act natural. Calm. Innocent.

Shit.

How calm and innocent could he look when he was sweating so much? Micah caught sight of his reflection in the station's grey windows. God, he looked rough. Creased shirt, hooded top with the zip at half mast, baggy shorts, trainers—no socks. Sunken, haunted eyes stared out from an unshaved face. His hair, dank and lifeless, screamed, "Look at me, I'm a drug smuggler!"

Pity's sake, Micah! Pack it in.

He looked no worse than any of the hundreds of hot and weary travellers wandering through the concourse. Who could remain cool on such a scorching, steaming day? No. He didn't stand out. He looked no more suspicious than anyone else.

Did he?

Micah swallowed the rancid, viscous spit and breathed deep. He could do this. Molly needed him to be strong. She was depending on him.

You can do this.

He pulled back his shoulders and marched through the main

entrance. There. Out of the burning sun and into the cool, shaded confines of the massive stone-and-tinted-glass building. Blinking against the gloom, he stood and shivered in his damp shirt. The shivering had little to do with the sudden drop in temperature.

Don't look back.

Another distorted announcement boomed through the cool air. With precious little understanding of French, he had no idea what the woman had said. Hopeless.

The electronic arrivals and departures board stretched out overhead, displaying hundreds of names and a dozen platforms. So bloody confusing. Despite the vaulted roof, lack of litter, and missing graffiti, the place reminded him of every UK railway station he'd ever been through. It smelled of decades-old dust, concrete, and decay.

Where to?

Micah reread the note the man with the scar over his eye had stuffed into his sweaty fist before dropping him off at the station. The note, half an A4 sheet printed on an inkjet, contained nothing but an address in London. How in the hell was he going to find his way to London from the depths of Toulouse? Eurostar or the cross-channel ferry? Which route would get him to London faster?

He searched the concourse area for a queue, and found one leading to a row of ticket machines. No signs of a ticket office or an information desk.

Bloody hell!

He'd have to wing it. How difficult could it be to buy a train ticket to England from France? He had no idea. Never done it before. He and Molly usually drove everywhere.

Micah joined the back of the fast-moving line and, after a wait where he did nothing but study his shuffling, dirt-encrusted trainers, eventually found himself in front of a modern electronic ticket machine. Mercifully, the welcome screen allowed him to select his preferred language and he tapped the area of the touch screen displaying the Union Flag in huge relief.

The process turned out to be far easier than he believed possible. Toulouse to London via Paris with a change at Paris Montparnasse to

Gare du Nord, and then straight through to London's St Pancras International. All being well, the eleven-hour journey—including transfers—meant he'd reach London by early evening, UK time.

A sliver of hope ran through him. Maybe he *could* do this.

Micah slid his bank card into the slot and punched in his PIN. He didn't even look at the cost of the one-way ticket. He'd have paid anything. He'd have paid the earth to save them. What good would all the money in the world do him if he lost Molly and ... and ... his whole world.

God. Don't go there, Micah. Don't go there.

The machine disgorged his ticket, a long, grey card with a detailed itinerary which included station names, platform numbers, and a QR code at the bottom.

Simplicity itself.

He stepped away from the machine, read the ticket, and found the designated platform on the departures board. He had thirty minutes to kill.

No. Stop that.

Why use that word? He had thirty minutes to *wait*.

Wait, not *kill*.

The mobile phone vibrated in his jeans pocket. He fumbled it free and read the caller ID, *Molly*. The evil bastards were using his wife's phone. Micah hit the green button and pressed the phone to his ear.

"Y-Yes?" he answered, his voice weak, terrified. He cleared his throat and repeated, "Yes?" This time he sounded stronger, more in control.

Control he didn't feel.

"Well done, *Micah*," Luc growled, his German accent thick, his voice a throaty rumble. "You now have your ticket and your travel itinerary. Your train awaits. Have a safe journey."

He knew.

The evil bastard *did* have people watching him.

Micah searched the concourse for anyone with a phone clamped to their ear. Couldn't help himself. Hundreds of passengers filled the station, many walked head down, concentrating on their phones rather than looking where they were going. Travellers sitting on benches or seated outside concession stalls also worked their mobile phones. None of them seemed to be looking in Micah's direction.

"Do not bother looking, *Micah*," Luc growled. "You will not find us. What time do you reach London?"

Luc didn't know. He hadn't been close enough to read the ticket machine. It meant he could be watching from anywhere in the station. Or someone else could be watching and relaying Micah's movements to him. It was hopeless.

"What time!" Luc repeated, increasing his volume to a near-shout.

Micah consulted the ticket and gave Luc his answer.

"Very good. My people will be waiting for you at the address in London," Luc said, reverting to his usual deep growl. "Do not keep them waiting. You know the consequences."

Micah took a breath. He had to take the risk.

"Will you let me speak to my wife?" Micah begged.

A deep rumble coughed down the phone line. Luc's version of a laugh. A heavy smoker's laugh.

"Say please," the evil bastard demanded.

"Please," Micah snapped. "I need to know she's okay."

"Very well, *Micah*. Since you asked so nicely. Wait."

The ensuing drawn-out silence cut thin slices through Micah's heart. All around him, the station bustled with normal life. A train's horn tooted its arrival, brakes screeched, and metal wheels clanked.

"Micah?" Molly asked, her voice timid, tearful.

Micah fought back his tears of fear and rage. He had to stay strong. Strong for Molly. Strong for them both.

"Yes, love. Are you okay?"

"I-I am." She didn't sound it.

"Have they hurt you?"

"No, no," she said, rushing the words. "They haven't touched me, but ..." Her words trailed into silence.

"But? What is it, love? What are they doing?"

"They're saying things. Horrible things. Threatening me. Threatening us." She broke down, her cries shredding Micah's innards.

"Stay strong, Molly. I can do this."

"Do as they say, Micah," Molly cried. "Please do what they say. And you must *trust* in the Lord. Remember that. We need to place our *trust* in God. He will see us through this. Pray to him. It's what Dad would have done."

Trust in God? Where's God in this?

"I will, love. I will. Be strong. I love you so much."

"Love you—"

Her words cut off mid-sentence and she yelped.

"Molly!"

"That is enough," Luc said, seething menace. "You have your instructions. Carry them out and we will reunite you with your wife. Fail us and she dies. Do I make myself clear?"

"Yes, yes," Micah said, desperately trying not to scream the words. "I'll do everything you say, but please don't hurt her."

The phone clicked and an ominous silence boomed through Micah's head.

"Hello?" he shouted. "Hello!"

Micah pulled the mobile from his ear and stared at the blank screen. He wanted nothing more than to redial the number and talk to Molly again, to hear her voice, to comfort her. But he couldn't risk it. No telling what Luc would do to her if he did call. While Luc held Molly, Micah was powerless. He could do nothing but follow their instructions and pray for a miracle.

A miracle.

Fat bloody chance.

Trust in God? Where the hell had that come from? Molly didn't even go to church, not since her dad's funeral.

Micah raised his head to the vaulted roof, desperate to hold back the tears that threatened to roll down his cheeks.

The bastards.

They'd probably kill Molly the moment he'd completed his task —assuming he made it through customs without being searched and caught. They'd probably kill him, too. Once he'd delivered the package he'd be of no further use to them, and neither would Molly. What would stop them? Nothing.

They would die, but what choice did he have?

He couldn't go to the police. Not a chance. Luc said they had the local police in their pockets. A lie, probably, but Micah couldn't take the risk. He knew nothing about the French police, except that they were routinely armed. The gendarmes he'd seen swaggered around the country, confident and superior. Nothing like the good old British Bobby.

Something tapped his shoulder. He jumped and jerked around, heart in his throat. A short, sixty-something woman looked up at him, concern written over her deeply tanned and heavily wrinkled face. She said something he couldn't understand.

"Excuse me?" he gasped.

"Ah," she said, smiling. "You are English?"

He nodded, swiping the tears from his eyes.

"Are you okay, *monsieur*?"

Micah nodded. "It's just that I hate saying goodbye."

The old dear smiled. "*Ah oui, je suis d'accord.* I understand, *monsieur*. But do as you are told, and all will be well. Molly will be returned to you." She dropped the smile and stared pointedly at him. Then she turned and strolled away before he could respond.

One of them.

Micah nearly collapsed.

2

Tuesday 30th May – Micah Williams

St Pancras International Station, London, UK

With his heart racing—it had been thumping hard since he'd left France and entered the UK—Micah stepped from the Eurostar train onto the platform. Again, the eyes of the world seemed to be focusing on him and his wheeled suitcase.

Don't look back. Don't look scared. Keep your head up. Look relaxed. Look normal.

He headed for the ticket barriers at the end of the platform, where he scanned his QR code and gained entry to the station concourse.

Despite his fears, the journey through France had passed without incident. Even border control at Paris Gare du Nord had been a simple case of strolling, almost breathless, through the European Citizens Green Lane—*Nothing to Declare*—and boarding the Eurostar.

Micah couldn't believe it. It had been a seamless entry into the UK. He would have sworn that the eye of every border guard had been drilling into the back of his neck the whole way through the quarter-mile parade, but no one stopped him. Molly once said he had one of those innocent faces that people naturally trusted. Perhaps that was why Luc had targeted them in the first place.

Head held high, he hurried through the concourse, carrying his dark suitcase and dodging in and out of the slow-moving throng. He reached the taxi rank in a much cooler station forecourt than the one he'd left behind in Toulouse, and stood in line, shivering the whole time. Again, the shivering had little to do with the early-evening temperature.

Finally, he reached the head of the queue and stepped up to the waiting black cab.

"Where to, guv?" the cabbie asked, a heavy-set, balding man in his mid-fifties.

Micah recited the address he'd memorised from the note Luc had given him.

"How long will it take?" he asked.

"This time o' night it'll be 'bout thirty minutes, guv. Cost you around twenty quid. Okay?"

"Yeah, that's fine."

The cabbie shot him a sideways look. "Didn't just come in on the Eurostar, did ya?"

"As a matter of fact—"

"You got any pounds sterling on ya?"

Micah frowned in thought. "No, I've only got euros. Can I pay by card?" He reached into his pocket, removed his wallet, and picked out his bank card.

The cabbie snorted through a smile. "If I 'ad a fiver for 'ow many times a fare told me that, I could've retired by now. There's a card reader in the passenger compartment. Contactless?"

"Yep."

"That'll work. 'Op in then, guv. Time's money," the chirpy cabbie said and added a wink.

Micah slid into the back seat and strapped himself in. The cabbie started the meter and nosed the black cab into the slow-moving traffic on Midland Road. They turned left onto Euston Road, and Micah stared out through the window, watching London roll past in a slow blur. Shops, pubs, office blocks, and small green spaces passed by almost unnoticed.

Ten minutes into the ride, while stopped at yet another set of traffic lights, the cabbie slid open the privacy panel.

"What me dad would've given for one of them things," he said.

"Sorry?" Micah didn't want to engage in conversation, but he didn't want to appear rude, either. Rudeness would have drawn attention to him. The last thing Micah wanted was to draw any attention onto himself.

"One o' them there card readers," the cabbie said, pointing over his shoulder towards the small grey machine attached to the door column. "Back in the day, before the ciggies took 'im way too early, me dad were a cabbie, too. You could call it the family business. The ol' man 'ated 'andling so much cash. Tallying up at the end of a shift were a nightmare, he reckoned. Dangerous, too. 'Andling all that cash, I mean."

The lights turned green. They rolled forwards and slowly picked up speed.

"Contactless payments, eh?" he said into the rear-view mirror, smiling. "Who'd have thought? Magic."

"Yeah," Micah said, "magic." He couldn't think of anything more to add.

Micah couldn't have cared less about the cabbie's dad. All he cared about was making the delivery and reuniting with Molly. The breath caught in his throat, and he tried not to think about what she'd been going through for the past day and a half. To mention her dad like she'd done on the phone showed how terrified she must have been. They hardly ever talked about the poor man these days. Far too painful. To have had his life snatched away by a madman, and him being so close to retirement.

Two months.

Two bloody months and he'd have been able to hang up his wings and retire to the country to tend his garden and take his campervan on short breaks in the British countryside. Two months and he'd never have taken to the skies again.

A criminal shame.

Killed by Ryan Kaine and his surface-to-air missile. What a waste of a life. A waste of so many lives. Heart breaking.

To take his mind off the tragedy, Micah glanced through the window, surprised to see so much greenery in the middle of the UK's capital city. Huge trees lined either side of the road, their canopy arching out over the traffic—reaching towards each other, trying to link arms. He'd read about them somewhere. London plane trees, planted by the Victorians to act as the lungs of the city.

Three large tower blocks climbed into the blue-grey sky, dwarfing the surrounding buildings. Micah caught sight of a sign, 250 City Road, London EC1. Born and bred in Blackburn, he had no idea where they were.

"You 'ere on 'oliday, guv?" Cabbie asked, still ever-so-cheery.

"No," Micah answered, reluctant to start up a conversation, but just as reluctant to appear rude. "Overnight visit. Then straight back to France."

I hope to God.

Cabbie nodded. He threw a thumbs up and shouted, "Whatcha, Beaky!" to the driver of another black cab passing them in the opposite direction. Beaky waved back and shouted something Micah couldn't catch.

"Cheeky so-and-so," Cabbie said, laughing.

He fell quiet, and they trundled along at little more than walking pace for a few minutes until they picked up another bus lane. The minutes passed in a tense silence.

"Won't be long now, guv," the cabbie said. "Traffic's worse'n I expected. Oh, an' that's Moorfields Eye 'ospital, by the way."

He pointed to a stocky grey-stone-and-red-brick edifice on their right.

"A sight for sore eyes, that place, eh?" He cackled at a joke he must have told a million times.

Micah tried to smile, but couldn't summon up the energy when he was a heartbeat away from bursting into tears of impotent rage. They swung a left, filtered into another bus lane, and their speed increased. After less than a mile, the bus lane petered out and they slowed again. Micah clenched his fists. He'd never felt so helpless in his life.

"You okay, guv?" the cabbie said into the rear-view. "Look a bit peaky."

"Been a long trip," he managed. "I haven't slept for nearly two days."

"Yeah," the cabbie said, nodding. "That lack of sleep's a real 'mare, eh? Still, you'll be 'ome soon. Able to put your feet up and chill."

If only.

"Hope so," Micah said, finally managing a weak smile.

If only he knew.

Micah expected this to be his first and last trip to London, and probably his first and last trip in a black cab. Once again, he fought back the helpless, angry tears.

3

Tuesday 30th May – Early Afternoon

Mike's Farm, Long Buckby, Northants, UK

Ryan Kaine dialled the number and waited, the mug of tea growing cold in his hand. He took a final sip and lowered the mug to the desk. The call rang and rang, but he held on. The recipients were busy doing important work and couldn't be rushed. Eventually, an answer rewarded his patience.

"Hillview Hospice," a friendly female voice announced. "How can I help?"

"This is Arnold Jeffries," Kaine said, using his latest alias—a retired naval officer who'd served with Mike Procter for many years. "I'd like to speak with Marion Hathaway, please."

"One moment, Mr Jeffries. I'll page her for you."

"Thanks."

Kaine settled in for another long wait.

Insanely busy, Marion Hathaway managed the hospice with great care and attention, but she'd certainly spare time for "Arnold Jeffries" who had recently stumped up a generous donation to their charitable cause. She didn't know it yet, but the hospice would receive a slightly lesser sum on a monthly basis, from Kaine's personal funds. Both she, and the hospice, deserved all the support he could provide.

A knock on the office door drew Kaine's attention. He hit the phone's mute button and called, "Come in."

The door swung inwards, and Will Stacy popped his head through the opening. His gaze landed on the phone in Kaine's hand.

"Can you talk?"

Kaine nodded. "I'm on hold."

"Lara's keeping you waiting, eh?" he asked, giving Kaine the rarest of rare things—a genuine Will Stacy smile.

Kaine shook his head and pulled the phone away from his ear.

"Hospice."

Will's smile faded. He'd only met Mike briefly, but understood the close bond between Kaine and the terminally ill retired Chief Petty Officer.

"Sorry," he said, "I can wait."

"No, no. It's okay. I imagine I'll be on hold for a while. What's up?"

Will stepped further into the small room.

"We've stowed all the gear and are about to have some grub. Will you be debriefing the men before heading off to Welsh Wales, boyo?"

Uncharacteristically, Will slipped into a cod Welsh accent. Clearly couldn't help himself. Still, they'd had a taxing night scrambling through a Northumberland forest on the way to their incursion of Belham Castle, and the long drive south that morning hadn't been much fun, either. In his exhaustion, Will could be forgiven for dropping his well-honed guard.

Will and the rest of the men were due some down time. Kaine, on the other hand, had another long drive ahead—a drive to the Brecon Beacons to meet with a certain former veterinarian. It would be a strained reunion. He still had fences to mend and bridges to rebuild.

"Yep. A short debrief before the off. It's been a long couple of days. Give me fifteen minutes, will you?"

"No probs. Who do you trust in the galley?"

Will didn't know the men very well and had yet to learn everyone's full skillset.

"They can all boil a kettle and make a brew, just about, but if you want something edible, ask Rollo or, at a pinch, Cough."

"Cough it is then," Will said, backing away.

"Rollo can cook, you know. He helps run a restaurant in France with his wife, remember."

Will pushed back into the room. "Yes, and that same wife has just survived a threat to her life. Rollo's desperate to bugger off back to France. Although I'm guessing he'd never tell you that himself."

Kaine winced. Having been too wrapped up in his own challenges, the attack on the restaurant had been driven to the back of his mind.

Unforgiveable. It went against the good leader's code—your troops came first, yourself second.

"Of course. Tell him to head off as soon as he likes. You and I can handle the debrief."

The phone clicked. Kaine pointed to it and waved at Will, who backed away and closed the door quietly.

"Mr Jeffries?"

Kaine cancelled the mute.

"Ms Hathaway, sorry to disturb you," he said. "I know how busy you are."

"That's not a problem. How can I help, sir?" she asked, politeness itself. She had a cheery voice and sported a Midlands twang.

"How's Mike doing?"

"Mr Procter is … as comfortable as can be expected," she answered after a momentary hesitation. "He's a very stoic individual."

Kaine knew all about Mike's condition. His old friend didn't have long, but he clung to life with the tenacity of a limpet.

"Would it be safe to bring him home?"

"That's not advisable, sir. As I understand it, he lives alone."

"Not anymore, Ms Hathaway. I've detailed two of my … colleagues to stay with him."

"Your colleagues?"

"That's right. My friends. Good people."

"Are they medically trained?" she asked. "Mr Procter needs round-the-clock care. He really is better off here, sir. We can make him much more comfortable."

"I promised to bring him home the moment I could, and I always keep my promises." Kaine paused for a moment before asking, "What would it take to make Mike's home suitable for his … respite care?"

Kaine couldn't bring himself to say "end of life" care.

"Mr Proctor needs a great deal more than respite care, Mr Jeffries. As I said, he needs round-the-clock cover with regular visits from an oncologist. Mr Proctor lives on a farm, doesn't he?"

"Yes," Kaine said. "Just outside Long Buckby."

"Ah, I see. Long Buckby is quite some distance from the nearest medical centre offering palliative care."

"I'd be happy to cover the cost of private nursing staff. Live-in staff if necessary."

"That would be rather expensive, Mr Jeffries."

"I understand. Who do I contact for private care staff?"

"We use Midlands Care Agency for support at times of high demand, Mr Jeffries. Would you like their number?"

"Yes, please. Fire away."

Kaine noted the number on a scrap of paper.

"MCA will also be able to provide a consultant oncologist," Hathaway said, "for a fee."

"Don't worry about that, Ms Hathaway. I have someone in mind to cover those duties. My men will be with you some time this afternoon. Please let Mike know he'll be coming home soon. Thanks for your time."

Kaine rang off, replaced the handset, and dialled another number, this one from memory, and using his burner phone of the day. Lara answered quickly.

"About time," she said, her voice an urgent whisper. "I've been worried about you."

"Can you talk?"

"Not really. Give me five minutes."

"Okay."

Kaine ended the call and dropped the burner onto the desk. He stretched his arms towards the ceiling and allowed himself a full-throated yawn. He cricked the stiffness from his neck and breathed deep and slow, luxuriating in the post-action calm down.

Raucous voices coming from the direction of the kitchen filtered through the office door. The enthusiastic sound of men who had prepared mentally for violent action only to find their expected enemy had turned tail and run, leaving behind the primary target—one Malcolm Sampson. That same enemy had left the terrified millionaire naked and tied, spreadeagled, to a four-poster bed with a ball gag wedged in his mouth. Malcolm Sampson had not survived his encounter. Kaine released a grim smile at the memory.

Kaine stood and worked his way through a series of exercises while he waited. In the middle of a hamstring stretch, the burner vibrated on the desk. He straightened, snatched up the phone, and accepted the call without checking the caller ID.

"Lara?"

"Hi," she said, slightly breathless. Happy birdsong in the background confirmed her as being outside, in the open.

"Everything okay? You sound a little puffed."

"I'm climbing the hills. I told the Cadwalladers I needed some fresh air. How are your hands?"

"A little tender, but on the mend."

"The rope burns were deep. Are you keeping them clean? Changing the dressings regularly?"

"Yes, love. I told you, they're fine," he said, almost snapping. "Really."

"Hmm. And the men?"

Kaine relaxed and dropped into the chair.

"Unharmed."

"What happened last night?"

He briefed her on all that had occurred overnight in the Evesham mortuary and in Northumberland. The abridged version took less than ten minutes.

"So, Sampson and Pinocchio won't be bothering us any longer," she said. No questions, no recriminations, just a simple statement of fact.

"That's right," Kaine said. "Not in this life."

"Good. In that case, why do you sound so low?"

Kaine sighed. How well she knew him.

"It's Mike …"

"Oh Lord. How is—"

"Close to the end."

Kaine couldn't sugar-coat it. As a medic, Lara knew Mike's condition and his prognosis better than Kaine did.

"Hillview Hospice is the best place—"

"I promised to bring him home as soon as I'd cleared up the Sampson mess."

"Yes, okay. I understand. Give me an hour to pack my things and say goodbye to Rhodri, and I'll be on my way."

"Thanks, love. I knew I could rely on you. By the way, have you ever heard of the Midlands Care Agency? They provide contract medical staff."

"No."

"No. Sorry. You're a vet, not a doctor. Mind giving them a call? Mike's going to need full-time support."

"Of course not. I'll ring them before leaving here."

"Thanks, love. I'll text you their contact number. If you leave within the hour, you should be here by the time we've collected him from Hillview."

Kaine smiled in relief. Lara's impending arrival made his intention to hotfoot it to Wales redundant. As always, it paid to keep his plans fluid.

"Oh," he said, "before you hang up, there are three things."

"Yes?" she asked, having to speak up over a gusting wind.

Kaine smiled. He'd trained in the Beacons often enough to know the prevailing weather conditions. The wind was often described as "lazy", in that it cut straight through an obstacle rather than slide around it.

"How's Rhodri bearing up?"

"Surprisingly well, considering what he's been through. His school is calling in a counsellor to help him work through the trauma, but he's a strong lad. He'll survive."

Thank God for that.

"Tell him I'll pop across to see him as soon as things calm down."

As if that's ever going to happen.

"I will."

"Is there any news of Mitch?" he asked, putting off the important third part.

"He's recovering nicely. I visited him yesterday after the surgery."

"Surgery?"

"He had reconstructive surgery to rebuild the side of his face. I reviewed the outcomes with the plastic surgeon. The prognosis is very good. Mitch is already sitting up and making light of the wound. Referred to himself as 'Ol' Scarface'. You know Mitch."

Kaine smiled. Despite everything that had happened to Mitch in the army, where he'd lost a leg to an IED, he was a fighter. If anyone could survive and thrive after being shot in the side of the face, it would be Mitch Bairstow.

"And the third?" Lara prompted.

"Sorry?"

"You said there were three things."

"Ah, yes. I did, didn't I."

"Yes," she said firmly. "You did."

"Third thing …" He paused. "I can't wait to see you."

"You can't?" she said, refusing to make it easy on him.

"No, I can't. We have a lot to discuss."

"Yes, we do."

"I love you, Lara Orchard. Don't you ever forget it."

"I … won't," she said. "I love you, too."

The warmth in her voice made Kaine's day.

"See you later, Ryan Liam Kaine."

"Count on it, Lara Belinda Orchard."

She ended the call.

Kaine jumped out of the chair, breezed through the office, and strolled into the kitchen, smiling the whole way.

"Who's manning the cooker?" he asked the crowd, rubbing his hands together. "I'm starving."

4

Tuesday 30th May – Micah Williams

Shoreditch, London, UK

The closer they drew to their destination, the harder Micah found it to draw breath. His stomach cramped, sweat formed on his forehead and under his pits, and his heart thumped against his ribs. It felt as though he was in the middle of a heart attack.

"'Ere you go, guv," the breezy cabbie announced. "Shoreditch. Be there in a couple o' ticks."

"Great. Thanks."

They turned left off Great Eastern Street and headed down the two-laned Commercial Street. A dirty, old redbrick wall to their left hid the railway lines, and a modern, ten-storey residential block loomed to their right. The area looked rundown, tired. In dire need of a facelift.

A quarter mile later, the cabbie indicated right, turned into Fleur

De Lis Road, and pulled up in a bay marked with a dashed red line. Unlike Commercial Street, the terraced row of houses with their mottled grey, red, and black brickwork, dark grey windows, and panelled front doors, looked expensive and well-maintained. Each house had a single, wide and bullnosed stone step up to the front door. Each step was worn smooth and bowed by decades of trudging feet. Not at all what Micah expected for a clandestine meeting place. No drugs den, this.

"Here you go," Cabbie said, twisting to face the rear. "Nice gaff." He pointed to the meter, which showed twenty-seven pounds fifty. "Bit more than I said. Sorry, guv."

"Not a problem. Can you round it up to thirty? I'd tip you in cash, but ..." He shrugged. "Euros, you know?"

"Cheers, guv. Much appreciated."

The cabbie grinned, did something with the taximeter, and the fare clicked up by another two pounds fifty.

Micah passed his bank card over the reader, and it bleeped its acceptance. He climbed out and onto the street, dragging the heavy suitcase with him. No way would he leave the suitcase behind. Molly's life depended on it.

The black cab pulled away.

Micah stood at the kerb and waited for the cab to turn right at the far end of the street and disappear around the corner. After another deep breath, he marched along the terrace, reading the numbers attached to the doors. The first house, Number 2, had an ice-white front door, beautifully painted and scrubbed clean, as were the windowpanes. Number 4, pillar-box red, slight chip on the lower left panel. Number 6, British racing green, let down by the heavy pitting to the letterbox and its handle. He stopped at Number 8, the door shiny black and spotless, its brass furniture polished and gleaming in the sunshine.

Micah stepped back and craned his neck to look up. Above the door, well out of reach, a surveillance camera with its green light glowing, stared down at him. He reached up to the brass knocker.

Before he had time to knock, the door swung inwards on silent hinges to reveal a wide man in a dark suit. The man glowered down at Micah through a pair of glacier-blue eyes. Blond hair shorn tight in a number-two razor cut allowed a pair of ears to stick out from the sides of his head like grab handles. His nose had been broken more than once and heavy scar tissue crumpled his left eye, making his glower appear even more aggressive. Not someone to argue with or take for granted, he stood over two metres tall and nearly filled the doorway. Micah felt small by comparison.

"Come!" the man growled, his voice deep and booming. He backed away, beckoning with a huge left hand.

Micah hefted his suitcase and climbed the single step. He entered a wide, high-ceilinged hallway, painted in a relaxing pale, mint green. The highly patterned, tiled floor looked original and very expensive.

The huge man backed into an open doorway on the right and waved Micah deeper into the hall. Once Micah passed him, the man growled, "Stop."

The front door slammed shut. Micah jumped and made to spin around, but rough hands grabbed the back of his neck and drove him into the left wall, pressing his cheek against the textured wallpaper.

Micah dropped the suitcase and cried out in shock and pain.

"Stay," the man whispered and his hot, coffee-saturated breath dampened Micah's cheek.

The hands released their grip and worked their way over Micah's body, patting under his arms, around his waist and back, between his legs, and down to each ankle. The search was fast and efficient—and intensely intimate. The big man seemed to pay an inordinate amount of attention to Micah's groin area.

"Bogdan?" a man called from deeper inside the house. "Is that our guest?"

The big doorman, Bogdan, pushed away from Micah, and the pressure on his back eased.

"Yes," he called. "It him. He not armed."

"Excellent, please show him through to the kitchen."

Micah turned towards the second voice. Bogdan backed further away and pointed to the fallen suitcase. Micah bent to pick it up, straightened, and hesitated. Bogdan punched him in the back, and he stumbled forwards. Inside, the hallway widened to allow room for a staircase with a polished and ornamental oak banister, complete with intricately turned spindles.

Bogdan, his hand planted in the middle of Micah's back, pushed him towards the only open door of four in the hallway.

The door led to a kitchen occupied by an elderly man in a smart three-piece suit, complete with a gold watch chain. Grey-haired and bearded, both neatly trimmed, he was nothing at all like Bogdan, and nothing like Micah expected. Instead of the mean Luc clone he'd been prepared for, the dapper gent could have passed for every family's favourite uncle. In fact, he bore a striking resemblance to Molly's late father.

"Mr Williams," the old man said, a broad smile on his distinguished face, "so happy to meet you at last. Come in, come in. I won't bite. Bogdan will stay outside. It will give us a chance to chat without being disturbed."

Bogdan gave Micah another shove. He lurched closer to "Uncle" and caught an expensive fragrance he couldn't put a name to. The old man's cologne hung heavily in the air between them.

In the time it had taken Micah to enter the kitchen, the smile had fallen from Uncle's gaunt face, he'd pulled out a handgun, and pointed it at Micah's chest.

God alive!

A gun. A real gun!

Micah shuddered.

"Please don't let the 'genial pensioner' guise fool you, Mr Williams," Uncle said, wafting his free hand in front of his slender frame. "If you make any move against me, not only will I shoot you where you stand, I will also instruct my German colleagues in France to kill your beautiful wife." The evil old man kept his voice low and relaxed, which made it all the more menacing.

"Don't ... please."

Dry-mouthed and quaking—outside of a TV crime show or a cinema screen, he'd never even seen a gun let alone had one pointed at him—Micah slowly lowered the suitcase to the flagstone floor. Equally as slowly, he straightened and raised his hands.

The old man flapped his free hand, the gesture dismissive.

"No need for that, Mr Williams. Lower your arms and relax as best you can. We're all friends here. Apart from Bogdan, of course. As far as I can tell, Bogdan doesn't have any friends." The amiable smile returned. "At least, none that I've ever met."

Micah dropped his hands to his sides and struggled to recover his breathing.

"Now, let me finish my threat and then we can get down to business. This gun"—he lowered the weapon and pressed it against his leg—"is rather heavy. In fact, guns are much heavier than they look on TV. I'm brandishing it to show you how serious your situation is—if you hadn't already gathered. In case you think you can overpower me and turn the tables, which is eminently plausible given the difference in our ages and our sizes, remember this. If, for any reason, I don't call the man you know as Luc with the prearranged signal, your wife dies. And she dies unpleasantly. It really is that simple. It is for this reason, I don't feel the need to keep Bogdan close. To be perfectly honest with you"—he leant closer and lowered his voice even further—"the man gives me the creeps. I only keep him on because he comes in handy to scare away the kids at Hallowe'en. I do so hate 'trick or treating'. Don't you?" Another smile stretched out his craggy face. He looked so pleased with himself. Micah wanted to rip the gun from his wrinkled hand and ram it down his scrawny throat, but fear held him paralysed.

If not for Molly, he'd have happily beaten the old man to a bloody pulp.

Oh God. Molly.

"Now, Micah," the old man said, speaking more normally. "Have I made your situation perfectly clear to you?"

Micah nodded, frightened to say anything that would betray his true feelings. His anger and his helplessness.

"Good, good. Now we have reached an understanding, you can

call me Abe," the old man said. "You don't need to know my full name."

Micah shuddered.

Abe's smile broadened.

"This must be awfully distressing for you, Mr Williams. Oh, that sounds overly formal. May I call you Micah? Since we're friends and business partners now, I really think we should be on first name terms, don't you?"

Micah couldn't speak. His dry throat wouldn't allow it.

"Take this," Abe said. "As a sign of my good faith." He raised the gun, turned it sideways, and offered it across. "Go on. Take it."

Micah shook his head.

"No. N-No. I can't. It might go off."

"And you'd hate for it to hurt your new friend, Abe. Is that right?"

And I don't want my fingerprints anywhere near it, arsehole.

"Y-Yes," Micah managed. "Yes, that's right."

Fingerprints?

Where did that come from?

Micah stood in danger of losing the plot completely.

Concentrate, man. For Molly, concentrate.

"Very good, Micah. Very good indeed. I'm so glad we've reached an understanding." He placed the gun on the table at his side, pointed towards the wall. "And not to worry. The gun's a Beretta and the safety catch is on. It can't be fired accidentally."

Micah stood with his hands at his sides, waiting. Helpless.

"Very well, Micah," Abe said, beckoning him closer. "Let's get this over with, shall we? Pick up the suitcase and place it on the table carefully. Before I can send you on your way, I need to check the merchandise."

Micah hoisted the heavy suitcase, and slammed it down onto the wooden surface.

"Stop that!" Abe yelled, raising his voice for the first time. "That table's an antique. It's worth more than you'll earn this year!"

"Sorry," Micah said, not meaning it.

"Open it," Abe snarled, dropping the mask of affability, and showing his true colours. "And be careful about it!"

Micah took the keys from his pocket, unlocked the catches, and threw back the top. He rifled through the contents, deliberately sliding the case over the table's precious surface, and removed the tin of talcum powder Luc had given him. He wiped it clean with the hem of his T-shirt, and, still using the hem, carefully placed it on the table next to the suitcase. Then he stepped away.

Abe snorted.

"You have been watching too many forensics shows on the TV, my friend."

Micah lowered his gaze.

"Don't worry, son," Abe said, reverting to his friendly and open persona. "No police-certified lab will ever lay hands on the merchandise." He stared at the tin. "Would you like to see what you've brought me?"

Micah shook his head.

"Not interested?" Abe asked, pushing out his lower lip.

Again, Micah shook his head.

"Can't say I blame you."

"What happens now?" Micah asked.

"Now, Micah," Abe said, picking up the tin. "I check the contents and make sure you've not tampered with them."

Them?

"I haven't."

Abe smiled. "It certainly appears that way, but I do have to make certain. I like to call it my 'due diligence'. Wait here. Make yourself a beverage if you wish. You'll find the makings of tea and coffee over there." He waved a hand towards the marble kitchen surface where an expensive-looking, chrome-and-black espresso machine stood next to the sink. "I'll be right back. Don't go away, now."

Clutching the package in his right fist, Abe hurried from the kitchen—and the Beretta—allowing the door to swing open and show Bogdan in the hallway. The minder stood, legs apart, hands clasped in front, sneering at Micah, a feral glint in his slits for eyes.

Micah turned his back on the hard-faced guard. He pulled a dining chair out from under the "antique" table and collapsed into it, all strength in his legs washing away. He sat, elbows on knees, head in hands, trying to hold himself together.

Somewhere in the house, a clock ticked away the minutes, which seemed to stretch out into forever.

5

Tuesday 30th May – Andrew Grantham

Elder Street, Shoreditch, London, UK

Andrew "Andy" Grantham stared down at Fleur De Lis Road from his obbo point, five floors up in a bedsit in the next street. He had a great view and could see the whole terrace. He yawned and tried to rub the grit from his eyes. Three hours he'd been there. Only three, but it seemed much, much longer. Nothing had happened. Bloody nothing. He'd lose another day's sleep thanks to this total waste of time. Sleep he'd never catch up on. He yawned again, so long and so hard, he nearly wrenched his jaw doing it.

Bugger.

"I'm so bored," he complained to the bedsit's four bare and tired walls.

The minutes ticked slowly by. Morning turned into midday and then into afternoon. He drained another cup of instant coffee, and almost spat it back into the cup. He bloody hated instant, but had no alternative. At least the bloody stuff helped keep him awake.

Movement below and to his left caused a spark of interest.

"'Allo, 'allo, 'allo," he announced to the empty room. "What's all this, then?" He snorted at the cliché.

A black cab pulled into the drop-off bay outside Number 2, and sat for a minute before disgorging its passenger. A man. Young, tall, dressed like a tourist, he waited for the cab to disappear around the corner before moving off. Pulling a wheeled suitcase behind him, the man headed towards the Pedersen house, staring hard at the numbers on each front door as he passed.

"First time visitor, are you?" Grantham mumbled, fully awake. "That's promising."

From his elevated position, Grantham had the perfect view of the man's approach. On the off-chance, he hit record on the camcorder and checked the picture on the viewscreen. The bright afternoon sunshine produced a pretty decent image. Grantham zoomed in on the face as close as possible without losing focus. It would do. No choice. It would have to.

The man arrived at Number 8 and stopped. He reached up for the brass knocker, but Bogdan beat him to it and ushered him inside.

"Bingo!" Grantham said, allowing himself a tight smile. "About bloody time."

He'd been watching the pigging house in rotation with the others for three days and finally, movement. He left the camcorder running on its tripod stand, grabbed his burner, and texted, *"Call me."*

He waited five long minutes for the mobile to buzz. He accepted the call and said, "Hi, boss."

"I don't have long. What is it?"

Typical of the boss. Always business. Never time for a pleasant chat.

"Pedersen just received a visitor."

"Describe him."

No, "Please"?

Grantham ploughed right into it. "Mixed-race. Early-to-mid-twenties. Long black hair, wearing blue jeans and a dark green hoodie. Wheeling a suitcase like he's coming back from his holidays."

"A courier, you think?"

"Looks like it."

"I knew it! The old sod's been holding out on us."

"What do you want me to do?"

"Stay where you are. Keep watch on the house and keep the camcorder running for a bit. Let's see if Pedersen keeps this visit quiet."

"Want me to follow him? The courier, I mean."

"If I'd wanted you to do that, I'd have told you."

Yeah. 'Course you would.

Would he ever get to stretch his legs?

"I'll send one of the others."

Fuck's sake.

"What happens if Courier buggers off before they get here?" Grantham asked, risking another snipe.

"Let me worry about that. Just do as you're told," the boss said, and rang off.

"Well, fuck you very much," Grantham muttered, after confirming the call had ended. He didn't want to risk a real bollocking. He lowered the burner to the table and yawned again.

When had life become so fucking pedestrian? He'd been pumped for action and had it snatched from him. Bloody boss ruled the roost with a rod of iron. Still, she knew best. Grantham had been raking it in recently. The rewards were worth eating all the humble pie—at least for the moment.

His empty stomach growled. He hadn't eaten a thing since breakfast. Lived on instant coffee and powdered milk since then. No bloody way for a highly skilled man to make a living.

Grantham sighed.

What the hell was Pedersen thinking? Why hide a drop from them? Such a stupid move driven by pure greed. Bloody idiot had to have known he'd been playing with fire. Must have known how it would end. Bloody madness. Overconfidence and arrogance would be the end of him.

Grantham expected to have been given the green light before now. Pedersen had been getting away with murder for too long. The old man was laughing at them. They couldn't afford to let things continue, but still the boss hesitated. No bloody need for it. No need to wait at all. The end couldn't have been any more obvious. Only a matter of time.

Grantham sighed and rested his hand on the carry case that held his Ruger 9mm PCC takedown rifle.

"Not long, baby girl. Not long now."

6

Tuesday 30th May – Micah Williams

Fleur De Lis Road, Shoreditch, London, UK

Eventually, what seemed like hours later, the old man returned without the package, a benign smile still playing on his thin lips. Micah jumped to his feet.

"Is everything okay?" he asked, embarrassed by how timid he sounded.

"Perfect, dear boy," Abe answered. "Absolutely perfect. The merchandise is all present and correct. You've done very well. Very well indeed."

"Can I go now?" he pleaded.

"You didn't fancy a coffee, I see."

"Well?" Micah said. "Can I go?"

"Of course you can go. There's nothing to stop you, but …" He arched a bushy eyebrow and allowed his words to trail off ominously.

Micah waited, holding his breath. The clock ticked louder in the threatening silence. In the hallway, Bogdan swayed on the balls of his feet and glowered at Micah as though desperate for the chance to tear him limb from limb. He pushed out as predatory and malicious a vibe as anything Micah had seen on a natural history programme.

"But?" Micah prompted, staring at the evil old man.

"Where will you go?"

Shit.

"I-I ... thought ... Toulouse?"

Abe shrugged his scrawny shoulders.

"Why would you return to Toulouse? Wouldn't you prefer to be with your wife?" Again he stretched out what he might have considered to be a charming smile.

The floor shuddered beneath Micah's feet. It felt as though he were falling.

"Oh God. You've moved her?"

Abe's shoulders dropped. "Of course we've moved her. Luc couldn't risk you calling the *gendarmes* and pointing them in his direction, now could he?" He paused for a moment to let the implications sink in. "I imagine you'd like to speak to her?"

Micah ground his teeth. He wanted nothing more than to wrap his fingers around Abe's skeletal neck, dig his thumbs into the old man's throat, and squeeze the life out of him, but where would that leave Molly? He forcibly relaxed his hands and sucked in a deep breath.

"Yes," he gasped. "Yes please."

"Feel free to call her," he said, wafting his right hand airily. "She's waiting."

"What?"

"You heard me, Micah. Call her. She *will* answer. And while you do that, I'll make us a drink. How do you take your coffee?"

Micah ignored the question, turned his back to the evil old git and his henchman in the doorway, and dragged the mobile from his pocket. Fingers that would have throttled the life out of the old man shook so much, they struggled to find Molly's number.

He pressed the phone to his ear. After a horribly long delay, the call connected.

"Micah?" Molly asked.

"Moll? Molly? Are you okay?"

"Scared out of my mind, but they haven't hurt me. How are you?"

"I'm okay, love. Terrified, but I'm fine. Really I am. What about you? Are you still in Toulouse?"

"No. I ... They took me in a car. We drove for ages. They blindfolded me. I-I think I'm in the country. It's really quiet here. Lots of birdsong. Oh God, Micah, I'm so sorry for getting us into this."

What? What did she say?

"It wasn't your fault, love."

"If I hadn't insisted on the holiday, we'd never have ended up here with these horrible men."

"But you didn't—"

"I needed to get away," she said, cutting through his words. Urgent. Insistent. "You didn't want to come, but I forced you. I did."

Micah shut his mouth and let her talk, even though she wasn't making any sense.

Molly continued, speaking rapidly, almost rambling, but certainly confused. "We hadn't had a holiday since ... well, not since Dad passed. It's been awful. *I've* been awful. Dad would have wanted me to see a counsellor, but I was too ... too bloody stubborn. I couldn't ever trust a counsellor with my mind. I-I needed to get away. Clear my head. I'm sorry, Micah. I'm so, so sorry." She paused, took a breath. "Micah? Can you hear me?"

"Yes, love."

"You found your way to London okay?"

"Yes, I'm here, and I've done what they wanted. I delivered their package."

"I-I know. They told me. Luc is signalling me to stop talking. I-I have to go. I love you, Micah. Remember this. *Trust* yourself. Trust yourself to do the right thing! You are a good man. I love you so, so much."

The catch in her voice brought Micah even closer to tears.

"I love you too, angel. We'll get out of this. I promise." The line fell silent. "Moll? Molly? Are you there? Hello?"

He tore the phone from his ear and stared at the screen. The call had lasted one minute and forty-two seconds. Too short. Far too short. Would he ever speak to her again? See her?

Oh God.

"Here you are," Abe announced, placing a silver tray loaded with cups and saucers, and the makings for coffee, on the table. "Help yourself to cream and sugar, dear boy."

"What happens now?" Micah asked, desperate to be away, doing something.

"Now, Micah," Abe said, "you return to France and your delightful wife ... and you go via Amsterdam."

"Amsterdam!"

Micah ground his teeth.

"Yes, Micah. Amsterdam. We need you to deliver one more package to complete the transaction. Just the one more delivery and this will all be over. Will you do that little thing for us? Yes, of course you will. You're such a sensible young man. After that, you'll be back with your delightful wife, and you'll be able to carry on with your lives as though nothing had happened. In fact, you might eventually look back on this whole episode as though it were an exciting adventure. Something *not* to tell your kids. Wouldn't that be lovely?"

"Amsterdam?" Micah gasped. "How the fuck do I get to—"

"Language, Micah," Abe chided, raising a reproving finger. "I know you're under a certain amount of stress, but there is no need to swear. It really is so unnecessary."

The old man lifted the carafe, filled his cup with coffee, and added a little cream. He stirred it with a tiny silver teaspoon.

"You have your driving licence on you, of course."

"Yes." Micah nodded.

"Good. We've hired a car for you through intermediaries. It's perfectly clean. A discrete little Peugeot 107. Not at all conspicuous." He took a delicate sip of his coffee and smacked his lips. "Delicious. You really should try some."

Micah shut his mouth and kept silent.

"Anyway, where was I? ... Ah yes, of course. The Peugeot. It's parked in a neighbour's garage. You will drive it to Folkstone, take the Channel Tunnel to Calais, and make your way north to Amsterdam. Door-to-door, it should take you little more than eleven hours, even allowing for delays at the Chunnel. At this time of the year, there won't be much in the way of traffic overnight, so you might even arrive earlier." He took another sip from his highly decorated China cup, index finger raised. "Now, take note. You must arrive before nine o'clock tomorrow morning. A moment later, and Molly dies." He paused to let the message sink in before continuing. "After that, you are free to go. From Amsterdam, it's a mere thirteen-hour drive to Molly in the centre of France. When you deliver the second package, Molly will call you with directions."

"Why?" Micah asked, shaking his head.

"Isn't it obvious? Without directions, how are you going to find her?"

"No. I mean, why are you doing this to us?"

"Ah," Abe said, raising his index finger once more. "I see what you mean. I could tell you to do as you're told and stop asking stupid questions, but I like you, Micah, and I feel you are owed an explanation." He smiled again, this one sad. "It's really quite simple, actually. I'm a cautious man. Very cautious. It's the reason I've been so successful for so long in this ... industry."

"Industry?" Micah snapped. "You're a bloody kidnapper and a smuggler."

Abe frowned at the interruption.

"Do you want an explanation or not?"

Again, Micah closed his mouth. He nodded.

"Very well. Things were becoming a little ... shall we say, difficult. People began to sniff around. I'm afraid you have our competitors to blame for your current predicament. It would appear that in recent months, certain very unpleasant and highly motivated individuals have become aware of our delivery schedules and our transportation routes. I have to say, we found this most disconcerting. I—and it was me, I'm afraid—felt the need to take some rather drastic action. Please, Micah. Sit down. Drink your coffee before it gets cold. I've a feeling you'll be needing as much caffeine as your system can handle over the next day or so."

Micah stayed where he was, in the middle of the kitchen, while a nattily dressed old man took another genteel sip of his coffee and dabbed his thin lips with a napkin.

"It really is delightful. You cannot beat a decent cup of coffee. Are you sure you won't have one?"

Micah shook his head. If he'd picked up his cup, he'd have struggled not to throw it in the supercilious old man's wizened face.

"Suit yourself." Abe grinned. "Anyway, where was I? Oh yes. We were worried about a potential interception, which would have upset not only us, but certain powerful individuals we deal with. Individuals who don't have any patience for failures in the distribution chain." Abe emptied his cup, sighed, and lowered it to its matching saucer. "So, we needed to find some new and completely independent couriers. Couriers with no links to either organisation, and that's where you and dear Molly—amongst others—come into the story. Your inclusion was quite random, actually." He smiled and took another sip. "To coin a phrase, you were in the wrong place at the wrong time. We considered using backpackers, but they can be a little flaky. Furthermore, they're amongst the first people searched at the border, don't you know." He sighed and leant back in his chair. "When you and Molly turned up at the café, you met our requirements to perfection. It was like a sign from the heavens. A twentysomething couple on holiday with no whingeing kids in tow." He shook his head, a faraway look in his eye. "It was so easy to disable your car. A simple hole in a radiator hose. Luc followed you for a few miles until your nice little Honda overheated. Offered you a lift to the nearest garage. And there you have it. You were so gullible."

A sign from the heavens?

"Still," Abe continued, "it's nearly over for you and Molly. As I said earlier, you have just one more little task to complete. After that, you and Molly can be on your way back home to live your perfect lives in peace."

"Our perfect lives!" Micah shouted, finally snapping. "You know nothing about us! Nothing at all."

"Luc has Molly's driving licence. We know where you live, dear boy," Abe said, speaking low, barely more than a whisper. "Remember that if you ever decide to make trouble for us after this business is all over. Rose Cottage, Broken Stone Road, Blackburn. Sounds like such a lovely place. Idyllic."

They knew where they lived. Of course they did. Again, Micah wanted to throw up. With an address, the bastards could get to them any time they wanted. He and Molly would never be free of these evil shits.

"Just let us go," Micah begged. "We'll say nothing to anybody."

"I know you won't. I was simply making a point, dear boy."

Micah swallowed the gorge rising to his throat. "One more delivery, you say?"

"Just the one."

"You promise?"

"I promise." The old man placed his liver-spotted right hand over his heart. "You have my word of honour. And Uncle Abe always honours his word. Famous for it the world over, he is." This time, the bastard didn't smile as he spoke.

As though Micah could ever accept the word of a man who'd organised their kidnap and threatened their lives. A man who smuggled diamonds across borders. Diamonds. Of course it had to be diamonds. The Amsterdam link said it all. What else could the tin of talc have contained? It wasn't big enough to carry the volume of drugs to make their abduction worthwhile. Kidnapping carried a huge risk. Smuggling a small tin of drugs wouldn't net nearly enough cash to make kidnapping a viable option. But diamonds. Yes. Diamonds were a different matter.

"A delivery to Amsterdam?" Micah asked.

"Yes. Just so." The old man nodded and set his cup and saucer down on the tray on the fancy antique table.

"And after that, I get Molly back." Micah made it a statement not a question.

"Exactly."

"Okay," he said, "I'll do it."

Of course he'd bloody do it. What choice did he have?

Abe broke out another cheery smile.

"Splendid. Splendid. Give me a moment to collect the second package, and I'll get Bogdan to show you the back way to the garage."

Abe stood, grunting as his knees creaked. He faced Micah, and had to look up to meet his eyes.

"Oh, a word of warning before I forget," he said, smiling and standing much too close for comfort. "Please don't try calling Molly again. Wait for her to contact you. Luc is in possession of her mobile, and he has a vicious temper when his sleep is disturbed. Do you understand what I'm telling you?"

Micah lowered his head and mumbled, "Yes. I understand."

Abe nodded, patted Micah's upper arm, and strolled out of the kitchen, leaving Micah alone to close his suitcase and stew in his own juices.

Five minutes later, the old man returned with a black plastic canister about the size of the pencil case Micah used in school. He placed it in Micah's outstretched hand, but held on to it.

"Take great care of this, Micah," Abe said before releasing the package. "Molly's life depends on its safe delivery."

The package weighed much more than the tin of talc.

"Are these the same diamonds I smuggled through France?"

"Diamonds?" Abe asked. "Diamonds? Who said anything about diamonds?"

"No one. I guessed."

"The Amsterdam connection, I assume?"

Micah nodded.

"Yes, well, I suppose it's a logical conclusion to draw. And in answer to your question, yes. They are the same diamonds. I've simply repackaged them and added them to a second consignment."

"A second consignment?"

"That's right, dear boy. Our last courier refused to complete his delivery. You don't need to know the details, but it didn't end well for the poor man, and it did leave us in a bit of a dilemma. Hence your enforced recruitment to the cause."

"Is that why you didn't send me straight to Amsterdam in the first place?"

"Exactly, Micah. I needed you to deliver both consignments. A little circuitous and time consuming perhaps, but needs must, dear boy. Needs must."

The old man tilted his head in a shrug and pointed to the brute in the hallway.

"And now," Abe said, "Bogdan will show you to the car. Please drive safely."

Micah hefted his case and followed the brute through to the back of the house.

7

Tuesday 30th May – Micah Williams

The A13, London, UK

The dark blue Peugeot 107 turned out exactly as Abe described—compact and discreet. A little too compact for Micah's six-foot-two-inch frame. His hair scraped the fabric roof, and his right shoulder regularly brushed the side window, but he'd driven worse cars. Smaller cars. In its favour, the Peugeot did have built-in GPS, which gave him an estimated arrival time at Folkestone of nine twenty-three. The car came with a quarter tank of petrol, which would never take him all the way to Amsterdam. He'd need to refuel at least once.

The GPS route took him east along the A13 towards the M25. As expected, the evening, post-rush-hour traffic was as light as he imagined it would ever get in London, and he settled in for a long and steady drive through the night. The journey gave him plenty of thinking time.

How had their once near-perfect lives fallen apart so badly?

Not so long ago, life had been good. Really good. They'd been happily renovating the cottage. They'd completed all the major construction projects and had started the decorating and homemaking phase when the wheels came off. Molly's dad, Chris, died in the plane crash and their cosy existence had crumbled into dust. Chris, a solid, hardworking, down-to-earth man, never raised his voice and was kind and generous to everybody. Such a terrible, sickening loss.

In the months immediately after the disaster, Molly had closed in on herself. She'd grown miserable, lost her sparkle. She rarely mentioned her father, and neither did Micah, for fear of picking at the scabs of her pain. Then, as the days lengthened into spring, the therapist had helped her to break through the despair, and she'd recovered some of her old energy. For a change of scene, they'd spent a weekend away from the house at a local hotel. Had too much to drink. Made love for the first time in months.

When she announced the pregnancy, the news came completely out of the blue. They were overjoyed. If it was a boy, they'd call him Christopher after Molly's father. If a girl, they'd name her Christine. Little by little, life started to recover. Molly thrived. Barely suffered any morning sickness. After the first trimester, Micah had the genius idea to travel. Why not take a holiday before the baby arrived and before Molly started showing? At first, she was reluctant, but he wore her down. He talked her into it.

"After all," he'd said one evening, "we won't be doing much travelling when the baby's here. All those nappies and toys. C'mon, love. A two-week driving tour. We can afford it."

He'd practically forced her into it. Without her knowledge, he'd booked the ferry, and the first two nights in an *auberge*—a small hotel in the outskirts of Caen. After that, he planned to follow their noses and maybe take in a vineyard tour or two—not that Molly would be able to sample the product in her condition.

"A driving holiday in southern France will be good for us both," he'd said.

In the end, since the ferry tickets and the hotel booking were non-refundable—another trick he'd used to ratchet up the pressure—she'd surrendered. Despite their growing bank balance, she'd always been the responsible one.

At first, the holiday had gone well. Then their engine overheated on a quiet road in the middle of nowhere and the world collapsed in on them all over again. Micah squeezed the steering wheel with grips of steel.

How naïve they'd been to be taken in so easily.

That was what had made Molly's interruption during their last phone call so strange.

He'd booked the holiday. *He'd* made all the plans. *He'd* practically forced her into it. All Micah's doing. The kidnapping was Micah's fault, not Molly's. So why had she taken the blame during the phone call? Why? It didn't make sense. Was she losing it again? She was still so fragile, had the terror broken her again?

Bastards. The evil fucking bastards.

Despite the anger flooding through him, Micah yawned. He rubbed tired, stinging eyes until they watered. So damn tired. He hadn't slept for nearly two days. Exhaustion spread over him like a heavy, dark blanket. Again, he yawned, long and hard. His stomach rumbled. When had he last eaten?

Headlights flashed in the rear-view mirror. Angry, insistent, repeated. A horn blared.

Shit. Now what?

The police?

Micah's heart lurched. His mouth dried.

Headlights flared again—the headlights of a bright green panel van. Not the police.

Thank God.

Micah checked his speed. Forty-five mph. He stamped on the accelerator, the Peugeot sprang forwards, and the speed increased to an acceptable sixty-eight. Micah signalled an apology to the driver he'd annoyed and pulled into the inside lane.

As the green van rolled past in the middle lane its driver threw him the finger.

"Up yours, too," Micah growled. "If you had my problems ..." He let the words trail off and the anger fade. Why waste the energy.

A blue sign showed the upcoming turn to the M25 at the same time as the GPS made the announcement for him to take the left lane. He followed the calm instructions of the disembodied voice and joined the M25 southbound, relieved to see a sign for the next services at Thurrock.

Ignoring the GPS' strident "recalculating route" announcement, he took the first slip road—a long, arcing S-bend—and found his way to the service station. He parked in front of the first coffee house and climbed out of the car.

After paying for his extra-large Americano, bacon bap, and a jam doughnut, he found an empty table in the corner and tried to tuck in, but it wasn't happening. Everything tasted of cardboard. He couldn't swallow a thing except the Americano.

So much for needing the energy.

The time on his mobile read 20:43. Leaving immediately would put him in Folkestone well before ten o'clock. The Channel Tunnel train crossing would take about forty minutes, meaning he would reach Calais long before midnight. Assuming the channel tunnel trains were running according to schedule, he had plenty of time. But what if there was a delay? What if the trains were full?

Micah pulled the mobile from the pocket of his jeans and tapped it into life. He tried not to look at the image on the home screen—Molly and her dad, hugging and smiling in better times—but couldn't stop himself. Tears blurred his vision. He swiped the screen, navigated to the web browser, and entered "Eurotunnel Bookings".

He followed the seamless reservation process and paid extra for a "Flexiplus" ticket which allowed him to roll up and board the trains at any time. Hang the cost. Money didn't matter. Thanks to the support and generosity of The 83 Trust, money would never be an issue for them ever again.

The 83 Trust!

Of course.

The realisation hit him with the force of a blow to the back of the head with a brick. Why the hell hadn't he thought of them before?

Molly. She'd been prompting him to call the Trust the whole time.

What had she said during the first call? Micah racked his brain for the exact phrase, which had stood out as weird. Something about "placing their trust in God" and "it's what Dad would have done." It had struck Micah as odd. Neither Molly nor her father were particularly religious. In fact, Molly was a confirmed and quite vocal atheist. So why mention God at all?

At the time, Micah had put it down to fear and stress, but Molly had been sending him a message. A message he was too bloody stupid—and exhausted—to pick up.

Fuck's sake, Micah. You bloody idiot!

He logged out of the Eurotunnel booking site, and keyed in *the-83.com*.

There it was, slap bang in the centre of the home page—the call-to-action he'd first seen back in November and laughed at in derision. He remembered wondering who would fall for such a line? It had to be a con. Who were they trying to kid?

Not laughing now, are you, Micah!

Over the months, The Trust had updated the page and changed the original message. This time there were two options:

If you are suffering financial hardship, **click here!**

If you are in personal danger, **click here!**

THE FIRST TIME they'd contacted The Trust, he and Molly had asked for a few thousand pounds to pay for Chris' memorial service and headstone. The following day, The Trust transferred funds into Molly's account—a hell of a lot more than they'd asked for, too. A smaller deposit had been made every month since. Money that had given them financial stability.

Micah shook his head. Fear and exhaustion had pushed The Trust clean out of his head. After all, they were nothing but a charity, a financial institution. Could they really do anything to help? Molly certainly seemed to think so.

She'd used the word "trust" during their latest phone call, too. The one he'd made at Abe's house. She said she'd never trust a counsellor with her mind, yet she'd been visiting a therapist every week since The Trust had started sending the money. She'd also said something like, "Trust yourself. You are a good man. I love you so, so much."

Bloody fool.

So many hints and Micah had missed them all.

Stupid bloody idiot.

Micah hit the second "click here!" button and completed the short questionnaire. It didn't take long. He added his mobile number to the end of the message, closed his eyes in prayer, and hit enter.

He didn't hold out much hope, but at least he'd done something other than blindly follow the instructions of the bastards who still held Molly. Somehow, his minor act of rebellion made him feel a little better. He left the bacon bap and the doughnut on the table, largely untouched, and headed for the car.

8

Tuesday 30th May – Evening

Mike's Farm, Long Buckby, Northants, UK

Kaine read the Enderby dossier for the third time, trying to find a weakness in the man's defences. As usual, Corky had done a bang-up job, and the material couldn't have been any more comprehensive. If they'd needed Commander Gregory Enderby's inside leg measurement for any reason, Kaine had no doubt that Corky would have found a way to provide it.

Enderby's whole life lay mapped out on six double-sided sheets of A4 paper, from his birth in a small village in Hampshire, through his moderately successful academic and naval careers, to his present role as Director of the National Counter Terrorism Agency, and his expected future promotion to Permanent Secretary, the Agency's head. His rise through the civil service ranks had been nothing short of meteoric. So meteoric for a man of Enderby's modest achievements, it raised clear suspicions. The commander either had friends in very high places—which didn't seem likely according to Corky's dossier—or he had compromising information on those same people in high places. If the latter, Kaine wanted eyeballs on the information in question.

Kaine turned to the final page. He preferred reading paper and ink and found it difficult to absorb information from a monitor. That sort of thing was best left to the younger members of his team, people like Connor Blake, who'd grown up with his nose riveted to a computer screen. When it became a viable option, Connor would no doubt be among the first in line to have a CPU surgically implanted where the sun didn't shine.

Kaine smiled to himself and turned to Will, another old school operator who preferred reading from the page.

"Any ideas?" he asked.

Will tore his attention away from the paper and turned his dark brown—some might say muddy—eyes on Kaine.

"Sorry," he said. "There are some possibilities, but nothing definite so far. You?"

Kaine shook his head and allowed his shoulders to sag.

Sitting in the state-of-the-art communications room Rollo had built in the loft of Mike's barn, under Corky's hands-off guidance, they fell silent again.

It had already been a long, long day.

* * *

KAINE, Connor, and Cough had liberated an exhausted and pained but appreciative Mike from Hillview Hospice and had reached the farm at the same time as Lara arrived from Wales. Without stopping to greet Kaine or the others, Lara supervised Mike's move from Range Rover to farmhouse, issuing orders to the troops as though she were an old-time drill instructor. While Kaine's strike team had made its assault on the hospice, the rest of the guys had turned Mike's airy front room into a hospital ward—working under Lara's telephoned instructions.

With Mike safely installed in his bed and hooked up to various monitors and a patient-controlled morphine drip, Lara beckoned Kaine to the office and they finally found themselves alone. They stood for a lifetime, facing each other, standing a metre apart, before she broke the spell and rushed into his arms. They kissed, long and hard.

"I missed you," she whispered, hugging him tight.

"Missed you too, love. I'm sorry about Paris."

She pulled away, shook her head, and pressed a finger to his lips. "Now's not the time. We'll work it through later. Mike's more important."

"Agreed. What did you arrange with MCA?"

"It's not good. They can't send a nurse until next week at the earliest."

"Really?"

She grimaced. "In-home care nurses are in short supply. MCA doesn't have any available at such short notice."

"You told them money wasn't an issue?"

"Of course, but it didn't help. I tried two other care providers before I left Wales. No luck. It's not a problem, though. I'll take care of him, and his regular home care package is still in place. We just have to reactivate it."

"Okay. And the guys are willing to help. I spoke to them earlier. Asked for volunteers."

"Volunteers?" she said, doubt clear in her hazel eyes. "Really? They volunteered ... I mean, voluntarily?"

Kaine threw his hands up and put on his innocent face. "I swear. No force required. They all love Mike like a father. Apart from the new man, Hunter, who's never met him before today. They all put their hands up. Even Hunter."

Lara leant in close again and he wrapped her up.

"It won't be necessary," she said. "I can handle all the medical care. Mike's no trouble, and it'll only be for a week or so."

Kaine's heart froze.

"Bloody hell," he gasped. "Is that all the time he has left?"

"No, you idiot. That's not what I meant at all." Lara speared him with her bright eyes. "I meant it'll only take a couple of weeks to find a good nurse."

Kaine's heart started beating again. "You could ask Nigel when he arrives."

"Nigel?"

"Yes. Mike's nurse. I met him a couple of days ago. Nearly shot him in the head ... long story," he said when she stiffened in his arms. "He seems like a decent enough bloke, and Mike's happy with him. We might be able to poach him from the NHS for a while. What d'you reckon?"

For the first time since her arrival, Lara's smile warmed the room.

"It might work. He could take a leave of absence. I'll ask him. Do you think we should ask Corky to do a deep dive first?"

Kaine thought for a moment before answering.

"Good idea, but Corky's a little busy at the moment."

"Working on the Enderby and Hartington situation?"

"Yes, but if you ask him nicely, he'll probably task Frodo to investigate our friendly nurse."

"Frodo?" she asked. "Who on earth—"

"Haven't I told you about Frodo?"

"No," she said, staring hard at him, "you haven't."

After a brief pause, she smiled and punched his upper arm in a familiar gesture that did more than anything else to demonstrate how much the ice had thawed.

"My darling girl, where do I start? Frederick 'Frodo' O'Dowd might just be the best computer hacker on the planet."

"What? Better than Corky and Sabrina?"

"Quite possibly, but I'd never let Corky hear me say it. Anyway, while we have a few minutes to ourselves, let me tell you about young Frederick O'Dowd." Lara allowed him to pull her into another hug and she moulded her body into his. "I met Frodo for the first time in the Presidential Suite at Belham Castle. The poor man was terrified. Curled up on the floor beside a cast iron radiator, hugging himself..."

* * *

Kaine started reading from the top of page one again, keen to work out a way to snatch Enderby without raising any alarms or harming any of his protection team. Eliminating the risk to innocent non-combatants happened to be at the very top of his rules of engagement. And in this instance, he included official, close-order protection officers—bodyguards—on the list of non-combatants.

"You definitely want Enderby undamaged?" Will asked after another extended pause.

"Unmarked, I said. He needs to be able to function, assuming we decide to let him return to his post."

"A traffic accident's no good then," Will mused, thinking out loud.

"That's right. Impossible to control all the variables."

"And you definitely don't want to risk injuring his bodyguards," Will said. "His *well-armed* bodyguards," he added unnecessarily.

"They're only doing their jobs. I don't want to risk innocents."

Kaine had hurt more than enough innocents in his time. The memory of the fireball he'd caused in the evening sky over the Humber Estuary, and the imagined pre-death terror of the eighty-three passengers and crew who died in it, rarely strayed far from his mind. The tragedy would haunt him for the rest of his life.

Will snorted. "Innocent bodyguards? Are there any such individuals?"

Kaine ignored the question and tapped the sheaf of papers in his hand. "Snatching him from his office is another no-no."

Will nodded. "Too much security. We'd never get past the front desk."

"Not without a full-frontal assault, which is totally out of the question, by the way."

"And even if we blagged our way in," Will said, "which we might be able to do with the right IDs and the right story—"

"We wouldn't be able to smuggle him out of the building without risking a firefight."

Again, Will nodded.

"An overnight incursion wouldn't get us anywhere either. The building's locked up tighter than a drum," Kaine added. "And Enderby doesn't strike me as the type to work into the wee small hours very often."

"You're not making this easy, Ryan."

"Nothing worth doing is ever easy." Kaine shot his long-time friend a wry smile.

"You can be really profound. Anyone ever tell you that? Really deep."

"Deep, that's me." Kaine sighed.

"The creep visits the local gym three or four times a week. Could we take him there?"

"Might be doable." Kaine scrunched up his face. "But there's always at least one minder in tow, and the gym will have internal monitoring and security. I'd rather not risk it if we can find a better alternative."

"We could pick him up at his home," Will said. "There'd be significantly less interference than at the office, and we're more likely to find something at his house. You did say you were looking for leverage, right?"

"I did."

"There has to be something incriminating somewhere. Corky hasn't found anything online, and there's no way Enderby became Director of the NCTA on his own merits. No bloody way." Will sniffed. "I met him during my time at MI6. Did I tell you?"

"No," Kaine said, hiking an eyebrow. "No, I don't think you did."

Kaine leant against the back of his chair both to look at Will and to ease a cramping lower back. The cheap office chair couldn't have been much more uncomfortable if it tried. He set a mental reminder to have one of the men pick up some more comfortable chairs.

Will frowned and scratched his chin. "Didn't I? How remiss of me."

"What did you make of him?"

"Oily bugger. Any slimier and he'd have left a trail in his wake like a snail or a slug."

"That nasty, eh?"

"Worse. Full of himself. Anyway, getting back to business. Is his home an option?"

Kaine flipped the pages until he found the section he needed.

"Penthouse Suite, Bideford Avenue, Holborn," Kaine read aloud. "Concierge-monitored twenty-four-seven. Alarmed door access linked to the local copshop, which is less than a ten-minute drive away. Wall-to-wall surveillance cameras outside and in. Enderby would have to escort us into the place, and I have no idea how we could arrange that. Do you?"

"Not within the terms of engagement you've outlined, no." Will shot him a trademark dead-eyed stare.

"If we look hard enough, we'll find a way."

Will twitched his right shoulder. His version of a shrug.

"All things are possible ... given time." He snorted. "It's not like we're on a schedule or anything. Oh no." He threw open his free hand. "We've got all the time in the world, right? There's only the little matter of a UK Government Grey Notice on your head, and with it, the risk of imminent and officially sanctioned death by a host of government funded and supported assassins. And who knows how many names will be added to the list when Malcolm Sampson's 'untimely demise' has been thoroughly investigated? Assuming it *will* be properly investigated. You never know, *my* name might even make it onto the list ... *given time*." He dropped his hands to the desk and sighed.

Kaine absorbed the tirade which had to be one of the longest continuous speeches the usually taciturn Will Stacy had ever delivered.

"Thanks to Corky, we have countermeasures in place to protect everyone's identities," Kaine announced quietly.

Will sat up straighter. He didn't seem to find his chair as uncomfortable as Kaine found his. At least, he didn't squirm around as much.

"Come again?"

"Corky has designed certain countermeasures. Didn't I tell you?"

"No, you didn't," Will said, twisting his head to push his right ear closer to Kaine. "What countermeasures?"

Kaine allowed himself an easy smile.

"He's modified the biometric data on all our military records. That includes our height and weight, our blood type, DNA, fingerprints, retinal scans. They currently look very little like us. He's also added a patch to the PNC, that's the Police National Computer—"

"I know what the PNC is, Ryan," Will interrupted, looking both impressed and surprised—a rare thing indeed for Will Stacy, whose poker face was legendary and flawless. Kaine had never been able to discover a "tell" and always refused to play him at cards.

"Of course you do," Kaine continued, still smiling. "So, the patch automatically modifies any computerised forensic evidence we leave at our 'crime scenes' to make sure that nobody can recognise a pattern that might link back to us. Basically, Corky has 'ghosted' us from every official database in the UK."

"Bloody hell," Will said. "He can really do that?"

"Apparently," Kaine said, tugging at his earlobe. "I don't have a clue how he does it or how it works, but I trust Corky to do what he says."

"That's ... quite fantastic."

"It is, isn't it." Kaine nodded. "I told you he was good. How do you think I've stayed free for the past nine months with the whole of the UK establishment out for my hide?"

"Exactly how many people have been 'ghosted'?"

"Everyone who's helped me, including Lara. And ..."

"And?"

"I've asked him to prep your records for similar treatment."

Will hiked his dark eyebrows. "Thanks."

"Only one issue."

"Which is?"

"Corky wants your permission to go ahead with the 'ghosting'. Says he'd never ghost anyone without their consent. Part of his own rules of engagement."

"Next time you speak to him, tell him I said he could crack on. I'm more than happy being ghosted. I've always considered myself a bit of a 'free spirit'."

In the middle of Kaine's groan, the largest monitor attached to the barn's gable end wall flashed into life, showing the round, smiling face of the computer hacker in question.

"Whatcha, Mr K and Mr S. How you both diddling?" He seemed back to his normal bubbly self after weeks of apparently being under the weather.

"Evening, Corky," Kaine said, "were your ears burning?"

"Huh? Why would they be burning? Was you talking about old Corky?"

"Nothing but singing your praises, my friend. In fact, I've just told Will about your nifty online countermeasures."

"And I am most impressed," Will said. "In fact, I'd be delighted if you could ghost me from the official record in a similar way."

Corky's grin widened. "Consider it done, Mr S. Consider it—crud." He looked off to the side and his smile melted from his mobile face.

"Trouble?" Kaine asked.

"A red flag on The Trust's website. You should be getting the relayed message in a tick."

"Financial issue or the other?"

"The other," Corky answered, head turned, clearly reading from a screen off to his left. "Give Corky a tick."

Kaine held his breath, preparing to leave, and mentally running through a pre-op checklist.

Corky's fingers rattled his keyboard, his eyes never leaving the screen to his left. After what seemed like an age, he nodded.

"Yep, Corky's confirmed the man's *bona fides*. He's a genuine 83. Hubby of the pilot's daughter." He turned his eyes to the main screen and threw Kaine a look of real sympathy. "His mobile phone number's kosher, too. Officially registered to him."

"He included his mobile number?"

"Yep." Corky nodded. "Looks serious." Corky typed something else. "There you go, Mr K."

A message flashed up on the screen adjacent to the monitor carrying Corky's face. Simultaneously, Kaine's secure mobile buzzed. He ignored the mobile and read the transcript from the screen. Will read the message, too. It didn't take either long to grasp its gravity.

"Bugger," Will said.

"Agreed," Kaine said, teeth gritted. His heartrate increased at the thought of what Micah and Molly Williams must have been going through.

"Genuine, d'you think?" Will said, frowning. "A kidnapping in southern France? Sounds a little farfetched. Could be a hoax to draw you out."

"He's a member of the 83. I *have* to respond." Kaine turned to the large screen. "Corky, do you have a location for Mr Williams' mobile?"

Corky nodded.

"He's stopped at the Thurrock Services on the M25. The message says he's on his way to the Chunnel. Looks kosher to old Corky. At least he's heading the right way from Shoreditch."

"Thanks, Corky. Can you program the GPS on my mobile to follow the signal?"

"Already on that, Mr K. So long as his phone's powered up and he'd got it with him, you'll be able to find the poor bloke no probs."

"How far from the Chunnel is he?"

Corky closed his eyes for a moment. "About an hour, maybe ninety minutes, this time of day."

"Hell," Kaine said. "It'll take me at least three hours from here."

Corky frowned. "You wanna intercept him 'fore he reaches France, I suppose?"

Kaine nodded. "If possible. I'd like to see whether he's being tailed. Is there anything you can do to hold him up? It can't look like Micah's waiting for anyone, though."

"That's a tough ask." Corky's frown deepened, and he scratched at the fluff on his chin that passed as a beard. "Leave it with ol' Corky for a bit. Let's see what he can come up with."

"Excellent. Thanks, Corky. I'll contact Micah on the way."

Kaine jumped to his feet. Will stood, too.

"Where are you going?" Kaine asked.

"With you, of course. After all, I am your wingman." He smiled.

Kaine shook his head. "No need. If the message is authentic, I'll be heading into France. If necessary, I can always RV with Rollo along the way."

"Rollo? He'll hardly have had time to reach Bordeaux yet."

Kaine grimaced. "I know, but he'd be really annoyed if I worked his home turf without at least checking in with him."

"And what do I do in the meantime? I can't be sitting here twiddling my thumbs like a numpty until you get back."

Kaine pointed to the Enderby dossier. "You already have a task, should you choose to accept it." He winked.

"And what happens if I *can* think of a way to intercept Enderby that meets your stringent code of engagement? What then?"

"You know what's required."

Will nodded. "I do."

"In which case, do what you do best, my friend. Now that Lara's here to look after Mike, Connor's available if you need a wingman of your own. You can use Hunter too, come to that. And the kitty will cover all expenses."

"We have a petty cash account?" As a recent member of Kaine's ad hoc team, Will had yet to learn the financial ramifications of working with The 83 Trust's well-resourced military arm.

Kaine grinned. "Don't forget to keep all the receipts."

"Oh yeah. I'm sure I can claim legitimate expenses on my taxes. You are such a funny man."

"He ain't joking, Mr S," Corky said, his expression deadly serious while he worked his keyboard. "Corky's got it all sussed. Set everything up as a charitable organisation, he has. Nobody wants to waste any dosh."

Kaine turned away, said, "Keep in touch, Will," and left the comms room without a backwards glance.

As he skipped down the barn's wooden staircase, Kaine made an instant decision. He'd allow himself a lightning-quick stop off to say goodbye to Lara, knowing she wouldn't ask to join him for once, not now she had Mike to look after.

9

Tuesday 30th May – Evening

Eurotunnel, Folkestone, Kent, UK

Kaine rolled his Range Rover to a stop at the automatic ticket machine which had read his car's registration plate. His latest cover name, Arnold Jeffries, appeared on the machine's screen, together with his car details and the date and time Corky had booked his crossing. Somehow, he'd managed to book the ticket three days earlier. The genius hacker always thought of everything. Kaine followed the screen's instructions, answered "yes" to the relevant questions, and the machine printed his ticket on a stiff card, which he hung from the stalk of his rear-view mirror. He nudged the car forwards.

A short, stop-start drive later, he showed his fake passport to the humourless border guard sitting inside a Plexiglass booth. She compared his face with the passport photo—always a tense moment—and appeared satisfied, then shone the passport's information page under a security light. After a momentary pause, she nodded and waved him through. He smiled at her, breathed again, and rolled slowly away.

No matter how often he tested Corky's false legends and the ID documents that supported them, the border crossing process always gave him the jitters. One day, the documents would fail. That day would test Kaine's determination not to hurt the innocent in his bid to remain free and clear.

Thankfully, that day had yet to arrive.

Kaine rolled his SUV forwards and parked behind a bright red Fiat Punto. Fortunately, he'd reached the high point on a downslope, giving him a good view of the station terminal. A double line of cars stretched out in a gentle right-hand curve into the distance. The queue filtered down to a single lane as it approached the platform. According to Corky's tracker app, Micah Williams' dark blue Peugeot 107 was towards the head of the queue, some one hundred cars distant. From his elevated position, Kaine searched the stationary cars until he found it.

With luck, they'd be boarding the same train.

Kaine reached over to the rear passenger seat, pulled a pair of binoculars from the side pocket of his Bergen, and raised them to his eyes. In the Peugeot, a man sat in the driver's seat, head in hands, long hair dangling. Even through the lenses and at a distance, Micah Williams looked distraught.

Once again, Kaine hesitated, putting off the dreaded moment of first contact with the latest endangered member of The 83. After the three-hour dash from Long Buckby to Folkestone, Kaine still hadn't worked out what to say. He'd rehearsed a dozen different opening pitches in his head, but each one sounded worse than the last. They were all ridiculous.

Micah and Molly Williams were in trouble. They needed his help, and Kaine couldn't even work out a way to introduce himself.

Such a bloody coward.

Micah would be terrified. No telling how a terrified man would react to his situation. The mistakes he might make. He needed help. He needed a friend. He needed Kaine.

C'mon, man. Get a grip. Do it!

Kaine snatched his mobile from the passenger seat, dialled Micah's number from the red flag message, and hit enter. The call took a while to connect, giving Kaine even more time to stew. Through the binoculars, he watched Micah jerked his head upright, scrambled for his mobile, and raised it to his ear.

"H-Hello?" Micah said, his voice timid, wary.

"Mr Williams," Kaine said, "you don't know me, but I'm from The 83 Trust."

There, he'd done it. Made the opening gambit. It hadn't turned out too bad.

"Y-You are? Really? Thank God. I-I'd given up hope," he said, the tension clear in his pinched and rushed words.

"Don't worry, Mr Williams. We're here to help."

"'Here'?" Micah barked. "What do you mean, you're here?"

"I'm here, at the Eurotunnel terminal. I can see you ahead of me in the queue. Please try to stay calm. ... No," he said, "don't look around. Try not to draw attention to yourself. There may be others in the queue with 'eyes on'. You understand?"

"Y-You can see me? Really?"

"Yes."

"How did you find me?"

"You gave us your phone number. I've been tracking you ever since you contacted us. Following your progress."

"Progress?" Micah snapped. "What bloody progress? They've cancelled the last four trains."

"Yes, I know. The Chunnel website calls it a 'minor glitch with the signals'," Kaine said. "The cancellations are precautionary."

Corky's ingenuity never failed to impress the hell out of Kaine, not that he could sing his praises to Micah. It might push the poor man over the edge, and it certainly wouldn't help Kaine build Micah's trust.

"I've been trapped in this bloody queue for the last two hours!" Micah raged. "It's killing me—"

"They've cured the glitch, Mr Williams—Micah. We'll be on our way really soon. Look at the signs."

The overhead information gantries—spaced at regular intervals along the terminal—that had been displaying apologies for the delays caused by "technical issues" changed to "Thank you for your patience. Boarding will commence in five minutes."

"Oh, thank God," Micah gasped. His voice wavered, clearly on the edge of tears. "Thank God."

Thank Corky, more like.

"One good thing, Micah," Kaine said, smiling. "The delay's given us a chance to reach you."

"Us?" Micah asked, sniffling. He wiped his nose with a tissue. "How many people are with you?"

"I'm alone at the moment."

"Alone?" Micah twisted in his seat and his head swivelled. "What can you do on your own?"

"Micah," Kaine said, speaking slowly, trying to radiate confidence. "Please keep calm. If necessary, I can call on operatives based throughout the Continent. But for the moment, I'll be working alone. It's for the best. Trust me, Micah. I know what I'm doing."

"But they have my wife. They're threatening to kill Molly. I-I don't … Maybe I shouldn't have called you. This is so dangerous. Oh God, I don't know what to do."

"I'm here now, Micah. You aren't alone. We can work though this together."

"But what if … what if they *are* watching me?"

"Just follow their instructions. You'll be okay."

"Will I?"

I hope so.

"Micah, does your car have a mobile phone holder?"

"What? Er … no. The car's not mine."

"Okay, so put it on speaker and place the phone on the centre console. We don't want you stopped for using a mobile while driving."

"Oh, right." Micah followed Kaine's advice.

"Can you still hear me, Micah?"

"Y-Yes. Just about. Don't know what it'll be like when we're driving, though."

"If it's a problem, we'll sort something out."

Moments later, the queue finally started moving. A gap grew between Micah's Peugeot and the car in front, and the understandably impatient driver in the Toyota behind blared his horn angrily. The Peugeot lurched forwards and stopped as Micah stalled the engine.

"Oh dear God," Micah repeated, the mobile picking up his fear and frustration.

He fired up the engine again, crunched the car into first gear, and jerked away.

"Try to relax, Micah," Kaine said. "I know that's easy for me to say, but you need to keep it together. I can hear you panting. Try to regulate your breathing. Make it slow, deep, and steady. I promise you it will help."

"I'm scared," Micah said, plaintive, voice faltering. "I don't know what I'd do if I lost her—if I lost my Molly."

The man was close to losing it. Kaine had seen the same thing happen many times in raw, untested recruits on the eve of combat. He'd seen many of those same timid recruits, once blooded, turn into battle-hardened veterans within minutes of the combat starting. Others though, failed the test and were often among the first to die.

On which side of the fence would Micah fall?

Micah pulled in a deep breath and released it slowly—the crystal-clear phone connection relaying every sound.

"Good, Micah. That's better. Keep that pattern going. It *will* help."

After losing sight of the Peugeot, Kaine followed the extended line of cars, entered the final carriage through a side door, and drove along inside the train until the car in front stopped and the shutter doors dropped into place.

"Micah, are you okay?"

"Yes, yes. I-I'm sorry. I panicked."

"I understand, Micah. I really do. This is challenging for you."

"Who are you? You haven't even told me your name."

"Today, I'm Arnold Jeffries. Don't laugh, but you can call me Arnie."

"Arnie? Not your real name, I suppose."

"Correct."

"Will I ever learn your real name?"

I hope not.

The train shuddered, started rolling, and picked up speed rapidly once they'd entered the tunnel itself.

"Micah," Kaine said, ignoring the question, "please stay in your car for the whole trip. Try to maintain the steady breathing. I'm going to have to hang up for a few minutes. I need to contact my colleagues, but I'll call you right back. Okay?"

"Please don't take long. I'm scared."

"I won't."

Kaine ended the call and puffed out his cheeks. That went better than he could have expected, but Micah's panic wouldn't help anyone. He tapped the fully charged earpiece once and waited. Three spare earpieces remained in their charging case, plugged into the car's USB port. Although the units retained enough charge to operate for six hours straight, spares always came in handy.

"*Whatcha, Mr K,*" Corky said, bright as a button. It made a nice change from his recent lacklustre performance. The magician had been off-key for a few weeks. In a quieter time, Kaine would try to find out what had happened, but the mission came first. The 83 always came first.

"*How can Corky help you this fine evening?*"

"Thanks for the 'signal failure'. You played a blinder, there. Over."

"*Too right. Corky surprises even himself sometimes.*"

Corky laughed and Kaine almost joined in.

"Okay, tell me. The house in Fleur De Lis Road," Kaine said, "did you find out who owns it? Over."

"*You'll never believe this,*" Corky said, cheerfulness bubbling in his voice, "*but the bloke's name is actually Abe. In fact, he's Abraham Pedersen. Turns out the geezer's owned the place for forty-three years.*"

"That's interesting. I expected it to be a rental. What do you have on 'Uncle Abe' Pedersen? Over."

"*He's retired. Been drawing his state pension for a couple of years. The geezer also has a small works pension from his time as a 'Jeweller to the Stars'. That's his old firm's tagline, not Corky's. He had a jeweller's shop in Hatton Garden which went bust about eight years back. Looks like the recession were bad news for him.*"

"And it seems he's now diversified into smuggling and kidnap. Over."

"*Fancy using his own gaff for the meet with Micah Williams. A bit dozy, innit?*"

"Overconfident, maybe. Or maybe a sign of desperation. What about police interest? Does Uncle Abe have a criminal record? Over."

"*Nothing found so far, Mr K. But ol' Corky ain't finished searching yet. The geezer pays all his bills and taxes on time. A model citizen, in fact. He's either been very lucky, or he has friends helping him keep under the radar. Or, he's a desperate amateur. 'Course, that don't mean his mate, Luc, ain't a real bad 'un.*"

"And dealing with desperate criminals is tricky. There's no telling which way they'll jump when pressed. Any lead on Luc? Over."

"*Nothing on the Toulouse address Mr Williams coughed up so far. It's an 'oliday let. And there's no one in Uncle Abe's records who fits the bill. No friends or associates even come close. Corky's gonna keep digging, though.*"

"Thanks. Can you run a deep dive on the old man? It'd be nice to know about his family, friends, and the like. Over."

"*Frodo's all over that.*"

Is he now?

"I meant to ask about our new colleague. How's he doing? Over."

"*Happy as a sandboy on a beach in the summer sun. There ain't no need to fret yourself on that front, Mr K. Corky knows how to press Frodo's buttons and keep him 'appy and peaceful. All it takes is a little Corky magic."*

Kaine managed a smile. It would appear that Corky had found a new friend. A like-minded soul mate.

"Anything on the Amsterdam connection? Over."

"Nothing yet. The language barrier's slowing things up a tad. But Corky and Frodo are working on that, too."

"Thanks, Corky. I appreciate all your help. I really do. Over."

"'Course you do, Mr K. Corky knows that. Laters." The earpiece clicked into silence.

Kaine changed tack, pressed a button on the steering wheel, and said, "Call Will Stacy."

The voice-activated system dialled the number and made the connection. Kaine briefed Will on progress so far.

"Want me to put a watch on Uncle Abe's place?" Will asked.

"Good idea, but keep it low profile. Slim and Larry are good at that sort of thing, and they've got nothing better to do since blowing their contract in Dubai. Tell them I said they'd be on the usual terms and conditions."

"What happens if Uncle Abe moves?"

"Have them follow him at a distance and report back. On no account are they to engage. Not while Molly Williams is still captive. Understood?"

"Understood."

"And what about you, Will. Any thoughts regarding Enderby?"

"Nothing concrete, but I'm working on it. Hunter and I are going to follow him for a while, see if we can't identify a weakness in his defences."

"Good idea. But don't do anything precipitous off your own bat."

"Precipitous? Moi?" Will said, in mock surprise. Kaine could almost see him pressing the flat of his hand against his chest. "If I knew what 'precipitous' meant, I'd probably be insulted."

Kaine grinned.

"Okay, Will. Keep in touch."

"Will do. Take care."

Kaine disconnected the call and dialled Rollo.

"Evening, Colour Sergeant," Kaine opened. "Where are you?"

"Home, sir," Rollo answered, wariness bleeding into his voice. "Marie-Odile collected me from the airport."

"Excellent, excellent. How is she?"

"A little, er … frazzled after what happened, but she's holding up well enough. We're just about to eat. This isn't a social call, is it."

"I'm afraid not," Kaine said and launched straight into a briefing on the Williams case.

To his great credit, after listening in silence, Rollo volunteered his services without hesitation—and without discussing it with Marie-Odile first. An omission he might live to regret if Kaine knew Rollo's new wife as well as he imagined.

"How long will it take you to reach Toulouse?" Kaine asked.

"About two and a half hours. Want me to head straight there?"

"No, no. Not yet. I'm just marking your card. Hopefully, it won't come to that."

"Of course it will. I'll have my go-bag ready. Let me have the word and the location, and I'll be on my way."

"Thanks, Rollo. Give my love to Marie-Odile."

"Will do, sir. Good hunting. I'll probably see you tomorrow."

"Hope not, but yes. Probably."

After hanging up on Rollo, Kaine redialled Micah.

"Hello, Micah, it's Arnie. How are you holding up?"

"Better thanks. The deep breathing helped. I'm still terrified for Molly, though. Can you tell me anything?"

Kaine paused for a moment, trying to decide how much to reveal.

"I have an associate helping with research. As it turns out, Abe actually owns the house on Fleur De Lis Road. Which means he's probably not going anywhere. My associate is also trying to identify any contacts he has in France. With luck, he'll find something before we reach Amsterdam."

"Is that likely?"

"My associate is good at his job, Micah. Very good."

"God I hope so."

"Stay strong, Micah. I'm with you. You aren't alone."

The Eurostar shot through the Chunnel at one hundred miles per hour. Amsterdam beckoned. Kaine closed his eyes and forced himself to relax. Like the earpieces in their case, Kaine needed to recharge his batteries, even if it was only for a few minutes.

10

Wednesday 31st May – Pre-Dawn

Eurotunnel, Calais, Hauts-de-France, France

Less than forty minutes after leaving Folkstone, the Eurostar exited the tunnel in Calais and slowed to a stop. Moments later, the internal shutter doors reopened, and the vehicles started disembarking.

"Arnie?" Micah asked. They hadn't spoken for a few minutes, but Kaine had kept the connection active.

"Yes?"

"A-Are we ever going to meet in person?"

"Yes, but not right away. I need to confirm that you don't have a tail."

"What should I do?"

"Exactly what Abe told you to do. Drive to Amsterdam, deliver the package, and then head for France. I'll be with you all the way."

"Okay."

Surprisingly, there were no passport checks on the French side of the border. They simply followed the line of cars through the station to the exit and headed northeast. They took the coastal road, the A16, driving towards Belgium.

Crossing the border into Belgium turned out to be a major non-event. No border control, no bells, no whistles, just a square road sign in blue with a circle of gold stars and the single word, *België*, in white. The French A16, became the Belgian E40.

Had they been driving in daylight, they would have been able to see the countryside of Flanders stretching out pan flat for miles on either side of the motorway. As it was, the darkness made the drive excessively tedious and fatiguing. To keep them both awake, Kaine maintained a casual conversation. At least as casual as he could, given the circumstances.

After having discussed their house renovations, Kaine asked about Molly and the couple's plans for the future, and Micah dropped the bombshell.

"Molly's four months pregnant."

Shit.

Kaine closed his eyes for a second, trying to take in the devastating news.

"We told Luc," Micah continued. "Begged him to let us go. Promised not to go to the police. But ... he didn't believe us. Said we were lying. Said we were trying to play to a conscience he didn't have. He actually laughed. Gave us a mocking round of applause. Molly's really slim, you see. She's barely showing yet. Just a little bump. Oh God, what are we going to do?"

At that point, Micah broke down. His sobs wrenched Kaine's heart and anger boiled within him. Anger aimed at the unknown German, Luc, anger at Abe Pedersen, and the valet, Bogdan. Evil men who had visited terror on the innocent. They deserved Kaine's attention. They deserved his kind of raw justice. And by God, they were going to receive it.

The bastards were going to pay. But first, Molly had to be safe.

"Micah," Kaine said, trying to keep his voice calm, comforting, "I'll do everything I can to get her back. Everything."

He fell short of turning the statement into a promise. Only a fool would make that kind of commitment.

After the revelation, the conversation ran out of steam. A few minutes later, Kaine ended the call with a promise to pick up if Micah needed him for anything, and the drive continued in silence.

They bypassed Bruges and skirted south of Ghent, picking up the E17 to Antwerp. In the dark, the only difference between France and Belgium was the language displayed on the road signs. Luckily, the pictograms overcame the language barrier and the GPS kept both Kaine and Micah on course to their fast-approaching rendezvous.

* * *

THREE HOURS INTO THEIR JOURNEY, Kaine's earpiece clicked once.

"Alpha One here, Control. What do you have for me? Over."

"Nothing new on Luc so far, but there is some good news."

"Excellent," Kaine said, making himself smile. "Good news is always welcome. Over."

"Corky thought you'd be happy 'bout that." He chuckled, just like the old Corky.

"So, what's the good news? Over."

"There ain't no sign of the Peugeot's infotainment and tracking system having been compromised or nothing. So, unless you've spotted a physical tail, it looks like you're in the clear. Corky's advice? When you stop, run the detector over the Peugeot, just to make sure."

"Will do, Control. Brilliant. That really helps. Thanks again, Corky. Over."

"No probs, Mr K. Laters."

Kaine reconnected with Micah.

"Hello, Micah. Not long now. How are you holding up?"

"How d'you bloody think?" Micah snapped. "I'm close to puking."

Kaine shook his head at his own idiocy. He couldn't blame the youngster for his outburst. In Micah's position, he'd suffer the same sense of anger, fear, and desperation. In fact, Kaine *had* been in Micah's position very recently, and he *had* felt exactly the same way.

"Sorry, Micah. Daft question."

"No, no. I'm the one who should apologise," Micah said, speaking quietly, more controlled. "You're only trying to help. I shouldn't have shouted at you, but ... God, Molly must be so scared. I can't imagine what she's going through. Without me. All alone."

Micah pulled in a long, staggered breath and resumed the deep breathing exercises.

Good man. We'll get through this.

"Micah, you won't believe me, but I understand what you're going through. I really do."

"Really," Micah coughed. "Your wife was abducted? Yeah, I believe you." Disbelief coloured his words, and anger bubbled just below the surface.

"Not my wife, Micah." *Not yet.* "My ... partner."

Kaine threw his mind back two, no, three days to relive the frantic motorway journey on the BMW K1300GT, still registered to the recently deceased John M Abbott. A journey during which he'd pushed the high-powered motorbike close to its limits in a frantic race to rescue Lara. The hopelessness, fear, and desperation he'd experienced at the time, the near-paralysis of thought and action, had to be close to the way Micah felt. The only real difference between the two men being Kaine's training and combat experience. In his life, Kaine had been in desperate, life-threatening situations many times. In some way, it had hardened him, prepared him for the trauma, but Micah had no such experience.

"Really?" Micah said, the doubt lessening. "What happened?"

"Sorry, Micah. I can't go into details, but she survived."

"And the people who took her?" Micah asked after a momentary delay.

"All I can tell you is they won't be abducting anyone else."

Not ever.

Micah tried fishing for more details, but Kaine refused to allow himself to be drawn and, once again, the conversation faded.

* * *

One hour from their destination, after passing Meerkerk, Kaine made the decision.

"Micah, pull into the next service station. We need a quick face-to-face."

"I'm not being followed?"

"Not a chance. I've been watching closely."

They pulled off the A27 at Junction 26, following the signs to Lexmond. The tree-lined, single-laned slip road curved sharply around to the right, and a left turn took them to Lakerveld. After negotiating a roundabout—anti-clockwise—they took a left turn into a small twenty-four-hour Van Zessen service station.

Micah pulled into the first pump and started filling his tank. Kaine rolled alongside the adjacent pump and climbed out of the car on apparently stiff legs.

Micah's disappointed double-take at Kaine's lack of bulk made him grin. He had the same effect on most people.

"What," he muttered across the gap between them, "you expected an Arnie lookalike?"

"Well, sort of," Micah answered. A flush rose up his neck and reddened his youthful face.

Dressed in heavy walking boots, blue jeans, dark blue polo shirt, and black zipped hoodie, Micah stood around ten centimetres taller than Kaine. With strong shoulders and a trim waist, he looked fit, but gaunt and tired. Dark lines circled his haunted eyes, and his long hair hung limp around his head.

"I'm sorry," Micah added.

"Not a problem," Kaine said, turning away, scanning their surroundings.

Theirs were the only cars on the forecourt and nothing seemed out of place. Three articulated lorries occupied bays in the distant car park, lights out, their drivers no doubt taking their enforced rest breaks. Two private cars–a mid-sized Fiat and a large Subaru— filled two other bays. The rest stood empty.

Micah's pump clicked and he replaced the filler cap.

"Park up and pay," Kaine said, head down as though fully absorbed in his task. "Buy yourself a drink and a snack. You look like you haven't eaten in a while. I'll join you in a minute."

Micah said something under his breath that Kaine couldn't quite pick up, but it sounded like a complaint. Nonetheless, the youngster slid back into his car, rolled it forwards, and parked in front of the shop. Then he climbed out and made his way through the single entrance door.

Kaine's pump finally clicked off—he'd been filling his tank slowly, having fully fuelled in Folkestone. He retracted the nozzle halfway and squeezed another few drops of premium unleaded into the already-full tank—playing the part of an overly cautious driver keen to squeeze the most of his opportunity to refuel.

In the minutes between Micah entering the shop and Kaine closing his filler cap and checking his tyres, nothing happened to tweak his senses. Vehicles raced past on the nearby A27, but the slip road remained empty and silent. The drivers of the two parked cars had finished their refreshment break and driven away in different directions.

Satisfied they were free and clear, Kaine strolled towards the shop. At the Peugeot, he stopped, took the bug detector from his pocket, and raised it to his ear as though it were a mobile phone.

He pressed the activation button, said, "Hello? Oh, hi there," and simulated a phone conversation while pacing up and down alongside Micah's car, waiting for the device to run through its search routine. In the middle of one lap, Kaine "accidentally" dropped his keys. He stooped to pick them up, giving the detector a chance to scan the Peugeot's floor pan, groaning as he straightened. After a full minute, having found nothing, the detector's red light flashed green. Clear.

"See you soon. Bye," Kaine said to no one, dropped the detector back into his pocket, and continued to the shop.

He pushed through the door and blinked against the harsh lighting. The man behind the kiosk screen welcomed him in English—his Range Rover's UK licence plate an obvious giveaway. Kaine paid and moved to the café counter where a dark-haired woman in her middle years with a full figure, waited to take his order.

"A large Americano, please. Black, no sugar."

"Anything else, sir?" she asked, trying to hide a yawn behind her hand.

He pointed to a chocolate-topped cereal bar. "One of those, please."

Smiling, she poured his drink and rang up his order. Kaine paid and turned. Micah sat in the corner, trying to make himself invisible. It wasn't working. He looked the image of a man living in fear for his wife and his life—pale, drawn, and twitchy.

Kaine carried his drink and cereal bar to the table alongside Micah's and lowered himself into the bench seat with his back against the wall, sighing while doing so. Micah had touched neither his drink nor his food.

"Eat," Kaine said, nodding towards the unopened plastic triangle containing a cheese salad sandwich on wholemeal bread.

"Not hungry," Micah whispered.

"Force it down," Kaine ordered. "You need the energy. You're out on your feet, and you've started to weave out of your lane. You're no good to Molly if you wipe yourself out in a car crash."

"Okay."

Micah tore open the plastic panel, pulled out the top sandwich, and nibbled at one end. He chewed and washed it down with a swig of his drink—a white coffee. A moment later, he took a proper bite and chewed with more enthusiasm.

"When was the last time you ate anything?"

Micah shrugged and worked the ball of food into the side of his mouth before speaking.

"Can't remember," he said. "Yesterday? The day before? I don't know. I stopped at Thurrock Services on the M25 to call you, but couldn't bring myself to eat anything. Frightened of throwing it straight back up. What day is it?"

"Wednesday."

The younger man blinked hard. "Is it?"

Kaine nodded.

"Molly and I ... had breakfast together on Monday morning. Since then ..." He broke off, blinking back the tears. "They took us around midday. I've been running scared ever since. Too terrified to eat. What were you doing?"

"When?"

"Outside," he whispered, still chewing, "by the car."

"Checking for a bug. The Peugeot's clean."

Micah nodded. "Thank God."

He resumed chewing. Kaine gave him time to swallow and take another pull on his coffee before speaking again.

"I'm here now," he said. "You're not alone."

"What can you do?" Micah said, looking Kaine up and down from the corner of his eyes, clearly unimpressed with what he saw.

"You'd be surprised," Kaine answered. "I know what I'm doing, Micah. I've handled hostage negotiations before. Many times."

"Really?"

Kaine nodded. "Before setting up The 83 Trust."

"You set it up?"

Again, Kaine nodded. He sipped at his coffee, which tasted much better than he had any right to expect, and unwrapped his cereal bar. He bit off a chunk and chewed. Again, it turned out far better than it looked, moist and not too sweet. The Dutch knew how to stock their petrol stations.

"Why?"

"It's simple, really. I'm a philanthropist," Kaine said, tilting his head to one side. "My friends and I came into some money, and we wanted to help the families of the people who died on Flight BE1555. People like you and Molly. We split our resources. Some of us deal with the financial needs of the 83, others deal with the more ... practical requirements."

Micah finished the first sandwich and pulled out the second. His colour had improved—a clear demonstration of the restorative effects of nourishment.

"I noticed the change you made to the website's home page," Micah said, nodding. "You have other people to help you?"

"I do."

"Are you going to call them in?"

"Not necessarily. I'll see what happens in Amsterdam."

"What do you want me to do?"

"Exactly as we discussed. You'll make the delivery before nine o'clock as Abe instructed. Wait for the call about Molly's location, and then head for France. Now, please take out your phone and lay it on the table."

Micah frowned in confusion, but did as Kaine asked.

"Thank you."

Kaine dug his own phone, the real one, from his pocket and called Corky.

"Whatcha, Mr K. I see you and Mr W have stopped at a petrol station. Are you together?"

"Yes, and his phone's right next to mine. Can you do the business please?"

"No probs. Open the app Corky downloaded to your mobile. It's called '123CopyMe'."

Kaine did as Corky asked.

"How long will it take?"

"Give it a couple of minutes. His mobile's operating system is from the Ark. Corky's gonna call you back."

By the time Kaine finished his cereal bar and his drink, his mobile phone chimed. He picked it up.

"Finished?" he asked.

"Yep. All done."

"Excellent, Mr C. Thanks."

Micah followed Kaine's action closely, but did nothing to interfere.

"What just happened?"

"I've just mirrored your phone. I'll be able to see and hear whatever's happening on your mobile. It works in stealth mode so no one will know I'm earwigging."

"How's that going to help?"

"Information is power, Micah. And for this situation, we need all the power we can get."

The last thing Kaine wanted was to tell Micah his plans. He had no idea how the distraught man would react.

Kaine pulled back his cuff and read the time on his watch. 03:13, which made it 04:13 locally. A brightening in the eastern sky signified the approach of dawn.

Kaine tucked the mobile into his pocket, removed one of the spare earpieces he'd taken from the Range Rover, and eased closer to the table. He picked up the laminated menu and pretended to scan the items—standard service station fare, chips with everything. After a few seconds, he placed the earpiece on the table and covered it with the menu.

"Did you see that?" he asked.

"What is it?"

"A comms unit. An earpiece. We'll be able to keep in touch more easily. Phones are too cumbersome and obvious. When I'm gone, grab it and take it back to the car with you. Place it in your ear—it doesn't matter which one—and tap it twice to activate. I'll talk you through the details when we're back on the road."

"An earpiece?" Micah stared at the menu and shook his head. "Are you kidding?"

Kaine ignored the question. He pushed his empty coffee mug away, leaned his elbows on the table, and hid his mouth behind his hands.

"Okay, so listen carefully. I'll be leaving now. Buy yourself another drink and something sweet. Wait here at least twenty minutes—"

"Wait here? But ... I can't be late. Don't forget the time difference. We're an hour ahead of England—"

Kaine opened a hand for silence.

"We're only forty-five minutes from Amsterdam. You have plenty of time to make the delivery. Please trust me. I do know what I'm doing." For the first time since entering the shop, he looked directly at Micah, and they locked eyes. "Listen carefully, Micah. I'm giving you fair warning. After we've confirmed the comms are operational, I'll be going dark. That means you won't be hearing from me for a while, but I can assure you, I won't be far away."

Micah leant closer.

"But I'm terrified," he gasped. "What if I mess this up? What if *you* mess—"

"You won't and neither will I. You're stronger than you think, Micah. You've got this far on your own. You've done brilliantly. We'll get through this together." He paused to let the message sink in. "Twenty minutes. Okay?"

Micah nodded through a gulp.

"Twenty minutes."

"Good man."

Kaine stood and strode from the shop without looking back.

11

Wednesday 31st May – Early Morning

Indische Buurt, Amsterdam, The Netherlands

Kaine confirmed the time. 07:26. Dawn had arrived warm and bright with a fuzz of wispy clouds shrouding the low sun. He'd parked his Range Rover with its tell-tale UK licence plates in a bay around the corner and hoofed it the one kilometre to near the delivery point, hiding himself among the early morning commuter foot traffic.

Overhead, black-headed gulls squawked and squabbled over food. The briny smell of the nearby canal mixed with the aroma of freshly ground coffee and warming croissants. Kaine's mouth watered, and his stomach grumbled. The cereal bar he'd eaten at the fuel stop hadn't made much of a dent in his hunger.

Follow what you preach, Kaine.

A crossroads on Molukkenstraat—a long, straight, two-lane thoroughfare—opened into a bicycle park and pedestrianised area bordered by a dozen or so five-storey residential blocks. Located diagonally across the square, the target block, Number 28, stood in full view of a corner coffee house.

Perfect.

Kaine picked an inside table with a good view of the square and block Number 28. He ordered a large Americano, two croissants, and a small pot of honey. For background colour, he picked up a local free paper and pretended to read while eating his light breakfast. At least he could look at the pictures and guess the gist of the story.

The comms unit clicked once in his ear.

Kaine lowered the paper, picked up his phone, and pretended to make a call while talking to Corky.

"*Whatcha, Mr K. Is you awake?*"

"Alpha One to Control. What do you have for me? Over."

"*The apartment is owned by a bloke called van Bleeker. Jan van Bleeker. And you'll never guess what the geezer does for a living.*"

"Don't tell me, he buys and sells diamonds? Over."

"*Nah, the geezer's what's called a lapidary. You know what one of them is when it's at home?*"

"A diamond cutter. Over."

"*That's right, Mr K. Got it in one.*"

"I can't think of a better way of dealing with smuggled gemstones than changing their shape. What else did you find on our new friend. Any police interest? Over."

"*Yep. There has been. Meneer van Bleeker served three years for handling stolen goods. That was back in the eighties. Been clean ever since though.*"

"Looks like he's up to his old tricks again. You have a description? Over."

"*Yep. Corky's just sent a profile and pic to your mobile. Long grey hair worn in a ponytail, bushy grey beard. Short guy. Five foot seven. And overweight. Huge, he is. Shaped like a rugby ball. You won't be able to miss him. Walks with a stick, on account of having a knackered right knee, which is probably down to him being so heavy. The bloke's saving up for a knee replacement, which is prob'ly why he's back on the wrong side of the law. Needs to pay for his surgery. One thing, though."*

"What's that? Over."

"Van Bleeker works alone. He's never had a minder or nothing. Should be easily intimidated—if you know what Corky means."

"I do. But that's not my intention at the moment. Anything else? No news of Luc, by any chance? Over."

"Nothing yet. Luc's likely a nickname. Sorry Mr K. Corky is working on it."

"Understood. Alpha One, out."

Kaine tapped the earpiece inactive and lowered his mobile to the table. He picked up the paper again and turned to the back pages to study the sports photos. The mobile dinged for an incoming email. Kaine opened the app and committed the picture of Jan van Bleeker to memory. It wouldn't prove difficult. Corky's rugby ball analogy covered it perfectly.

The earpiece clicked twice. Then twice more. Micah was showing his impatience and a lack of trust with the comms unit. Kaine couldn't blame him. The bone conduction system took a little getting used to, even for someone familiar with radio comms.

"Hello, Arnie? Is that you?" Micah asked, hurrying his words. *"Hello? Are you there?"*

"Okay, Micah, I can hear you," Kaine answered, covering his mouth with the coffee mug. "There's no need to shout. Where are you? Over."

"Sorry," Micah said, lowering his voice to a near whisper. *"Er, I'm on Zeeburgerdijk. About to turn left onto, er, Molukkenstraat."* He hesitated over the pronunciation, and who could blame him. *"I'm a few minutes away. Where are you?"*

"I'm in position. Over."

"Where's that?"

Kaine flinched. He'd forgotten what it was like to work with an amateur. As a result, he relaxed his radio protocol.

"I'm across the street from the drop-off point. Don't look for me.

I'll see you coming. There are a few empty parking spots outside the apartment block. You should be able to park without a problem."

"Right, okay."

He sounded nervous. Terrified.

"You can do this, Micah. The man you're going to see is disabled. He's no threat. Just hand him the package and leave … Hang on."

"What's wrong?"

Across the square, the front door to Number 28 opened. A round man with an ebony walking stick, complete with a silver tip, squeezed through the opening. He had to turn sideways to complete the manoeuvre. He turned to face Kaine and hobbled along the pavement which ran between the road and the cycle path, heading directly for the coffee house. The bulbous man—long grey hair tied back in a ponytail, Santa beard—limped along the pavement, favouring his right leg. A baggy grey sweater hung from his rounded shoulders, its wide hem dangled around his chubby thighs and fluttered in the breeze. Loose black trousers flapped around his legs, hiding his footwear.

"What's wrong?" Micah repeated with more urgency.

"I have eyes on the target. He's heading towards me."

"Oh God. Has he spotted you?"

Brakes squealed and a car horn blasted through the comms. Micah cursed.

"What was that?" Kaine asked.

"N-Nothing. I nearly ran into the back of a van. It's okay. No damage. What's the, er … target doing?"

"Take it easy, Micah. Keep it together for a little longer. There's no problem. I'm sitting in a coffee house, and our target has just walked in. He's standing in line. Hold on." Kaine waited for the fat man to work his way to the front of the small queue. "He's buying a large coffee and a bag of pastries. Did I tell you he's a large individual?"

"No. No, you didn't."

"The man looks like a bowling ball trying to pass himself off as Father Christmas," Kaine said, trying to lighten the mood. Failing.

"I'm on Molukkenstraat, now. Where's your coffee house?"

Van Bleeker said something to the barista which elicited a hearty laugh, handed over a banknote, and waved away the change. The barista smiled, nodded his thanks, and dropped the money into a small tip jar that nestled on a shelf behind the counter.

"Don't worry about that, Micah. Just head for Number 28 and wait in the car for a few minutes. Our man's paid for his breakfast. It's a carry-out. Means he'll be heading straight home. The speed he moves, you'll arrive at more or less the same time he does."

Van Bleeker hugged his brown paper bag of treasure to his fleshy chest and waddled through the café, brushing past Kaine on the way. A waft of strong soap and pastries tickled Kaine's nose.

From the left, Micah's dark blue Peugeot rolled into view. He matched the car's pace with Santa van Bleeker and kept glancing at him through the car window.

"Micah, don't stare," Kaine snapped. "Keep going and find a place to park."

"*Sorry,*" Micah said. "*Sorry.*"

Keep it together, son.

Micah turned his head to face forwards and increased speed. He pulled away, but stopped at the junction and allowed a stream of cyclists to cross before rolling forwards again. He eventually found a parking bay on the same side of the street, and a couple of hundred metres beyond Number 28.

"Not long now, Micah. We're nearly there. Wait for my signal."

Gasping, his shoulders rising and falling like a marathon runner nearing the end of a race, van Bleeker reached the entrance to his apartment block. He keyed the door and pushed his way through. Again, he had to turn sideways to squeeze through the opening.

The time on Kaine's watch showed 08:12.

Kaine hoped van Bleeker lived on the ground floor. If he owned an apartment on the top floor, they might miss the nine o'clock deadline. He waited a full five minutes.

"Okay, Micah. Time to go. Van Bleeker will have reached his apartment by now. I don't see why we shouldn't interrupt his breakfast. Do you?"

Micah groaned.

"*Okay ... I'm going.*"

Ahead, the Peugeot's door opened, and Micah climbed out, his head on a swivel. He searched both sides of the street, clearly nervous. He looked like a man with something to hide.

"Try to relax, Micah," Kaine said. "You'll be fine."

Micah reached up and fiddled with his earpiece.

"*This thing's so uncomfortable. How the heck do you wear it all day?*"

"You get used to it."

The comms crackled and the sound levels dipped.

"Micah. Leave the earpiece alone, please. I want to record your conversation with van Bleeker. Assuming there is one."

"*Sorry.*"

Micah slammed the Peugeot's door shut. He leaned his back against it for a moment, breathing deep through an open mouth, before pushing away and turning towards Number 28, towards Kaine. His face pale and drawn, his lips pulled into a thin line, the youngster looked close to collapse.

"You can do this, Micah."

He stopped walking. Closed his eyes.

"*My ... chest is tight. I-I can't breathe.*"

Panic attack?

"It's just nerves, Micah. You can get through this."

Micah opened his eyes again, the whites large, oval. He blinked twice, breathed in deep, and puffed out his cheeks.

"You do have the package?" Kaine asked.

Micah frowned, raised his hand to his chest, and patted the outside of his jacket.

"*Yes,*" he said. "*Yes, I've got it.*"

"Just checking."

"*Thanks. I-I mean it. Thanks. Without you here ... I don't know how I'd have coped.*"

"Time's passing, Micah. Keep going."

Micah nodded and stepped forwards, his strides long and more confident. He reached the door to Number 28, searched the intercom system for the number Abe had given him, and pressed a button. The electronic chime rang out loud and clear through Kaine's earpiece.

That's it, lad. Nice and easy does it.

12

Wednesday 31st May – Micah Williams

Indische Buurt, Amsterdam, The Netherlands.

Dry-mouthed and breathing heavily, Micah stopped at the metal-framed and wire-reinforced glass door. He read the labels on the entry system, found the one he was looking for—*Appt 1a, van Bleeker*—and pressed the corresponding button. A chime echoed through the entrance hallway beyond the glass. He waited.

Nothing happened.

Micah checked his watch, just gone eight thirty. He'd reached the place well ahead of schedule. Where the bloody hell had van Bleeker disappeared to?

He pressed the button again and held it down for a count of three.

The intercom bleeped.

"Who is that?" a man asked, his voice higher pitched than Micah had expected.

God. Who am I?

"Er, ... Abe sent me."

"*Over verdomde tijd.* About bloody time. I expected you earlier. Enter."

The security system buzzed, and the front lock disengaged. Micah pushed the stainless-steel handle and the door opened inwards. He stepped inside and found a stark white entrance hall with one black door on either side of a wide stairwell. Polished concrete floors, immaculately clean, led to the grey-tiled staircase. The left-hand door opened to reveal the bulbous figure of Jan van Bleeker. The fat man scowled and pulled the door wide.

"Williams?" he whispered, glancing around and behind Micah to confirm he was alone. "Don't just stand there, man. Enter."

Leaning on the walking stick, he backed into the entrance hall and summoned Micah inside with his free hand.

Micah took a hesitant step forwards and stopped before reaching the threshold. He dug the black plastic package from the inner pocket of his jacket and offered it out.

"Do you know where my wife is?"

"Put it away, man," van Bleeker hissed, flapping his hand and staring through the glass door behind Micah. Anger flashed in his eyes and sweat shone on his fleshy face. "Come. Now!"

Micah hid the package inside the flap of his jacket and followed van Bleeker into the apartment.

The hall, warm with a deep-pile, dark grey carpet, and light grey walls, opened out into a large living space. Two oil paintings hung on the inner walls. Cityscapes showing Amsterdam in all its night-time glory.

"Close the door behind you and follow me into the kitchen."

Van Bleeker hobbled through an open door and lowered himself slowly and carefully into a dining chair, groaning and grunting with every movement.

The kitchen-diner was much larger than Micah anticipated. Sunlight flooded through a landscape window, looking out over a nicely maintained communal area to the rear of the building. A neatly trimmed lawn bordered by raised beds full of flowers made a colourful display, and not a tulip amongst them.

"Do you know where my wife is?" Micah repeated. Inside, he cringed at how pitiful and weak he sounded.

"No. I do not. At some stage, you will receive a telephone message with directions," van Bleeker said, disinterest and boredom marked his words. "I have nothing to do with that part of the ... business. When Abe told me what he had done to you and your wife, I cannot say it surprised me, but ..." He shrugged a pair of heavy, round shoulders. "As I said. It is nothing to do with me. I have my own concerns." The big man's right hand slid down and touched his right knee.

Micah ground his teeth.

"Do not look at me like that!" van Bleeker snarled. "I will not discuss it further."

When van Bleeker looked up at Micah, it made the rolls of fat at the back of his neck bulge.

He sighed and held out his hand. "If you ever want to see your wife again, we need to complete the delivery. Pass me the package, and you had better pray that the seals remain undisturbed."

"I haven't opened it. If that's what you're worried about." He clutched the plastic cylinder tight. As his only direct link to Molly, he didn't want to give it up easily. "Where's my wife?"

"The package. Now."

The earpiece clicked. Micah jerked his head and hid the action by tugging at his hair.

"*Micah,*" Arnie said, the word so clear the man could have been standing at his shoulder, "*ask him if he knows Luc.*"

Micah swallowed. How far could he dare to push the fat man?

"The man who has Molly, Luc," Micah began, "do you know him?"

"No. I do not. Not personally. I only have a telephone contact number. When I am satisfied with the package, I will call that number and confirm its safe arrival. Now"—van Bleeker snapped the fingers of his outstretched hand—"the package, Meneer Williams. Give it to me."

"*Ask for the phone number.*"

"Give me the phone number, and I'll give you the package."

Van Bleeker looked up from his chair. His pudgy forehead creased into a frown.

"The phone number is of no use to you. There is a certain form of words I must use."

"A code?"

Van Bleeker nodded. "Exactly. A passcode. I will not give it to you. Do not ask again." His voice deepened, its tone becoming more strident. "We are wasting time. If I do not call the number before nine o'clock, I cannot be responsible for what will happen to your wife. Now, the package."

"*Give it to him, Micah.*"

Micah pushed out his hand. Van Bleeker snatched the package and studied the seals carefully. Eventually, he nodded.

"Very good, Meneer Williams. It is undamaged. Now you must leave."

"*Get him to call the number now.*"

"Not until you call the number."

Van Bleeker's shoulders sagged even further. He released a long sigh and nodded.

"Okay. Very well. I understand how you must be feeling. Pass me my mobile phone." He pointed to the kitchen counter behind Micah.

Micah snatched it up and handed it across.

"My knee." Flinching, he placed a meaty palm on the joint. "Arthritis. Standing is difficult for me. Painful."

Micah couldn't give a crap.

Van Bleeker pressed the home button and the mobile's screen lit up. He worked the touchscreen for a few seconds, dialled, and raised the phone to his ear. He waited for what seemed like an age for the connection. The phone clicked.

"*Allo? ... Oui, c'est moi, JVB. ... J'ai les fleurs. Juin sera parfait, maintenant.*"

Micah's rusty French mangled the translation. Something about flowers and June being perfect.

Van Bleeker listened to a curt reply, ended the call, and fixed his bulging eyes on Micah.

"There. We are finished now. He will call you with the location of your wife within the next hour. I suggest you leave and head towards France."

Micah hesitated, uncertain.

Van Bleeker flapped his free hand in dismissal. "Go, go. I can do nothing more for you."

"Okay, Micah. Leave him. We've traced the call."

"You have?" Micah blurted out, without thinking.

Van Bleeker sat up a little straighter, the belly under the loose sweater wobbled from the effort.

"Excuse me?"

Micah coughed.

"You have ... nothing else for me? Are you sure?"

"Yes. You must go."

Grunting, he leant on his stick and used it to help him to his feet. He wobbled forwards, crowding Micah out of the kitchen and ushering him along the hall. Micah allowed himself to be pushed out of the apartment and into the foyer.

Van Bleeker shuffled backwards half a step and slammed the door in Micah's face.

Micah stood, staring at the highly polished black panel.

"What do I do now?" he wondered aloud.

"Micah, it's okay. Really. Go back to your car and set the GPS for Schiphol. Drive slowly. I'll catch up with you along the way."

"Schiphol? You mean Amsterdam airport?"

"Yes. Van Bleeker called a landline. We've confirmed the address, Micah. We have Luc's address."

Micah gasped. He spun away, tore open the metal and glass door, and raced towards his car. For the first time in two long days, fractional hope fluttered in his chest.

13

Wednesday 31st May – Morning

Indische Buurt, Amsterdam, The Netherlands.

Kaine folded the local paper neatly and placed it on the table beside his empty plate. He drained the last of his coffee, set the mug on its coaster, and stood.

Corky's announcement had improved his mood immensely.

He watched a distant Micah Williams explode out of the apartment block and race towards the Peugeot.

"Slow down, Micah," he said aloud.

The desperate man ignored him. If anything, he increased his pace. He reached the Peugeot and fumbled in his pocket for the keys. Eventually, he ripped open the car door and dived inside.

"Micah, slow down. Remember your breathing."

"*Fuck my breathing!*" Micah screamed. "*It's okay for you to tell me to calm down, you arrogant prick. Molly's not your wife. She means nothing to you!"*

Kaine let the man rant. He needed to blow off steam and screaming at a stranger gave him ample opportunity. At least the Peugeot hadn't moved. The engine had fired up and the brake lights had flared, but the car remained stationary. Kaine allowed the silence to grow.

"*Hello, Arnie? Are you still there?*" Micah asked, slightly calmer.

"I'm here," Kaine answered.

"*I-I'm sorry. I didn't mean … You've done nothing but support me. You didn't deserve that. I shouldn't have shouted at you.*"

"It's okay. I know the pressure you've been under. Believe me. I do know."

Micah breathed deep and blew out an extended exhale. Kaine waved goodbye to the barista and exited the coffee house, still searching the area for signs of anyone tailing Micah—or taking an undue interest in Kaine. Nothing seemed out of place. No one stood out as being interested in anything but themselves and their own lives. Whether anyone sat behind any of the windows watching the square, he would never know—hopefully.

Micah continued his deep, rhythmic breathing.

Outside, the day had warmed by a few degrees in the forty minutes he'd been sitting in the coffee house. The air smelled fresher than most capital cities he'd visited, a testament to the low numbers of internal combustion engines in the area, and to the volume of cyclists pedalling through the streets. The nearby canal seeped moisture into the air, humidifying the atmosphere, and loosening his lungs.

"*Did I hear you right?*" Micah said in the gap between the deep breaths. "*Y-You know where Molly's being kept?*"

How should he answer? The truth. The only way to build trust.

"Not necessarily. We know where Luc took the call from van Bleeker. I have a colleague on the way there right now."

"*You do? Oh God. You have people in France?*" Hope and relief hurried his words.

"He's a three-hour drive away. Don't worry, he's a good man. He won't do anything rash. He has a watching brief until we reach Toulouse—"

"Toulouse?"

"Yes, that's right, Toulouse." Kaine didn't reveal the address. He had no idea how Micah would react to the news that Luc hadn't moved from the place he'd first held Molly and Micah. "My man won't interfere unless he has to," Kaine added.

"Why would he have to interfere?"

Think about it, son.

Kaine deliberately changed the subject. "It's a twelve-hour drive from here to Toulouse, Micah," he said. "But a lot faster by plane. Head for Schiphol Airport. I'll meet you there."

Kaine turned away from apartment block Number 28 and the Peugeot, and retraced his steps towards his Range Rover. He walked quickly. Playing the part of a commuter hurrying to work, he checked his watch regularly.

"Is there a scheduled flight to Toulouse this morning?" Micah asked, his tone incredulous.

"Who said anything about a scheduled flight? Program your GPS for the private jet terminal."

"A private jet. Are you joking?"

"I rarely joke, Micah. And never in a situation as serious as this one."

* * *

THE DRIVE from Indische Buurt to Schiphol private jet terminal took fifty-five minutes at the height of the Amsterdam rush hour. The GPS had originally allocated twenty-five-minutes for the journey. A delay that gave the pilots, who'd been on standby since six o'clock that morning, plenty of time to register their flight plan to Toulouse-Balgnac Airport.

Kaine smiled.

After saving his granddaughter's life, Maurice LeMaître,

Chairman of ESAPP, had placed his company's private jet at Kaine's semi-permanent disposal. Not wanting to abuse their friendship, he vowed to only make use of the jet, a Gulfstream G550, when absolutely necessary.

Kaine and Micah met at Schiphol airport's exclusive private car park. Micah climbed out of the downmarket Peugeot and looked around him, eyes wide, obviously impressed by the location.

"Never thought I'd see the inside of a private jet," he said, his voice hushed in awe. "But the cost must be ..." He slowly shook his head and puffed out his cheeks.

"The Trust is covering all flight costs," Kaine said, pointing him towards the terminal building, an angular glass-and-steel structure that could have passed muster on the set of a sci-fi blockbuster.

Micah matched Kaine's hurried pace, stride for stride.

"I was talking about the environmental costs," Micah muttered.

"So was I. We're buying carbon credits to offset the emissions. Three times as many as the system calls for." Kaine glanced sideways at his latest client. "The next scheduled flight to Toulouse doesn't leave until seven o'clock this evening and that's fully booked. There aren't any free seats until tomorrow evening. I don't know about you, Micah, but hanging around Schiphol airport all day isn't my idea of fun. And neither is a fifteen-hour drive south through western Europe."

They reached the entrance and waited impatiently for the automatic double doors to open wide enough for them to step into a luxuriously appointed terminal. A twentysomething woman in a smart blue uniform greeted them with a bright smile.

"Mr Jeffries?" she asked, looking at Kaine.

"Yes," he said. "And this is Mr Williams."

"Welcome to Schiphol Airport. I'm Peta. Pre-flight formalities have been completed, and your flight is ready to depart. Please follow me."

She turned and led them through the lounge, bypassing the border control kiosk.

"They don't need to see our passports?" Micah asked Kaine quietly.

Peta half-turned. "As yours is an internal European flight, and you are both Europeans, passport control is not necessary."

She led them through a second set of double doors, out onto a concrete apron, and straight to the only aircraft on the ground. A gleaming blue-and-white jet with the impressive ESAPP livery on its tail. Peta waited at the foot of the staircase and formed a solitary guard of honour while they climbed the ten steps and entered the belly of the sleek beast.

The moment they sat in their well-padded leather swivel seats, an unseen member of the ground crew rolled into action. The outside door actuators whirred, the curved panel rose, and the lower half of the staircase folded into the upper half. The unit clicked into place and snapped tight against the fuselage.

An electronic warning dinged, and the seatbelt light glowed bright yellow above the cockpit door.

"Good morning, gentlemen," a French-accented female voice said. "I am Captain Katherine Gamay. Your co-pilot today is Captain Alain Christian. Please fasten your seatbelts. We will be departing immediately. Our flight will last approximately one hour and forty minutes. We hope you have a pleasant flight." The electronics dinged again, and the comms unit fell silent.

"Less than two hours from Amsterdam to Toulouse," Micah said. "Astonishing. I wish ..." He closed his eyes and left the sentence hanging.

"You wish Molly was here?"

Eyes glistening, Micah blinked away the tears. He nodded and turned his head away.

"When we recover your wife, I'll ask Captain Gamay to fly you back to England. Will Manchester Airport do you?"

Micah's eyes opened wide. He stared at Kaine.

"Are you ... you must be joking?"

Kaine shook his head. "I told you, I rarely joke. This jet is at my beck and call. I imagine you and Molly would be keen to sleep in your own bed tonight."

Micah arched his eyebrows.

"I won't care where we sleep so long as Molly's safe and we're together."

Kaine nodded. "I understand."

The Gulfstream's twin Rolls-Royce BR710C4-11 engines whispered into life, the power wound up quickly, and the plane started rolling.

Micah gripped his seat's armrests so hard, Kaine feared for the integrity of the leather.

As the jetliner hurtled along the runway, building to its take off speed, Kaine reclined his seat and settled back for an essential pre-operation snooze.

"You're going to sleep?" Micah asked, his eyes popping in disbelief.

"If I can. I haven't really slept for a while. We all need rest, Micah."

Five minutes after they reached cruising altitude, and with sleep eluding Kaine, Micah's mobile vibrated. Kaine opened his eyes.

Micah snatched the phone from his jacket pocket and read from the screen.

"Unknown caller," he said, holding it out, his hand shaking. "It's Luc. It has to be. What do I do?"

"Answer it. Nothing else you can do."

"Wh-What do I say?"

"Micah, answer the call. And put it on speaker."

"Yes. Of course. Of course."

Micah thumbed the green icon and hit the speaker button.

"H-Hello?" he said.

"Micah?" a disembodied voice asked. A man's voice.

"Yes. Yes, it's me."

"Well done. You have completed your task," the man said, his voice deep, the accent German. "Molly will be very pleased … when I tell her."

"Please may I speak to her?" Micah begged. "Please?"

"No. Not yet, but soon."

"Where is she?"

"Safe, Micah. She is safe."

"But—"

"Don't interrupt again. There is a strange noise in the background. Where are you?"

Micah stared at Kaine, who mimed holding a steering wheel and driving.

"I-I'm in the car, heading towards the ..."

Kaine mouthed, "A2 motorway."

"... the A2 motorway. I'm in an ... underpass."

"You have jumped the gun, I see." The man who must've been Luc laughed. A cruel, mocking laugh. "I fully understand, Micah. In your position, I believe I would do the exact same thing. Okay, continue to drive south. Head towards Toulouse. I will call you again in ten hours with further instructions. Oh, and one more thing, Micah."

"Yes?" Micah asked, eagerness itself.

"Drive safely, my friend. Molly is waiting." Laughing, Luc ended the call.

Micah stared at the dead mobile for a while before lifting an enquiring gaze to Kaine.

"Wh-What do you think?"

"It's promising," Kaine said, hoping the youngster believed him.

"Yes," Micah said. "It is. He kept his promise to call."

Kaine nodded. "You'll be with Molly soon."

Mentally, Kaine crossed his fingers.

* * *

AN ELECTRONIC DING jerked Kaine awake. The "Fasten Seatbelts" sign above the cockpit door shone bright in the subdued cabin lighting. He rubbed the sleep from his eyes and read the time on the digital clock above the cockpit door. They'd been in the air sixty-five minutes. From the angle of flight, Kaine surmised that the plane had already started its long descent into Toulouse. He yawned.

In the seat opposite, Micah stared at him, an angry scowl darkening his youthful face.

Click.

"Whatcha, Mr K. How ya diddling?"

"Alpha One to Control. I hear you. Over."

"Corky's identified Luc."

"How? Over."

"The call Micah received from Luc came from the same landline van Bleeker called to confirm the receipt of the package. These dickheads are overconfident, Mr K. Arrogant, Corky would call it. They screwed up. The phone is registered to a block of flats in Balma, a suburb of Toulouse. And, get this, there's a bank opposite. A bank with an external surveillance camera facing out onto the street."

"And you've accessed the pictures? Over."

"Sure did, Mr K." Corky chuckled—a welcome sound that Kaine had missed. "Corky grabbed historic shots of all the tenants entering and leaving the block over the past five days. Facial recognition identified the bloke with the scar."

"Who is he?"

"Maximilian Luca Schiller. Born in Germany. You'll be receiving a link to his bio and pic on your phone soon. And a nasty dollop of excrement he is, too. Europol's file on him is way thick. He's wanted for aggravated kidnap and murder in three countries. Germany, Slovakia, and the Czech Republic. Looks like he's set up business in France."

"Any known associates?"

"Another German geezer called Jakob Essen. Big guy. Used to be in the Stasi—the old East German secret police. And you know what those buggers were like. Evil through and through the lot of them. There's an older woman in the frame, too. A Marta Braun. She sometimes pretends to be Luc's mother but isn't. Another nasty piece of work. They've been operating as a unit since the fall of the Berlin Wall. Better watch out with this lot, Mr K. They may be arrogant, but these ain't your usual half-assed bad guys."

"Thank you again, Control. I'll take care. Alpha One, out."

Kaine tapped the earpiece inactive and absorbed Micah's angry glare.

"What's wrong?" he asked, keeping his voice low, calm.

"How could you just fall asleep? Molly's in danger. Don't you care?"

Kaine loosened his seatbelt a shade and rotated some of the stiffness from his neck and shoulders.

"Believe me, Micah. I do care."

Micah spun his seat to face Kaine head on.

"But you fell asleep!"

"Like you, I've been awake all night."

And for most of the previous night, too.

"Would you rather I be exhausted when I come face-to-face with Max Schiller?"

The frown lines on Micah's forehead deepened.

"Who?"

"The man you know as Luc, is Maximilian Luca Schiller."

"You've identified him?"

Kaine nodded. "And his associates." His mobile phone chimed with an incoming message. "Hold on a moment. This is important."

He opened the message. Clicking the link took him to one of Corky's "access once and self-destruct" websites. Kaine read Luc's bio and showed the mugshot to Micah.

"That's him! That's Luc."

Micah craned his neck, trying to read the text below the mugshot, but Kaine clicked to the next page and scan-read Jakob Essen's bio. It told him no more than he would have surmised from Corky's overview. The mugshot showed a bald, fifty-nine-year-old man with a back fringe of close-cropped white hair and a nose broken more than once. Hooded hazel eyes drilled into the camera's lens, giving away nothing of the man.

He showed Micah the photo, and Micah shook his head.

"I didn't see that man."

Kaine clicked again and read Marta Braun's bio. The mugshot

showed a middle-aged woman with dyed brown hair cut in an overly youthful, shoulder-length, pageboy bob.

"What about this woman?"

Micah studied the photo for a moment and shook his head. "No ... Hang on. Yes. I saw her at Toulouse railway station. She was behind me in the queue when I bought my ticket. She was the one following me. The haircut was different. Grey and longer. The evil bitch looked much older, too."

Kaine navigated out of the website, touched his contacts app, and dialled Rollo. It took an age for the call to connect.

"Hello, Quartermaster," Kaine said, avoiding using Rollo's name. The fewer personal details Micah had, the better. "This is Arnie, I'm on speaker. Where are you?"

"Morning, sir. I'm on the outskirts of Toulouse now. ETA in Balma, fifteen minutes."

Micah's eyes widened.

Damn.

Rollo shouldn't have mentioned Balma. Micah would be able to work out the location.

"Excellent. You made good time. Take a watching brief only. We should be with you within the next two hours."

"Very good, sir."

"You have all the equipment we need?"

"Yes, sir."

Kaine ended the call and slid the mobile into his pocket.

The plane's intercom chimed, and Captain Gamay announced their imminent arrival at Toulouse-Blagnac Airport. She ended her announcement with the inevitable and largely superfluous, "Captain Christian and I hope you have had a pleasant flight."

How could anyone fail to have had a pleasant flight aboard a multimillion-pound private jet?

Kaine pressed the red intercom button on the arm of his seat.

"Captain Gamay, the flight has been excellent, thank you. Most relaxing." Again, Kaine absorbed Micah's angry scowl. "My compliments to you and Captain Christian. Mr Williams and I have urgent business in Toulouse for the next day or so. Unfortunately, we can't give you an exact departure time, but the next flight will be to the UK. Manchester Airport. We'll need you on standby until then. Will that be acceptable?"

"Yes, Mr Jeffries. We are at your disposal."

"Thank you. I'll give you as much warning as possible."

Kaine released the call button, retightened his lap strap, and settled down for what the statisticians suggested to be one of the two most dangerous parts of any flight.

This part, he wouldn't sleep through.

14

Wednesday 31st May – Early Afternoon

Balma, Toulouse, Haute-Garonne, France

Kaine rendezvoused with Rollo in a near-empty car park in the centre of Balma, in the shadow of the nineteenth-century Saint-Joseph Church. The sun blazed down from a cloudless, deep blue sky, searing the streets, and bouncing up off the concrete pavements in heat haze waves. The oppressive warmth kept most of the locals inside, in the shade, leaving the streets almost deserted—not the best thing for a stranger who wanted to stroll along the sun-baked pavements unnoticed.

He parked his hired Renault Captur alongside Rollo's dark red Peugeot 208 and beckoned him inside. The Renault's door opened, and its soft suspension deflected under Rollo's weight.

"What do you have for me?"

No need for a greeting. Not when they were working.

Rollo showed Kaine the screen of his mobile.

"This is the live view from the surveillance camera in the bank across the street from the target block. No one's entered or left the building since I arrived. Everywhere is closed for lunch now, though. You know how much the French love their two-hour lunch breaks. The place is dead."

Kaine studied the image. It showed a five-storey concrete and red-tiled apartment block, *Maison Haute*. Black veranda railings outlined the extent of each apartment. On the ground floor, a food shop, an insurance office, an estate agency, and a hairdresser proudly showed their best—but closed for lunch—faces to the world.

"Not the easiest location for an obbo," Rollo said. "The surveillance camera hook-up is the only way to go. A stakeout is a non-starter. Strangers would stand out for miles in a place like this. We can't stay here for too long, either. Fact is, it's not the ideal spot to hold a kidnap victim, either. Too built up, and too many surveillance cameras."

"Agreed. They moved Molly yesterday. She spoke to Micah by phone. She thinks they've taken her to the country."

"Makes sense," Rollo said, nodding. "So, we follow Schiller to Molly and snatch her back?"

"That's the general idea. Assuming he's still in the apartment."

"Sounds simple enough," Rollo said, and they fell into a waiting, watchful silence.

Kaine took in the view through the side window.

Across the road, on the sunlit side of the street, a door opened, and an elderly woman appeared wearing a loose-fitting black dress. She attacked the front step with a stiff broom, looking around the whole time. A window in the adjacent house swung open. Its glass caught the sun and threw a blinding golden flash into Kaine's eyes. He blinked the orange afterimage away. A second woman leant out of the window, dressed in light grey. She rested a pair of chubby forearms on the sill and the two women turned to face each other. The first stopped her vigorous sweeping and opened the discussion. The animated conversation ebbed and flowed in energetic bursts.

Although their voices carried clearly in the near silence, Kaine could understand about one word in every twenty. After ten minutes of the babbled back and forth, the woman in the window flapped her hand and pulled back inside her house. She left the window wide open. The first woman swiped her broom over the step one last time, stepped back inside, and closed the door behind her.

Kaine smiled to himself.

"What happened to our client?" Rollo asked, breaking the extended silence.

"I booked him into a hotel at the airport," Kaine said. "Told him to sit tight and wait."

"That can't have been easy on him."

"He wasn't best pleased. Begged to tag along."

Kaine glanced at Rollo and gave him the eye.

"I can imagine. Still, he's better off in his hotel room festering than getting under our feet."

"That's more or less what I said," Kaine said through a wry smile. "I even used some of the same words."

Rollo lowered the mobile to his lap and kept his eyes on the screen. "I thought you'd be bringing Will with you. An extra pair of hands might prove useful, given who we're facing."

"Will's busy."

"Enderby?" Rollo glanced up from the phone and quickly lowered his gaze again.

"Yep." Kaine nodded. "Will's looking for a chink in the commander's defences."

"If anyone can find one, Will's the man. None of the others fancied a trip to *la belle France*?"

"Hunter is backing Will up, and Slim and Larry are keeping tabs on Abe Pedersen."

"Paddy?"

"Back in Ireland. He still has some mopping up to do after all the fireworks he set off the other day. I'm keeping the others in reserve at the farm in case we need them. Lara could do with help on the farm and the lads need the exercise."

"So, that leaves you and little old me," Rollo said, still studying the growing activity on the small screen.

"Has anyone ever referred to you as 'little'?"

"Not recently." Rollo snorted. "Although I was quite small as a kid. Shorter than average. A growth spurt in my teens put an end to that, though."

Must have been one hell of a growth spurt.

"I never had one of them," Kaine said, ruefully.

"What? A growth spurt?"

Kaine nodded.

"You haven't done too badly, sir." Another smile stretched Rollo's lips. "For a little 'un."

Kaine settled back and allowed the silence to ease out again.

A battered Citroën rumbled past the car park. It trundled down the hill towards the church, belching acrid blue smoke from its cracked exhaust. The traffic lights guarding the crossroads turned red, and the Citroën squealed to an eventual stop on dodgy brakes. Its loud backfire could have passed for a gunshot. Exhaust smoke billowed in the otherwise pristine air. It took an age for the lights to turn green and even longer for the ancient Citroën to build up enough revs to pull away. The driver, apparently oblivious to his single-handed assault on the local air quality, turned left and rattled away, the car's engine note coughing and spluttering through the town.

"How did Marie-Odile take it?" Kaine asked, turning his head to follow the trail of blue exhaust fumes into the distance.

"What? My bugging out on her so soon after getting back?"

Kaine nodded. "Yes, that."

Without taking his eyes from the screen, Rollo flinched.

"She's ..." He twitched his massive shoulders. "Well, she's Marie-Odile. She'll forgive me ... eventually. At least we had one night together." Rollo gave up a reflective smile, still without tearing his eyes from the screen.

"Sorry," Kaine said, "but I had no real alternative. Not at such short notice. You're local, and you speak the best French in the team."

Rollo snorted. "My French is pitiful, and you know it."

"It's better than mine."

"True enough. The doc speaks French pretty well," Rollo offered.

"Granted," Kaine said, nodding, "but she has her hands full with Mike."

Rollo frowned. "How is he? I meant to ask."

Kaine shook his head. "Not good, but happy to be home."

"I bet."

They fell silent for a few minutes before Kaine twisted in his seat to face his old friend. "Listen, Rollo. As soon as we reunite Micah with Molly, I'll let you go. You're long overdue some leave—"

Rollo raised his hand. "It's okay, sir. I understand. France is my turf. To be honest, I'd have been a tad miffed to learn that you'd been in France on a jolly without inviting me along for the craic."

"Cut the bull, Colour Sergeant. It won't wash."

Rollo finally looked up at him.

"Bull, sir? Me, sir?" he asked, feigning shock and confusion. "I have absolutely no idea what you mean, sir."

"Never mind, Rollo. Just know I appreciate your help. After this, you'll be excused boots for a while. I promise. You can have a well-earned rest. Take Marie-Odile away somewhere nice. So, we'll draw a line under it, shall we?"

"You brought the subject up, sir." Rollo smiled. "Not me. Oh, look." He pointed at the screen. "Movement."

"The target?" Kaine asked. He stretched closer, trying to catch the view, but the image was too small, and he gave it up as a lost cause.

"Nope."

"Can I have a commentary, please?" Kaine asked when Rollo failed to elaborate.

"An old biddy's just popped into the hairdresser for a blue rinse and a blow dry. I imagine." He smiled at the image. "Oh, and a car ... a Citroën ... has pulled up outside the insurance agents. Wait a minute," Rollo said, simulating a breathless excitement. "A bloke in a suit and tie is climbing out of the Citroën . Headed straight into the insurance agents. And ... a middle-aged man in a white T-shirt and baggy shorts—dear Lord, he shouldn't wear shorts with those legs—is pushing his bike along the pavement outside the grocery shop. This is so intense." Rollo looked up and grinned. "Had enough yet, sir?"

"Okay, okay. Just let me know if the target shows himself."

"Roger that, sir."

Kaine read the time from the digital clock on the dashboard. 14:09. He compared it with his watch. The hour's difference confirmed the car as being on local time. He sat and waited.

A few minutes later, more signs of locals waking from their heat-enforced siestas showed in greater traffic and an increase in foot traffic. In five minutes, three cars and a van rolled past the car park, two drove up the hill, and two travelled down. During the same period, Kaine counted eleven pedestrians descending or climbing the hill. Most of the individuals who climbed carried at least one unwrapped baguette.

The dashboard clock clicked over to 14:20.

"Okay, that's long enough," he said wringing his hands. "I'm going to take a quick shufty. Be right back."

"Are you sure that's a good idea, sir?"

Kaine shrugged. "I need to stretch my legs and, to be honest, I'd like to find out how much the houses cost around here." He pointed to the image on Rollo's phone screen. "The estate agents are open, right?"

Rollo frowned.

"I'll be careful."

"Of course you will. You have everything you need in case you bump into him?"

Kaine grinned and patted his jacket pocket.

"Yep."

"Good hunting, sir."

Kaine climbed out of the Renault and stepped into the searing afternoon heat.

15

Wednesday 31st May – Early Afternoon

Balma, Toulouse, Haute-Garonne, France

After sitting in the air-conditioned car for so long, Kaine had underestimated how scorching the day had become. Within ten paces, sweat formed under his arms and started trickling down the middle of his back. He peeled off his lightweight summer jacket, threw it over his shoulder, and reduced his pace to a slow, downhill amble. He wandered past a mini-market and a closed pizza place and carried on downhill towards the church which stood at the crossroads.

Kaine turned right at the crossroads and paused in front of the uninspiring religious monstrosity constructed out of red bricks and large concrete blocks. Playing the interested tourist, he took a picture of its bland façade with his mobile phone. He stared up at the pointed spire, nodding his false appreciation. To the left, a two-storey building with a bakery on the ground floor and a residential unit on the first, separated the church from *Maison Haute*.

A solid-looking metal gate—padlocked—barred access to a narrow alley between the bakery and the target building.

Hunching his shoulders and dipping his head to make himself appear even shorter, Kaine shuffled on, favouring his left leg. He stopped in front of the estate agents' window, studying the offerings—stunned by the low cost of a three-bedroom detached house. It wouldn't have bought a closet-sized bedsit in London. It would barely pay for a week's board in an upmarket hotel either.

Click.

"Movement to your right," Rollo said, ignoring radio protocol for expediency. "*The front door's opening. Hold on. ... It's Schiller. Identification confirmed. Over.*"

Hunched over and squinting hard at the sale offerings, Kaine watched Schiller from the corner of his eye. The German kidnapper lowered a suitcase to the ground and double locked the front door. He picked up the suitcase and turned to his right, heading towards the row of shops, towards Kaine.

Excellent.

The setup couldn't have been better.

Kaine waited. Timing was everything. It had to be perfect.

Schiller drew closer, his stride long and confident. The suitcase hit his left leg with each step.

Five metres separated them.

Four ... three ... two.

Now!

Kaine stepped backwards and looked up. Schiller slammed into his side. Kaine stumbled, grabbed at the lapel of the German's jacket, held on tight.

"*Bouge, connard,*" Schiller growled. A straight arm jab shoved Kaine to one side.

"*Move, arsehole?*" *How charming.*

Kaine staggered, stopped himself falling.

"*Desolé, monsieur. Desolé,*" he gasped, backing away, lowering his head in submission. He coughed for good measure and raised his arms to apologise—and to hide his face.

The square-built man—slightly taller than Kaine with longish salt-and-pepper hair and broad shoulders—snarled something rude in German and marched towards a row of parked cars directly across the street from the shops. He didn't so much as shoot Kaine a backwards glance.

So rude.

Schiller pointed a set of keys at a big, dark blue Citroën C5 Aircross, and the central locking disengaged. He yanked open the passenger door and unceremoniously threw the suitcase inside.

In a hurry, Schiller?

After a quick glance around, the German cranked open the driver's door, slid behind the steering wheel, and fired up the engine seemingly in one continuous movement.

"*Bravo One to Alpha One, are you receiving me? Over,*" Rollo said, reverting to protocol.

"Loud and clear, Bravo One. Over."

"*Nicely done, sir. Over.*"

"Thank you, Bravo One. The target is armed. Shoulder holster. Right armpit. Over."

The man was also heavily built and solid throughout. Obviously kept himself in shape. He hadn't run to fat in his middle years.

"*Means he's a leftie, which doesn't show on his bio. Knowing that might come in handy later. Want me to come and collect you? Over.*"

"Hold tight for a second. I don't want to tip our hand. Over."

Still hunched over, Kaine brushed off his jacket and watched the big Citroën in the reflection cast by the estate agents' window. The car pulled out of its parking spot, hung a sharp U-turn without indicating, and roared through the town, heading towards the crossroads. At the lights, he turned left—again without indicating—and disappeared behind the red brick monstrosity, climbing the hill towards the car park and Rollo.

"Bravo One, he'll be passing you in a second. Follow him at a distance. I'll catch up with you later. Alpha One, out."

The angry roar of the Citroën's diesel engine faded into the distance. With no need to maintain the pretence, Kaine straightened to his full height. He stepped into a fast march and turned left, heading for where he'd parked the Renault.

A car raced up from behind him, travelling almost as fast as Schiller's Citroën. Tyres squealed as it took the left-hand turn too fast. The car drew alongside him, and Kaine caught sight of the driver.

Micah Williams!

Hell!

"Micah!" Kaine yelled, holding up his hand. "Stop!"

As he passed, Micah shot a glance at Kaine but ignored his barked order and continued up the hill.

"Stop!" Kaine screamed and broke into a flat-out, uphill sprint.

Micah's car, a small black Fiat, pulled further into the distance.

"Bravo One," Kaine yelled, gasping, "he's here. ... Micah Williams is here! ... Black Fiat. ... Intercept him. Over."

In the distance halfway up the hill, Rollo's dark red Peugeot pulled sharply out of the car park, ahead of the little black Fiat, blocking the road. Brake lights blazed, the black bonnet dipped, and all four wheels locked and squealed. The Fiat stopped a metre from Rollo's Peugeot.

Micah blared his horn, lowered his window, and popped his head though the opening.

"Move, man!" he yelled. "*Allez! Allez!*"

Rollo raised his hand in apology and seemed to struggle with his gears. The Peugeot juddered and stalled.

Schiller's Citroën had disappeared into the distance.

"He's getting away!" Micah screamed, slamming his fist into the steering wheel.

As the gap between Kaine and the cars closed, he slowed to a fast walk, controlling his breathing. A round woman stepped through an open doorway. She glowered at the cars blocking the road outside her place of business, a dress shop, and shook her head at Kaine who shrugged.

"*Si bruyant,*" she said.

"*Oui*," Kaine answered, not knowing what she'd said, but imagining it needed his agreement. Breathing hard, he carried on towards the vehicles causing so much disruption to Balma's afternoon tranquillity. Across the street, the woman in grey appeared in the open window once again, gawking at the scene with avid interest. She and her neighbour would have something interesting to discuss the next time the step needed sweeping.

Micah opened his door and pushed his leg through the opening in preparation to jump out.

"Will you please move!" he screamed.

Kaine skipped around the back of the Fiat and dropped a hand on Micah's shoulder. Micah twisted at the waist, fear etched into his youthful face until recognition arrived.

"Arnie? What the fu—"

"Easy, Micah. You're drawing attention to us."

"But this fool"—he pointed a trembling finger at Rollo—"won't move. Luc ... he's getting away."

"No, he isn't," Kaine said, lowering his voice. "Now, calm down."

"I won't bloody calm down!" Micah tore his shoulder from Kaine's grasp. "He's getting away!"

"Micah," Kaine snapped. "Cool it. We've got this under control."

"We? What do you mean 'we'?"

"That 'fool'"—Kaine nodded at Rollo—"happens to be a very good friend of mine."

"What!" Micah jutted out his jaw and curled his fingers into fists, fighting to retain control.

Kaine waved Rollo back into the car park. Rollo nodded, fired up the Peugeot, and reversed out of the road and into his original parking spot next to Kaine's car.

"I'll explain everything," Kaine said, "but first, you need to get in your car and follow him. We can't stay out in the open like this. People are taking an interest."

A stoop-shouldered man had joined the woman in the shop doorway. Both studied the commotion with interest. A second-floor window in the building next to the dress shop opened and an elderly woman leant out, her head of curly grey hair waving in the gentle breeze. Excitement shone in her pale eyes and a gap-toothed smile formed on her shrivelled face. She waved to the woman in grey across the street, and the woman in grey returned the greeting.

"But Schiller's getting away."

"No," Kaine said. "I promise you he's not getting away, but we can't talk about it here."

Micah turned and stared in the direction he'd last seen Schiller's Citroën. The air exploded from his lungs and his shoulders sagged. Tears filled his brown eyes and threatened to spill.

"I'll never find the bastard now," he gasped.

Kaine took hold of Micah's arm and encouraged him back into the car. The youngster dropped into the driving seat and gripped the wheel with both hands.

"Park over there," Kaine said, pointing towards Rollo's Peugeot, "and I'll tell you what's happening."

Micah sighed, selected first gear, and drove into the car park. He parked alongside Rollo's Peugeot and cut the engine.

Kaine followed him on foot and slid into the passenger's seat beside Micah. He nodded to Rollo and tapped his earpiece.

"Off you go, *Adrian*," he said, using Rollo's most recent identity—the one he'd assumed in Wales, Adrian Bennett. "I'll follow you in my Renault. Over."

"*Roger that, sir. Bravo One, out.*"

Micah swiped the tears from his eyes.

"Where's he going?" he asked, his voice catching.

"Not sure exactly. He's following Schiller."

"How ... How's he going to manage that?"

Kaine smiled. "I planted a tracker on him," he said quietly. "On Schiller. We won't lose him, Micah. I promise."

"A bug?" Micah twisted in his seat to face Kaine. "You bugged him?"

Kaine nodded.

"A bug!" Micah closed his eyes and raised his face to the Fiat's roof. "Thank God. No wonder you were so chilled. ... The bug," he said, turning and fixing his eyes on Kaine's, "what sort of range does it have?"

Good question.

It showed that Micah's head was clearing enough for him to think straight.

"It's a GPS system," Kaine answered. "There are no range limitations. We can follow it on our mobiles wherever there's a phone signal."

Kaine drew the mobile from his pocket and opened the tracker app. He waited for the system to lock on to the signal and canted the screen towards Micah.

"The red dot is Schiller's Citroën," Kaine said. "The green one is Adrian's Peugeot."

The gap between the red and green dots remained fixed as the map scrolled beneath them. After a few moments watching the dots' progress north, Kaine lowered the phone.

"Micah," Kaine said.

The youngster looked up and met Kaine's steady gaze.

"We know what we're doing. We have the experience and all the resources we need at our disposal. And … I asked you to leave this to us."

"I couldn't. Molly's my wife. My responsibility."

"What were you planning to do?"

Micah's shoulders sagged and he hung his head. "I don't know. Follow him."

"And then what?"

Micah raised his head and stared blankly at the sunlit view through the windscreen.

"I don't know." He let out a deep sigh. "I have no idea. I just had to do something."

"I do understand," Kaine said, "but you could have done more harm than good. What would have happened if he'd spotted you? We'd have lost any advantage the Gulfstream gave us."

Micah pulled in a staggered breath. "I'm sorry. I just … Oh God, I'm worried for Molly." Again, he locked eyes with Kaine. "What she must be going through. They aren't going to let her go, are they? They can't afford to release her, can they?"

No. They can't.

Schiller, Essen, and Braun were holding Molly and would use her to lure Micah into a trap. They couldn't let either go free.

"Micah," Kaine said, maintaining eye contact, "now if I ask you to stay here, will you?"

"No." Micah shook his head. "No way."

"I could always make you."

"Will you?"

Kaine sighed. Of course he wouldn't.

"It would be better if you stayed here. You might get hurt, or get in the way again."

"Please don't make me stay. It's worse not knowing what's happening. I promise to do anything you tell me."

"Okay, stay here." Kaine shot him a deep scowl.

Micah stared, stone-faced, straight back. "Apart from that."

Kaine imagined the tabloid stories an aggrieved member of the 83 could write after being locked in the boot of a car by the "leader" of The 83 Trust. He shook the thought from his head. One thing, though. He did have to give Micah points for bravery, and keeping him close might be the only way to keep him safe.

"Right," Kaine said, decision made. "We'll use my car. This Fiat's no good. Not enough power."

He pushed open the Fiat's door and climbed out into the stifling air. Micah followed Kaine to his Renault and slid into the front passenger's seat.

Kaine clipped his mobile into the universal holder stuck to the windscreen and pressed the ignition. The dots on the mobile's screen remained motionless, and the map still scrolled beneath it. Kaine selected first gear and pulled the powerful Renault out of the car park. They turned left up the hill, and rolled out of the quiet little suburb of Toulouse.

16

Wednesday 31st May – Afternoon

Corbarieu, Tarn-et-Garonne, France

Kaine and Micah trundled along the D21, a flat, minor country road servicing villages and farms some nine kilometres south of the historic town of Montauban. They'd been driving for fifty minutes before the tracker's map had finally stopped moving some eight kilometres distant.

By the time they rendezvoused with Rollo, the red dot on the screen had been stationary for a full fifteen minutes.

Kaine consulted his mobile's screen. Schiller's Citroën had come to a halt at the top of a densely wooded hill overlooking a wide river valley full of farms and fields, and little else.

Zooming in on the satellite map revealed a single building at the end of a winding track that split off a lane that itself spurred from the D21. It lay some six kilometres outside the picturesque village of

Corbarieu. The track petered out at the building, which couldn't have been much more isolated if it tried. An ideal spot to hold a kidnap victim.

Rollo had found a quiet place off the lane, the *Chemin de Montamar*—a lay-by surrounded by trees and low bushes at the foot of the valley. It was the perfect place to meet without drawing the attention of any inquisitive locals—not that the valley was heavily populated. Judging by how overgrown the grass verges were and the lack of rubbish in the single litter bin, Kaine would have been surprised if a vehicle had parked in the lay-by so far that year.

Rollo climbed out of his Peugeot and joined them in the Renault. He sat in the middle of the back seat. Kaine made the introductions.

"Micah Williams, meet Adrian Bennett, one of The 83 Trust's senior security officers."

Rollo smiled.

"Call me Ade," he said.

Quick on the uptake, Rollo didn't even look sideways at Kaine. He pushed his meaty right hand between the front seats. Micah took hold and they shook briefly.

"Ade?" Micah said. "I imagine that's no more your real name than his is Arnie, right?"

Rollo ignored the question and turned to Kaine.

"I thought he was staying in the airport hotel."

"So did I. Some people simply won't do as they are asked."

"He's a liability," Rollo said, fixing his gaze back on Micah.

"I know,' Kaine said, shooting him a wry grin, "but short of hitting him over the head with a brick and leaving him in Balma, what else could I have done?"

"A brick would have worked for me, sir." Rollo shot Micah a stiff smile.

"Excuse me," Micah interrupted, waving a hand in the air between them, "but I'm right here."

"We know," Kaine said. "And you shouldn't be. That's the whole point."

"What are we going to do with him?" Rollo asked.

"We'll leave him here in the car."

"You can't!" Micah shouted. "I won't stay. I'll follow you. Molly needs me."

"She needs you to do what's best for her," Kaine said, "and that's to stay here and let us do our thing."

"But I can help!"

"You've already cost us time, Micah. Too much time. Adrian, please convince him to stay in the car."

Rollo reached out and ensnared Micah's right wrist in his bear-like fist.

"Let me go!"

The youngster tried to fight Rollo off, tried to pull his arm free and pry open the iron grip with his left hand, but Rollo held the wrist tight without seeming to expend too much effort in doing it. He pushed the arm towards Kaine and handed him a heavy grey cable tie. Kaine looped the tie around the struggling man's wrist and the steering wheel, and pulled it tight. Micah yelled and cursed the whole time.

Once secure, Kaine sat back.

"You bastards!" Micah screamed. "Let me go!"

Red faced, Micah wrenched his tethered arm, trying to break the ratchet catch. The sharp plastic tie dug deep into his wrist. Panting and still cursing, he gave up before the tie had a chance to draw blood.

"Keep your bloody noise down, man!" Kaine shouted, and cuffed the back of Micah's head.

Shocked by the stiff blow and the harsh words, the youngster fell quiet.

"That's better," Kaine said, gently. "I'm sorry about this, but you do need to stay here."

"Bastard," Micah growled, tucking in his chin.

"Don't even think of sounding the horn. Sound travels on the wind and we don't need to give Schiller any warning. Understand?"

With his free hand, Micah rubbed the top of his head.

"We'll be back as soon as we have Molly."

Kaine patted the lad's shoulder, grabbed the mobile from its holder, and backed out of the car, signalling for Rollo to join him outside.

"Bloody hell, Captain, that was almost as bad as trying to convince the doc to keep her head down and stay safe," Rollo said when they'd gained enough distance to speak without being overheard and without having to listen to Micah's angry shouting. The Renault swayed and bounced under Micah's assault, but he wouldn't be able to keep it up for much longer. Already the car's rocking had started to subside.

"Not funny, Colour Sergeant."

"Wasn't meant to be, sir." Rollo shrugged.

Kaine consulted his mobile. Schiller's Citroën still hadn't moved.

"Ready?"

"Always."

Kaine pointed towards a turning off the lane, a heavily rutted track that climbed the northern slopes of the valley, leading deep into the woods.

"Do we go now or wait for dark?"

Kaine glanced towards the west. The sun remained high. They had at least three hours before it reached the western hills, and at least another ninety minutes after that before anything like full darkness would descend.

"I'd rather wait for night, but that's hours away. I don't like the idea of leaving Molly a second longer than we have to."

"Agreed. Those woods look dense enough to give us decent cover and, according to the map, there isn't another house for a couple of clicks."

"Are you armed?"

"Glock 17," Rollo said, patting his left armpit. "Rarely leave home without it. You?"

"Of course. Give me a second."

Kaine spun and headed back to the Renault, which had stopped bouncing. At the risk of re-igniting Micah's anger, he opened the driver's door and leant inside. A panting Micah glowered at him from the front passenger's seat. His long, dark hair was plastered to the side of a sweaty face.

"Do you and Molly have an animal, a pet?" Kaine asked.

"Why?"

"Molly will be terrified. Won't know us from Adam. We'll need a safe word. So, do you have a pet?"

Micah swiped the lank hair out of his eyes.

"A dog," he muttered.

"What's its name?"

"Rambo."

"An Alsatian? Doberman?"

"No, he's a cockapoo."

Of course he is.

"Thank you. Try not to worry. We'll be back as soon as we have her."

Kaine closed the door softly and returned to Rollo with the password.

"Rambo the Cockapoo?" Rollo said, rolling his eyes towards the cloudless sky.

They turned their backs on the cars and headed towards the track, hugging the shadows of the woods.

17

Wednesday 31st May – Afternoon

Corbarieu, Tarn-et-Garonne, France

Rather than clamber through the dense undergrowth and waste precious time, Kaine took a calculated risk and opted to take the more open route. The track. Although it increased the chances of running into the opposition if they decided to evacuate, the time gained might prove vital. To minimise the risk, Kaine kept a constant eye on the mobile's screen. The second the red dot showed any signs of movement, they would dive into the undergrowth and lie in ambush.

Kaine and Rollo had been in similar situations before. Each knew his role. Kaine would take the left flank, and Rollo the right, to cover both sides. If it came to a shootout, Kaine would open fire first.

They jogged up the steep winding track, hemmed in on both sides by the densely wooded slopes. The sun, high to their left, flickered and glinted through the trees. Deeply rutted grooves in the dirt track and protruding boulders showed the effect of heavy traffic over time. It also showed how little maintenance it had received in recent years. On either side, deep ditches acted as open drains to carry away runoff during the worst of the winter storms.

A light wind huffed through the leafy canopy, allowing a stippled, flickering light. Insects buzzed around their heads, birds cawed and twittered, and gravel crunched underfoot. Below them in the valley, the occasional vehicle raced along the distant D21. Otherwise, the only sounds came from their heavy breathing, their footfalls, and the wildlife. Mercifully, no descending cars interrupted their headlong climb.

Towards the top of the hill, they slowed and hugged the inside of the track.

They rounded a corner—the penultimate rising bend according to the tracker's map. The trees thinned, and the sky opened out above them, bright and cheerful, and empty.

Kaine dropped into the nearside drainage ditch, and Rollo climbed in behind him. They carried on the ascent, reducing speed, and taking greater care over the broken ground in the bottom of the overgrown ditch.

Up ahead, close by, a heavy door slammed. A man shouted. The words echoed and swirled above them, distorted by the terrain. Kaine couldn't make out what he said. A female answered, higher-pitched, curt. Another man, older than the first, his voice deeper, more guttural, possibly Jakob Essen, called out, *"Ja, schnell. Lass uns gehen!"* Again, the hollow shout echoed strangely through the trees.

The extended double click of a car's central locking system releasing sounded close. Above their heads, but very close.

Kaine leant towards to Rollo and whispered, "They're leaving."

Rollo nodded.

They hugged the side of the ditch, taking cover in the ferns, moss, and shrubbery. Damp earth, leaf mould, and twigs released their ripe odours. Worms slithered into the rich and broken soil. The mottled sunshine warmed Kaine's neck and shoulders. Sweat leaked out of him, and he swallowed past a parched throat.

In broad daylight, they were vulnerable. Exposed.

After a quick nod from Kaine, Rollo interlaced his fingers and cupped his hands. Using it as a stirrup, Kaine stepped into it. Rollo boosted him out of the drainage ditch and into the woods high above. Leaving his legs dangling over the edge, Kaine grasped the exposed roots of a nearby tree. He held on tight and called out a quiet, "Go!"

Rollo scrambled up Kaine's legs and torso, and rolled into the undergrowth beside him. After a nod to each other, they started crawling. Deeper into the undergrowth. Ever deeper.

Chestnut, oak, and beech trees interspersed with dark, wax-leafed shrubs and deep green ferns climbed up around them, both hampering and shielding their progress.

After ten metres, Kaine paused in the wide bowl of an oak. Rollo pulled in at the other side.

Kaine held his breath. Listened.

German words and phrases rattled and echoed strangely through the air, some of which Kaine understood. Some, he didn't. The woman, probably Braun, mentioned *das Mädchen*—the girl. Spoken as a question. Schiller shouted his answer. Abrupt. Angry. An internal door slammed. Schiller called again, telling Braun to get on with it. His rough, distorted words were greeted with a heavy silence.

Kaine looked at Rollo and raised his eyebrows. Rollo dipped his head in a brief nod. He understood as much German as Kaine.

"Schiller ordered Braun to get the girl, Molly," Kaine whispered. "I think they're moving her."

"Taking her to draw Micah out, you reckon?"

Kaine tilted his head. "Possibly. Let's go."

They wormed their way past the oak, heading towards the hazy brightness that signalled a break in the woods.

After a twenty-five-metre scramble—their movement masked by the noises up ahead—they ran into a dense line of hydrangeas in full leaf and heavy bud, making ready to flower. Kaine skirted to the left, Rollo headed right.

Ahead, through gaps in the bushes and trees, sunlight glinted on glass, and the dark red tiles of an A-framed roof fanned out below them. Built on a terrace cut deep into the hillside in a tight horseshoe curve, red rocks exposed, the bungalow commanded a spectacular view of the sunlit slopes of another valley that stretched out below.

Kaine and Rollo had climbed above the terrace and looked down into the rocky-faced opening.

An internal door slammed shut, gunshot loud in the near silence. The sound reverberated and distorted through the humid air. Kaine finally understood. The terrace's horseshoe curve explained the unnerving hollow echo of the German's words. Its vertical rock face stretched and twisted the sound, playing acoustic tricks with every noise.

They had emerged above the western side of the bungalow. The Citroën stood to their right, part-hidden by the corner brickwork. Schiller emerged from the house, carrying a large and heavy suitcase, his back to Kaine and Rollo. He loaded the case into the back of the car next to the other one, lowered the tailgate, and turned towards the house.

"*Lass uns gehen!*"

"He said, 'Let's go'," Kaine whispered, translating for Rollo.

Rollo nodded. "Yes, I got that."

A woman appeared at Schiller's side—Marta Braun. Slightly built and in her early sixties, she had to lift her chin to meet his hostile stare.

Schiller said something Kaine couldn't catch.

"*Ja,*" Braun said. She nodded and looked away.

"Are you ready?" Schiller asked.

"*Ja. Ja.*"

Schiller grabbed her upper arm.

"The girl?"

They were talking about Molly again.

Again, Braun nodded, and again she looked away.

"It's done," she said just loud enough for Kaine to catch.

"Good," Schiller said.

A hollow opened out in the pit of Kaine's stomach.

Oh God, no!

Schiller released Braun's arm and waved her towards the car.

Kaine shot a look at Rollo. The big man's jaw muscles bunched, and his eyes burned with fury. Despite his weak German, Rollo had worked it out, too.

"She's dead!" Rollo whispered. "Molly's dead!"

18

Wednesday 31st May – Afternoon

Corbarieu, Tarn-et-Garonne, France

The bastards had killed Molly! Cleaning up after themselves, they'd shot Molly in cold blood.

Bastards!

Kaine and Rollo had arrived too late. Seconds too bloody late. Not a door slamming to a loud echo, but a gunshot. An execution. Schiller had forced Braun to do his dirty work.

Too late. They were too bloody late.

Kaine clamped his jaws together to stop himself screaming. He wanted to rage at the world. Another innocent victim he couldn't save. How could he have allowed it to happen?

A dark cloud hovered overhead, hiding the sun and matching Kaine's mood. Teeth gritted, blood boiling, he leant to his left, lowered the zip on his jacket, and drew out his SIG. Slowly, under a control he didn't feel, he pulled back the slide and levered a bullet up the spout. On the other side of the bushes, Rollo did the same with his Glock. He caught Kaine's eye.

"On three," Kaine mouthed. He raised his left hand and showed three fingers.

"Essen?" Rollo hissed. "What about Jakob Essen?"

Essen. Damn it.

What the hell was wrong with him? In his rage, he'd forgotten all about the ex-Stasi killer. He lowered his hand and clenched it into a fist.

Below them, the Citroën's starter motor churned, and the engine caught instantly. A second engine ahead of the Citroën, and out of sight around the front of the bungalow, roared. Another diesel. This one heavier. Jakob Essen. They were leaving in convoy. Getting away.

No, damn it. No!

"Three!" he yelled.

Kaine scrambled forwards, exploded through the bushes into the daylight, and reached the edge of the cutting where the rock wall dropped four metres vertically. He spun, lowered himself legs first, pressing his chest against the crumpled rock wall, using friction as a brake to prevent an uncontrolled plummet. He hit the uneven ground, gave at the knees, rounded his back, and parachute-rolled backwards onto his feet in a single, flowing movement.

Off and running, leading with the SIG, Kaine felt rather than heard Rollo at his back.

Together, they darted around the side of the bungalow and emerged at the front of the building. Ahead, the track curved around to the right, falling steeply away in a tight switchback. The two vehicles rolled in front of them, less than twenty-five metres distant, heading down the steep slope and getting away. Jakob Essen took the lead in a bronze Nissan Navara.

Fish in a barrel.

The bald Essen looked up towards them. His eyes widened and his upper lip bared in a snarl. His right hand scrambled inside his jacket, the impetuous movement jerked the steering wheel. The

Nissan lurched to the right. The nearside front tyre caught the edge of the track and dipped towards the drainage channel. Panicked, Essen tried to counter the slide, but at speed on a dirt track, and with only one hand on the wheel, he lost the fight. Never had a chance.

The Nissan's nose dipped, the rear wheels lifted, and the pickup swerved sideways into the ditch, its engine screaming. Still on the move, Kaine took aim and fired. The bullet smashed through the Nissan's side window and ploughed into Essen's open mouth. Blood and brains decorated the inside of the driver's cab.

The Nissan's engine stalled. The truck blocked the track.

Behind Kaine, Rollo's Glock barked three times.

Brake lights flared. Schiller's Citroën shuddered to a sideways halt, centimetres before it smashed into the Nissan's rear bumper. Schiller scrunched low behind the wheel. Lightning fast, he threw the big car into reverse. The engine screamed. Front wheels spun backwards. Dust and gravel flew, rattling into the engine's splash guard.

Finally, the tyres bit into the dirt, gained traction, and the dark blue Citroën reversed up the hill, racing for the bend in the track. Racing for safety. The Citroën bounced and weaved as Schiller jerked the steering wheel, trying to minimise the target.

Still on the run, Kaine aimed and fired twice. Rollo's Glock cracked in unison.

The Citroën's windscreen shattered, and the nearside front tyre exploded. Kaine had targeted a head behind the windscreen. Rollo chose the wheels.

A woman's scream pierced the air, mingling with the high note of a racing diesel engine.

The Citroën's front end wobbled. It reversed over the far drainage ditch. The rear end crumpled as it slammed into the ditch's far wall and scraped to the bottom. Four airbags exploded, engulfing the cab in protective white pillows. The passenger's airbag turned pink as it moulded itself around Marta Braun's bloodied face.

Schiller screamed. Powerful arms tore away the white fabric on the driver's side. His left hand held a H&K USP Compact semi-automatic pistol. Matte black, polymer-framed, and in the right hands, deadly. Still howling, Schiller started shooting, randomly and apparently unaimed. Wild but still lethal.

Bullets whistled past Kaine's head. Some high and wide. Some close. Too close for comfort.

He dived headlong into the dust. Rollo grunted and slammed into the dirt at Kaine's side.

Kaine slithered towards the grass verge at the edge of the terrace, keeping low and flat, his chest and knees scraping rock and gravel. Rollo gasped and took his time to join Kaine at the edge. The high ground gave them the advantage. Lying prone, they were out of sight of the track. Protected.

Rollo coughed. A muffled curse exploded from his lips. His heavy breathing blew dust into the air around them.

The USP stopped firing.

Out of ammo?

Kaine hadn't been counting the shots.

"I'm hit," Rollo breathed. He coughed again.

Oh God. No.

"How bad?" Kaine asked.

"It's nothing," Rollo gasped. "A scratch."

Another crack split the silence. The bullet flew high and wide.

Kaine turned onto his side, searching Rollo for a wound. Rollo lay prone to Kaine's right, his left side showing. No signs of blood.

"Where?"

"Right shoulder," Rollo answered, his face pale, pained and sweaty.

"Bad?"

Rollo's dark green eyes narrowed, and his lips stretched into a tight line. He shook his head.

"Stings like a bitch. I've had worse, but I can't feel my right hand. Can't hold my Glock properly."

"Let me see."

"No." Rollo scowled. "Concentrate on the arsehole doing all the bloody shooting."

Kaine shook his head. Rollo was making sense. First things first. Keeping flat, he crawled forwards again, edging closer to the terrace's verge. He pushed the SIG outwards and peered through the tufts of weed and grass that hid him from the track below.

The Citroën's front door stood open, the driver's seat empty. Schiller had taken his chance. He'd gone.

Bugger!

With no pressure on the accelerator, the Citroën's engine had slowed to a gentle idle.

The airbag covering the front passenger seat moved, tugged away by a bare and skinny arm.

"*Hilf mir,*" Braun cried, her voice weak, stilted, barely carrying the distance between them. "*Bitte ... h-hilf ... mir.*"

"Help yourself, you murdering bitch!" Kaine muttered.

Gasping, blood pouring from a neck wound, Braun raised her arm towards Kaine.

"*Bitte* ... p-please." The voice faded.

The arm fell, her head slumped back against the head restraint, and her chest moved rapidly.

"Braun?" Rollo asked, panting hard. "Is she ...?"

"Hanging on. Just about. But she's going nowhere."

Kaine twisted.

A patch of crimson the size of a side plate glistened on Rollo's right shoulder.

Shit.

Far worse than Rollo made out. Kaine scrambled backwards.

"Schiller?" Rollo asked. "Where's—"

A gunshot exploded from the bushes on the far side of the track. The bullet whistled over Kaine's back. Close. Very close.

Schiller hadn't gone far.

A second shot cracked the air. The bullet nearly parted Kaine's hair, and he stretched out lower, hugging the rocky ground.

Bloody good accuracy for forty-five metres—approaching the limit of a USP's maximum accurate range. The man could shoot. By God, could he shoot.

Kaine crawled alongside Rollo, placing himself between Schiller and his injured mate.

"Move, Rollo. Bloody move, will you!"

"What?"

"Get further away from the edge. Head for the bungalow."

Rollo blinked, shook his head, shook himself aware. "Oh, right. Yeah, sure."

Grunting, blood oozing from the wound, he squirmed around and slithered towards the safety of the bungalow's solid walls.

Still prone, Kaine spun to face the track. He pushed out his SIG again and searched the woods, looking for a sign. Any sign.

Another gunshot boomed. The bullet slammed into the front wall of the bungalow and ricocheted away, its point of origin higher than the first two. The trees!

Schiller had climbed a tree.

"I'm safe," Rollo called. "Around the side of the house."

Another gunshot cracked. Behind Kaine, a window shattered. The echoes bounced off the terrace walls and rumbled through the valley. The USP coughed again. The bullet thumped into the grass and dirt in front of Kaine's face. A cloud of dust rose, and the wind blew grit into his eyes.

It stung. Stung like hell. He blinked, trying to clear his eyes.

Shit.

Kaine rolled to his left, down the hill. Moving the target.

Tears filled his eyes, and his vision swam. He blinked again, hard, fast, desperate to clear his eyes. Grit scoured his eyeballs with each blink and each eye movement.

They kept watering—the body's defences working overtime. He continued blinking, rapid and firm.

Slowly, his vision recovered.

Another crack, and another bullet struck the bungalow behind him. Kaine raised his head a centimetre. Below and to the right, in the trees, gunsmoke billowed. Behind it, a pair of blue eyes glistened in a sneering face. A sneer or a grimace, Kaine couldn't tell for certain.

Kaine pulled in a deep breath. Released it slowly. Forced himself to stop blinking. Ignored the sharp and stinging pain scorching his eyes.

He raised his SIG, chose a spot thirty centimetres below the face, aiming for centre mass. He squeezed the trigger three times. The blue eyes narrowed, and the sneer disappeared along with the face. Branches whipped and cracked. A dark mass fell through the trees.

Eyes still streaming, Kaine took two snap shots, following the line of the plummeting lump. Two definite hits. The body slammed into the undergrowth at the foot of the chestnut tree. A red spray splattered the chestnut's bark, and air exploded from lungs. Schiller grunted and groaned, then fell silent.

Kaine held his breath. He lined up the SIG's sights on the area where the dark mass had landed and fired four more times, keeping the pattern close and tight.

"Did you ... get ... him?" Rollo asked, gasping, the pain clear in his stilted words.

"Yes. At least three hits. Probably more."

"Dead?"

"Should be. How are you?"

"I'm fine. Stop worrying."

Like that's going to happen.

"How's the bleeding?" Kaine asked, keeping his focus on the patch of vegetation where Schiller had landed. Apart from the leaves fluttering in the wind and the fair-weather clouds sweeping across the sky, nothing moved.

Could he afford not to confirm the kill?

Hell no.

He took aim at the spot where the heavy shape landed and unloaded three more shots in a second closely spaced grouping. The slide locked open. The gunshots' loud echoes resonated through the valley. Kaine let them fade away to nothing. He replaced the empty magazine with a full load and worked a round into the breach.

"Schiller!" Kaine shouted. "Maximilian Schiller! Can you hear me?" It was worth a try, but he didn't expect a response.

He waited a few seconds before trying again.

"Schiller," he yelled. "Armed police are on their way. Give yourself up and I'll see you're treated well. Even if I missed you, that fall must have hurt."

He rolled five metres downhill and paused to listen. Nothing.

"Rollo?" he called quietly. "Is it safe to leave you?"

"Yes," Rollo said, the response instant, his voice stronger, more controlled. "It is. Go. Confirm the kill. The bugger knows where Micah lives."

"If I return to find you've bled out, I'll be putting you on a charge. Understood?"

"Ha!" Rollo coughed. "Don't make me laugh, sir. It hurts when I … bloody laugh. The bleeding isn't that bad. It's almost stopped. I'm applying pressure."

"Okay. Can you break into the bungalow and confirm Molly's … condition?"

"Yes, sir. Will do."

"I'm heading out. Switching to comms."

"Roger that."

Without removing his gaze from the target area, Kaine pushed himself to a low crouch and held his breath.

Birds twittered in the tree canopy, recovering quickly from the rattling shock of the gunfire.

Kaine fixed the chestnut tree's location in his memory. He pushed the SIG into its holster and scrambled sideways, further back from the edge. He raised his chest and knees from the ground and kitty-crawled down the track, moving fast and silent.

He kept going.

After twenty-five metres, the track dipped into a shallow hollow before making its sharp turn to the right and passing in front of the bungalow. Thick tufts of grass grew along the edge of the verge. The long blades waved in a stiffening breeze. Kaine stopped. He lowered himself to the track, drew the SIG, and pushed it forwards, through the grassy tufts. Below and to his right, thirty-five metres distant, the large chestnut stood proud and strong, dominating the surrounding trees.

Kaine fired again. Five shots, all centred one metre to the left and slightly below the memorised position. He rolled two metres to the right. Uphill. Stopped.

Holding his breath, Kaine waited, counting slowly to thirty. The gunshots' angry echoes faded and died—lost to the humid afternoon air.

Silence fell. Kaine breathed again.

The earpiece clicked.

"Bravo One to Alpha One. Do you hear me? Over."

"Alpha One here. I hear you. Molly? Over."

"She's gone, sir," Rollo answered, his words slicing through Kaine's heart. *"Single gunshot to the chest. At least it was quick. Over."*

Oh dear God!

Kaine closed his eyes. He wanted to be wrong. Hoped he'd mistranslated the Germans' conversation. A desperate hope. A hope that lay in tatters. How the hell could he break it to Micah?

"How are you, Bravo One? Over."

"Sore, but holding up, sir. The shooting earlier," Rollo said, *"Didn't you finish him before? Over."*

"Insurance," Kaine said. "I'm going down now. Wait there for my return. Alpha One, out."

Kaine scrambled backwards to the outer side of the track and dipped into the drainage gully. The deep ditch enabled him to stand at the crouch and still remain hidden from the kill zone. Or what he hoped was the kill zone.

He headed downhill, avoiding the trip hazards, taking his time, moving carefully, using the sun at his back to estimate his distance from the target.

The chestnut tree's wide and dappled shadow gave him the location. That, and the stench of warm blood and faeces. Even when fresh, human corpses had their own distinctive smell.

SIG outstretched in a two-handed grip, pointed into the shadows, Kaine straightened at the knees.

A heavy tangle of large-leafed ferns, thick brambles, and red bushes couldn't hide Schiller's corpse. His mangled, bloody face—steel blue eyes open, staring wide, but seeing nothing—peeked out through the dense undergrowth.

Kaine lowered his SIG and slipped it into its shoulder holster—he wouldn't be needing it. Not for Schiller.

He reached up to a low-hanging branch, used it to haul himself out of the ditch, and trampled down the brambles surrounding the body. Seven black and bloody holes punctured the corpse. One through the throat, one shattered the left shoulder, the rest were grouped centre mass. Kaine nodded. Happy with the accuracy but not with the outcome. Schiller had died quickly. Too bloody quickly for Kaine's tastes. He would have preferred it to be slow and painful.

Kaine backed away, slid into the ditch, and climbed out the other side. Eyes still streaming, still stinging, but less so than earlier, he lifted his face to the sky, and soaked in the warmth of the late-afternoon sun. He pulled in a deep, cleansing breath and tapped the earpiece active.

"Alpha One to Bravo One. Kill confirmed. Over."

"*Good ... job, sir. What next? Over.*"

"I'll check on the other two and go fetch the car and Micah. You stay put. Over."

"*What are you going to tell him? Over.*"

What indeed?

"The truth. Over."

"*You can't do that, sir,*" Rollo snapped. "*You ... can't tell him we arrived too late because ... because he held us up!*"

"No, Bravo One. I'll go easier on him."

Somehow.

"Alpha One, out."

Kaine tapped the earpiece inactive, turned downhill, and left Schiller's corpse to rot in the undergrowth where it had fallen. Where it belonged.

19

Wednesday 31st May – Afternoon

Corbarieu, Tarn-et-Garonne, France

Kaine found Micah where he and Rollo had left him—sitting in the Renault's front passenger seat with his wrist cable-tied to the steering wheel. As Kaine raced towards the car, Micah glared out at him through the windscreen, thin-lipped and close to exploding. Kaine slowed his pace and jogged the final few steps, unable to meet the youngster's eye.

During his race down the track, Kaine had been trying to work out what to say, but everything he came up with sounded trite. He still didn't have a clue how to break the news.

"Where is she?" Micah yelled as Kaine approached. "Where's Molly?"

Kaine tore open the driver's door, slid inside, and took a breath.

"Well?" Micah demanded. "Where is she?"

Still not making eye contact, Kaine pulled the Fairbairn-Sykes knife from its sheath on his right calf and sliced through the cable tie. Micah snatched his arm towards his chest and rubbed at the red welt left by the plastic binding.

Kaine finally met Micah's gaze and slowly shook his head.

"Micah," he said, "I'm so, so sorry, but we were too late. Molly's ... gone."

Pitiful. Was that the best you could come up with?

"Gone?" Micah shook his head. "She's dead? No, she can't be. You promised. Y-You promised to bring her back. *You promised!*" He screamed the last two words.

No, Micah. I didn't promise.

Micah's face crumpled. Tears burst from his dark brown eyes, streamed down his cheeks, and pooled in his stubble.

"She can't be dead."

"I'm so sorry, Micah."

Kaine reached across and rested a hand on the youngster's shoulder. Micah slapped it away.

"She isn't dead!" he roared. "You're lying. She isn't dead! She can't be dead." Ready to explode, Micah's hands bunched into fists. "She can't be!"

Kaine fired up the Renault and notched the selector into drive. The seat belt alarm bleeped.

"Seatbelt," Kaine ordered, fixing his strap into place.

Micah, eyes glazed, acting on autopilot, tugged the strap across his lap and clicked the buckle into its holder.

"Where are we going?"

"I'm taking you to Molly. You need to be with her when the police arrive."

"The police?"

"Did you hear the shooting?"

Micah frowned through the tears. "Shooting? What shooting?"

The peculiar setup at the top of the hill with the deep-cut, rocky terrace and the gusting wind must have carried the sounds away from the valley and into the next. Away from the nearest village, Corbarieu.

The vagary of acoustics.

"Wh-What happened?"

"We were too late," Kaine repeated, unable and unwilling to say more.

He nudged the Renault out of the lay-by and turned left onto the deeply rutted track. They wound quickly up the side of the steep valley, Micah in tears the whole way up. Near the top, as the track reached the wide left-hand curve, Jakob Essen's Nissan Navara blocked their path.

Kaine stopped the Renault, activated the parking brake, and turned to his distraught passenger.

"We'll have to walk from here."

Kaine unfastened his seatbelt, pushed open the driver's door, and stepped out onto the track.

With the stilted actions of a robot, a tearful Micah followed Kaine's lead and extricated himself from the Renault.

"Who did this?" he asked, without emotion. He stared blankly at Essen's bloodied corpse, seemingly unmoved by the man's death.

"They tried to escape." Kaine pursed his lips. "Adrian and I didn't let them. Come with me. Try not to look at them."

Desperate to learn the extent of Rollo's injury, Kaine rushed up the hill. Micah followed close behind, panting as they climbed towards the battle-scarred bungalow.

"You ... you shot him?" Micah asked, tugging at Kaine's sleeve.

"And her," Kaine said, nodding as they passed the crumpled Citroën, jammed into the drainage ditch on the far side of the track. Marta Braun's head barely showed above the twisted bodywork.

"She's the woman who followed me to the railway station," Micah announced. Tears still tumbled from his eyes, but his flat, detached speech showed that his emotions were shutting down as shock set in.

They hurried past the last mortal remains of Max Schiller—his bloodied corpse mercifully hidden by the undergrowth—and reached the horseshoe terrace to be met by a white-faced Rollo. He stood, leaning against the bungalow's bullet-pocked front wall, his right arm cradled in a makeshift sling made from a curtain tie knotted at the neck. A bulging right shoulder showed where he'd packed his wound with a cloth. His right hand hung limp from the sling, white and immobile.

Micah tried to dart forwards, but Kaine shot out an arm and held him back. He tried to break free, but Kaine gripped him tight.

"Micah, wait."

"Let me go!"

The youngster screamed and threw his whole weight behind a wild right cross, aimed at Kaine's jaw. Kaine ducked beneath the arcing blow. Micah lost his balance and stumbled into Kaine's encircling arms. Kaine hugged tight, fell to his knees with the kid in his arms, and allowed him to cry it out.

"It's okay, Micah. It's okay. Let it go, son. Let it go."

Micah howled and his body shuddered, racked with sobs. From his knees, Kaine stared up at a pale and clearly pained Rollo, who nodded as if to say, "Good work, sir. Nicely done."

* * *

It took Micah five minutes to settle, with Kaine holding him the whole time, mumbling words that meant nothing and did even less.

Rollo looked on in silence, leaning fast against the wall as though worried that if he slid down to the ground, he'd never be able to get up again.

"Micah," Kaine said after the lad's sobbing had eased, "would you like to see her?"

The lad shook his head.

"No—I-I mean, yes. I-Is she as ... bad as those ... the others?"

Kaine looked at Rollo, and raised his eyebrows in question.

Rollo shook his head. He closed his eyes and pressed the back of his left hand to his right cheek. Miming sleep.

"No," Kaine said. "She isn't."

"I'll take you to her," Rollo said.

He levered himself away from the wall, staggered a little, and threw his good hand against the bricks for support. Kaine jumped up and raced to his old friend's side.

Micah climbed more slowly to his feet. His desire to be with Molly fighting with his reluctance to confirm her death, the battle showing on his crumbling face. He approached them and hesitated, unwilling to enter the house.

Kaine ducked his head under Rollo's good arm and draped it over his shoulder. Rollo sagged and Kaine willingly took the heavy load. He helped Rollo through the front door. Micah stopped at the entrance, loath to step over the threshold.

"Where is she?" Kaine whispered.

"Spare bedroom," Rollo gasped. "Third door on the ... left."

The first door stood half open and revealed a spartan kitchen. It contained a cheap dining table with a Formica top circled by four hard-backed metal chairs. Kaine led his burden inside and lowered him into one of the chairs. Rollo sighed as he collapsed against the chair's hard back, flinching with every movement.

"Thanks," Rollo gasped. "Give me a minute to recover. I'll be okay."

"Thirsty?" Kaine asked.

"Parched," Rollo croaked and cleared his throat.

Kaine searched the cheap wall units over the stainless-steel sink and found a group of mismatched crockery and a couple of cracked mugs behind the third door he opened. He ran the cold tap long enough for it to run clear. He rinsed out a mug, filled it, and placed it on the table near Rollo's good hand.

"Drink it all," he ordered. "There's plenty more in the tap."

Kaine returned to the sink, opened the cold tap fully, and splashed the chilled water over his face and into his eyes. They stung like hell on contact with the water, but he had to clear the remaining dust or risk permanent damage.

A ragged, soulful, gut-wrenching howl erupted from deeper inside the bungalow.

"Molly! Oh God. No!"

Rollo tried to stand, but Kaine held up a hand, and he settled heavily into his chair.

"Drink. I'll handle this," Kaine said.

"Go easy on him, sir," Rollo said, stretching out a trembling left hand to the chipped mug.

What else would I do?

Kaine turned away and stepped out into the corridor. The third door along stood wide open. The wailing erupted from inside. Kaine hurried forwards.

A sobbing Micah knelt on the bare floorboards to the side of a single bed. Hands on knees, backside resting on his heels, the distraught youngster stared at the figure lying on the bed. Part-covered by a bloodstained sheet, her head and shoulders were exposed, face pale, lips bloodless, her eyes closed as if in sleep. Micah turned his head and stared up at Kaine.

"She ... She looks so ... peaceful," he said, lower lip trembling, cheeks wet with tears. "Could be sleeping."

He leant forwards and reached a hand towards the translucent face of his dead wife.

"No," Kaine said quietly. "It's better not to touch her."

Micah snatched his hand away.

"Why not?" he asked, choking on the words. "F-Forensics?"

Kaine fully entered the room.

"No, Micah," he said, standing over the grieving man. "She'll be ... cold. It's better for you to remember her as she was before. Warm. Vibrant. Alive."

Micah's shoulders sagged and he sank back on his heels. Once again, he tore his tear-filled eyes from the body and turned them on Kaine.

"What am I going to do?" he asked, the plaintive words full of pain.

"You'll carry on living," Kaine said, keeping his voice low and his tone soothing. "You'll survive. It may not seem possible now, but eventually, you will remember the good times. You *will* remember her smile. ... I promise."

Micah blinked. More tears flowed.

Kaine wanted more than anything to find words that would help. A hopeless task.

"You've lost people you loved?"

Kaine studied the youngster as he struggled to come to terms with his loss. The trauma had shredded him, torn him apart. It would take weeks, months, for him to crawl up and out of the pit of despair—assuming he ever did.

Danny's face floated onto the screen in the back of Kaine's mind. Danny, with his infectious smile and naïve optimism. Danny, the latest of many friends to pass.

Kaine recalled the first of a growing list. Gus. Sub-Lieutenant Angus McBride. The friendly, impossibly young Scot with perfect teeth and the naïve positivity of a true believer. The Second Gulf War. A mortar had blown him into tiny pieces in front of a very young Kaine. It had taken him weeks to reach some sort of balance, some sort of normality. Weeks.

Yes. He'd lost people.

"Too many," Kaine said. "Come"—he held out his hand—"let's leave her in peace."

After a moment's hesitation, Micah grabbed the offered hand and allowed Kaine to help him up. Micah stood over the deathbed, made the sign of the cross—Kaine didn't—and they left the room. Kaine closed the door quietly behind them and steeled himself for the difficult part. The extrication.

They returned to the kitchen to find a stronger-looking Rollo gulping down another mug of water and sitting more upright in the hardbacked chair. A little colour had returned to his cheeks.

Micah followed Kaine on stiff legs, walking like an automaton, stunned at his loss. Like Rollo before, Kaine helped him into a chair and placed another mug of water on the table. Micah left the drink untouched.

Kaine allowed the silence to stretch out, giving Micah as much time as possible. Five slow minutes passed before Kaine encouraged Micah to drink the water. He couldn't wait any longer—he had no idea when a local would contact the gendarmes about the unexpected gunfire they'd heard rolling around the valley. Gunshots might have been mistaken for the hunt, but Kaine had no idea when hunting season started in that part of France.

"I-I've lost ... everything. Everything," Micah said, staring at his hands. They trembled in his lap.

"Micah," Kaine said, keeping his voice low. "Listen to me."

The lad lifted his eyes and looked directly at Kaine for the first time since leaving Molly.

"I've got nothing left to live for," he moaned, chin trembling, tears streaming again.

"Stop that, Micah. Stop," Kaine said, firmly. "Those bastards"—he pointed through the kitchen window towards the remains of battle outside—"were planning to kill you, too. You know that, right?"

"They were?"

"Yes, they were." Kaine pulled a chair next to the lad and sat. He leant close and lowered his voice. "They would have lured you into the middle of nowhere and shot you dead. Don't let them win, Micah. Don't!"

"But ... Wh-What am I going to do?"

"You, Micah," Kaine said, "are going to stay here and wait twenty minutes before calling the police."

Micah stiffened. "The police?" Momentary confusion showed on his face before understanding struck. "The police ... the gendarmes. Okay. Yes. The gendarmes. Right." He nodded, his gaze vacant.

"That's right, Micah. Remember. Wait twenty minutes before calling them. The emergency number in France is 1-1-2, and all the operators speak English. Tell them what happened and wait for the police to arrive. I don't think they'll take long."

Not with four dead bodies on their hands.

Micah's eyes gained focus, and they turned on Kaine once more, imploring, begging for help. "Wh-What should I tell them? How can I explain all this ... all this ...?" He allowed the question to trail away.

"Don't say anything at first. Hold off for as long as possible."

"Why?"

I need time to reach Pedersen.

"You're in shock. Act like it. Keep quiet. Play dumb. They'll offer you medical care. Take it. In a few hours, maybe tomorrow, you can start talking. Tell them everything that happened. Reveal it slowly. You need to tell them everything you did, everything you saw, everything you heard, but …"

Micah blinked and waited for Kaine to continue.

"But?"

"Leave out the part about calling The 83 Trust."

Confusion returned to the youngster's face.

"What?" he said. "Why?"

Here's the crux.

Could he convince the youngster?

Kaine leant further forwards and rested his elbows on his thighs. Rollo sat up a little straighter, clenching his jaws at the effort. They had to wrap this up quickly. Rollo needed urgent medical attention, and Kaine needed to pay Pedersen a quiet visit.

"Think about it, Micah," Kaine said. "If The Trust is embroiled in a police investigation, we won't be able to help the other families."

Not that we've been of much use here.

Micah glanced at Rollo before facing Kaine again.

"But how do I explain you and Adrian … and the flight in the private jet?"

"Tell them exactly what happened. Give them our names as you know them, Arnold Jeffries, and Adrian Bennett. Repeat them, Arnold Jeffries, and Adrian Bennett."

Micah recited the names and Kaine continued.

"Tell the gendarmes I intercepted you when you were refuelling outside Lakerveld, on your way to Amsterdam. You remember that place, right? We had drinks and a snack."

"Yeah, yeah," Micah said, nodding slowly, vacantly. "I remember. Of course I remember. It was only last night … For God's sake. Was it only last night?"

Kaine nodded.

"There were surveillance cameras. Plenty along the route, too. They'll confirm your story."

Micah rubbed the tears from his eyes.

"And how did you convince me to let you help?"

Kaine smiled. Time for the embellishment and an out-and-out lie. He ran through it, working off the cuff.

"This is the part you don't know, because I haven't told you yet." Kaine leant away from the table and fixed Micah with a dead eye. "Adrian and I work for Europol."

"What?" Micah raised a sceptical eyebrow and blinked twice.

"We work for Europol."

"You do?"

"We do?" Rollo asked, then nodded, his expression turning from surprised to serious. "Yes, we do. Europol. Most definitely."

"That's right. Our department focuses on organised crime and pays particular attention to the illegal trade in conflict diamonds. In fact, we've had eyes on Pedersen for the past few months."

"Who?"

"The man you met in London, Abe. His surname is Pedersen. Abraham Pedersen."

"Oh." Micah nodded. "Right. I see."

"When you turned up at his house the other morning, I decided to follow you and make the interception. I showed you my credentials—"

"You did?"

"Yes, indeed. I showed you my credentials and you convinced me that you were the victim of a kidnap scheme and had been coerced into acting as a courier. If you hadn't, I'd have arrested you on the spot for smuggling gemstones."

Micah blinked as though having difficulty taking it all in. "And the private jet? How do I explain that?"

"You don't. You were simply following my instructions. You just need to tell the gendarmes exactly what happened. We'll deal with any fallout as and when it occurs."

Micah frowned. "How? There'll be a trail. A flight plan. Surveillance cameras at the airport."

Kaine sighed.

"Micah," he said, "we flew on a jet owned by a major French armaments company. I think ESAPP will have plenty of ways to wrap the police investigation up in red tape for months and months. Don't you? They'll also be able to bring pressure to bear on the authorities. I'll make sure they help you, Micah."

"But ... How do I explain what happened up here ... to ... Molly?" Micah's lower lip started trembling as he slid closer to the edge of losing control again.

"You don't," Kaine said. "You have no idea what happened after we left you tied up in the Renault. Look"—he pointed to the red welt running around Micah's exposed wrist—"you have the injury to prove it."

Micah held up his arm and stared at the wound as though he'd forgotten all about it.

"H-How did I ... escape?"

"You didn't," Kaine said. "Tell it the way it happened. I came back and released you. Then we drove up here and left you alone. And ... that's it, really. We told you to call the gendarmes. Then we disappeared."

"Just like that?" Micah asked, still gazing at the red welt through tear-filled, dark brown eyes.

Kaine nodded. "Just like that. And remember this. The vast majority of what you say will be the absolute truth."

"The absolute truth ..." Micah rubbed the side of his injured wrist with his left thumb and didn't seem to feel any pain. A faraway look entered his eye.

Kaine leant forwards and dropped a hand on Micah's shoulder. The lad jumped and his attention returned to the room.

"Micah," he said, adding some urgency to his voice. "There are only two things you have to remember."

"What's that?"

"You didn't call The 83 Trust."

Micah closed his eyes and nodded. "Okay. Got that. And the other thing?"

"We got the bastards who killed Molly. They'll never hurt anyone else ever again. Okay?"

And who's going to give a damn about three dead killers?

Micah teared up again, Molly's name causing pain, as it would for a long while. Probably forever.

"That's it, Micah," Kaine said. "Sorry, but we need to go now."

He stood and offered a helping hand to Rollo, who waved it away and levered himself upright, grunting with the effort. Kaine turned the hand towards Micah and the young man grasped it as though it were a lifeline.

"Y-You can't go."

"I'm sorry, Micah, but we can't stay."

Micah's grip strengthened.

"But, I-I need you."

Desperation flashed on his tear-stained face.

Kaine eased his hand out of the youngster's grip.

"Be strong, Micah."

"But Abe ... Pedersen ... h-he knows all about us. He knows where we"—he winced and shook his head—"where *I* live."

Kaine grasped Micah's upper arm and squeezed it tight.

"Don't worry, son. I haven't forgotten about Abe Pedersen."

Not for one minute.

20

Wednesday 31st May – Afternoon

Corbarieu, Tarn-et-Garonne, France

Kaine allowed Rollo through the front door first and stepped alongside, ready to catch him if he stumbled, but the rest and the water had done some good. Rollo didn't falter.

"Is it safe to leave him?" Rollo asked.

"We don't have any choice." Kaine glanced back at the bullet-damaged bungalow before facing forwards and fixing his eyes on the track ahead. "What else can we do? We can't be here when the gendarmes arrive, and there's no way we can take him with us."

"True enough." Rollo shuddered and shook his head. "I doubt he'd leave Molly, anyway. Will he keep The Trust out of it, d'you think?"

"No idea. I hope so. If he doesn't we can always close it down and open another charity. Let's hope it doesn't come to that."

They reached the first turn and passed the undergrowth hiding Schiller's corpse.

"Nasty piece of work," Rollo said, nodding towards the area.

"I doubt anyone's going to miss him, or the other two."

"By the way, Europol?" Rollo snorted. "I mean, Europol?"

Kaine frowned. "What's wrong with Europol?"

Rollo shook his head. "Don't know how you do it."

"Do what?"

"Make up all that stuff on the fly. Ever thought of writing fiction?"

"When would I have the time?"

"Good point." Rollo sighed and nodded. "It has been a little full-on lately. To be honest, I could do with a bit of a rest."

"You're getting one. I'm putting you on sick leave until you're fully recovered."

"This"—Rollo waved his good hand at the patch of red still seeping from the wound—"is nothing. I'll be ... right as rain in a couple of weeks."

The medics and Marie-Odile will be the best judges of that.

"A couple of weeks, Colour Sergeant? Hell no. I'll give you seven days, no more." He smiled.

Rollo stumbled. Kaine threw an arm around his trim waist and stopped him falling. He ducked low and draped Rollo's heavy left arm over his shoulders, buckling slightly as he took the weight again. They continued slowly, Rollo growing heavier with each shuffled pace.

"Bloody hell, Rollo," Kaine gasped, the muscles in his legs, back, and shoulders burning under the load. "Ever thought of going on a diet?"

"No," Rollo said, teeth gritted. "You ever ... thought of doing some ... strength work ... sir?"

"Ha, ha. Very funny, Colour Sergeant. Another crack like that, and I'll place you on a charge. Insubordination will do. Or mutiny, maybe." Kaine tried to smile, but couldn't manage one through clenched teeth.

They skirted around the battered, nose-dived Nissan and finally reached the Renault. Heavily winded, Kaine fed Rollo into the front passenger seat as gently as possible. He helped the big man fasten his seatbelt and turned to study the carnage—two damaged vehicles and three bloodied corpses. The aftermath of a small-scale skirmish in an isolated beauty spot.

"What are you thinking?" Rollo asked, panting. Sweat formed at his hairline and ran down his forehead. The struggle downhill had taken more effort than he wanted to admit, but at least the shoulder wound hadn't opened up again.

"I've had an idea. Can you reach your Glock?"

"Sorry?"

"Your Glock," Kaine said, beckoning with his fingers. "Can you reach it?"

Rollo eased over to his right. He squeezed his eyes shut and the breath caught in his throat. "Sorry, sir. It's a little awkward."

"Where is it?"

"Left jacket pocket." He straightened and breathed again.

Kaine leant closer and plucked out the weapon.

"Thanks," Kaine said. "Don't move. I'll be right back."

Rollo puffed out his cheeks.

"I'm going nowhere, sir. This seat's really comfortable."

Kaine closed the door carefully to avoid jolting his mate, pushed away from the car, and jogged up the track until he'd passed Jakob Essen's Nissan. Twenty metres beyond the Navara, he reached the point where Schiller's Citroën more-or-less intersected with the trajectory of the shot that had killed Essen. Kaine turned, raised the Glock, aimed, and shot the dead man for a second time. The bullet followed a similar path to the original, entered Essen's open mouth and drove through the back of an already-shattered skull. It smashed through the driver's side window and carried on into the undergrowth beyond. With any luck at all, the Glock's bullet would have destroyed all trace of the original wound. Not that it mattered if it didn't. What mattered was the confusion and delay it brought to the police investigation.

Above him, the bungalow's front door creaked open.

"What was that?" Micah shouted, his voice pitched high in fear.

"Don't worry, Micah," Kaine called. "It's only me. Arnie. I'm cleaning up. Go back inside."

A few seconds later, the door slammed shut.

Kaine returned to the Nissan, tore open the front passenger door with the hem of his shirt over his hand, and climbed into the cabin. After pausing a moment to survey the latest damage to Essen's head, he pulled his SIG from its holster, took a wad of tissues from a box that had fallen into the passenger footwell, and wiped the gun clean of his prints. Then, he placed the SIG in Essen's right hand, making sure the man's prints and his palm touched all the right places. Finally, he pushed the dead man's index finger through the trigger guard. Leaning as far away as possible, he pointed the SIG through the smashed driver's window and fired three times, depositing gunshot residue over Essen's hand, sleeve, and lap.

Good enough.

Kaine reversed out of the Nissan, climbed back up to the track, and carried on uphill until he reached the large chestnut tree. Using the same low-hanging branch as before, he pulled himself up the runoff ditch and into the ferns and brambles. The familiar iron-rich taint of blood filled the air over the corpse. Flies fizzed around the bullet-riddled body, feasting on the blood, and finding rich, moist conditions in which to lay their eggs.

"Excuse me," Kaine said, smiling at Schiller's heavily scratched face, "but I need this more than you."

Taking care to disturb as little of the undergrowth around the body as possible, Kaine leant down, ripped the USP from Schiller's left fist, and replaced it with Rollo's wiped-clean Glock. Then he reversed into the gully and climbed back up to the track.

One more thing to do.

At the damaged Citroën, Kaine cleaned the USP and planted it in Martha Braun's lifeless hand. He fired it through the shattered windscreen, depositing more gunshot residue and dropping another shower of glass granules into the cabin and over his head and shoulders.

On his way back to Rollo and the Renault, he brushed the glass out of his hair and from his T-shirt, and climbed into the driver's seat.

Rollo stared at him for a moment before asking, "What was that all about?"

Kaine smiled. "Thought I'd bring a little confusion to the enemy."

"The enemy in question being the local ... gendarmes, I suppose?"

"That's right. It can't hurt to muddy the waters a little."

"I suppose not."

Kaine fired up the Renault's engine and selected reverse.

"Where to now, sir?"

"First," Kaine said, twisting at the waist and throwing his arm over the back of Rollo's seat, "we're going to find you a medic."

Rollo grunted as Kaine slipped the clutch and the car rolled backwards down the hill, pain written large on his pinched face.

"Where are we going to find a tame medic in this neck of the woods?"

"No idea," Kaine said, "but I think I know someone who does."

After reversing through a tight lefthand curve, Kaine slowed as he reached a passing spot cut into the woods. He worked through a tight five-point turn—doing his best not to jerk the car too much—and drove forwards down the deeply rutted track, keeping the speed down and the gear low. Despite the crawling pace, the Renault bucked and wallowed, and worked the suspension to its limits.

Eyes and mouth tight shut, his face blanching, Rollo clung tight to the grab strap. He didn't make a sound until they reached a relatively straight and smooth part of the track.

"Don't tell me," Rollo said. "Corky knows a French medic?"

"Does he?" Kaine asked, smiling.

"He doesn't?

"No idea." Kaine dropped down a gear to negotiate another sharp and uneven righthand bend, and passed the lay-by where they'd left Micah and Rollo's Peugeot 208. At the T-junction with the D21, he turned right and headed towards Corbarieu. Slowly, smoothly, he worked his way up the gears and increased speed until they'd reached the heady heights of eighty kph—a whopping fifty mph. Fast enough to avoid drawing attention to themselves, but slow enough to minimise the strain on Rollo.

"Well, who does?" Rollo asked.

"Who does what?" Kaine asked. Occasionally, he did enjoy playing the wind-up merchant.

"Who *does* know a local medic? And please ... pack that in, sir," Rollo groaned. "I'm really ... not in the mood."

"Sorry, Colour Sergeant." Kaine dropped the smile. "I was trying to lighten the mood."

"It's not ... working."

"Yes, I know. But to answer your question, that would be Maurice LeMaître."

"Sabrina's grandfather?"

"I don't see why not. After all, this is his neck of the woods." He waved a hand towards the lush green countryside rolling past the windows.

"And he does ... owe you a favour after ... that business in Arizona."

"I'd never remind him of that."

"You'd ... never have to."

An approaching junction seemed a reasonable place to pull off the road. Kaine slowed the Renault and indicated right.

Rollo reached up to the grab strap again and steadied himself while Kaine made the tight turn onto a narrow farm lane running downhill into thick woods. Kaine pulled in at a bulge in the track that acted as a passing place.

"And second?" Rollo said.

"Sorry?"

"Back at the bungalow, you said, *first* we find a medic. What do we do second?"

Kaine shot Rollo a knowing glance. "*We* do nothing. You go home and recuperate with your lovely wife, and I visit an elderly gent called Abe Pedersen, after a brief stopover in Amsterdam."

"Ah," Rollo said, nodding. "I somehow ... thought you might. Is that why you asked Micah to keep quiet for a while?"

"Yep."

Kaine killed the engine, reached for his mobile, dialled a number from memory, and hit the speaker button for Rollo's benefit. The call connected quickly.

"*Bonjour,* Ryan," a bright female voice said. "How are you, *mon ami*?"

"Sabrina?" Kaine said. "Is that you?"

"It is."

She sounded much stronger and healthier than the last time they'd spoken.

"*Bonjour,* Sabrina. I expected your grandfather."

"*Grand-père* Mo-Mo is indisposed at the moment," she said after a momentary hesitation.

"Is he okay?"

"Yes. A minor illness. Against his wishes, I sent him to his bed. So, how can I be of assistance?"

"Before I ask for your help, how are you?"

"Recovering, thanks to you. The American doctors gave me permission to return to France. However, I'm under strict instructions to remain in quarantine for another two weeks. It doesn't mean I can't answer the telephone though. So, tell me. What is it you require?"

Kaine told her where they were and what they needed.

"How bad is the wound?"

"Not sure. The stubborn fool won't let me check him over. Doesn't look good, though. He's lost a lot of blood."

"It's not ... that bad," Rollo growled. "Nothing but a scratch. A couple of stitches and some antibiotics should cover it."

Kaine flapped his hand to silence him.

"Does he need hospitalisation?" Sabrina asked, her voice carrying over the clicking of a keyboard.

"Yes, definitely. But isn't a bullet wound notifiable in France?"

"Officially, yes," she said, sounding a little distracted.

"And unofficially?"

"Ah," she laughed. "That, *mon ami*, is a different story. One moment ... I nearly have it. ... Ah yes. You are not far from me here in Limoges. I'll send you an address to program into your GPS."

"Limoges?"

Kaine had heard of the place, but had never visited.

"It is approximately three hundred kilometres north of your current location. The journey should take you less than three hours."

"What's in Limoges?"

The mobile dinged with an incoming text.

"Cafés, restaurants, medieval architecture, and many other wonderful tourist attractions, *mon ami*. And outside of the city, ESAPP has a medical research facility. Sergeant Rollason will receive the very best of medical care in complete secrecy. No questions will be asked. I shall talk to the chief medical officer and warn her of your impending arrival."

"Medical research?" Rollo gasped. "I'm a ... bloody guinea pig now?"

Sabrina laughed. "The Limoges facility focuses its research into the treatment of battlefield trauma, *Rollo*. You will receive the very best medical care available anywhere in the world. I can assure you."

"One more thing, Sabrina."

"*Oui?*"

"Does Limoges have an airport?"

"Yes, of course," Sabrina said, a smile in her voice. "Would you like me to have Captain Gamay fly the Gulfstream to meet you there?"

Kaine smiled. She thought of everything.

"Yes please."

"And her ongoing destination ... for the flight plan?"

"Schiphol International. I have a lapidary to revisit."

"A lapidary in Amsterdam? But of course. I will call you back if I need more details. *À bientôt, mes amis.*"

"Cheers, Sabrina. And thanks for everything."

"No need to thank me, Ryan. I will be forever in your debt."

Sabrina disconnected the call before Kaine had the chance to respond. Rollo gave him the "I told you so" look, which Kaine studiously ignored. He opened Sabrina's text and entered the coordinates into the car's built-in GPS. The ETA showed two hours, fifty-one minutes.

"I don't know what you're looking so smug about, Colour Sergeant," he said, smiling.

"Me? Smug?" Rollo said. "I'm ... sitting here with a ... bullet hole in my shoulder and a numb hand ... and you think I look smug? What the hell have I ... got to be smug about?"

"Absolutely nothing, Rollo. You still have to call Marie-Odile." Kaine tried not to snigger.

"Oh God."

The low sun threw a blinding light into the cab, making it difficult to see tonal differences, but Kaine could have sworn Rollo's face lost a few more shades of colour. He pressed the mobile into his friend's left hand and grinned. Couldn't help himself.

Kaine fired up the Renault, reversed out of the passing spot, and headed back up the hill to pick up the D21 again. Once they'd reached cruising speed, he shot Rollo a sideways glance.

"Call her, Colour Sergeant. She needs to know."

Rollo shook his head.

"I'd rather face Schiller and that bloody UPS again."

"You can't put it off any longer."

Rollo held up the mobile and made a half-hearted attempt to open the telephone app.

"It's no good," he said. "I'm useless with my left hand. It'll have to wait."

"Coward."

Rollo sighed.

"Guilty," he rasped. "Guilty as charged."

Keeping his eyes on the empty road ahead, Kaine held out his hand. "Pass me the phone."

"Hadn't you better concentrate on your driving?"

"The phone, Rollo. Now!"

Reluctantly, Rollo handed the mobile across, grunting with the effort of moving. Without looking, and keeping the phone in his lap and out of sight, Kaine held down the home button long enough to access the phone's virtual assistant.

"Call Marie-Odile's mobile!" he ordered, loud and slow.

"*Would you like me to call Marie-Odile's mobile?*" the naturalistic voice responded.

"Yes please," Kaine answered and turned to look at Rollo. "Isn't modern technology wonderful?"

Rollo groaned.

Still grinning, Kaine handed the phone across. "I'll try not to listen."

"No fair, sir," Rollo growled. "No fair at—ah hello, love. ... I'm using the captain's phone. ... No, I haven't lost mine. How are you?"

Kaine tried to block out the conversation and focus on his driving, but Marie-Odile's emotional voice blasted around the cab as loud as an artillery barrage.

21

Wednesday 31st May – Early Evening

ESAPP Medical Centre, Limoges, Nouvelle-Aquitaine, France

Kaine and a flagging, pale-skinned, and sweating Rollo reached the outskirts of Limoges fifteen minutes ahead of the original ETA—thanks to light traffic and Kaine pushing beyond the maximum speed limit. They followed a convoluted route to the ESAPP Medical Centre which occupied one sector of a small industrial zone to the southwest of the ancient city.

Lit by night-into-day floodlights attached to tall gantries at each corner, surrounded by a three-metre-tall, stainless-steel mesh fence topped with razor wire, and with twin blast gates at the entrance, the centre positively screamed, "High Security Military Research Facility". However, a modest sign on each gate—one in French, the other in English—carried the medical logo, the Caduceus, and read:

ESAPP Medical Research Centre
No Unauthorised Entry

"Bloody hell," Rollo grunted, shifting uneasily in his seat. "Impressive, or what?" He took another sip from a bottle of water and wiped his mouth with the back of his hand.

Apart from the occasional grunt or gasp when they'd negotiated a sharp corner or hit the very occasional pothole, he'd been silent for most of the drive. Evidently, the call to Marie-Odile had rendered him speechless as much as the injury.

Kaine drew the car to a stop at the barrier, lowered his window, and pressed the only button on a stainless-steel intercom system. A raucous bell rang deep within the compound.

"*Oui? Qui êtes-vous?*" A man's voice. Abrupt and official.

"*Smith et Jones. Nous sommes d'Angleterre,*" Kaine answered in his stilted French, following the instructions given by Sabrina during their race north.

"Ah, welcome. Please enter and follow the green signs to Building B," the voice said in perfect English, its tone warmer and much more welcoming. "It is to the rear of the complex."

A warning alarm chimed before the blast gates split in the middle and rolled apart. As soon as the gap had opened wide enough to accept them, Kaine punched the Renault through, and the gates rolled closed behind them.

A two-lane service road circled the research facility, and Kaine followed the green signs as the disembodied voice had instructed.

A pair of low buildings dominated the space inside the security fence. Single storey, sleek and modern, with narrow vertical stripes of glass and zinc, and flat roofs, they were pure modernist works of art.

Kaine took it all in, impressed by what he saw.

The green signs led them around the back of the artwork to a wide grey door marked with a large white sign that read, *Bâtiment B*, and nothing else. Ten parking spaces—all but four empty—lined the entrance. Kaine reversed into the nearest empty space to the grey door, slid out of the Renault, and darted around the front of the car to help Rollo release his seatbelt.

Before Kaine could ease Rollo from the car, the grey door swung open, and a man wearing a white lab coat and a white cotton facemask appeared in the opening. He stood behind a wheelchair.

"Won't be needing the chair," Rollo called, groaning as he pushed himself out of the Renault and waved away Kaine's offered arm.

"Don't be an idiot, Rollo," Kaine barked. "Let him help."

Rollo snapped his mouth closed and growled.

The medic pushed the wheelchair towards them. As he cleared the entrance, a second figure appeared in the opening. A woman. Slim-built and young, she also wore a facemask, but hers matched the shade of her dark blue business suit. She followed the man in the white coat. The way she carried herself, shoulders back, head held high, Kaine recognised her immediately and smiled in greeting. While the duo approached, Kaine gripped Rollo's good arm, holding him upright, keeping him steady.

"Stay right where you are, Colour Sergeant."

The man with the wheelchair stopped in front of them and activated the brakes.

"*Monsieur* Jones," he said. "If you please." He helped a reluctant Rollo into the chair, released the brakes, and started wheeling him towards the building.

Rollo leant to his left, protecting his injured shoulder, but trying not to show how much pain it gave him. Kaine frowned.

Typical.

The woman stepped alongside Kaine and looked up, a smile crinkling the corners of her bright eyes.

"Evening, Sabrina," Kaine said. "Didn't expect to see you here."

Sabrina pulled him into a surprising hug, and Kaine responded in kind. Kaine caught a fragrance he couldn't identify, something expensive and probably exclusive—a distinct improvement over the last time they'd met.

"I've been recuperating here ever since returning from the USA," she said. "It's the ideal place to recover and not feel too isolated. Here, I have access to both medical care and a world class IT infrastructure."

Sabrina lowered her mask and leant in to kiss his cheek. Clever use of makeup had done wonders to mask her bruises, but it couldn't quite hide the swelling around her eyes, or the partially healed cut on her lower lip.

She stepped away and wrinkled her nose. "You smell of battle."

Kaine shrugged an apology. "Sorry. We didn't have time to freshen up."

"You have a change of clothing?"

"Just a sec." Kaine left her and grabbed his and Rollo's go bags from the rear seat of the Renault.

"Shall we?" Sabrina said, pointing towards the retreating wheelchair.

She replaced her facemask, handed Kaine a fresh white one, and led the way into Building B. The doors swung closed behind them on electric motors.

By the time they reached the clinically clean reception area behind the entrance doors, Rollo and his white-coated medic had disappeared into the bowels of the building.

"Don't worry, Ryan," Sabrina said in answer to his worried frown. "Rollo is in good hands. The operating theatre has been prepared and is waiting to receive him. Dr Meniere is head of this facility. A world-class surgeon. The surgery will commence immediately after Rollo has been to the scanner. I promise, we will take great care of him."

"Dr Meniere pushed the wheelchair?"

Again, Sabrina smiled behind her mask.

"That was Nurse Alphonse. He is taking Rollo to the imaging centre. Dr Meniere is already in theatre, scrubbing up. As I said, Ryan, our friend is in good hands. And talking about scrubbing up, please follow me." She pointed down the corridor and headed off.

"Where are we going?" Kaine asked, stepping alongside her.

"You need a shower."

He nodded, unable to argue the point.

"And your eyes. They are red and look sore."

"I copped a little dust," Kaine said, blinking rapidly. "They don't hurt much."

"You will find a medical kit in the changing room. There will be eye drops. Please, help yourself."

He nodded his thanks.

They passed three closed doors before stopping at the fourth. Sabrina took a plastic rectangle from her pocket and passed it over a wall scanner. The lock disengaged. She pushed open the door and stepped back to allow Kaine through first.

He entered a bright, but starkly furnished room. The walls were clad in white floor-to-ceiling tiles, a row of grey metal lockers lined the opposite wall, and bench seating ran along two of the other three. A white door broke into the final wall.

"The shower room is through there. I shall see you in reception. Fifteen minutes?"

He nodded, dropped his bag on the nearest bench, and handed Rollo's to Sabrina.

She smiled, passed him the entry card, and left the changing room. The door closed softly behind her.

* * *

AFTER SHOWERING AND CHANGING CLOTHES, Kaine found the medical kit and the sealed pack of eye drops. He bathed his eyes with the soothing drops, and snaffled a few of the plastic vials for later. Then he made his way back to the entrance area to find Sabrina seated behind the reception desk, talking into a phone. She spoke rapidly and quietly in French. He waited on the other side of the desk, trying to be patient, but churning inside. He hated not knowing the full extent of Rollo's injury.

Sabrina ended the call and dropped the receiver into the cradle, looking at Kaine the whole time.

"What's happening?"

Sabrina stood and stepped around to the front of the desk.

"Dr Meniere is reviewing the scans."

"He's been through the scanner already?"

"*Oui*, Ryan. As I said, Rollo is receiving the best of care."

She smiled beneath her facemask and touched his upper arm as she brushed past him on her way to the rear doors.

"You're leaving?" Kaine asked.

Sabrina ignored his question and pressed a button on the wall beside the rear entrance doors. The locks disengaged. She pushed through the doors and headed outside into the glare of the floodlights.

"Come on," she said, beckoning him towards her.

Frowning, he approached in time to see a pair of car headlights rake the inside of the security fence and turn into the parking area. The car, a dusty white Citroën, screeched to a stop in the middle of the access road. The driver's door opened, and Marie-Odile jumped out. She raced towards the open doors and fell into Kaine's arms.

"Where is he?" she cried, her cheeks wet, mascara smudged. "Where is my Rollo?"

* * *

The waiting room could have been created by a film set designer. Stark and clean, but soulless. It didn't even have the usual array of out-of-date magazines. Sabrina sat in a corner with Marie-Odile, comforting the distraught woman. Kaine hadn't been able to answer any of Marie-Odile's medical questions and refused to discuss the operation that resulted in Rollo's injury. Details wouldn't help. Plausible deniability stretched to family members.

Originally, Kaine had planned to leave Rollo and Marie-Odile in Sabrina's care and take off in pursuit of his prey, but Dr Meniere's pre-operative report had forced a change of plans. Rollo's injury proved much more serious than Kaine had imagined.

Five minutes after Marie-Odile's dramatic arrival, Sabrina took the surgeon's call from the reception desk. She received the news in silence, but her expression told the tale.

"What is it?" Marie-Odile demanded, barely recovered enough to have stopped crying.

Sabrina answered in French and Marie-Odile fell silent, struggling to retain control.

Kaine stared at Sabrina, in a silent demand for information.

She took him to one side, out of Marie-Odile's hearing.

"It is bad, Ryan," she said, voice low.

It has to be.

"Tell me."

Sabrina swallowed hard, turned her back to Marie-Odile, and spoke even more quietly.

"The bullet tore through Rollo's rotator cuff and shattered his shoulder joint on the way through. There is the possibility of some nerve damage. I asked Dr Meniere for a prognosis, but"—Sabrina shook her head—"she would not be drawn."

"Dear God. Can she save the arm?"

"If anyone can, it is Dr Meniere."

Kaine returned to Marie-Odile and held her tight.

* * *

UNABLE TO SIT AND STEW, Kaine spent the better part of five hours pacing the ten-by-five-metre waiting room, formulating a plan of attack. Abraham Pedersen, the man ultimately responsible for Molly's death and Rollo's injury, deserved Kaine's close attention. But a direct approach wouldn't be easy. The old man would be well protected and on his guard. Slim and Larry might have found a decent view, but Kaine held off contacting them until Rollo's surgery had finished and he'd regained consciousness. They'd want to know his condition.

A little before midnight, a male orderly interrupted Kaine's pacing with a tray of drinks—coffee for everyone and individual packets of dry biscuits. Kaine accepted the coffee, but ignored the uninspiring wafers.

Another seemingly endless hour later, the waiting room door

opened, and a short, slim woman entered, dressed in purple medical scrubs. She looked tired, her eyes drawn. Sabrina jumped to her feet and introduced the new arrival as Dr Meniere. Marie-Odile sat up straighter and grasped the arms of her chair.

Kaine stood at Marie-Odile's side, ready to offer whatever comfort he could.

Sabrina and the surgeon spoke quietly for a few moments, in French. Marie-Odile, straining to hear the conversation, gasped. Her shoulders sagged. She buried her face in her hands and burst into silent tears.

Oh God. No!

Sabrina turned to face them. A relieved smile plumped her cheeks and tears filled her dark eyes.

Still seated, Marie-Odile wrapped her arms around Kaine's waist and wept—tears of joy.

"You saved the arm?" Kaine asked the clearly exhausted surgeon.

"*Oui, monsieur,*" Dr Meniere answered, her French accent thick, her voice deeper and chalkier than her slight frame promised. "It was not ... easy. *Le plexus brachial*—the network of nerves that carries signals from *la moelle épinière* ..." She looked towards Sabrina for a translation.

Sabrina had returned to Marie-Odile's side and sat beside her, a joyous grin part-hidden behind the mask, but her eyes showed the emotion clearly. She looked up at Kaine and said, "The spinal cord."

"Ah *oui*," Dr Meniere said, nodding, "the spinal cord." She tilted her head to one side and offered up a Gallic shrug. "Please excuse my poor English, *Monsieur* Smith."

Nothing in her expression suggested the surgeon considered the name an alias, but her tired, creased eyes twinkled.

"As I was saying," Meniere continued, hiding a yawn behind a hand with long and delicate fingers, "the *plexus brachial* transmits ... messages from the ... spinal cord to the arm and hand. One of the nerves had sustained *dégâts importants* ... significant damage, as did a number of the blood vessels in the area. I ..."

Dr Meniere sighed, shook her head, and gave up the translation.

She turned to Sabrina and Marie-Odile and spoke for a while in French.

Kaine stared at Sabrina.

She smiled. "Dr Meniere repaired the damaged blood vessels, which she claims is a relatively easy procedure."

"And the nerve?"

"This is where it becomes complicated."

"*Oui. C'est compliqué, Monsieur Smith,*" Meniere said, nodding. "*Le pronostic est moins certain.* Less certain. We may not know the outcome for some time."

"What's the worst case?" Kaine asked, barely able to form the question.

Meniere cranked out another tired shrug.

"He may lose some function in his arm," she said. "Or there may be some lack of sensation in his fingers. But this will not be clear for some time."

"Hours?" Kaine asked. "Days?"

"Days," Meniere said. "Perhaps weeks. It will take a ... little time for *le gonflement*, the swelling, to reduce. Only then will we know the full extent of *le fonction compromise*. At this stage, it is too early to ... tell the outcome. You understand?"

Kaine nodded.

"But he is strong," Marie-Odile said, speaking for the first time since receiving the news. "He will recover fully."

Kaine nodded. "Yes, he will."

He wished he felt as confident as he made himself sound.

Marie-Odile stood and smoothed out the creases in her green sweater. She asked Meniere a question. The surgeon nodded, opened the door, and escorted Marie-Odile through. Sabrina and Kaine stayed where they were.

After the door closed, Kaine spoke. "Without the full use of his right arm ..." He trailed off, unwilling to finish the sentence.

"But as Marie-Odile said, Rollo is strong, and Dr Meniere is highly skilled. We can only hope for the best."

Kaine nodded towards the door. "She's taking Marie-Odile to

Rollo?"

Sabrina nodded.

"How long will he be out?"

"Out?" She shook her head in confusion.

"Unconscious. He had a general, right? A general anaesthetic?"

"Ah, I see. I'm afraid I have no idea."

The door opened and the orderly who'd provided the coffee appeared. He spoke to Sabrina who nodded and thanked him.

"Rollo is awake," Sabrina said, smiling. "And he's asking for you."

"That was quick. Can I see him?"

"Of course. *Suis-moi.*" She turned and marched away.

With tension clutching at his guts, Kaine trailed her down a pristine white corridor that echoed to their footsteps and seemed to stretch on forever. They turned right at the end and stopped at a door marked, *Salle de Réveil #3*. Sabrina knocked quietly and stepped inside. Kaine hesitated a moment, worried about what he'd find. He took a breath, fixed a hopeful smile onto a reluctant face, and stepped into the recovery room.

With his right shoulder thickly bandaged and his arm in a sling, a white-faced Rollo reclined on a hospital bed in a private room, hooked up to machines that clicked and bleeped. A bag dripped a clear liquid into a vein in his left forearm. Antibiotics, Kaine assumed.

Marie-Odile sat by the bed, holding Rollo's left hand in both of hers, smiling up at her husband.

Kaine stood in the doorway with Sabrina, unwilling to disturb the scene.

Rollo turned his head towards him and blinked.

"Captain?" he croaked.

"What's all this malingering, Colour Sergeant?" Kaine said softly, stepping further into the recovery room. "Should be ashamed of yourself."

Sabrina remained by the door.

Rollo tried to smile but didn't seem to have the energy to hold it for long.

Kaine stopped at the foot of the bed and studied his friend. Sweat shone on his brow. He swallowed and licked his lips. Marie-Odile released her grip on his good hand and fed him water from a plastic cup fitted with a lid and a straw. He took a short pull and nodded his thanks. She dabbed his lips with a white cloth and returned the cup to the side table.

"Why are you still here?" Rollo asked, his voice slightly stronger after the water.

Kaine frowned.

"Where else would I be?"

Straining from the effort, Rollo jutted his jaw and raised his head from the pillow. The numbers on the heartrate monitor increased from seventy-seven to ninety-three, and the respiratory rate hit thirty-six.

"Uncle Abe," Rollo gasped. "He's due a visit."

The heartrate climbed to one hundred and three, and Rollo's head flopped back on the pillow.

Kaine leant forwards and gripped the steel rail on the foot of the bed.

"Pedersen can wait."

Rollo shook his head.

"No," he said, "he can't. ... He might not know about the Germans yet. Go get him, sir. ... Get him before he disappears. Or before the gendarmes try to extradite the bugger."

Kaine stared at his injured friend. They locked eyes. Understanding passed between them, unspoken but clear. Kaine dropped his gaze to Rollo's pale right hand, which lay across his chest. Slowly, his right thumb and index finger formed a circle.

God alive!

"Okay, Rollo," Kaine said, grinning in delight, the relief overwhelming. "I know when I'm superfluous to requirements."

"About time," Rollo said, stretching out a tired smile.

Kaine turned to face a beaming Marie-Odile. She'd seen it, too.

"Take care of him," he said to her. "Make sure he follows his doctor's orders."

"I will," she gushed. She grasped Rollo's left hand again—squeezing tight—lifted it from the bed, and pressed it to her lips.

Kaine dipped his head to her and turned away, unable to hold back the grin. Sabrina followed him from the recovery room and into the corridor.

Once she'd closed the door behind them, Sabrina took hold of his arm and spun him to face her.

"Why are you smiling?" she demanded, clearly worried for his state of mind.

"You didn't see it?"

Sabrina's smooth forehead creased. "See what?"

"Rollo's right hand."

"What about it?"

"He moved his fingers."

"Really?"

Kaine nodded and allowed his grin to stretch wider. "When he raised his head, his fingers moved."

She shook her head. "I did not see it, Ryan. But it might mean nothing. When he lifted his head, the movement may have caused his arm to move involunta—"

"No, Sabrina. He formed a circle with his index finger and thumb. It's the diver's version of a thumbs up sign. He was telling me he's going to be okay. Giving me permission to leave."

"You're going to visit this Pedersen chap?"

"Yes," Kaine said. "After a brief stopover in Amsterdam."

"Care to explain?"

"It's complicated. Maybe another time?"

She raised her chin in a nod of understanding. "I'll hold you to that, Ryan." She leant forwards, lowered the cotton facemask, and brushed her lips to his cheek. "I shall tell Dr Meniere about the hand signal. She will wish to know. Can you find your way out from here?"

"Yep. Will I need this?" Kaine held up the plastic pass card.

She smiled. "To access the changing room only. You will need to collect your ready bag. Leave the card on the desk at reception when you go. *À bientôt, mon ami.* Good hunting."

22

Thursday 1st June – Early Morning

Indische Buurt, Amsterdam, The Netherlands.

Kaine collected his Range Rover from Schiphol private jet terminal and completed the night-time drive to Indische Buurt in less than half the time it had taken during the previous morning's rush hour. The Gulfstream had shaved eight hours off his journey from Limoges, and it would save more time on the trip into London. Using a private jet had left a bitter taste in terms of the damage it wrought on the environment, but Kaine promised himself the private flight from Amsterdam into Heathrow would be his last for a while. Hopefully.

Kaine parked near the spot Micah had used for his Peugeot—a few metres beyond Jan van Bleeker's apartment building—and sat for a moment to settle his thoughts and his breathing. While waiting, he opened another vial of the eyedrops—his third—and treated his eyes again. The stinging soreness had eased during the flight, and his vision had recovered to near normal. His eyes still watered a little, but he would be able to operate effectively.

He closed his lids and regulated his breathing.

The blood-pumping rage that had overwhelmed him when he'd seen Molly Williams' body on the bed had cooled to a dark fury. A thirst for revenge. The animals who had snatched up Micah and Molly, and forced them to do their bidding—and had likely done the same to other innocent souls—had paid with their lives, but other players remained. The likes of Jan van Bleeker, Bogdan, and Abraham Pedersen deserved a similar retribution. As did anyone else associated with the operation. Pedersen wasn't necessarily the gang's head man. Others might be involved, and they were going to pay. By God would they pay. And Kaine would be the one to extract the fee. The image of Rollo lying injured in his hospital bed with a distraught Marie-Odile at his side only added fuel to Kaine's cold rage.

He adjusted the rear-view mirror to give him a better sight of the building's entrance. A dim night-light shone inside the empty foyer. Otherwise, the place showed no signs of life. As expected in the middle of the night, none of the front-facing windows displayed any lights. As far as he could tell, the building lay dormant, its occupants asleep.

Perfect.

Time to go.

Kaine opened the car door, climbed out, and pulled in a deep breath of the cool, moisture-laden air. He stretched his legs and back, easing the stiffness that had built during the short drive through the city. He'd managed a refreshing sixty-minute doze during the short flight north. Not enough, but it would have to do. The channel-hop to London would allow him to catch a little more shuteye. Sleep before action could be as important as food and drink, and Kaine had become a master at snatching recovery naps at every opportunity.

In the middle of the night, Indische Buurt stood deserted, the streets, bars, and cafés dark and quiet, devoid of life. He straightened, pushed away from the car, and turned his back on van Bleeker's apartment block. He strolled along the tree-lined pavement between the road and a cycle path on a spotlessly clean Molukkenstraat, following the route he'd picked out on his mobile's street map. He passed dozens of front doors, all painted gloss black. Two hundred metres later, he turned right onto Niasstraat, and then turned right again on Makassarstraat. Fifty metres further on, he stopped and listened to the night. In the middle distance, to the north, traffic thrummed along an arterial route which probably never stopped. Locally, the roads stood silent and empty.

Opposite, dimly lit by orange streetlamps, a small park—a rectangle of grass and a children's play area, complete with conical climbing frames built out of logs—remained vacant and graffiti free. Kaine breathed deep again and carried on until he'd reached the end of the street. The GPS map showed him directly behind van Bleeker's apartment block. Black railings guarded a small communal garden, again dimly lit by the same orange streetlamps that illuminated the deserted park. Kaine turned to investigate.

"*Hé! Wat ben je aan het doen, klootzak?*"

A man's voice. Deep, angry, the words slurred.

Bugger.

Movement in a shaded doorway to Kaine's right coalesced into a large shape. It loomed over Kaine, dark and ominous.

"*Geef antwoord, klootzak,*" the man said, louder, angrier—a few decibels below a shout.

A second figure materialised behind the first, this one smaller and leaner than his mate.

"*Antwoord mijn vriend, man.*" The second man smiled, showing a pair of brown and broken front teeth.

Kaine turned to face them. He opened his hands and kept them in front of his body, in an apparent offer of surrender.

"Sorry, guys. I don't understand a word you're saying," he said, keeping his voice calm, quiet.

"Ah," the second man said. "English?"

Kaine nodded, taking half a pace back, letting himself appear intimidated. The two men eased closer, stepping out from the shadows and into the pale orange light.

"Ari asked what you are doing here, man?"

"Wh-Why does Ari want to know?" Kaine asked, allowing a tremor to weaken his words.

"This is our turf, man. Anyone coming through here has to pay a toll."

Kaine swallowed hard and lifted his hands a little higher—moving into a full defensive stance without making it obvious.

"How much?"

Broken Teeth shot a sly glance at his mate. "Fifty euros."

"Fifty euros?"

Ari nodded.

"*Ja, gozer. Vijftig euro.*"

"Oh, right. Okay."

Kaine dipped his left hand towards his jacket pocket. The one with the broken teeth slid past his large mate and edged even closer, an eager smile allowing Kaine another glimpse of his damaged gnashers. The man stood close enough for Kaine to smell the booze on his breath. The sweet and sickly odour of stale sweat wafted out from the self-styled toll collectors. Broken Teeth's right hand moved. A steel blade glistened in the lights. He waved the knife under Kaine's nose.

You piece of crap.

The image of Molly Williams lying in her death bed flashed into Kaine's head. Anger flared. His blood boiled.

Kaine shot out his open right hand and rammed the heel of his palm into Broken Teeth's chin. The blow's shockwave shot up his arm, and the rope burns screamed in complaint. Broken Teeth's head snapped back, his feet left the pavement, and he flew backwards, slamming into his large mate, Ari.

They fell in a heap of tangled limbs.

Evil bastards!

The back of Broken Teeth's head cracked against the pavement. The knife shot from his hand and skittered away into the shadows.

Kaine stepped back, the red mist of fury still coiling around him. His right hand pulsed with pain. Breathing hard, fighting the need to wade in and bludgeon the would-be muggers into oblivion, he pushed out his hands and beckoned Ari with his fingers.

"You still want your money?" Kaine growled, jaws clenched, teeth gritted. "Come on then, arsehole. Come and get it."

The red mist continued to wash over him.

Ari bellowed. He rolled out from under his friend and scrambled, unsteadily, to his feet. He spat onto the pavement and drew the back of his hand across his mouth. Broken Teeth lay still at the big man's feet—an unmoving bundle of dirty rags.

"I will break your neck, asshole!" Ari snarled. He spat again. The dark glob landed close to Kaine's right boot.

The big man stalked forwards, shoulders hunched, fists raised, leading with his left. He adopted a boxing stance—or what passed for one in Ari's mind.

Kaine allowed him to draw close.

Still moving and unbalanced, Ari started swinging, aiming at Kaine's body and face. He telegraphed each wild blow. Kaine absorbed a right hook on his forearm, and slid inside a left jab. He slammed a straight right into Ari's face, and a left uppercut to the jaw. Both blows landed full and flush.

The lumbering tax collector grunted, staggered backwards. Blood poured from a shattered nose. His eyes watered. He blinked the tears away, shook his head, and swiped at the blood with his forearm. Again he spat onto the pavement. Again he roared and stalked forwards. He stopped at arm's length and threw a long, raking left hook at Kaine's ribcage.

Kaine slipped inside the blow and drove a half-power straight left into Ari's flabby gut. Kaine stepped back, taking his time. Ari grunted, screamed, and launched an arcing right cross at Kaine's jaw.

Kaine stepped into the punch, dipped at the knees, and twisted at the waist. The right cross grazed the top of Kaine's head, parted his hair, and flailed at empty air. Ari overreached and toppled forwards.

Kaine ducked beneath the collapsing giant. As Ari's belly brushed his back, Kaine straightened his legs and sent the big man flying. He landed flat on his back, gasping, winded.

Kaine darted forwards, dropped, and drove the point of his knee into the man's midriff. Foul air exploded from Ari's open mouth, along with a stream of vomit.

The bloodlust raged again, Kaine snarled. He grabbed Ari's greasy hair and slammed the back of his head into the concrete slab. The big thug's eyes rolled up into his skull, and his jaw flopped open. Kaine raised the head again and stopped short of smashing the foul-smelling man's skull into pulp—but only just. He released the oily hair, sank onto his heels, and rolled back and away.

Kaine stood over the large and comatose body and pulled in a deep and steadying breath. He shook his head and stared at his trembling hands, trying to remember the last time he'd lost control so badly.

Denmark, probably.

Yes, Denmark.

His mind flashed back to the college changing room and the big blond South African who'd attacked Lara, Hardy Krüger. Kaine had lost control and had nearly lost the fight. Nearly lost Lara, too.

Bloody idiot.

Two nights, no, three nights earlier, he'd smothered Malcolm Sampson to death with his own pillow, but he'd been cold and calculating, in total control. He'd ended Sampson's life in the same cool way he might have killed a fly with a flyswat. But this? These two fools?

Easy, Kaine. Take it easy.

Kaine took in another deep breath and released it slowly, forcing the control to return. Taking pity on the lumbering ape, he stepped forwards and rolled Ari into the recovery position. He lifted the big man's chin to open his airway, used one of his hands to hold it in place, and stood back. His right palm throbbed. He turned it to the light. The biggest scab remained intact. No bleeding. Given time, the injury would mend—assuming he didn't keep fighting.

To the side, Broken Teeth groaned. His right arm lifted from the pavement and flopped down again.

Kaine closed the distance between them, lifted his foot, and pressed the sole of his boot on the man's dirty fingers—the fingers that had recently held the shiny knife. For control, Kaine rested his heel on the pavement and added a little pressure to the sole. Not enough to crush the bones, but more than enough to gain the attention of the man with foul breath and brown teeth.

Broken Teeth yelped.

"What's your name?"

No response.

Kaine added a little more weight to his foot.

The man yelped again.

"Name!"

"Jens," he whimpered. "Jens de ... de Kuiper."

Kaine removed his boot from the hand and stepped back. Crying, de Kuiper pulled his right hand to his chest and cradled it in his left.

"Ask me again for fifty euros," Kaine growled. "Go on. I dare you!"

De Kuiper sniffled and shook his head, whimpering the whole time.

"I-I'm sorry."

Kaine stepped closer.

"What was that? I didn't hear you!"

"I'm sorry," he repeated, louder than before. Tears flowed down his cheeks and snot ran from his nose. "I-I am sorry. Sorry."

"Apology accepted, Jens de Kuiper." Kaine smiled. "Now, what lesson have you learnt from this episode?"

De Kuiper's frown deepened, and his lower lip quivered.

"Huh?"

"The lesson, Jens. What did you learn?"

"I-I ..."

Kaine bent and wagged a finger in front of de Kuiper's running nose. "Stop trying to rob strangers at knifepoint. You really aren't any good at it. *Agreed*?" Kaine snarled the last word.

De Kuiper nodded.

"A-Agreed."

"Do you have a mobile phone?"

De Kuiper shuffled to a seated position, blinking rapidly. Still hugging his hand, he propped himself upright on his elbow. "Y-Yes. I do."

"In that case, you'd better call an ambulance for poor old Ari. He took a bit of a pounding, I'm afraid. Needs some medical attention."

Kaine straightened and tugged out the creases in his jacket. "Crack on, Jens. Crack on. But"—Kaine lifted a finger in the air—"stay on the ground. Try to stand before I'm out of sight, and I'll come back and teach you another lesson."

De Kuiper nodded. He leant back and dipped his good hand into his pocket.

In a window on the second floor of van Bleeker's building, a light blinked on. Another glowed on the third floor. Elsewhere in the block, a window opened, and a man shouted something Kaine couldn't understand.

Damn. Mission aborted.

Kaine left de Kuiper and Ari to their woes. He'd have to change to Plan B—the direct approach.

23

Thursday 1st June – Early Morning

Indische Buurt, Amsterdam, The Netherlands.

A cool-headed Kaine sipped his third cappuccino, finished his second buttered croissant with honey, and dabbed his lips with a paper napkin. The door he'd been watching since the café had opened at six-thirty finally cranked inwards and his quarry hobbled through the opening, leaning on the black cane.

Kaine read the time off his watch. 08:13.

Early today. Poor man must be hungry.

He studied Jan van Bleeker as he limped from his apartment along the pavement and all the way to the crossing place where he gave way to the red "Don't Walk" light. If anything, the lapidary leant even more heavily on his cane than the last time Kaine witnessed his stuttering progression from the apartment block to the café. He wore the same baggy black trousers as before, but had changed the capacious grey sweater for an equally large one in bright yellow. Van Bleeker paused at the crossroads for a tram. As the grey steel tram passed in front of the bright yellow sweater, the reflected light dimmed in much the same way as it would during a solar eclipse.

Van Bleeker nodded to a passer-by and the two stopped at the crossing for a brief chat before van Bleeker laughed and pointed towards the café. The passer-by, an angular man in his fifties with close-cropped hair, clapped the round man on the shoulder and hurried off. Meanwhile van Bleeker continued on his faltering way in the opposite direction, still smiling. Apart from the obvious discomfort given by his right knee, van Bleeker looked as though he didn't have a care in the world.

Once again, the image of Molly Williams lying dead in a filthy bed in a French bungalow and a distraught Micah kneeling in front of her drove a skewer through Kaine's heart.

Calm down, Kaine!

Kaine tried not to scowl at van Bleeker's slow advance and lowered his eyes to study his paper.

Van Bleeker crossed the cycle lane, advanced along the pavement, shuffled into the café, and waited in line to place his order. Five people stood ahead of him in the queue.

Time to go.

Kaine folded his paper and dropped it on the table. He stood and exited the café, turning right after pushing through the door. He continued at a brisk pace until he'd passed the café's window, where he slowed to a saunter. At the first junction, he crossed the road and studied the goods on offer at a jewellery shop—eyeing a small silver bracelet that a certain vet-turned-medic might appreciate—and waited. Two minutes and five departing customers later, van Bleeker eased through the café door, clutching his paper bag of pastries and a large takeout mug of what would be overly sweetened coffee, assuming van Bleeker remained true to form. The lapidary could easily be described as a creature of habit.

In no condition to rush, van Bleeker took his time checking for traffic before recrossing the road. Kaine turned his back on the silver bangle in the shop window and strolled towards the crossroads, setting his pace to intercept his target as he rejoined the footpath.

Their journeys met at the point where van Bleeker stepped onto the drop kerb and mounted the pavement. Kaine, looking away, apparently distracted by an attractive window display, collided with the limping man, and sent him staggering backwards into the road.

"*Mijn knie!*" van Bleeker screamed.

Kaine shot out a hand to catch the man and stop him falling into the path of a rumbling tram. Bracing himself against the heavy mass, Kaine pulled on a fleshy forearm and dragged van Bleeker onto the pavement. The cup tumbled from van Bleeker's hand, the top popped off, and coffee splattered into the gutter at their feet, but he maintained a firm hold on the bag of pastries and the walking stick.

"*Jij verdomde sukkel,*" van Bleeker shouted, tearing his arm free of Kaine's grasp.

"Oh my goodness," Kaine gasped, holding up his hands and adopting an expression of shock and mortification. "I'm most terribly sorry. Are you okay?"

"English?" van Bleeker growled. He whimpered and reached down to brace his right knee with his free hand. The paper bag with the pastries rustled with the movement.

"Yes," Kaine answered. "English. I'm sorry wasn't looking where I was going."

"My coffee—"

"Let me buy you another."

"No," van Bleeker said, clenching his jaw. "That won't be necessary."

"But I insist. It's the least I can do."

Van Bleeker groaned as he straightened. He planted the tip of the cane into a crack between the paving slabs and leant on the handle. His fist blanched as his grip tightened.

"No," he said. "I cannot face the walk. I need to get home—to sit down." He waved a hand towards the apartment block. "Get out of my way."

"Can I help?"

"No."

"At least allow me to accompany you home. You look rather pale and shaken. I'd hate for you to fall again." Kaine rounded his shoulders, made himself smaller, and offered the rotund Dutchman an apologetic smile. "And afterwards, I'll go back to the café and fetch you a replacement drink. Coffee, was it?" He smiled an ingratiating apology. "As I said, it's the least I can do."

Van Bleeker looked Kaine up and down, took a sharp breath, and nodded, no doubt seeing the awkward Englishman before him as totally harmless.

"Yes, yes. That might be for the best. I am a little shaken."

"One moment," Kaine said. "Don't move."

Kaine scooped up the fallen coffee mug and deposited it and the lid into a nearby rubbish bin. He returned to van Bleeker and held out a hand.

"Can I carry that for you?" Kaine indicated the brown paper bag full of goodies.

"Yes, okay." Van Bleeker handed over the pastries and started walking—grunting and groaning with every step.

Kaine took up a position on van Bleeker's left and offered his right arm for support. The heavy man grabbed Kaine's forearm and latched on tight. Kaine relaxed his forearm muscles in an effort to appear weak and innocuous.

"Knee or hip," Kaine asked, pointing at the offending right leg.

"Knee," van Bleeker said after two more painful steps. Panting deeply, he paused for a rest at the side of the walkway. "Worsens every day."

"That's awful. My barging into you can't have helped." Again, he stretched out an apologetic grin, this one even more sympathetic.

"No. It did not."

"Can anything be done? Treatment, I mean."

"I need a knee replacement, but I am allergic to anaesthetic, and the cost …" Van Bleeker broke off and shrugged. "Astronomic."

Kaine dropped the grin and stared at the fat man. "A friend of mine has just undergone a shoulder operation. We were so worried, but at the moment, it looks as though he'll make a full recovery."

Van Bleeker sniffed and looked away, clearly disinterested in anyone else's suffering but his own. He sucked in a deep breath, grabbed hold of Kaine's forearm again, and they pressed on towards the nearby apartment block.

Van Bleeker stopped at the pair of wire-reinforced glass doors. He reached into the pocket of his roomy trousers and pulled out a set of keys.

Kaine looked up, studying the building's five floors.

"Is this it?" he asked, deliberately stating the obvious.

The Dutchman stared hard at him but didn't answer.

"Nice. What floor are you on. I mean, is there a lift?"

"A lift?" van Bleeker asked, frowning, and shaking his head.

"An elevator."

"Ah, I see. No. No elevator. Not necessary. I am on the ground floor."

With trembling fingers, van Bleeker inserted the key into the lock and pushed through the door. Kaine followed close behind, and they entered the vestibule. He smiled at his target's back. Gaining entry to the apartment had turned out far easier than he'd expected. There'd been no need for an overnight incursion after all.

Van Bleeker turned towards the left-hand door, selected a different key, and slid it into the lock. He pushed the door open and placed his right foot over the threshold.

Kaine rammed his palm into the big man's back and drove him through the open door.

Van Bleeker screamed as he fell, crashing headlong to the floor, sending his silver-tipped walking stick flying, along with a small occasional table.

Kaine followed him inside and slammed the door shut behind them. He dropped a knee into Van Bleeker's lower back, grabbed the howling man's ponytail, and tugged hard. Van Bleeker's head snapped back, neck stretched, throat exposed.

"Shut up!" Kaine hissed into van Bleeker's ear. He jabbed an index finger into the pressure point behind the fat man's jaw.

Van Bleeker's scream cut short mid howl. He gasped, struggling for breath.

"That's better," Kaine said. "Wouldn't want to alert the neighbours now, would we."

Kaine removed his finger from the pressure point and released his grip on the ponytail. Van Bleeker's head flew forwards, stopping short of faceplanting onto the tiled floor—but only just. Kaine stood over the downed man, tugged the SIG from his belt, cocked the gun, and levelled it at the back of van Bleeker's head.

"Get up!"

Van Bleeker pushed himself up on his arms, twisted, and caught sight of the SIG. Eyes wide, mouth open, blood drained from an already pallid face. Sweat popped out on his forehead and ran into his eyes. He blinked, hard and fast.

"What—"

"This is a SIG P226." Kaine curled his index finger through the trigger guard and lowered the gun until it pointed at the back of van Bleeker's right knee. "Piss me about and you'll need more than a new knee."

Van Bleeker's mouth snapped shut and his lower lip quivered. Tears spilled down his round cheeks, mingling with the sweat and dampening his grey beard.

"Can you stand?"

Van Bleeker's lips compressed into a thin line. He shook his head and the lank ponytail flapped behind him.

"N-No ... I d-don't think so."

"Okay. Fair enough. Crawl into the front room."

"I-I can't," van Bleeker wailed. His chin trembled and the tears flowed afresh. "M-My knee. I can't."

Kaine stepped over the prostrate man and opened the first of four closed doors in the hallway—a kitchen. The second door revealed an airy front room complete with a well-upholstered leather settee. He stooped to grab van Bleeker's left arm and dragged the screaming man along the shiny floor and into the room. The plush carpet offered too much friction and prevented further movement. Kaine dropped the arm.

"I'm not lifting you," Kaine said, teeth gritted. "Climb into the settee or stay on the floor. Makes no difference to me either way."

Kaine stood back and watched van Bleeker crawl further into the room—hand over hand, left leg bent, right leg stretched out behind him, a useless appendage. Grunting and sobbing, van Bleeker worked his corpulent body up and onto the crumpled leather settee and flopped onto his back. The leather sagged and squeaked under the enormous load.

"I-I don't have any money," van Bleeker cried. "I'm a cripple. I-I live on state handouts."

Kaine tilted his head and stared down at the sweating, gasping man.

"Bollocks."

"I-It's true. I have nothing of value. N-No money."

"I'm not after money, Jan. I'm after diamonds. Conflict diamonds."

"Diamonds?" Van Bleeker shook his head violently. Again the ponytail swished behind him. "I don't have any—"

"Shut up!" Kaine snapped.

He pointed the SIG at van Bleeker's right knee and added a little pressure to the trigger. It wouldn't take much more to end the man's sorry life.

The lapidary raised his trembling hands. Sweat flowed. Dark stains showed under the arms of his yellow sweater. A sharp scent of body wash hung in the room, barely masking the sharp tang of stale sweat.

"N-No," he squealed. "No, please. I-I don't have any diamonds."

"What happened to the ones in the package?"

Van Bleeker frowned.

"Wh-What package?"

"The one Micah Williams gave you."

The fat man gasped, and his arms flopped to his sides as though they'd become too heavy for him to hold aloft.

"Y-You know about—" Van Bleeker snapped his mouth shut.

Kaine lowered the SIG a little.

"I know everything. I know how you bastards work. You kidnap innocents and force them to smuggle diamonds across international borders." Kaine scowled. "Bad business."

"I-I had no idea."

"Liar."

Kaine levelled the SIG at van Bleeker's forehead.

Van Bleeker lifted his arms again and waved his hands.

"No! No! I'm not lying," he blurted. "I know nothing about the operation. The ... the diamonds. I-I just cut them. That is my only role."

"I don't believe you."

Kaine fired. The SIG barked loud, and the bullet slammed into the padded leather millimetres away from van Bleeker's left ear. The Dutchman squealed. A damp patch spread around the crotch of his baggy trousers.

"Please!" he begged. "Don't shoot. Please!"

Kaine lowered his aim, targeting the knee once more.

Van Bleeker's monstrous belly clenched and rippled. He retched, gagged, and threw a hand to his mouth in a desperate effort to stop himself vomiting.

Kaine grabbed a metal bin from the carpet beside the settee and threw it to the fat man. Van Bleeker fumbled the catch, caught the bin on the second attempt, and held it under his chins in time for it to accept the load of puke. He retched a second time and released another deposit, this one mostly liquid. Kaine waited for the fat man to recover before speaking again.

"Aren't you going to ask how they are?"

"H-How who are?" van Bleeker asked, wiping his mouth on the sleeve of his yellow sweater.

"Micah and Molly Williams."

Van Bleeker's head dipped as he swallowed, and his long beard crumpled.

"H-How are they?"

"Molly's dead."

"Dead?" van Bleeker gasped, covering his mouth with a hand.

"Marta Braun shot her under Max Schiller's orders."

"Oh my God. I-I didn't know."

"Liar."

"B-But he promised," van Bleeker cried. "He promised no one would get hurt."

More tears fell from van Bleeker's brown eyes. These seemed genuine. Tears of loss? Tears of guilt by association?

"Who promised? You spoke to Schiller?"

"No, no. I know nothing about the Germans. I have never met them. I-I mean Abraham," van Bleeker whispered. "Abraham Pedersen. He's the one behind this. The boss. He promised no one would ... Oh God. Dear God."

Where's God in this?

Kaine fought to stop the anger overwhelming his senses again, struggling to win the battle.

Van Bleeker slumped more heavily into the settee, and his shoulders sagged. He grunted, lowered the bin to the side of the settee, and peered up at Kaine through soulful brown eyes.

"That is terrible. And Micah? I-Is he?"

"Devastated, but alive and safe. He'll be talking to the gendarmes about now."

"Thank God he's alive. But his poor wife ... I-I didn't know what they planned. You must believe me!"

"Why?"

Van Bleeker's bushy eyebrows knitted together. Confusion creased his round and bearded face.

"Excuse me?"

"Why must I believe you?"

Van Bleeker's lower lip trembled.

"B-Because it's the truth. I-I had no idea what Pedersen had planned. Months ago, he contacted me. Told me about the consignments and about how the Germans were forcing people to work for him. But he said they would be unhurt. He promised they would all be safe."

Kaine's left hand curled into a fist. The right hand tightened on the SIG's textured grip.

"All? How many?"

Van Bleeker shook his head slowly.

"How many?" Kaine repeated with more force, allowing the anger to bleed through. He jerked the SIG.

"Four," Van Bleeker said, staring at his trembling hands which rested in his lap. "Four couples in total. Micah and Molly from England, another couple from the Netherlands, and two from France. D-Do you think they are dead, too? ... Do you?"

Kaine didn't respond, but they both knew the answer.

"*Mijn God!*" Van Bleeker sat up straighter. Fear struck again, revealed in his expression and in each tick and shudder. "It is over."

"What do you mean?"

"It is finished." He lifted his eyes to meet Kaine's. "*I* am finished. Pedersen told me the latest consignment would be the final one. As soon as I've finished work on this shipment, they will have no further need for me. It means the Germans will come after me next."

Kaine lowered the SIG further and shook his head. "Schiller and Braun aren't in any position to come after anyone."

"You killed them?" van Bleeker asked, his gaze falling on the SIG once more.

"I did."

"But there is another. A man called Jakob—"

"Jakob Essen's dead. I killed him, too."

The emotion on van Bleeker's expressive face changed. Fear and resignation transformed into awe mixed with a little hope.

"You killed them all?"

"I had help."

Van Bleeker glanced behind Kaine, searching for an accomplice.

"Don't worry, Jan. You and I are alone for the moment. I don't need help to deal with scum like you."

"I am not scum," Van Bleeker barked, finally showing a little backbone. "I am a man in pain, trying to earn enough money for an expensive operation. I need a new knee. I am horrified by what happened to the Williamses and the others. Truly. And I'm glad you killed Schiller and his ... his associates. Delighted. They deserved nothing more." He paused for a moment before adding, "Are you going to kill me now?"

"Can you give me a good reason not to?"

Van Bleeker paused for a moment before shaking his head. His face lost all expression. He seemed resigned to his fate.

"No," he said. "I cannot."

"Have you started working on the latest shipment?"

"I have." Van Bleeker nodded and wafted a hand towards the open door. "My workshop is in the back of the apartment. Second door on the right. There are twenty-five raw gems plus the one I am currently working on."

"Are they in a safe?"

"Yes. When I am not working, I keep them locked away the whole time." He held out his right hand. "If you pass me my *wandelstok*—my walking stick—I will open it for you."

Kaine tilted his head and shot the large man a wry grin.

"Don't even think about trying anything stupid."

"I will not. I have neither the strength nor the inclination. You are welcome to the diamonds. In their current condition, they are worth very little. Blood diamonds are illegal throughout Europe. Even after I have made them beautiful, they will still be worth far less than if they were legal. Please take them away. I want nothing more to do with the evil things. There is blood all over them."

Kaine took hold of van Bleeker's outstretched hand—hot and slimy—and heaved him to his feet. The heavy man tottered for a moment and threw out a hand to brace himself against the nearest wall. Kaine pointed the SIG at van Bleeker's damaged knee, backed out of the room, collected the walking stick, and handed it to him.

"Don't think I won't shoot you, Jan. This apartment is well insulated. No one's going to hear a second gunshot."

Van Bleeker hung his head.

"You have nothing to fear from me, *Meneer*."

"I know."

Kaine backed away and waited for van Bleeker to shuffle into the hall and lead the way to the workshop.

* * *

BACK IN THE front room with the resealed package safely stowed in his jacket pocket, Kaine leant against a wall, staring down at van Bleeker's crumpled and bloated form. The heavy man stared up at him from the settee, panting from his minor exertions. His right foot rested on a stool, the leg stretched out straight in front of him. He didn't look particularly comfortable or pain free.

"You will shoot me now, I think?" van Bleeker asked, his tone flat, emotionless.

"Probably. Unless …" Kaine said and let the word hang in the air between them.

Killing the pitiful creature in cold blood had never been an option, but he couldn't leave him alive and unguarded either. The man would undoubtedly warn Pedersen if only to curry favour and try to save his skin. As if in answer to his thoughts, the earpiece clicked three times.

Kaine listened to the message and smiled.

"Unless?" van Bleeker asked, eagerness adding strain to the word.

"How do you contact Pedersen? By phone?"

Van Bleeker nodded.

"Yes. We video call, and I show him the results of my work. He sends couriers to collect the product and deliver my fee. Video calls are the only interactions we have."

"Do you know where he lives?"

Van Bleeker lifted his round shoulders and let them fall, the shrug as heavy as any Kaine had seen.

"London, I assume. I have never visited. These days, I do not travel much," he said, waving a hand over his knee.

The doorbell rang.

Kaine bunted himself away from the wall, decocked the SIG, and replaced it in the pancake holster under his left arm. He held up his hand and motioned for van Bleeker to keep still.

"I am not expecting anyone," van Bleeker said.

"No, but I am. Stay right where you are. Don't you dare move."

Van Bleeker nodded, clasped his hands tight to his chest, and appeared to shrink deeper into the leather.

Kaine rushed along the corridor and pressed the button to release the entrance latch. After unlocking the internal door, he returned to the front room. Van Bleeker hadn't budged.

The internal front door creaked open, and a deep voice called out, "Hello?"

"In here," Kaine answered.

On the settee, van Bleeker dropped his hands into his lap and frowned. He didn't have a clue.

Seconds later, a well-muscled black man with a shaven head and a serious expression entered the room. Dressed in black jeans and a dark blue polo shirt under a black leather jacket, he carried a backpack slung over one shoulder.

"Morning, sir," Connor Blake said. Despite a little puffiness around his eyes—the legacy of a long drive through the night—a beaming smile revealed a set of perfect white teeth.

"Morning, Sergeant. You made good time."

Connor dropped the backpack to the floor. "Not much traffic overnight, sir. Roads are nice, too. Don't think I saw a single pothole the whole way here. How come they can do that over here, but we can't do it back home?"

By way of an answer, Kaine shook his head and shrugged.

"Come and meet your host."

Kaine turned to face van Bleeker. "Jan van Bleeker, this is Jim Smith. He'll be looking after you for the next day or so. Don't give him any trouble, he's not as soft as he looks."

Connor canted his head to one side.

"Soft?" he said, jabbing a thumb into his chest. *"Moi?"*

Kaine turned his back to van Bleeker and winked at Connor.

"Don't let van Bleeker get to you, Smith," Kaine said. "The bloke keeps banging on about his poorly knee."

"I won't, sir." Connor scowled at his prisoner. He sniffed the air over the settee. "Bloody hell. Smells like puke in here."

"Yep," Kaine said. "Some people throw up when they're shot at."

"Funny how often that happens, eh?" Connor said, his smile expanding. "I wondered about the bullet hole in that cushion. Took the gunshot poorly, did he?"

"He did indeed."

"Talking about taking things poorly, how's the colour sergeant holding up?"

Kaine frowned. "It's early days, but the surgeon is hopeful. I spoke to his wife a little while ago. He's asleep now, working on his recovery."

"Glad to hear it, sir."

Kaine pointed to his ear. "I'll let you know when you can stand down."

Connor rubbed his hands together and took in the room.

"Take as long as you need, sir. I've stayed in plenty worse billets than this." He grinned, clearly pleased with what he saw.

Kaine patted him on the shoulder and left the room without a backwards glance at the tubby man with the dodgy knee.

24

Thursday 1st June – Anthony Simms

Elder Street, Shoreditch, London, UK

Anthony "Slim" Simms noted the time on his tablet—11:00—and stared through the dirt-encrusted bedroom window at the view that had changed very little since they'd started their obbo. He yawned deep and long. On the single bed in the corner, "Fat" Larry Kovaks—one of the skinniest but strongest blokes Slim had ever known—tried to fight the desire, but gave up and yawned in sympathy.

"To think," Slim said, "this time last week we were in Dubai, sunning it with the rich and powerful."

"Yep, and arseholes, they all were, too. The bloody lot of them," Larry said, covering his mouth to hide another gaping yawn. He chomped into a chocolate biscuit and spoke with his mouth full—one of the few things Slim disliked about his best mate in the world.

On the other hand, Larry's mouth was rarely empty of food. Waiting for his gob to empty would have rendered him largely mute.

Inwardly, Slim smirked.

"I bloody hated having to suck up to all those arrogant pricks just to earn a crust," Larry added. "Why is it that every millionaire in the world turns out to be an absolute fu—"

"The captain's a millionaire," Slim interrupted what promised to be another of Larry's revolutionary rants, "and he's decent enough."

"Granted," Larry said, holding up a hand and showing Slim the remaining half of the bickie before popping it into his gob. "Still, there's always an exception that proves every rule. But he's not really a millionaire, is he. All those millions he 'liberated' from SAMS is for the 83, right?"

Slim turned away from his mate and resumed his watch. The sun broke through a thin layer of bulbous cloud and threw its warm yellow light over the city, casting Fleur De Lis Road into deep shadow. He dipped his head and peeked through the Canon's viewfinder. No good. He screwed a neutral density filter onto the front of the EF 75-300mm auto-focus zoom lens to counteract the sun's brightness. It gave him a clearer view of the target.

"Yeah," he said, blinking to moisten his dry eyeballs, "but there's more than the SAMS money in the kitty, don't forget. There's all that moolah we've taken from the bad guys over the past few months." Slim smiled wickedly at the remembered image of the gangland boss and multiple murderer, Teddy Tedesco, strapped to a concrete post in his own basement garage, awaiting his fate. With the help of the elusive genius, Corky, they'd emptied Teddy's bank accounts and distributed the bulk of it to the gangster's victims. Under the captain's orders, they'd used part of the remains to cover ongoing incidental expenses and salted away the rest to bulk up the guys' individual retirement pots. The captain looked after his people. Always had, always would. Without doubt, the captain was the best damned officer Slim had ever had the good fortune to work for. Bar none.

Slim sighed. Southampton seemed like the distant past. So much had happened in the meantime. Six months could be a lifetime in their game.

"Any action?" Larry asked, waving a hand at the window. He swallowed and reached for yet another biscuit, his fifth. Nibbling around the edges, he worked his way to the middle.

Where the hell does he put it all?

Slim shook his head. "Not a thing."

"Shame we can't get no closer. I'd love to know what's going on inside that gaff."

"Yep. That old sod's responsible for what happened to the colour sergeant. I hope the captain lets us in on the take down. Rollo's a decent bloke."

"Hear, hear," Larry said, nodding and chewing at the same time. Whoever said booties couldn't multi-task? "Best drill sergeant I ever served under. Any idea how he's getting on?"

"Nope. I expect we'll hear as soon as there's any news."

Bloody hope so.

Larry finished his biscuit, drained the rest of his coffee, which must have been ice cold, and lowered the mug to the floor next to the pile of junk food wrappers. He swung his legs off the bed, sat up straight, and stretched his arms out in front of his narrow chest. After another yawn, a shoulder roll, and a neck stretch, he shot to his feet.

"Want a spell?"

"Thanks."

Slim stood to give up the seat to his mate, but movement in the street below caught his attention.

"Hello, who's this?"

"Action?"

Larry appeared at Slim's shoulder.

"Could be."

Slim dropped back into his chair and put his eye to the Canon's viewfinder, pointing the lens at the man knocking on the target's door. He pressed the shutter button and held it down. The motor buzzed and the shutter clicked five times. Not the best angle, but at least they had a couple of half-decent shots of the man's face as he looked around the street while waiting for someone to answer his knock.

The man, lanky and comfortably dressed in dark cargo shorts and black hoodie, carried a cardboard envelope in his right hand. It looked heavy. A large wheeled trolly butted against his leg.

"Delivery man," Slim said, unable to prevent the disappointment leaching into his voice.

"Another courier?" Larry asked, staring over Slim's shoulder.

"Doubt it. Would a courier carry a consignment of diamonds in plain sight like that?"

"Good point." Larry leant closer to the dirty window, angling for a better view.

"Nah," Slim said, "Pedersen's ordered himself a smutty book off of the internet. That's why it needs the plain brown envelope." He laughed. "Wanna do the business with the mic?"

Larry raised the sash window a crack, pointed the parabolic disk microphone towards the black door, and picked up the headphones. He held one cushioned pad to his left ear and let the other dangle for Slim to listen in.

Below them on Fleur De Lis Road, the messenger raised his hand to the brass knocker and rapped again, three times. The triple crack pulsed through the headphones loud and clear.

"*Parcel for Mr Pedersen,*" the messenger called in answer to a question from inside the house, a question the microphone didn't pick up. He showed the package to the surveillance camera fixed to the wall high above the shiny black door and read the label.

"*It's from Foyles, mate.*"

Slim winked. "A book. Told you."

"Can't be smut, though," Larry said. "I doubt Foyles sells dirty books. At least not over the counter."

In the street below, the delivery man read the time from his wristwatch, the picture of impatience.

"*C'mon, mate,*" he said. "*I don't got all day.*" He pushed out an ear to listen, and his shoulders dropped. "*No can do, mate. It's registered. I need a signature.*"

The parabolic mic picked up the messenger's aggravated sigh, and muttered curse.

Five seconds later, the shiny black door opened inwards and Slim caught his first sight of the Polish minder, Bogdan, who turned out every bit as large and every bit as ugly as Micah's description suggested he would be.

"That's one nasty-looking individual," Larry mumbled, never one to shy away from stating the obvious.

"*Where sign?*" Bogdan demanded, his voice deep and his tone angry.

"Blimey," Larry gushed. "It actually speaks?"

"Evidently," Slim said, "but what's the betting he'll mark his name with an 'X'."

"*Right here, mate,*" the messenger said, holding up his tablet to Bogdan, who towered above him on the single step.

Slim took a few pics of the transaction, focusing the shots on the minder.

Bogdan took the stylus in his right hand, signed his name on the tablet, and ripped the package from the delivery man's outstretched hand.

"*Take it easy, mate,*" the messenger said, flexing his fingers.

Bogdan slammed the door in the messenger's face.

"*Rude fucker!*"

The door jerked open again, and Bogdan pushed out onto the doorstep.

"*What you say?*"

"*Nothing, mate. Nothing.*"

The messenger grabbed the handle of his trolly and hurried away. Bogdan sneered at the man's back and closed the door, quietly.

"Wrong!" Larry said, closing the sash window and folding away the mic. "So wrong."

"Who is?"

Larry winked. "You is."

"I am? In what way?"

"He signed his name properly." Larry smiled and hung the headphones on the edge of the mic's dish.

"No one's right all the time, Larry. Not even me."

"Once in a while would make a nice change."

"Spin on this, arsehole." Slim shot Larry the finger.

"That's one of the things I like most about you, Slim," Larry said.

"What is?"

"Your eloquence." Larry winked again.

Slim clapped his mate's shoulder and peeled away from the lookout post at the window, the place with the best view of the house that contained the evil bastards who had caused so much pain. The evil bastards who had become the focus of the captain's fury. Slim almost pitied them. Almost, but not quite.

"Take over here, mate. I need a break. My backside's killing me."

"Happy to, big guy."

* * *

THE MORNING TICKED SLOWLY into afternoon. Below them, pedestrians wandered along Fleur De Lis Road, using it as a cut through between Commercial Street and Shoreditch High Street. None of them stopped at the shiny black door. None of them so much as looked at it.

Slim had decided that their current job, although well paid, had to be the most tedious mission since the long-range patrol in Chad, during which they'd seen nothing but sand and the sun-bleached bones of dead livestock. Chad! As far away from the sea as anyone could imagine. Not a wave or a squall in sight, and he'd joined the SBS because he'd been the best swimmer in his old unit. No one could underestimate the hairbrained irony of the military officers' mind.

"Anything?" Larry asked, this time munching on an apple. Choosing the healthy option for a change.

Before Slim could think of a caustic enough response, the earpiece clicked three times.

"*Alpha One to Charlie One. Come in. Over.*"

Slim tapped his earpiece open.

"Charlie One here. As is Charlie Two. Over."

Larry sat up straighter and tapped his own earpiece.

"*Anything to report? Over,*" the captain asked. Rumbling and rattling in the background suggested the captain was sitting in a train carriage.

"That's a negative, sir. The targets haven't moved since we arrived yesterday afternoon."

"*Where's the OP? Over.*"

"Number 14J, Elder Street. It's between Commercial Street and the target house. Top floor flat. We're renting it by the week. You won't believe how much it costs, sir. Over."

"*Expenses will cover it. Make sure you keep receipts. How good's the view? Over.*"

The deep tone of a London Underground train horn confirmed Slim's guess.

"Not too bad, sir. We can't see the whole street from here, but the target's house is in full view. Over."

"*So, they've not had any visitors? Over.*"

"Only a messenger with a package." Slim gave the captain a blow-by-blow account. "Want me to send you the shots we have of Bogdan? Over."

"*Yes please. Over.*"

"I've heard nothing from Control, sir. Have you? Over."

"*Yes, he's monitoring the target's internet and telephone traffic. The internet's been inactive all day. An hour ago he received a call from an old friend—no one of interest to us. He arranged a dinner date for Saturday, which he won't be making. Over.*"

"Boring, isn't he, sir. Over."

The captain grunted. "*Remember what he's done, Slim. What he's responsible for. Over.*"

"I haven't forgotten, sir. What do you need from us? Over."

"*Just keep eyes on. If the target leaves the house, follow him, and let me know where he goes. Over.*"

"Will do, sir. Over."

"*Alpha One, out.*"

The captain ended the call. Slim shot Larry the eye.

"Bloody hell," Larry said. "Haven't heard him sound so pissed for ages. Not since he arrived too late in Southampton. Poor woman."

Angela Shafer's vicious assault had weighed greatly on the whole team. The payback they'd all helped deliver to the Tedesco mob couldn't have been any more justified. No need for a trial or a jury.

Slim nodded.

"Got to pity Pedersen and Bogdan, eh," Larry said.

"After what they've been involved in?" Slim sneered. "Those buggers don't deserve your pity, mate."

Larry shifted on his chair. "Fair comment."

"Hope he lets us in on the action. I'm fed up with just sitting here watching."

"Nah, mate." Larry curled his lips and shook his head. "Wouldn't surprise me if the captain goes it alone. He won't want us involved. Whatever he does, it'll be illegal."

Another fair comment.

Slim sighed. "At least we'll have a bird's-eye view of the entry."

Larry snickered and took another large bite out of his apple.

"Can't wait," he said.

25

Thursday 1st June – Afternoon

Braithwaite Street, Shoreditch, London, UK

"Alpha One to Charlie One. I'm approaching the target," Kaine said into his mobile, holding it to his ear like the majority of the pedestrians wandering London's pavements. The easiest way to blend in imaginable. "Any change? Over."

"*No, sir,*" Slim reported. "*Nothing since the delivery. Over.*"

"Okay. I won't be long. Over."

"*Are you coming here, sir? Only if you are, we need to tidy up a bit. Over.*"

Kaine snorted.

"No, Charlie One. I'm heading straight to the target. Keep an eye out for me. Alpha One, out."

Kaine ended the call, marched out of the darkened underpass, and emerged into the bright afternoon sun. After the airconditioned luxury of the Gulfstream, and the highly filtered air of the underground train carriage, the grim city dust clogged his nostrils and stuck his nose hairs together. He'd almost forgotten how much he hated the city. Give him the salty sea air of the coast any day.

He left Braithwaite Street and picked up Wheler Avenue which joined Commercial Street diagonally across from Fleur De Lis Road. Kaine stopped on the opposite side of the road and pretended to study the window display of a shop selling gold and silver trinkets. None of the displays showed price tags. Again Kaine snorted. If the punters had to ask the prices, they couldn't afford to shop there.

More jewellery.

The universe was clearly sending him a message.

The window's reflection gave him a decent view of the Pedersen house some seventy-five metres distant.

He tapped his earpiece once.

"Alpha One to Control. Over."

"*Corky's here, Mr K. How you diddling?*"

"I'm in position. What's the news from France? Over."

"*Not much. Micah's still with the gendarmes, trying not to say anything. Tell you what's interesting. There hasn't been a single thing on the airways about anyone finding three bullet-ridden Germans in the middle of the French countryside. Looks like the French media don't have the story yet. Weird, huh? As for Rollo, Corky's French counterpart is making sure he's having a nice rest. Rollo's wife is all over that, too. Truth is, Corky's feeling a bit sorry for the poor bloke. Proper henpecked he is.*" Corky's chuckle gave a lie to the idea of him feeling any empathy for Rollo's plight.

"Thanks, Control. What's happening in Amsterdam? Over."

"*All quiet there, too. You won't believe it, but the Con-man's having a great time playing chess, of all things. Turns out that him and the jewel cutter are dab hands at the game. Who'd have thought it? Corky's been eyeballing their play. First five games ended up drawn, but the Con-man's well on top in the sixth. Bloody good they are, too. Not up to Corky's standards of course, but how many are?*"

Corky played chess. Kaine would never have guessed.

"Any movement from the uncle? Over."

"Not a sausage. He ain't used his phone since receiving that call earlier. He don't spend much time on the internet, neither. Bit like your old mate DCI Jones used to be back in the days before he dragged himself into the Information Age." Another bright chuckle hurtled down the earpiece. "If Corky were a betting man—which he ain't, by the way—he'd put money on Uncle Abe not knowing diddly about his German mates being goners yet."

"Unless they've missed a scheduled communication. I need to move before the uncle gets a sniff of their demise and heads for the hills. Did you have any luck with his internet search history? Over."

"Yep. Corky looked back a couple of days like you asked. And you're right, Mr K. Corky did find summat you can use."

"Excellent. Fire away, Control. Over."

Kaine listened to Corky's report, smiling when he reached the interesting part.

"Thanks, Control. That's really helpful. Alpha One, out."

Kaine tapped the earpiece once. In the jeweller's display, a small, silver, heart-shaped pendant inset with a single diamond dangled from a thin silver chain. Draped on a purple cloth, the diamond—assuming it was a real diamond—caught the light and drew Kaine's attention.

Given the current mission, the sparkly stone seemed to be calling to him.

Unable to resist the urge, he stood in front of the shop's glass door, waiting for the shopkeeper to check out the cut of his jib. She clearly didn't take him for a robber and hit the lock release switch behind the counter. He entered and the smartly dressed forty-something woman behind the counter smiled a welcome.

"Good afternoon, sir. How can I help?"

Kaine pointed out the item he wanted.

The woman gave him the price, straight-faced.

"How much?" Kaine asked, staring at the pendant again, totally incredulous.

She repeated her answer and still didn't bat an eye.

"For a silver heart and chain?" he asked.

"It most certainly is not *silver*, sir," she said, as though it would be beneath her to stock items made from such an inferior material. "One moment, please."

She removed the pendant from the display shelf, and placed it on a cloth-covered tray that sat on the counter. The piece sparkled under the lights.

"This, sir," she said, leaning over the pendant, "is twenty-four carat white gold, with rhodium protection. The round, brilliant cut, diamond is half a carat. It rates a G in terms of colour, and an F for its clarity. The diamond is also set in a platinum bezel."

"Oh, I see," Kaine said, not having a clue what she was talking about, and the confusion must have shown on his face.

The woman's stiff expression softened.

"Is this your first jewellery purchase, sir?"

"No, not really," Kaine said, "but the first time for this ... person."

She smiled knowingly. "A special gift for a special person?"

Kaine returned her smile. "Very special."

"I understand, sir. Would you like me to explain?"

"Yes please."

The rhodium protection ensures the stunning shine of the piece and protects the gold from daily wear. The colour scale ranges from D, pure and colourless, down to Z. As such, a G on the scale is quite literally brilliant. In terms of clarity, the F grade confirms it as being flawless. The bezel setting enables the wearer to go about their daily routine without fear of dislodging this exquisite stone."

The words "brilliant, flawless, and exquisite" had been perfect convincers. The woman could have been describing Lara.

Pack it in, Kaine. You old softie.

"Okay, you've got me," he said, smiling. "I'll take it. Can you add an inscription ... to the back?"

"Certainly, sir."

He wrote down the six-letter inscription, made sure she knew he wanted it in italics, and paid the extortionate price without further quibble. The highly appropriate platinum credit card he used for the transaction—registered to the fictitious Arnold Jeffries—was valid, but could never be traced back to either Kaine or The 83 Trust.

"How long before I can collect it?" he asked after the woman had registered the sale and printed off the receipt.

"It will be ready within the hour, sir. Our engraver is onsite. He's very good."

Kaine checked the time on the clock hanging on the wall behind the jeweller. 14:55.

"What time do you close?"

"Half past five, sir."

"Excellent." Kaine nodded. "I'll be back in plenty of time. Now, this might seem a strange request, but do you have an empty box I could have? I'm about to visit an old friend and we like winding each other up."

The woman frowned. "A box, sir? How large?"

"Large enough to hold something like a mobile phone and its charging cable." He pointed to a sleek black, chrome, and glass clock on the shelf behind her. "The box that clock came in would do."

The woman turned and did a double take.

"That, sir," she said, facing him again, "is an eight-day, Kilinger Triple Chime, Limited Edition table clock with a Tourbillon Escapement."

Is it really?

"And?" Kaine asked, completely underwhelmed. To him, the thing simply looked like a clock.

"It retails at nine thousand pounds, and the chest is classed as an essential accessory, sir," she said, her expression deadly serious.

"How can a box be an accessory?" Kaine asked.

"Kilinger chests are handmade and structurally reinforced. Customers use them to return the clocks ... for servicing."

"Ah, I see. Don't suppose I could borrow it for a couple of hours if I promise to look after it?"

"I'm afraid not." The woman hiked up her eyebrows. "Of course, you could add the clock to your order, take the empty chest with you to your friend, and collect the clock when you return for your pendant."

"That would be a rather expensive joke."

"It would indeed, sir." She smiled. "There is an alternative."

"There is?"

"You could pop into the mobile phone shop five doors along." She pointed through the window and indicated to her right. "I'm sure they'll have an empty box or two. If not, a prepaid mobile will only set you back a few pounds."

Kaine nodded. "I think that's probably a much better idea. Thanks. I'll be back long before you close."

"Have a good day, sir."

I plan to.

He left the shop and turned right. Five doors along, he found the phone shop in question and bought the cheapest prepaid mobile they stocked—twenty-three pounds ninety-nine. The server stiffed him a pound for a padded envelope, but gave him a sticky label free of charge. Not the same smiling service he received from the jewellery shop, but he didn't have to shell out nine grand for the short-term use of a box, either.

Back outside, nose-to-tail traffic crawled along Commercial Street in both directions. Its slow progress gave him plenty of opportunity to jog across the road without trudging to the nearest official crossing.

Kaine tugged down the peak of his baseball cap and stepped off the pavement. He dodged between a small white van and a sleek Mercedes Benz and made the safety of a pedestrian island between the lanes. He paused for a moment to allow a large truck to rumble past, belching blue-black exhaust gases.

Okay, Uncle Abe, time for a little payback.

26

Thursday 1st June – Afternoon

Fleur De Lis Road, Shoreditch, London, UK

The black lacquered door on the quiet street looked solid and formed a stout defence, armed with brass furniture and a steel-ringed spyhole.

Feeling the eyes of Slim and Larry drilling into the back of his neck from high across the street, Kaine reached up with his gloved hand and rapped the brass knocker against its base. The metallic clacks echoed in the vault behind the door. He took a pace back from the threshold, held up the package he'd bought from the mobile phone shop, and adopted an expression of impatient boredom.

A red light flashed on the surveillance camera attached to the wall high above the door, well out of reach of grasping hands.

"Who there?" a voice growled through a speaker built into the camera. Bogdan.

"Delivery for a"—Kaine tilted the package towards the light and pretended to read—"Mr Abraham Pedersen." He looked up again and shot the camera a look of abject boredom.

"What it is?"

Kaine sighed. "Dunno, mate. But I'm guessing it's a mobile phone, given the shop's logo that's printed on the envelope." He held up the package and waved it at the surveillance camera.

"Leave on step," the Polish minder said, his thick accent almost impenetrable.

"No can do, mate. This here's a registered package. Someone's got to sign for it." Kaine shrugged and made a point to check his watch. After all, he was a busy delivery man and didn't have all afternoon to wait for some ignorant numpty to pull his finger out and open a pigging door.

"Stay," Bogdan ordered. The camera's speaker clicked, and the red light snapped off.

By the time the light behind the spyhole darkened, Kaine's count had reached twenty-three. He sighed deeply and shuffled from one foot to the other, impatience itself.

The lock clicked, and the black door opened inwards. Bogdan—huge and bald, wearing shiny shoes and a dark grey suit—stared down at him.

"Where sign?"

Kaine held up a notepad and mumbled, "Alphabet stew."

"What?"

Bogdan canted his head to one side, pushing his left ear closer to Kaine.

"Alphabet stew," Kaine repeated, equally indistinctly.

The big man bent at the waist, leaning even closer.

Kaine dropped the package, rammed his right fist into the man's midriff, and followed up with a ringing, open-handed slap to the exposed left ear. Bogdan's head slammed against the door jamb, and he toppled backwards into the hall.

Kaine followed Bogdan into the house. He kicked the door closed behind him and drew his SIG before the man in the nice grey suit had time to recover. He racked the slide and lined up the SIG's sights on the fallen man's gashed right cheek—gashed where it had connected with the sharp leading edge of the door jamb. Bogdan lay on his side on the richly patterned floor tiles, eyes closed, mouth open, out for the count.

"Bogdan?" a man called. "Who is it?" The man had an older voice and a smooth English accent.

Deep inside the house, a door opened, and the grey-haired Abraham Pedersen stepped into the hallway. He turned towards the front door, stared bug-eyed at Kaine and his fallen minder, and dived back into the room he'd exited. The door slammed shut behind him.

Kaine took off, reached the internal door, and crashed through into a larger-than-expected kitchen.

Pedersen, his back to Kaine, stood in front of a kitchen unit, his right hand reaching into a half-open drawer, the fingers scrambling, searching. Kaine darted forwards and booted the drawer shut, slamming Pedersen's hand inside.

The older man's scream cut short when he spotted the SIG in Kaine's steady hand—pointed at the centre of his chest.

Smiling, Kaine tugged open the drawer.

"Good evening, Mr Pedersen. So nice to meet you at last. Please step away from the cabinet."

Grunting, Pedersen ripped his right hand free, covered it with his left, and hugged it tight to his chest. Anger and pain showed in his misty blue eyes. He backed away from the cabinet and kept staring at the SIG.

"Who are you? How dare you break into my home and attack my valet!"

Kaine allowed his smile to fade. "What's in the drawer, Abe?"

He tore it fully open and found a black Beretta M9 together with two spare magazines, both fully loaded.

"What were you going to do with this popgun?"

Pedersen braced his shoulders and took another step backwards. Glowering eyes searched the kitchen for an opportunity to assert his dominance. Kaine knew the type. Pedersen was a dangerous and calculating man wrapped in an apparently feeble and innocuous package.

"I have every right to defend myself from intruders."

"And you have a licence for the Beretta, I suppose?" Kaine asked, pointing to the M9 before sliding the drawer shut.

"A licence?" Pedersen shot back, cold anger bubbling beneath the words. "Do you have one for the SIG?"

Touché.

"No. But I don't need one," Kaine answered, keeping his voice low, threatening. "I'm not the one trying to claim self-defence. And besides, nobody will know I was ever here." To underline his point, Kaine lifted his left hand and waggled his fingers inside the thin, flesh-coloured Nitrile glove.

Pedersen shut his mouth and ground his teeth together.

"Take a seat," Kaine ordered, pointing the SIG at the dining chairs gathered around a large and imposing oak table.

Still clutching his crushed hand, Pedersen followed the instruction and lowered himself carefully into the chair at the head of the table. He sat, feet planted flat on the flagstone floor, preparing himself for an instant take-off.

Kaine backed away and leant against the kitchen counter. He crossed his arms and pointed the SIG at the ceiling, keeping his ears open for movement in the hallway. He had no idea how long Bogdan would remain out of the picture. Depending on the thickness of the man's skull, the blow to the head might be minor, or it might prove fatal. No telling with head injuries.

"My hand," Pedersen said, jaw still clenched. "I think it's broken." Spittle formed at the edges of his mouth.

"Tough."

Kaine couldn't have cared less. Molly Williams would never feel pain again.

"Call an ambulance," Pedersen demanded. The spittle flew from his mouth and dropped to the flagstone at his feet.

"Shut up."

"I demand you call an ambulance!" Pedersen repeated, raising his voice to a near shout.

Kaine took aim and squeezed the SIG's trigger. The bullet smashed into the tabletop at an acute angle. Splinters flew. One, the size of a pencil, embedded itself into Pedersen's right wrist, adding insult to his recent injury. A smaller one caught in his shirtsleeve, high up on his forearm.

He yelped.

"My table," he gasped, gaping at the furrow the bullet had ploughed into its surface. "It's antique. What's wrong with you?"

"Oops. Sorry 'bout that," Kaine said, his tone dry.

Pedersen fixed Kaine with an angry glare for a moment before ripping the first splinter from his wrist. The second fell out as he moved. He gasped and lowered his eyes to stare, apparently fascinated by the blood seeping from the wound and dripping down the front of his shirt.

"I need an ambulance," he repeated.

"It's not serious. An ambulance can wait."

Pedersen leant against the back of his chair, flinching from the pain caused by the movement. He stared through the open kitchen door.

"Are you alone?"

"No," Kaine said. With the earpiece in place, he was never truly alone. He tapped it three times. "Alpha One to Charlie One, did you hear that? Over."

"*Charlie One receiving,*" Slim responded. "*Hear what, sir? Over.*"

"The gunshot. Over."

"*A gunshot? Didn't hear a thing. Is everything under control? Do you need us? Over.*"

"That's a negative, Charlie One. Things are running according to plan. Alpha One, out."

He tapped the earpiece inactive, stared at Pedersen, and shook his head.

"No," Kaine said, "I'm not alone. Just wanted to confirm my assessment of the acoustics in here, and I was right. With these thick internal walls"—he waved his SIG around the kitchen—"and the double-glazed windows, the sound of the gunshot didn't carry. No one heard it. We won't be disturbed."

Kaine settled himself more comfortably against the kitchen counter and studied the evil old man sitting in the dining chair, panting. The splinter wound still bled, and the red stain on his shirtfront grew. The shirt was ruined.

Such a shame.

"Who sent you?" Pedersen asked, teeth gritted. "The Dutch?"

"No. Micah Williams."

"Michael who?" Pedersen shot back without hesitation. His eyes widened, innocence itself.

"*Micah,*" Kaine snapped and added, "Micah Williams." He added it slowly.

"I don't know anyone called Micah," Pedersen said, frowning and shrugging his narrow shoulders. "Nope. Sorry. My mind's a complete blank."

"Liar," Kaine said, calm and considered.

Pedersen shook his head. "I'm not lying. I've never heard of anyone called Micah—"

Kaine shot the table again. More splinters flew. This time, none lanced into Pedersen.

"Please," Pedersen cried. "Please, stop that."

"I'll stop when you've finished lying."

"This fellow, Micah Williams. He sent you?"

"Yes. As did Molly—in a roundabout way."

"Sorry, that name doesn't ring a bell either," Pedersen announced, again without hesitation and without lowering his eyes from the SIG.

"How about Max Schiller, Jakob Essen, and Marta Braun?"

The old man jerked, but tried to hide it with a grunt.

Finally, a reaction.

"Who sent you?" Pedersen gasped.

"And we can't forget Jan van Bleeker, now. Can we?"

Pedersen's shoulders slumped.

"Okay, okay. I admit, I know them. So what? You're here on behalf of Micah and Molly Williams? Yes, I admit. I do know of them, but I only met Micah in person, and then only the one time. We had a ... a business transaction. Nice people from what I understand." Pedersen nodded slowly. "Perhaps a little naïve for their own good. How are they, by the way?"

"Molly's dead."

Pedersen's eyebrows lifted a fraction. "Ah, I see."

"Marta Braun killed her ... on Schiller's orders."

Pedersen raised his chin in a nod.

"I see," he repeated. "And where are they now? Schiller and Braun, I mean. Dead, I suppose?"

Kaine arched an eyebrow. "Yes. As is Jakob Essen. I shot them with a gun very much like this one." He patted the SIG against his upper arm.

"And you're here to kill me, I imagine." No emotion. A statement of fact, nothing more.

"Perhaps. That depends."

"On what?" Pedersen pricked up his ears, no doubt sensing an opportunity for survival.

"On what happens in the next few minutes."

Pedersen swallowed and looked around the kitchen. A large vehicle rumbled past the front of the house. It barely made a sound. The thick walls of the terraced house absorbed the vibration, deadening the noise.

In the hallway, Bogdan groaned.

Kaine pointed the SIG at the old man and flicked its muzzle upwards.

"Up you get!"

Pedersen shook his head.

"No. I'm in pain," he gasped. "You'll have to shoot me."

"Do it!"

Kaine steadied the SIG, took careful aim, and squeezed the trigger. A red scorch line appeared at the tip of Pedersen's left ear and the bullet drilled into the wall behind his head. Plaster exploded from the wall and dusted Pedersen's short, grey hair. He yelped and shot to his feet.

Kaine smiled. "That's better."

"You bastard!"

"Tut, tut. No need for the foul language, old chap." Kaine beckoned with his fingers. "Come here."

Still cradling his right hand against his chest, Pedersen shuffled forwards, meek as a kitten. Kaine grabbed the scruff of the old man's collar and pushed him, squealing, into the hall.

Bogdan, on hands and knees, heaved a stream of yellow fluid over the floor tiles. He dropped his head, and dribbled more of the liquid into the puddle.

Pedersen gagged against the tightness of his collar.

Bogdan turned his head slowly. Vomit smeared his damaged face and solid lumps matted his hair. Blood ran out of his left ear and dripped into his collar.

"Oh dear," Kaine said. "He looks in a bad way."

The valet straightened his arms and sat back on his haunches, swaying and groggy. His eyes lost focus and he slumped against the wall, arms loose at his sides, hands still, chin dropped to his chest.

"What did you do to him?" Pedersen gasped.

"Introduced his face to the doorjamb. Looks like a heavy concussion to me. Might have a fractured skull, too. Such a shame. Not much of a minder, is he. Never *mind*."

Kaine groaned at the pitiful pun. Sometimes, he disappointed himself.

Pedersen released his injured hand and tugged at his collar, desperate to undo the top button of his shirt.

"Please," he choked, "I-I can't breathe."

Kaine released his grip and Pedersen sucked in a huge breath.

"What's in there?" Kaine asked, pointing to a closed hallway door.

"The front room."

"Show me."

Pedersen stretched out his left arm, grabbed the brass handle, and twisted. The door opened inwards to reveal a well-appointed reception room, containing a three-piece suite, shelves full of books, a low coffee table, and a drinks cabinet. Comfortable and cosy. No sign of a TV.

"Keep going."

They repeated the process with the door opposite. This one opened into a room decked out as an office. It contained an old, leather-topped desk complete with a steam-driven desktop computer, a modern telephone, a swivel chair, and more bookshelves.

"All these books," Kaine said. "You consider yourself an educated man?"

"What of it?" he asked, eyes lowered.

"An educated man with a side business of smuggling, kidnapping, and murder."

"I'm a retired businessman. Nothing more."

Kaine grabbed Pedersen by the upper arm and pushed him fully into the room. The old man tried to angle towards the well-upholstered swivel chair on the far side of the desk, but Kaine steered him to the austere-looking visitor's chair.

Gingerly, Pedersen lowered himself onto the minimally upholstered seat and sat up straight. The injured hand had already started swelling, suggesting he'd broken at least one metacarpal. Painful, but not life-threatening. No, Kaine would be the one to threaten lives.

Kaine dropped into the swivel chair and tugged at each desk drawer in turn. None opened.

Fair enough.

He pulled the keyboard closer and tapped the spacebar. The computer's screen woke to reveal an interesting screensaver—a picture of a smiling, waving family posing in a long, narrow garden. A forty-something couple and two teenage children, one of each, both fair-haired. The husband looked like a young version of Abraham Pedersen.

"What now?" Pedersen demanded, still fighting for control.

Kaine leant back. The swivel chair squeaked as he altered position.

"Now, Pedersen, we discuss your future." Kaine shot him an icy smile. "And by that, I mean whether or not you actually have one."

27

Thursday 1st June – Afternoon

Fleur De Lis Road, Shoreditch, London, UK

Pedersen shuddered and Kaine dropped his smile.

"You can't kill me," Pedersen gasped, disbelief written all over his angular face.

Kaine frowned and jerked back his head. "Really? Why not?"

"You ... You'll never get away with it."

Kaine hesitated a beat before asking, "Why should that matter to you?"

"You'll be caught. The surveillance camera at the front door, it took your picture as you arrived. The police will know it was you."

Kaine raised his left index finger and pointed it towards the ceiling. "That, Abe, is a very good point."

Without taking his eyes off the man in the uncomfortable straight-backed visitor's chair, Kaine tapped his earpiece once.

"Alpha One to Control. Have you done it? Over."

"*Yep. Corky deleted all the surveillance footage taken today. Made it look like a glitch. Corky also mirrored the system in case the old man tries to wipe his files later. They're safe in the cloud.*"

"Thank you, Control," Kaine said, looking at Pedersen to confirm he was listening. "Thanks for confirming that you've accessed the security system and deleted today's footage. When I leave, please repeat the process. Alpha One, out."

Kaine tapped the earpiece inactive and snapped open his fingers.

"And *poof*," he said, grinning. "There goes the video evidence of me having been here. All gone."

"I have money," Pedersen said, his tone pleading. "Plenty of money."

Kaine smiled. "So do I, but mine wasn't earned through smuggling, kidnap, and murder."

No, but by blackmail and coercion.

But his victims weren't innocent non-combatants. The difference couldn't have been clearer. Kaine felt no guilt over it.

Still cradling his injured hand, Pedersen leant forwards and eased out of his chair.

"But ... I didn't murder anyone. That was all down to Schiller," he said, becoming more strident, his voice increasing in pitch. "H-He was out of control. The woman, Marta Braun, too. They forced me to do their bidding. I-I was terrified of them. I'm as much a victim as poor Micah and Molly. Schiller made me work for him. Blackmailed me into it. You have to believe me!"

Pedersen held out his left hand in supplication, keeping his bruised and swollen right clamped against his chest.

Kaine shook his head.

"No, I don't."

"But ... I don't want to die," Pedersen sobbed and made a good stab at appearing scared. "Please don't kill me."

The tears almost looked genuine, but Kaine couldn't believe a word spewing from the old man's mouth.

"What about the others?"

Pedersen frowned. "Wh-What others?"

"The other victims. One couple from the Netherlands, and two from France. What about them?"

Pedersen shook his head and shrugged.

"I ... I have no idea what you mean."

Kaine scowled and waved the pitiful creature back into his chair.

"Stow it, Pedersen. It's not working. You're a miserable piece of filth."

"Yes, I-I know. I probably am." Pedersen sighed, giving up the act and hitching up another shrug. "So, what happens next?"

"I'm probably going to kill you," Kaine announced, matter-of-fact.

Pedersen pulled in a deep breath, his gaze searched the room, probably looking for an escape route. Unable to find one, he slumped back in his seat and dropped his shoulders. Finally, he stared at Kaine.

"If you kill me, it makes you no better than Max Schiller. Could you live with yourself?"

Kaine snorted.

"Yep. Without a doubt. I could shoot you and set it up to look like you and Bogdan had a falling out. It's easily done, but ..." Kaine allowed his words to trail off as though a different option had recently come to mind.

"But?" Pedersen prompted, sensing a possible alternative.

"Killing you would be far too quick. Too easy on you. In fact, I've just had a better idea. I want you to suffer for your part in killing Molly Williams and the others. Yes, there is another option." Kaine snapped his fingers as if to confirm his new idea.

"There is?"

"Care to hear it?"

Pedersen tilted his head to one side, pushing out his ear as Bogdan had done in the doorway. "I'm all ears."

"I leave you here alive, and when I'm gone, you wait one hour. A full hour," Kaine repeated. "Then you dial 9-9-9 and ask for an ambulance for Bogdan. At the same time, you ask for the police. You will then confess all your sins to the police. Every single one of your sins."

Abraham Pedersen's jaw dropped.

"But … but that's preposterous. You can't be serious."

Kaine shook his head. "On the contrary. I'm deadly serious. And you'll call them on that desk phone"—he nodded towards the handset—"so my colleagues and I can overhear the conversation. It should prove enlightening and highly entertaining."

"Why on earth would I confess to the police?"

"It's your only option. The only way you survive this meeting."

Pedersen squeezed his eyelids together and shook his head as though trying to clear the cobwebs from his mind.

"Okay, okay. Wait a minute. So, let's say I agree. Let's say I promise to do as you demand. Why would you trust me? What's to stop me promising you the world and then running off into the sunset the moment you leave? I have an exit strategy. Of course I do. You'll never find me."

Kaine snorted his derision.

"Oh, we'll find you alright," he said. "In fact, we know everything about you. For example, we know about your little bolt hole in the Bahamas, and we know all about your offshore accounts. The Caymans. The British Virgin Islands. All of them."

Again, Pedersen's jaw dropped. He stared at Kaine, eyes wide, unblinking.

"But," Kaine added, "you aren't going to run."

"Why not?" Pedersen asked, looking decidedly confused. Confused and unwell.

"If you run, we'll go after Paul instead."

"Paul?" Pedersen gasped. The remaining colour drained from his gaunt face.

Kaine reached out and swivelled the computer monitor to show Pedersen the screensaver.

"Such a lovely family," Kaine said, keeping his voice low, menacing. "Paul, Elizabeth, and we mustn't forget the kids, Ginny, and Grant. Such a lovely house they live in, too. Nice quiet street on the outskirts of Basingstoke. A rather pleasant town, I understand. Not that I've visited it … yet."

Pedersen jumped to his feet and threatened to launch himself across the desk. Kaine stopped him with a jerk of his SIG, and the old man slumped back in his chair. Defeated.

"Y-You're bluffing," Pedersen whispered. Tears pooled in his pale eyes—these were definitely genuine.

"Call him. Call your son now. Their home phone number ends with zero-two-four. Tell him if he looks through his front window, he'll see an old silver Audi. Inside the car will be two men. My men. Go on, use the landline." He pointed the SIG at the desk phone. "I'll wait." He added a tinder-dry smile.

Pedersen snatched up the handset and dialled with the shaking index finger of his left hand. He misdialled, grunted, and repeated the process, this time successfully.

Kaine stretched out in his chair and waited for the call to connect.

Seconds passed slowly, the old man's growing anguish clear in every twitch, gasp, and tremble.

"Hello, Elizabeth?" Pedersen shouted, leaning forwards, eyes locked on the SIG held rock steady in Kaine's fist. "It's Abe ... Yes, I'm well, thanks. Is Paul there? ... Oh, yes. Of course, of course he is. When are you expecting him home? ... Ah, okay. What about the kids? ... No, no, don't disturb them. Homework's important. Listen, Elizabeth, I need you to do something for me. Go to your front room and look through the window. Tell me what you see. ... Don't ask questions, woman," he barked. "Just do as I bloody say. ... Yes, yes. I'll hang on."

Pedersen closed his eyes and waited, the handset pressed tight to his ear, the knuckles of his left hand blanching under the force of his grip. After a few moments he jerked upright, and his eyes snapped open.

"Yes, I'm still here. ... A silver Audi?" The old man's tear-filled blue eyes locked on Kaine's. He blinked and the tears fell again. "Okay ... No, no. Lock and bolt the doors. ... Just do what I tell you, please. ... When Paul gets home, tell him to call me. I'll explain everything. But whatever you do, stay inside. Don't let the kids out, and don't open the door to anyone but Paul. Understand? ... No, don't ask any questions, I'll explain everything to Paul. Bye Elizabeth. Send my ... my love to the kids."

He dropped the handset into its cradle and stared at Kaine, his eyes pleading.

"Please don't hurt them. They're innocent. Paul's an accountant and Elizabeth's a primary school teacher. They don't know anything about my ... business activities."

Kaine stared the old man down.

"Micah and Molly were innocent, too. Molly's dead and Micah will grieve for the rest of his life. By the way, Molly was four months pregnant."

"Oh God. I didn't ... I didn't know."

Pedersen's late show of regret seemed authentic.

"Would it have made any difference?"

Kaine sneered at the man sitting across the desk. The man who had caused so much suffering. The man who wouldn't suffer half as much as he deserved, but he would suffer.

"So, do you accept my offer? Life over death?"

Pedersen nodded.

"Say it aloud."

"Yes, yes," Pedersen said. The words sighed through the air between them. "I accept. I'll hand myself over to the police and confess everything. I-I promise."

"Good. The moment you contact the police—and I'll know when you do"—he pointed first to his earpiece and then to the desk phone—"I'll call off my people in the Audi. Oh, and I almost forgot."

Kaine stood, reached into his trouser pocket, and pulled out the packet of rough diamonds he'd taken from van Bleeker. He tossed them onto the middle of the desk. Pedersen stared at the bundle, clearly recognising what it was and where it had come from.

"Hand these over to the police when they come to pick you up. It'll help them take you seriously."

"Y-You took these from van Bleeker?" Pedersen asked, eyes focused on the black package.

Kaine nodded.

"I-Is he ...?"

"No. He's still alive, for the moment. There's no need to keep him out of your confession, either. He's equally culpable. And don't forget your suppliers. Europol will be interested in learning all about them."

Pedersen nodded his understanding and his submission.

"Can I ask a question?"

"You just did," Kaine said, unable to resist the age-old joke. "But carry on. I'll give you one more question. Might even answer it."

"Who are you?"

Kaine sniffed.

"You don't need to know that, but remember this." He leant closer to the old man who looked a damn sight more frail than he had when Kaine first barged into his home. "Micah Williams is under my protection, and he always will be. If anything unpleasant ever happens to him, anything at all, I'll blame you, and I'll take it out on your family. Do I make myself perfectly clear?"

"Yes," Pedersen said, nodding slowly, a defeated man. "I-I understand. Please don't hurt my family."

Kaine smiled as pleasantly as he could. "You keep your promise, and I'll keep mine. You have my word of honour."

He turned his back on Pedersen and left the office. Once out in the hallway, he closed on Bogdan and stood over the injured man.

The valet had fallen onto his side. He lay folded at the waist, eyes closed. His chest moved, showing signs of life. Blood dripped from his ear into the pool of vomit.

Kaine stepped over the man's bent legs, opened the front door, and surged out into the warm afternoon sun. He picked up the package he'd dropped earlier, stuffed it into his pocket, and stepped down onto the pavement. A pedestrian rushed past, head down, eyes focused on the screen of her mobile. They almost collided. Without looking up, she marched on without offering an apology.

A sign of the times.

He looked up and signalled the all-clear to Slim and Larry in the building opposite, turned right, and headed towards the busy Commercial Street. He had one final errand to run.

* * *

Kaine smiled through the window, waved, and waited for the security lock to release before pushing through the jeweller's shop door. The same attractive and well-dressed woman welcomed him with a high-wattage smile.

"Hello, sir. That was good timing. I was just getting ready to close."

Kaine returned her smile. "Sorry. Lost all track of the time. My business took a shade longer than expected."

"Did your friend enjoy his present?"

"Yes, thanks. At least I think so. Is the pendant ready?"

"Yes, sir."

She opened a drawer below the glass counter, withdrew a small jewellery box covered in red leather—at least he assumed it was leather—and slid it towards him. He flipped open the lid and confirmed that the inscription on the back of the heart said what he wanted it to say.

"That's wonderful, thanks."

"You can read it?"

"Yes. Why not?"

"The script is ever so small. I thought you might need this."

She held up a jeweller's loupe.

"No need. My eyesight's pretty decent, thanks."

"You're lucky. I have to wear contact lenses. My eyes are rubbish."

"Not from where I'm standing," Kaine said, and meaning it.

She smiled prettily.

"I don't suppose you have time to gift wrap it?"

"Of course, sir. Happy to," she said without glancing at her wristwatch or at the ridiculously expensive mantelpiece clock on the shelf behind her.

Kaine closed the leather box and handed it back. She took a purple velvet sack from the open drawer, dropped the box inside, and tightened the drawstring.

"Will that do?" she asked, handing it across.

"That's perfect. Thanks."

Kaine slid the package into his jacket pocket.

"Is it for a special occasion? An anniversary?" the woman asked.

"No," Kaine said, "nothing like that. It's just long overdue."

"She's a lucky woman, if you don't mind my saying."

Kaine smiled and shook his head.

"No, I don't mind, but you're wrong. I'm the lucky one."

He tipped the peak of his cap to her and turned to leave.

At that moment, a heavy diesel engine growled, and a large white shape appeared outside the window. It raced forwards and smashed through the door. Glass exploded, and the front of the shop caved in.

28

Thursday 1st June – Afternoon

Commercial Street, Shoreditch, London, UK

A concrete ceiling support collapsed, smashing into the floor at Kaine's feet. He dived backwards and slammed against a display cabinet, jarring his left shoulder. The woman screamed. Alarms wailed. Pins and needles shot down Kaine's left arm, and his hand spasmed.

Engine howling, the white shape—a Toyota Hilux complete with a reinforced bull bar—reversed. Gears crunched and the truck slammed forwards again, competing the job of destroying the shop front and creating a new opening.

Kaine scrambled around and behind the cabinet, hands and knees crunching on glass granules. His left arm ached, the hand numb.

"Get down," he shouted.

The woman stood transfixed, hands covering her mouth, staring at the damage to her little shop. She sucked in a deep breath and let it out in a scream.

The Toyota's front doors cranked open, and two men dressed in black boilersuits and tan work boots jumped out. Hooded, masked, and wearing yellow safety glasses, they carried heavy lump hammers. Cloth bags hung on straps from their shoulders. The one from the passenger side raced towards the serving counter. His mate, the driver, peeled to his right, and swung his hammer into a glass-fronted display cabinet. Glass exploded into a million pellets. He dropped the hammer into the tray and started piling expensive sparklies into his sack.

"Stand back!" Passenger howled. "Stop fucking screaming, woman!"

The shop owner's piercing scream cut short, but the burglar alarms still wailed loud.

Kaine stood, threw his right arm up and out, hand open. His left arm didn't want to move.

"Easy," he called over the noise of the alarm. "We're doing nothing."

"Too fucking right you're not. Get back from the counter, arsehole."

Kaine stepped away and to his right, sliding in front of the woman. He half-turned, reached out, and pushed her towards the office door, hoping she'd take the hint. Her screams had turned into tears.

Kaine's heart raced.

He gritted his teeth.

Leave them to it.

They'd be gone in minutes, and the shop would be insured. His left arm wasn't working properly. A liability.

Leave them, Kaine. Leave them.

Something warm and wet dripped from Kaine's left ear and ran down his neck into his collar. Blood. He'd been cut, although he felt nothing. Nothing but rage. He clenched his fists, forcing movement through the pain.

Don't! Don't do anything.

Passenger stepped closer, his shining eyes focused on the glittering watches under the glass of the serving counter—Rolex, Tag Hauer, Cartier, Breitling—each worth thousands. A fortune just sitting there waiting for him. Passenger raised his hammer.

No!

Left arm trailing, Kaine sprang, vaulted the counter, and rammed his boot heels into the man's face. Passenger's head snapped up and around. He collapsed backwards, his head slammed into the corner of a cabinet, and he landed, face-up, in a pile of broken glass. Kaine's momentum carried him forwards, onto his feet, facing the driver.

Driver spun. The eyes behind the safety glasses widened in shock and anger.

"You stupid bastard!" he screamed.

Driver released his cloth sack and snatched up the club hammer from the shattered display cabinet. The sack fell to his side and dangled from its strap. He lowered himself into a crouch and stalked forwards, leading with the hammer.

Kaine stood his ground, waiting for an opening.

Yep. Such a stupid move.

"I'm gonna—"

Driver straightened, lunged. He swung the hammer in a downward arc, aiming for Kaine's head.

Kaine jagged left. The hammer sailed past his right shoulder. It grazed his arm on the way through, tugging the sleeve of his jacket.

Driver roared and raised the hammer again, opening his stance and his guard.

Slightly off balance, Kaine booted him in the nuts, his aim off, but not by much.

Driver buckled, collapsed in on himself, mouth open, gasping for breath. Kaine swivelled and drove the point of his right elbow into the side of Driver's face. His jaw crunched under the force. Driver fell to his knees and toppled onto his face alongside a prone Passenger, who still hadn't moved.

Kaine stepped back, flexing the fingers of his left hand. Feeling had returned. Painful and reluctant, but sensation and movement just the same. He turned to the shop owner. She stared at him, unblinking, mouth hanging open.

"You okay?" he shouted.

She raised her hand to her mouth and nodded.

"Y-Yes."

In the street outside, a huge man in a baggy, olive-green parka with the hood up strode into view. He carried a long-handled axe, and held it in both hands at chest height. Patrolling the street, he screamed at the growing crowds and the slow-moving traffic.

"Get back!" he bellowed. "Get back! I'll fucking kill anyone who comes near the shop. Drop them phones! Stop filming. Stop fucking filming!"

Parka hoisted the axe and sprang forwards, swinging. He drove the blade into the roof of a slowly passing Vauxhall Astra. The head buried itself up to the cheek. Screaming in terror, the Astra driver scrambled over the passenger's seat, dived through the door, and raced to the far side of the street. Once there, he stopped and turned to face his ruined car. Gasping, he bent forwards, resting his hands on his thighs, the blood draining from his face. Parka laughed at the terrified man, levered the axe from the Astra's roof, and turned to face the shop's destroyed frontage.

Nasty bugger.

His blood boiling, Kaine scooped up Driver's fallen lump hammer and picked his way through the wreckage. He stepped out into the late-afternoon sunshine and closed on the man in the olive-green parka.

"Drop the axe, mate," Kaine said, speaking quietly, his tone almost conversational. He shook some more life back into his left arm. The pins and needles returned. His fingers tickled and stung.

"Who the fuck are you?" Parka roared, eyes wide, pupils dilated, running high on adrenaline—or something else. His chest heaved, breathing hard from the effort of swinging the axe and extracting it from the Astra's roof.

Kaine smiled.

"I'm the man who told you to drop the axe."

"Fuck you!"

The cool air stung Kaine's left ear. He reached up and found a sticky patch. His fingers came away bloodied.

"I'm afraid you owe me for a new jacket and shirt. I'll never get the bloodstain out."

"Fuck off," Parka thundered, definitely a man with a limited vocabulary.

Parka edged closer to Kaine, who backed off, leading the man away from the crowded street. Parka held the throat of the axe handle in his right hand and bounced the belly in his left. He stepped out of the sun and into the shadows, and stopped two metres from Kaine, out of reach.

Three motorbikes—bright green Suzuki Bandits—screeched to a stop behind the battered Hilux in squeals of burning rubber. Revving hard, the bikers raced their engines, the high-pitched mechanical screams adding to the deafening chaos. Parka smiled behind his white cotton facemask. As getaway vehicles in London, motorbikes beat cars hands down.

One of the bikers sounded his horn and pointed to his wrist. He shouted something that Kaine couldn't make out.

"Time's up!" Parka yelled to his mates in the shop. "Where are you!"

"I'm afraid they won't be coming," Kaine called.

"What?"

"I said, they won't be coming," Kaine shouted, waving Driver's lump hammer at him.

Parka glared at the hammer and screamed, "You bastard!"

He raised the axe over his left shoulder and charged. The axe blade whistled through the air, swinging in a downward arc.

Kaine stepped inside the blow, timing his spin to match Parka's movement and cramping him for space. The axe head swiped in front of Kaine's face and clanged into the paving slab. Sparks flew. From inside Parka's guard, Kaine drove the head of the lump hammer backwards into the man's standing knee, and back-butted him in the face.

Parka howled. Kaine dived forwards, headlong into the empty road. He rolled to his feet and turned in a single, flowing movement, hammer raised.

Blood spurted from Parka's shattered nose and his knee bent backwards, working against the natural movement of the joint. He looked down, shrieked, and toppled forwards. The axe fell from his grip, and he crumpled to the pavement. His agonised howls drowned out the high-pitched wails of the racing motorbike engines. The lead biker shouted something unintelligible to his mates, stomped his bike into gear, and screamed away. The other two followed close behind, abandoning their mates in the shop, and the crumpled mass on the pavement.

Breathing hard, Kaine stepped back into the shadows. He stood over the squealing Parka, who lay on the filthy, chewing-gum-spotted paving slabs. Face contorted, bent double, he clamped his hands around his shattered knee, trying to hold it together.

"You smashed my fucking knee!" he wailed, spraying blood onto the pavement.

"Tough," Kaine said, through a tight smile. "You cut my ear."

"Did you see that?" a nearby onlooker yelled over the wailing alarm.

"Bloody brilliant!" another in the growing crowd called.

"Never seen nothin' like it!" the man beside him yelled.

Someone across the street near the junction with Fleur De Lis Road started clapping. Others joined in.

"Like watching something out of Hollywood," someone else added, having to shout over the growing applause.

One of the drivers in the slow-moving traffic sounded his horn. Others followed suit. Kaine raised a hand to cover his face from the ubiquitous mobile phones and turned towards the shop. Once again, he picked his way through the wreckage.

Inside, Driver and Passenger lay where they fell, head to tail in the builder's rubble. Driver showed some signs of recovery. His knees pulled together, and his hands moved towards his groin. Passenger didn't look at all well and his face carried a green tinge. Neither man presented any immediate danger.

Kaine returned to the relatively unscathed back of the shop and found a stunned owner with her mouth hanging open.

"Are you okay?" he asked.

She nodded, closed her mouth, and swallowed. She blinked and started hard at him.

"You're hurt," she said, pointing to his ear.

He caught sight of himself in one of the few undamaged mirrors. A patch of dark red stained the left side of his neck and coloured his collar. Otherwise, he was unmarked. Thankfully, his left arm had recovered, although his shoulder still throbbed.

"It's nothing," he said, scrubbing at the stain with the back of his right hand. "A scratch."

She pulled in a deep breath. "Who are you?"

Kaine smiled. "Arnie Jeffries. It's on the sales ticket."

"What you did"—she waved a trembling hand towards the rubbish on the floor—"it ... it was fantastic."

Kaine shrugged. "I got lucky."

"Lucky?" She gasped. "That had nothing to do with luck."

Wailing sirens broke through the high-pitched warble of the burglar alarm.

Time to stride off into the sunset.

"Is there a back way out of here?" Kaine asked, looking towards the office door behind the intact counter.

"Yes. But aren't you staying? The police will want to—"

"Ask me a million questions," Kaine interrupted, "and tie me up for hours. I have places to be. They might even arrest me for attacking those bozos. Who knows?"

Paranoid much, Kaine?

"They won't do that, I won't let them. But they will want to know who you are and how you did ... that." Again, she stared at the human rubbish groaning in brick dust and shattered glass.

"You have CCTV in the store, don't you?"

"Yes, but ..." she shrugged.

"Show it to them. That ought to cover it."

The sirens grew louder as the police drew ever closer to the crime scene.

Kaine edged his way around to her side of the counter.

"Can I go through?" He pointed to the office door.

"Yes, yes." She nodded, long hair bobbing behind her. "Of course."

"The engraver. I'm guessing he's already gone home?"

She continued her nod. "He leaves at five. Go straight through the workshop and the storeroom. You'll find a door through to the back yard. It's alarmed but …" Her shoulders hitched in a tight shrug. "That doesn't matter now, I suppose."

Kaine smiled. "Thanks. I'm sorry about the mess."

"Why? It wasn't your fault. And thanks to you, they didn't get away with any stock."

Kaine reached the internal door, grabbed the handle, and nodded goodbye.

"What am I going to tell the police?"

"It's okay, just tell them what happened. Don't leave anything out."

"But I have your credit card details. They'll be able to trace you."

Again, Kaine smiled and added a nod. "I know."

"Do you want me to hide it from them?"

"No. They'll see the transaction on the till receipts. And I'm all over the CCTV images."

"But you're running from them." She winced and looked away in embarrassment before catching his eye again. "The transaction is valid, isn't it? You haven't robbed me, have you?"

"It's valid. I promise you. I'm no thief."

He patted the pocket where he'd placed the pendant. The police sirens grew raucous, and flashing blue lights coloured the single pane of unbroken glass in the destroyed shopfront.

"Tell the police I promised to call them when I have a spare moment. Good luck with the clean-up."

Kaine touched the peak of his baseball cap and pushed his way through the unlocked office door. On his way through the workshop, he zipped up his jacket and pulled out his mobile. Holding it to his left ear during his stroll to the car would hide the blood from any inquisitive pedestrians. Perhaps not the greatest camouflage in the world, but the best he could think of at short notice.

29

Thursday 1st June – Andrew Grantham

Elder Street, Shoreditch, London, UK

The black door to Number 8 opened, and a bearded man dressed in black jeans and a dark hoodie stepped out of the house and into the road—a man Andrew Grantham didn't recognise. Not Pedersen nor Bogdan, and none of the people on his watch list.

"What the fuck?"

Head lowered, the man with the beard tugged his peaked cap down over his eyes, picked up a package from the step, and turned towards Commercial Street. He wandered off, arms swinging free, his stride jaunty.

Where the fuck did he come from?

"Shit!" Grantham hissed. He'd missed the entry. It showed the problem with running a single-person stakeout. The boss would throw a huge wobbly.

Grantham stopped the recording, hit the rewind button, and the camcorder did its thing. Pedestrians comedy-walked backwards into and out of frame, some dodging around each other, most carrying on unhindered. Cars and a delivery van reversed into and out of shot at breakneck speed. All the while, the black door remained closed.

The recording reversed through twenty-one minutes of movie madness until it reached the part he wanted. Grantham stopped the rewind and hit play at normal speed.

The bearded man stopped at the door, reached up, and worked the brass knocker. A few seconds later, his head tilted up and Grantham could see nothing but the top of the man's dark blue baseball cap. He spoke to the surveillance camera above the door and showed it the package he carried.

Grantham almost relaxed.

A delivery man. Not the problem he feared, but why had he been inside the house for so long? Twenty-odd minutes to make a delivery? Unlikely.

The black door opened, and Bogdan appeared. The delivery man said something. Bogdan leant out and ...

"Jesus, fuck!"

Grantham jerked forwards. Everything happened so fast, he'd missed the action. He reached out, rewound the scene, and hit slow-motion replay.

He watched in disbelief as the delivery man smashed Bogdan's head into the doorframe, barged his way into the house, and slammed the door shut behind him. He left the package where it fell, on the front step.

Grantham replayed the scene and checked the timer. The whole episode had taken seven seconds from the moment Bogdan opened the door to it closing again. Seven seconds.

Bloody hell.

He replayed the scene again and again. The "delivery" man hadn't missed a beat. Although way smaller than Bogdan, he'd taken Pedersen's thick-set minder apart, using the advantage of surprise. A professional. No doubt about it.

Grantham fast-forwarded the recording to the point where the delivery man exited the house and then played it at half speed. Nothing. At no point did the man look up towards the camera. The only exposed part of his face was the bearded chin. Useless in terms of facial recognition.

"Bugger."

The boss needed to know, but how the hell could he explain missing the bloody entry? Grantham slumped back into his uncomfortable chair and took a moment.

"Ah shit," he said to the wall opposite. "Go for it, Andy."

He picked up his burner, keyed in, *"Call me"*, and hit send. The boss would call when ready and not before.

Grantham settled in for the nervous wait.

* * *

IT TOOK eight minutes for the phone to vibrate, by which time Grantham had almost nodded off—again. The solo obbo had cost him crap knew how many hours in lost sleep. At least the money was building up. Wouldn't be long before it paid for an early retirement in the sun. A worry-free retirement.

Now wouldn't that be a fine thing.

He snatched up the phone on the fifth buzz and hit accept.

"Hi, boss."

"What is it?"

Typical. No greeting, not a wasted word. All business.

"The target's had a visitor. Unfriendly."

"Explain."

He gave a blow-by-blow of the forced entry, and the boss listened in silence until he'd finished.

"When did this happen?"

Grantham read off the time of entry from his notes.

"What the hell! That's over half an hour ago. Why'd it take you so long to report?"

Grantham cringed.

"Sorry, boss," he said, realising how pitiful it sounded. "Still got the runs after last night's curry. I was in the loo when the fucker arrived. I didn't see him."

The loo part, he'd made up. It sounded better than the truth—he'd nodded off in the chair in front of the window. He hadn't even made it to the lumpy bed.

"I didn't know the bugger was inside until he left."

"So, let's see if I've got this straight," the boss said, anger building with each word. "An unknown assailant overpowers Bogdan and breaks into Pedersen's house. He stays inside for twenty minutes, and then hoofs it. Am I right?"

"Yep. That's about the size of it."

"And you've no idea what went on inside?"

"Of course not. How could I?"

"No gunshots? No screaming? No neighbours in the road wondering what's going on next door?"

"Nothing like that. I'm too far away to hear any gunshots fired inside the house. Pity we couldn't bug the place like I suggested."

"Not a chance. Pedersen hasn't left the house in days."

"What's our next move?"

"*My* next move is to do some thinking. *Your* next move is to stay there and keep your bloody eyes open for a change."

Fuck.

More bloody waiting. More lost sleep.

"Yes, sure," he said to a dead phone. "Way to go, Andy. There goes the proficiency bonus."

30

Thursday 1st June – Abraham Pedersen

Fleur De Lis Road, Shoreditch, London, UK

A shattered and trembling Abraham Pedersen sat at his desk, cradling his aching and swollen hand, which throbbed with every beat of his racing heart. When he tried to move his fingers, the pain flared as the bones ground together. Broken. Definitely broken.

God it hurts.

Brought tears to his eyes.

The evil bastard had crushed the delicate bones with the kitchen drawer. Abe needed an ambulance, but had to wait. The bastard was setting the agenda, and Abe had no choice but to follow his instructions.

Christ alive. What a mess.

The burner vibrated in his pocket. He ignored it.

Fuck. What now?

Only one person knew the number, and a fat lot of good they'd been. So much for their so-called protection. He'd paid their extortionate demands and they'd proved useless. Still, one good thing would come of the bearded bastard's treats. Abe's confession would take the arseholes down, too, and he wouldn't give a damn.

The burner stopped vibrating. They wouldn't leave a message. Of course they wouldn't. That would be professional suicide.

Groaning from the hallway outside showed that Bogdan was still alive. Alive and suffering. Well, sod him. Let the useless meathead suffer. He'd let the bearded bastard in. Into Abe's home. Into his sanctuary. As a bodyguard, Bogdan had proved himself worse than useless. The moron deserved all the pain in the world. Deserved more pain than he was currently suffering.

Abe watched the clock on the computer screen tick away the seconds. Twenty-three minutes had passed since the bearded animal had left. Twenty-three minutes. It seemed more like twenty-three hours.

Another groan erupted from the hallway, this one drawn out, long and hollow.

Moron.

Abe gritted his teeth. He took a deep breath, released his hold on the broken hand, and used the good one to push himself out of his comfortable chair. Abe staggered as a hot wave of nausea washed up from the depth of his stomach. He steadied himself, took another long breath, and exhaled slowly. His stomach heaved again, then settled.

More groans wormed their way into Abe's head. Into his mind.

Useless piece of shit.

What did he care about the Polack? The evil fucker had threatened his family. His son and his grandchildren, for God's sake. Abe shuffled through the door, into the hallway, and stood over the meathead who'd been found wanting. He glowered down at the useless lump, focusing his anger, blaming the man for everything.

Bogdan's eyelids fluttered half open. His vomit-smeared face lifted from the pool of puke. He groaned, mumbled something in Polish that might have been "hospital".

"Shut the fuck up, you useless piece of crap!"

For balance, Abe pressed his good hand against the wall and kicked the Polack in the face, once, twice, three times. Again and again, the toe of his shoe slammed into Bogdan's flat, square face.

Four, five, six times.

Frustration, anger, and pain added power to each kick until, panting and exhausted, Abe stopped and leant against the wall. He bent at the waist, gasping for breath, staring down at the Pole's shattered face and lifeless body.

"Not fucking groaning now, are you! Not begging for the hospital now, are you! You useless fuck!"

Abe moved his finger to point. An involuntary action. His right hand flinched, and a white-hot lance of agony shot up his arm. He groaned and held the hand close to his chest again. Sweat poured out of him, soaking his bloodstained shirt, dripping from his forehead and into his eyes. Stinging like a bitch.

The phone in his office trilled.

Paul!

Abe gasped, levered himself away from the wall, and stumbled through the open door into the office. He slid carefully into his chair—the one so recently vacated by the evil, dead-eyed bastard—and grasped the handset. Again, the movement jostled his broken hand and drove another sheet of flame up his arm. Again, his stomach heaved.

He pressed the phone against his ear.

"Dad? Dad?" Paul asked, worry clear in his voice.

"Yes, it's me. Listen—"

"Elizabeth's terrified. What's this about the Audi?"

"Is it still outside?"

"Yes. It's still there. I'm calling the police—"

"No, Paul. Don't, please! You mustn't. They ... the people in the Audi ... are dangerous, but they won't hurt you. I promise. I'm ... dealing with it."

"Dad, you're worrying me."

"I'm sorry, but listen ... you must listen."

Paul's heavy breathing tore at Abe's heart. In the background Elizabeth's sobs had less effect. The bloody woman always overreacted to everything. Paul had married beneath him. Abe had known it from the first time Paul introduced her to the family. On the other hand, she had produced two lovely grandchildren. Something to the lowbrow broodmare's credit.

"Okay, Dad. I'm listening," Paul gasped, clearly struggling for control.

The clock on the computer ticked forwards. Thirty-three minutes gone. Twenty-seven left. So little time, but so much to say. Where to start?

"Paul," he started, forcing through the catch in his voice, "very soon, you're going to hear some things about me. Some very bad things, and ... it's all going to be true ... all of it ..."

* * *

ABE STARED at the computer's clock. It ticked ever more slowly.

He'd told Paul and the kids he loved them, and gave his apologies for what was to come. With nothing left to say, he'd ended the call and sat back in his office chair to watch the time tick away. To watch his freedom slip away.

During the phone call, he didn't go into specifics. Over time, the media would unearth the full story. They'd dribble out the details piecemeal. Each one would be more damning than the last. Abe was ruined. His carefully constructed façade, the cultured and educated face he showed to the world, would be shattered. He'd be laid bare. Ruined.

Ginny and Grant would, no doubt, be shunned by their classmates the moment the media broke the news of their grandfather's fall from grace, his crimes. He felt for them, but they were young, and a change of name and a new home would solve everything.

When the clock reached forty-five minutes gone, Abe briefly

considered heading to the kitchen for the Beretta. A bullet to the brain would have made a swift end to his pain. His suffering. But he dismissed suicide. He dismissed taking the "easy" way out. It wouldn't satisfy the bastard with the beard, who wanted Abe to hurt. He'd made it clear. Demanded it. If Abe topped himself, the bastard would feel cheated. Maybe cheated enough to carry out his threat to hurt Paul and the kids.

No, Abe couldn't take the risk. So, he sat in silence, watching the fucking clock on the fucking computer screen tick away to the end of his life. To the end of his freedom.

Tick, tick, bloody tick.

* * *

Fifty-six minutes gone. Four remaining.

Fuck it.

Abe couldn't stand it any longer. He leant forwards, snatched up the handset, and dialled 9-9-9. The call clicked through in an instant.

"Emergency. Which service?" the voice asked. Female. Cool and calm. Professional.

"Er…"

Abe paused. The whole time he'd been watching the clock tick down to the end of his freedom, the end of his life, his mind had been full of other things. He hadn't run through the call in his head.

"A-Ambulance," he stuttered, his voice cracking. "Ambulance, please."

"One moment. I'll put you through."

The line clicked and clicked again.

"Hello, caller." A man this time. Equally cool. Equally calm. "Is the patient breathing and awake?"

"No. Not any longer."

Not with his head kicked in.

"Are you certain, caller?"

"Yes. I'm sure."

"What telephone number are you calling from?"

Abe told him and could hear the man typing.

"What is the address of the emergency?"

Abe gave him the address, too.

"Do you know the patient?"

"Yes. He's my valet."

"Your valet?" A change in the cool delivery.

"He's dead, but I need the ambulance. My hand is swollen. I think it's broken."

"What happened?"

"My ... valet smashed it in a kitchen drawer."

"Your valet smashed it in a drawer?" the call handler repeated, incredulity entering his tone. The typing continued, seemingly faster and definitely louder.

"Yes. He went ballistic. Attacked me. Which is why I had to restrain him. Which is also why he's no longer breathing, and why he's bleeding all over my beautifully tiled hall floor."

"Can you see your valet now, caller?"

"No," Abe said, sighing. "He's outside in the hall, and I'm using the phone in my office. I'm in a great deal of pain, here. Can you hurry?"

"An ambulance is on its way, caller. We're treating it as a Category One emergency. It should be with you soon."

"How soon?"

"It's difficult to say. We're experiencing a heavy call volume at the moment. Would you like me to stay on the line?"

"No. Don't bother. I'm going to call the police now."

Abe ended the call, redialled the emergency number, and received the same response.

"Police, please. I'd like to report a murder. A series of murders, actually."

"One moment, caller."

Abe couldn't be certain, but she sounded like the same operator as earlier.

"Police. What is your emergency?" A different woman asked, her accent pure east end of London.

"I am a diamond smuggler, and I've just killed my valet."

"Say again, caller," the operator asked, after a momentary delay.

Abe repeated his confession and added, "After he attacked me, by crushing my hand in a kitchen drawer."

"Is there a weapon involved?"

"Apart from the kitchen drawer, my right shoe," Abe said, feeling a little light-headed. The pain from the broken hand and the shock of the bearded fucker's ultimatum were taking their toll.

"Your right shoe?" the operator asked, sceptical. The professionalism slipping.

"Yes, I kicked him to death. My valet that is. Can't have servants attacking their employers, now can we."

"Where are you, sir?"

Abe recited his address.

"Are you there now, sir?"

"Where else would I be?" Abe snapped and grunted as another involuntary movement shot agony through his damaged hand.

"When did this happen?"

"About an hour ago."

"An hour ago?"

"That's what I said, isn't it?"

"Why did it take so long to call us? Are you hurt?"

"Yes. My hand's broken. I just told you."

"How old are you, sir?"

"None of your damned business. Send the police. I'm confessing to a crime here. Oh, and by the way, I have a gun in the house. A Beretta M9. It's in my kitchen drawer. The same drawer Bogdan crushed my hand in."

"A Beretta?"

"Yes. Why are you making me repeat myself?"

Abe smiled, trying to imagine what the operator made of her latest caller. A raving lunatic probably.

"Sir," she said, "do you know the penalty for making a prank emergency call?"

"Not offhand," Abe said, dry as bone, "but I imagine its more than a rap on the knuckles. Which, in my current condition, would be extremely painful. I did tell you I have a broken hand, didn't I?"

"You did, sir. Have you called for an ambulance?"

Abe released a long sigh.

"I have, and one is apparently blue-lighting its way to me as I speak. No idea when it'll arrive though. I'm in a great deal of pain. Did I tell you that?"

"Yes, sir. You did."

"So, are you going to take me seriously or not? I *do* have a gun, and I *did* kill my valet. I take it this call is being recorded?"

"It most certainly is, sir."

"Good. Let's make this official, shall we? My name is Abraham Miles Pedersen, I am a diamond smuggler, and I'm confessing to killing my valet, Bogdan Kowalski. I've also been involved in the deaths of at least seven others. Furthermore, I have a gun in my house. A Beretta M9. If you don't come soon, I don't know what I'm going to do."

"Okay, sir. Okay," the operator said, sounding flustered. "I'm referring your call to my supervising officer."

"Good. I'm hanging up now. I'm going to rest for a while. After that, I'll be sitting on my front step, waiting."

Abe ended the call and spoke to the dial tone.

"Did you hear that? Were you listening?"

Although he didn't expect a response, Abe held his breath. Nothing happened. He breathed out.

"I've held up my end of the bargain, you bastard. You hold up yours."

Moments later, a window appeared in the centre of the computer screen. It opened to reveal the backlit outline of a man with long wavy hair. The bearded arsehole!

God alive!

A green light shone in the top centre of the monitor. Someone had activated the system's built-in camera.

"I heard you, Pedersen," the backlit image said, a smile in his voice. "I'm a man of my word. I've just stood down my team in the

Audi. Call Paul to confirm if you like. I'm sure you have time before the police crash through your front door."

Abe lunged for the phone, but the bastard held up his hand.

"But before you do," the bastard added, "remember this. Don't even think about reneging or pleading diminished responsibility. We'll be watching." He paused again. "We will *always* be watching!"

The window dissolved from the screen as though it had never been there. Abe shuddered. Left hand trembling, he reached for the phone and dialled.

Paul took an age to answer. With each ringtone, Abe expected to hear the approaching wail of police sirens.

Come on, Paul. Answer it.

The phone line clicked.

"Paul?"

"Dad?" Paul gasped. "It's gone. The Audi's just driven off. Are we safe? Are my kids safe?"

"Yes, Paul. You're safe. You're all safe. I promise."

31

Thursday 1st June – DCI Graham Spicer

Shepherdess Walk, Shoreditch, London, UK

DCI Graham Spicer jotted notes into his day pad and listened to the telephoned report in silence.

"...a mini war zone down here, sir," Detective Inspector Callum Hinds said, having to shout over the sirens flooding the background of his call. "A Toyota Hilux is half-buried in the shop front. Broken glass and rubble all over the place. My sergeant's called in a tow truck, but it'll be a while before it can get here."

Callum, one of the more experienced DIs under Spicer's command, sounded more animated than Spicer had heard him in years.

"We've cordoned off a section of Commercial Street and set up a diversion around Shoreditch High Street," he added, "but the traffic's backing up here."

"Do you have enough officers?" Spicer asked.

"I could do with some more bodies for crowd control if you have any. There's a bunch of rubberneckers hanging around getting in the way. More uniforms would come in handy to snaffle any mobile phone footage of the raid. Even a few warm bodies will help."

Spicer added another note.

"We're a little stretched right now, but I'll see what I can do. Meanwhile, do what you can."

"Thank you, sir," Callum said, clearly unimpressed with Spicer's response.

"Three suspects in the bag already, you said?" Spicer asked, deliberately moving the subject along to better news.

"Yes, sir. One's in a bad way. Looks like a shattered kneecap. Nasty, it is, but he was the one brandishing the axe and threatening the crowds. The other two suspects are walking wounded. All are hospital cases. Ambulances are on their way."

Someone shouted something over Callum that Spicer couldn't make out.

"What was that?" he asked.

"Reporters, sir," Callum said. "Bloody morons expect me to stop what I'm doing and give them a fucking interview." Spicer chose to ignore the obscenity Callum added at the end. "They keep asking if we know the name of the 'have-a-go-hero' who foiled the raid."

"And do you?" Spicer asked, without any expectation of a positive response.

"Actually, we do," Callum said.

"You're kidding."

"Nope. He was a customer, and his name is ... Arnold Jeffries. The jeweller, Ms ... hang on, sir. I've written it down." He paused for a moment, presumably to read through his notes. "Ms Gillian Golding. Understandably, she's in shock, but she's been really helpful. She's given us a copy of Jeffries' sales receipt. Lucky for us, the bloke paid by card. Jeffries isn't short of a few quid, either. Wait 'til you see what he paid for the trinket he bought."

"What happened exactly?" Spicer asked.

"Like I said, sir. Jeffries took on the three raiders. By all accounts, the guy was all over the bandits like a ninja warrior. After he wiped the floor with them, he scarpered through the back of the shop. And you won't believe this."

Probably not.

"Tell me."

"We've got the whole thing on the shop's surveillance cameras. Everything, sir. All the action inside and outside. It's ... well, brilliant. Crystal clear, too. Wait 'til you see it."

"Looking forwards to the viewing, Callum. If it's as good as you say, I'll even provide the popcorn."

Callum laughed.

"We have them done up like kippers, sir. All three. Everything we need for a conviction. The CPS will lap it up. Guaranteed. This'll be the sweetest case I've ever worked. All we need are the bikers and we'll have a clean sweep."

"Bikers? What's that about bikers?"

"The getaway drivers, sir. Three scrotes on motorbikes. They scarpered as soon as Jeffries laid out the one with the axe."

Spicer nodded to the blind phone. "Motorbikes. Right. I wondered how they were hoping to clear the scene."

"A bit old school 'smash and grab', but the buggers had it planned down to the second. They'd have been free and clear if Jeffries hadn't waded into action. I'd like to shake the man's hand and offer him a commendation."

"Me too."

"I wonder why he ran?"

"Could be he's special forces. They like to keep their heads down. Or maybe he's shy," Spicer said. "You can ask him when you pick him up for an interview. Okay, colour me intrigued. I'll be there in fifteen, and I'll be bringing some more troops along for the ride."

"Excellent. Thank you, sir."

The second Spicer replaced the handset, the phone burst into life with the intermittent ring of an internal call.

Spicer snatched up the phone.

"Spicer here," he said, warily. "I'm just off out. This had better be important."

"It's Jenny in the Control Room, sir. We've had a call put through from the emergency operator."

"A call," Spicer said flatly, trying not to sound too annoyed or bored.

"It's a strange one, sir," Jenny said. "Interesting."

How could it be as interesting as Callum's ram raid?

"Interesting?" he said, cautious. "In what way, interesting?"

"The caller confessed to having kicked his valet to death. He also claimed to be complicit in the murder of seven others."

His valet? Yeah. Right.

"Listen, Jenny. If this is some kind of a joke designed to wind me up it's in particularly bad taste. You've heard about the ram raid—"

"We have, sir. And we'd never do that, sir. We all know you had the mandatory humour bypass when they made you a DCI ... sir," Jenny said, a smile in her delivery.

"Oh, very funny." Spicer grinned. "Okay, so the caller's likely one sandwich short of a picnic. Did he give his name?"

"Yes, sir. ... Abraham Pedersen."

Spicer stiffened and his level of attention reached the ceiling. Maybe it *did* trump Callum's call.

"Abe Pedersen? Fleur De Lis Road?"

"Yes, sir. Right around the corner from the ram raid. A coincidence, do you think?"

"Probably, Pedersen's no ram raider, but we can't rule it out yet."

"Would you like me to call DI Taylor? He's one of Amazing's targets, isn't he?"

"He is, but there's no need. I'll collect her on my way—assuming she's still around."

"You're going over there?"

"Yes."

"Be careful, sir. Pedersen says there's a gun in the house. A ... Beretta. He claims it's his and he wants to hand it in."

A weapon. Now she tells me.

"Fast track two Trojan Units to the house."

"Yes, sir. Will do."

"Okay, I'm heading out. Do you have Pedersen's phone number?"

"Yes, sir. I've emailed it to your phone along with a recording of the emergency call."

"Thanks, Jenny."

Spicer dropped the handset into its cradle, grabbed his jacket from the hook on the back of the office door, and marched out. In the hall he turned left and barged through the double doors diagonally across from the poky little cupboard that passed for his office. Sparsely populated on account of DI Hinds' mob dealing with the ram raid, the open-plan office echoed to his footsteps. In the far right-hand corner he spotted a familiar figure sitting alone at her desk, and angled his approach to close on her.

He stopped a few metres from her desk, not wanting to crowd her. He'd witnessed far too many of the younger men do that and earn a justified tongue lashing for their pains.

"Working late, Inspector Taylor?" Spicer said. "That's not like you."

Inspector "Amazing" Grace Taylor stopped typing and looked up from her screen. When she caught sight of him, she frowned in apparent annoyance. "Off early again, sir? The privilege of rank, eh?" The frown morphed into a cheeky and highly attractive grin.

"Watch your impudence, Inspector."

"Yes, sir," Grace said, still grinning. "Sorry, sir." She all but added a mock salute.

"What's happening with the Pedersen case?"

Grace's grin faded.

"Nothing, sir. Officially, my team's still working on it, but ..." She shrugged. "We've drawn a big fat zero so far. Why?"

"Nothing?" Spicer asked. He edged closer to her tidier-than-average desk. "Nothing at all?"

A tidy desk demonstrated a tidy mind. At least, that's what he'd always been told. Not that it reflected in the way he kept his own desk, with the piles of paper scattered all over its surface.

Grace hesitated for a moment before answering.

"Plenty of rumour and gossip, but nothing useful or actionable, sir. A couple of weeks ago, when you were on leave, I asked Candy—sorry, I mean Commander Overton, to stump up the funding for a two-week covert obbo on the Pedersen house, but she practically laughed me out of her nice top floor office. Chuffing bean counter." Grace's hand shot up in an instant apology. "Sorry, sir. I know you and the Commander go back a long way, but ... bloody hell. How does she expect me to work with one hand tied behind my back? Do you know how many active cases my team is working on right now?"

Spicer cocked an eyebrow. "Absolutely no idea, Detective Inspector. Do tell."

Grace shook her head, her dark fringe fell into her eyes, and she flicked it away with her little finger. A grin returned, this one edged with embarrassment.

"Sorry, guv. Of course you do."

"I spend half my day pleading the case for more funding, and the other half juggling the lack of resources I already have."

"I hear you, guv. If you don't mind my asking, what's the sudden interest in Abe Pedersen?"

"Ten minutes ago, he phoned 9-9-9 and confessed to murdering his valet."

"He did what?"

Grace shot forwards in her chair. Her hands gripped the edge of her desk as though preparing to jump to her feet.

"You heard. I didn't even know he had a valet. Did you?"

"Yes, sir. Bogdan Kowalski. A rather large Polish gentleman. He's registered as a valet, but he's more like a minder. Uncle Abe killed him? How?"

"No idea. Maybe he shot the man. On the phone Pedersen said he had a gun and wanted to hand it in. Fancy a trip to Fleur De Lis Road?" he asked, pointing towards the exit doors. "I'm heading over there right now."

"Pedersen's gaff? Try stopping me, sir. One moment."

She logged off her computer and grabbed her jacket from the back of her chair.

"Want me to drive, sir?"

"No thanks, Grace. I know all about your driving."

She sighed and shook her head.

"Honestly, I run one patrol car into a brick wall, and no one ever lets me forget it." Again, she rewarded him with a bright smile.

Lord, she was a beauty.

"And no one ever will."

Spicer started walking and Grace caught up with him at the doors.

"We could always jog there," she said. "Fleur De Lis is only around the corner. Not far from the ram raid, in fact. You don't reckon there's a link, do you?"

"That was my first thought, but there's no reason to think so. And as for jogging, not a chance. My jogging days are over." Forever the gentleman, Spicer held open the door and allowed her through first.

Outside, on the landing, Spicer made his way to the fire exit to avoid the unreliable and rickety lifts. Grace hesitated at the head of the stairs.

"Sorry, guv. Do you mind?" She pointed to the toilets. "If I'm going to be standing around in the cold all evening, I'll need the loo first. I can follow you in my car if you don't want to wait."

"No, no. That's okay. I'll see you on the ground floor in ten minutes. I need to stop off at the ops room to assign some more troops. Oh, and do you mind picking up a couple of vests from the stores on the way?"

"Not at all, sir."

They separated at the landing. Grace turned towards the toilets. Spicer pushed through the fire doors and jogged down the stairs. While he liked to play the "doddery old man", he also liked to keep himself fighting fit.

32

Thursday 1st June – Andrew Grantham

Elder Street, Shoreditch, London, UK

Grantham yawned, scrubbed some life into his face, and wiped the grit of sleep from his eyes. Thirty-five minutes and the boss still hadn't called. The drawn-out tension exhausted him, but he'd snap out of it when called into action. Always had in the past. Always would in the future.

He lived for the moment. It didn't happen so often these days, but when it did ... hell, what a rush.

Sirens and flashing blue lights on Commercial Street were the first signs of police activity. Shock rippled through him. He watched them cordon off the far lane of Commercial Street and manage the stalled traffic.

"What the bloody hell's going on?" he asked the empty bedsit, but as usual, it didn't answer.

Grantham stared at the burner phone, willing it to vibrate, but it remained stubbornly silent.

He flicked the power switch on the radio, tuned into LBC, and listened to the non-stop overexcited jabber. The outside broadcast reporters were covering the lead story of the day—a ram raid on a Commercial Street jeweller that had been foiled by a civilian.

Bloody hell.

Just around the corner from Elder Street and he'd missed it.

For a moment, he considered breaking cover and reporting in, but he held off. The boss had told him to await instructions and that's exactly what he would do—at least for the moment.

Ten minutes of frenzied activity later, uniformed cops started running out police tape across either end of Fleur De Lis Road. More cops in hi-vis jackets marshalled pedestrians clear of the pavements.

What the fuck were they doing that for?

Fleur De Lis Road had nothing to do with the ram raid. Had he missed something? Worry reared its ugly head.

Grantham started to feel hemmed in. If the cops caught him with the Ruger ... No, it didn't bear thinking about.

Time to go, Andy.

He stood and started packing up.

The mobile on the side table finally buzzed. He snatched it up and accepted the call without checking the screen. Only three people knew the number, the boss, Herriot, and Rathbone.

"Yes?" he asked, breathless with nervous energy, all signs of fatigue gone.

"Do you see all the police activity?"

"Of course. Could hardly miss it. They've closed off the streets. I was getting worried 'til I listened to the news. It's about the ram raid, yeah?"

"Some is, the rest isn't."

"What?"

"Don't ask questions. Just listen," the boss snarled. "Pedersen's going to be leaving soon. Keep your eyes open. When he shows himself ... do it."

Grantham beamed.

About bloody time.

33

Thursday 1st June – DCI Graham Spicer

Commercial Street, Shoreditch, London, UK

Spicer and Grace were stopped by a uniformed constable manning a temporary road barrier near the junction between Fleur De Lis Road and the much larger Commercial Street. Spicer found a space to park his Volvo behind a police transit van and they climbed out to soak in the scene. Callum Hinds hadn't exaggerated. The place was a war zone.

Dozens of police vehicles, blue lights circling, blocked two ends of Commercial Street. Uniformed officers sweltering in hi-vis jackets marshalled pedestrians, syphoning them away from the crime scene. A set of metal barriers blocked off Fleur de Lis Road from Commercial Street and separated the two scenes. On the offside lane diagonally across from Fleur De Lis, a recovery truck was wrestling with an off-white Toyota Hilux, the front half of which lay buried inside the wreckage of what had been an up-market jewellery shop. Behind the pavement barrier, a crowd of people stood enjoying themselves, pointing their mobile phones at the action.

The heavy boned DI Hinds, together with his partner, the tall and impeccably dressed DS Paulo Dragoni, stood back, watching as the Hilux recovery process destroyed even more of their crime scene. Still, if the surveillance footage and eyewitness testimony turned out half as conclusive as Callum had claimed, losing some of the forensic evidence wouldn't hamper the case too much. Either way the Toyota needed removing and Commercial Street needed reopening as soon as possible. The city's traffic had to flow again, or the career prospects of someone higher up the police food chain than Spicer would take a severe dent.

As Spicer and Grace approached, Callum caught sight of them and mumbled something to Paulo. The Italian shot Grace an appreciative look that was one step short of a leer, and replied out of the corner of his mouth.

Spicer sighed. He could only imagine the hidden conversation. Women as good looking as Grace Taylor had a lot to contend with.

"Hullo, sir," Callum drawled, "you've come just in time. We'll have access to the shop in a few minutes." He nodded at Grace. "Afternoon, Amazing, what are you doing here? Not trying to poach my case, I hope."

His accompanying gentle laugh tried to make it sound like a joke, but the underlying subtext stood out clear enough. Callum was playing the seniority card and might as well have screamed, "Hands off, bitch. This one's a slam dunk and it's all mine."

At his side, Paulo stared at Grace, saying nothing.

"Don't worry, DI Hinds," Grace said, smiling just as sweetly—and just as falsely, "your case is safe. I'm here to help the guv'nor with a much more important matter."

"More important than armed robbery?" Callum scoffed, glancing at Spicer, who allowed the verbal jousting to play out.

"I think arresting a multiple murderer trumps it. Don't you, DCI Spicer?"

Callum dropped his snide smile and turned a pair of shocked, pale blue eyes on Spicer. "Is she serious, guv?"

"Yes, Callum. As it happens, she is," Spicer answered, nodding.

"Who's she talking about?"

"Abraham Pedersen," Grace announced. "My case. Hands off."

"Pedersen?" Callum scoffed. "A murderer? Bugger off."

"That's what he's confessed to," Spicer said. "And mind the language, Detective Inspector Hinds. There are members of the public around."

"Sorry, sir. My mistake." Callum turned to his oppo. "Can you believe this?"

Paulo shrugged. "Pedersen must have blown a fuse."

Callum shot a look over Spicer's shoulder. "He lives over there, doesn't he? Fleur De Lis?"

"That's right," Grace answered, nodding.

"Well, there's your answer," Callum said through a sneer. "All these blue lights have fried Pedersen's circuitry. He's pulling your chain."

"That remains to be seen," Spicer said, "but he's confessed to killing his minder. He also claims to have a handgun in the house, and we have to take it seriously. The Trojan Units will be here soon."

"Crap," Callum muttered.

"Does that mean we have to pull back, sir?" Paulo asked, frowning. "It's a little crowded here, as you can see." He gestured to the crowd hemmed in behind the pavement barrier, although the road itself had finally been cleared of civilian traffic.

"Not necessarily," Spicer said. "You'll have to push the crowds further back though. But we're just about out of sight of Pedersen's house from here so you can continue working unless the Trojan team leader sees it differently."

"Crowd control?" Paulo said, nodding. "I'm on it, sir."

He peeled away and marched towards a uniformed sergeant standing near a metal barrier strung with police "Do not cross" tape. He shouted and waved at the pedestrians. The uniformed sergeant nodded and issued instructions to his officers.

The crowds complained about being herded back, but reluctantly shuffled further away. A man in a white shirt called out, "What's happening?"

"This is a crime scene, sir," the uniformed sergeant answered. "Please step away." He was met with more grumbled complaints.

Spicer returned his attention to Callum.

"Where's the jewellery shop owner, Ms Golding?"

"In the café," Callum answered, pointing to a coffee house four doors along from the destroyed jewellers, and one back from a place that sold mobile phones. "She complained of feeling queasy. Delayed shock, I reckon. I sent her for a coffee and a sit down. Petra's looking after her, sir."

"Good," Grace said. "DC Blackburn knows what she's doing." She smiled and muttered, "Someone in your team has to," under her breath loud enough for Spicer to hear, but not Callum.

"And the suspects?" Spicer asked, scowling at Grace who ought to have known better.

"On their way to St Thomas' A&E, sir," Callum answered. "They're all in cuffs and being guarded by two uniforms a piece. I don't think they'll be in any condition to answer questions for a while, though. Our man, Jeffries, worked them over pretty well, God love him. It'll give us more time to work the scene. The forensics techs are waiting to gain access. Assuming the Trojan boys give us their permission, of course." He sneered, no doubt disgusted at the idea of being prevented from doing his job.

Paulo returned and took up his earlier position alongside his gaffer.

"Oh, and by the way," Callum added, "Paulo's uploaded the surveillance footage to the PNC. I tell you, sir, it's brilliant. Fancy taking a look while we're waiting for the glory boys with their fancy guns to make an appearance? Paulo can run it for you now if you like."

Paulo held up his tablet.

"Thanks, Paulo, but it can wait. Okay, Callum, carry on. I'll be setting up a command post over there if you need me." He jerked a thumb in the general direction of his Volvo.

"Thank you, sir," Callum said. "Mind how you go, Amazing." He slipped her a wink, which she blanked.

Spicer wheeled away from the joker and headed back to his car. Grace followed him, a deep frown showing her annoyance.

"Don't let him get to you, Grace."

"He's a Neanderthal, sir."

"Maybe a little 'old school', but he's a good, solid officer."

She sniffed, but fell silent and matched her pace with his.

Keeping to the shaded side of Commercial Street—the same side as the jeweller's shop—they reached the junction with Fleur De Lis Road and paused long enough to take in the scene.

The black door of Pedersen's house, Number 8, stood closed. No sign yet of the man who claimed to be a mass killer and a diamond smuggler, and who'd promised to sit on the doorstep and wait for the police.

More blue lights and a siren's wail announced the arrival of another ambulance, this one for Pedersen and Kowalski. The uniformed officer at the lead barrier held up his arm. The siren cut off—to the great relief of Spicer's pummelled hearing—and the blue lights stopped rolling. The paramedics didn't look too pleased with the idea of being held up from their duties, but they'd get over it. No way the police could allow them through until the Trojan units had declared the scene safe.

While the green-clad driver spoke into a handheld radio, reporting the delay to his control room, his partner—a man with grapevine tattoos crawling up his neck—opened a plastic lunchbox and pulled out a bread roll. He licked his lips and started munching, making good use of his enforced break. The driver lowered the radio, sat back, closed his eyes, and rested his head against the seat restraint, settling in for the long haul.

"Seen enough?" Spicer asked.

"Yes, sir."

"Good. Let's go."

They crossed the street and marched towards Spicer's Volvo. He pressed a button on his key fob and the tailgate lifted. They removed the ballistic vests that Grace had requisitioned from the armoury and pulled them on over their jackets—Standard Operating Procedure for calls with even the hint of firearms involvement.

"What now, guv?" Grace asked, keeping her voice low, barely audible above the increasing clamour of pedestrians railing against the police pushing them further away from the action.

"Now," Spicer said, "we wait for the cavalry. After that I plan to give Pedersen a call."

"Sounds like a good idea."

"Don't worry, though," Spicer said, grinning, "I'll put it on speaker. Can't have you straining to eavesdrop with all this background racket going on. I'll also call from inside the car. Wouldn't want the media pointing parabolic microphones at us."

"Paranoid much, sir?" She grinned at her own question.

Spicer scanned the gathering mob who were hoping to witness some activity. Anyone with a mobile phone could upload film clips to social media and "go viral" with a video scoop. How many of the same individuals would be affiliates of the world's media?

Bloody people.

Moments later, a pair of Armed Response Vehicles—blue lights flashing and two-tone sirens wailing—screeched to a stop behind the ambulance. They powered down their blues and twos and left a ringing silence in their wake. Doors flew open and three officers dressed in black tactical uniforms and decked head-to-toe in body armour, emerged from each BMW. Tailgates opened and the officers withdrew weapons from gun safes bolted to the floor pans.

An onlooker in the front row of the nearest crowd greeted their arrival with a whoop. The same man tried to start a round of applause, but nobody took up the cause and he lapsed into silence.

One of the firearms officers—heavy-set and boasting a pair of legs so bandy they could only belong to Inspector Rick Jarret—peeled away from the group and jogged towards them. The holster strapped to his left hip held a Glock 19, and he carried his H&K G36C assault rifle at port-arms, its muzzle pointed at the cloudless sky.

Once hidden behind the protective barrier of the Volvo, Jarret lifted the clear visor of his paramilitary helmet and nodded to Spicer and Grace in turn.

A thin film of sweat glistened on his face, and he breathed heavily from his brief exertion. The mass and insulative property of the body armour had its effect on even the fittest of individuals. During a long-ago training course, Spicer had worn the full Trojan battledress—for all of an hour. He'd nearly collapsed under the weight of the stuff and melted under the thermal load. Never again. He had nothing but praise for the men and women of the Specialist Firearms Command, MO19, who wore the kit and walked the walk, day and night—and in all weathers.

"Evening, sir," the grim-faced Jarret said. "Fancy meeting you here."

"Thanks for coming," Spicer said.

"Nothing else important on, sir," Jarret said. He shot Grace a cheery smile, which she returned. "No kittens stuck up trees or little old ladies to help cross busy roads."

Grace sighed and shook her head. On another day and under different circumstances, she might have given him the benefit of an eye roll.

"Busy here, eh?" Jarret said, casting his eyes over the scene and fixing them on the recovery operation. "That's the ram raid, isn't it?"

"Yes, but there's no link between the two shouts. At least, none that we know of. Can you treat them as separate incidents?"

Sweating under the helmet, Jarret rolled his gaze around the scene and bared his teeth in a grimace.

"Complicated, isn't it, sir. Never had a double incident like this before. Are you happy that this scene"—he nodded towards the jewellers shop and the Hilux recovery operation—"is secure?"

"I think so, Rick," Spicer said, mirroring the younger man's grimace. "We're holding the crowds well back, the traffic's already been rerouted, and everything's out of sight of the Pedersen house. Agreed?"

Jarret scanned both scenes some more. Eventually, he nodded.

"It's not ideal, but agreed," Jarret said. "It's not like we can clear the whole area, and we can't hang around all day, either. What do you need, sir?"

"Not sure yet. I was just about to call Pedersen. Do you mind scoping the area out? Consider the best ingress options and then give me your report. We'll chat when I know more."

"On it, sir." Jarret tipped his helmet in salute and returned to his officers, ducking low as he crossed the open gap between the cars.

"Okay, Grace," Spicer said, "with me, please."

34

Thursday 1st June – DCI Graham Spicer

Commercial Street, Shoreditch, London, UK

Back behind the steering wheel of his Volvo, Spicer dialled the number given in Jenny's email. He didn't have to wait long for an answer.

"Hello, who is that?" a man asked. Although well-spoken, his voice trembled, whether from emotion or fatigue, Spicer couldn't tell.

"Abraham Pedersen?" Spicer asked.

"Yes," the man sighed, "that's me."

"Mr Pedersen, this is Detective Chief Inspector Graham Spicer from the Metropolitan Police. Did you call the emergency number a short while ago?"

"I did. Where are you?"

"We're at the junction between Fleur De Lis and Commercial Street."

Pedersen grunted. "You made good time. I expected to have a longer wait."

"Shoreditch police station is only around the corner, sir. And when you mentioned a Beretta M9 it did ramp up the urgency a tad. Your call led me to fast-track the operation."

Pedersen grunted again, although it might have been his version of a tired laugh.

"I rather thought it might. In fact, that was the whole point," Pedersen said.

Interestingly, Pedersen made no mention of the ram raid. He had to be deaf not to have heard the police sirens. Spicer filed the information away for later questioning. At that stage, he had no idea what to make of the man.

"During your emergency call, you said something about a valet."

"Bogdan, yes. You've heard a recording of the call, I imagine?"

"Yes, sir. I have. In the car on the way over here."

"In that case you'll know I confessed to killing him. Along with certain ... other crimes."

"Were you being serious, sir?" Spicer asked, keeping eyes on the Trojan Units.

Jarret and his team stood in a close-knit group near the BMWs, heads bowed deep in tactical conversation.

"Of course I was being serious!" Pedersen barked, showing real emotion for the first time. Anger.

Spicer didn't respond, letting Pedersen take the lead.

"Forgive me, Officer," Pedersen said after a moment. "I didn't mean to snap, but I am a little ... tense. This is a serious matter. As is the rest of it."

"The rest of what, sir?"

"The rest of my statement. I kicked Bogdan to death—"

"Please don't say any more, Mr Pedersen. It would be better if we talked face-to-face. In any event, I advise you not to make a statement until you're under caut—"

"Please listen to me, Officer," Pedersen said, his tone reverting to dull and lifeless. Tired. "I have to tell you this right away. I, Abraham

Pedersen, smuggled conflict diamonds from Africa into the Netherlands, and, apart from killing Bogdan, I am directly involved in the kidnap and murder of at least seven innocent people."

Pedersen sounded lucid, but who confessed to multiple murders over the phone?

"Mr Pedersen, are you alone? Are you being coerced in any way?"

Pedersen breathed in deep and released it in an extended sigh.

"Officer," he said, "apart from Bogdan, whose dead body is festering in the hall in a pool of his own blood and vomit, I am alone. No one is forcing me to do anything, I can assure you. I have had enough of my miserable existence. Enough, I tell you. I've done so many terrible things, my conscience can't take the pressure anymore. Forgive the cliché, but I would like you to lock me up and throw away the key. Please."

God above. The man is a nutcase.

"At this stage, sir, I should caution you—"

"There's no need to bother with that. I formerly waive my right to remain silent and my right to a solicitor. Is that okay? Can I do that?"

Over by the BMWs, Jarret pointed towards the far end of Fleur De Lis Road. A sergeant and two other men jumped into the second BMW and raced away, without lights or sirens.

Where are they off to?

"Well, Officer?" Pedersen asked. "Can I?"

"That is your prerogative, Mr Pedersen, but I still have to read you the caution. I'd prefer to do it in person, though. Face-to-face."

Pedersen sighed again. "Okay, Officer. Have it your way. What happens next?"

"Can you come to the door? We'd rather not have to break our way in."

"That sounds eminently reasonable. I'll hand myself over to you personally, but ..."

Grace shook her head and mouthed, "You can't do that."

Spicer nodded. Regulations would never allow him to step out into the open and expose himself to danger. That's what the Trojan units were created for.

Pedersen groaned yet again. "Excuse me, Officer. I'm in a bit of discomfort ... my hand ..."

"It's broken I understand."

"Yes. Bogdan slammed it in a kitchen drawer, which is one of the reasons I killed him."

"Please, sir. Don't say anything more for now. I need to protect your rights even if you've waived them."

"Okay, okay," Pedersen said, sounding more exhausted with each interaction. "Have it your way. Oh, before I forget. I did ask for an ambulance."

"It's outside the police cordon, sir. We can't let the paramedics through, though. Not when there's a threat of gunfire."

"No. I suppose not. So, how do we do this?"

"You need to open your door and hold up your hands. Make sure we can see that they're both empty."

A grunt ripped down the phone line.

"Don't worry, officer. I'm in no condition to even carry a gun, let alone use it. The weapon is safe in my kitchen at the back of the house. I'll be out shortly. Be patient, though. It might take a few moments. I'm not feeling too sprightly right now. I'm a little unsteady on my feet."

"As quick as you can, sir. There's a bit of a crowd gathering out here."

"I ... can imagine," Pedersen said, and the call clicked into silence.

Spicer hit the red button and slid the mobile into his inner jacket pocket. He turned to Grace.

"You're not seriously thinking of going out there are you, guv?" she asked, stunned disbelief written all over her young face.

"Of course not. I just want him out of the house. Jarret's in charge here until then. What do you make of Pedersen?"

She hitched up one shoulder.

"He sounded lucid enough. I didn't pick up any lunatic vibes off him. In fact, he sounded tired and in pain. And impatient. What did you think? Is he coming out all meek and mild?"

"I hope so. Let's bring the expert back in. Take some advice."

Spicer pushed open his door and slid out of the Volvo into the growing mayhem of an ever-more-teeming Commercial Street. Standing tall, he signalled for Jarret to join them again. The armed inspector cut away from his remaining men and jogged forwards.

"What did Pedersen have to say, sir?" Jarret asked, breathing deeply.

Spicer nodded towards the black door in the middle of the well-maintained terrace.

"He pretty much confirmed what he said during the emergency call," Spicer said. "He claims to have killed his valet, amongst others, and he says there's a gun in the house."

"A nut job, or a lonely old geezer tired of life and seeking a little ... I dunno, excitement?"

Spicer half expected Jarett to use the phrase, "suicide by cop". Thankfully, he reined himself in.

"He came across as lucid but exhausted," Spicer countered, keeping his eyes fixed on the black door some seventy-five metres away. "Hopefully, we'll find out soon enough. Pedersen promised to open the door and give himself up."

"So where is he, then?"

"He's elderly and injured. Give him time." Spicer paused a moment before adding, "I see you've split your troops, Rick. Is there another emergency somewhere?"

"Nothing that trumps this one, sir." Jarret's grim face cracked a thin smile, and he aimed it at Grace. "I sent Sergeant Patel's team to the far end of Fleur De Lis. They should have a good line of sight from over there. Maybe a better one than we have here. They'll be slightly closer, too." He pointed to his large black earpiece and the attached boom mic. "He'll let me know the moment he's in position."

"Right," Spicer said, nodding. "Sounds like a plan. You have a good sightline from here though, right?"

"Definitely. My men will be ready to move as soon has he shows himself, sir."

They fell silent, watching the black door. The time stretched out.

"What's taking him so long?" Jarret muttered. His gaze roved the area, and he puffed out his cheeks. "I hope he opens up soon. It isn't the easiest house to force entry. Satellite imagery rules out a rear entrance. There's no real garden out back, just a small yard, and a full-frontal assault would be dicey since we won't have a chance to clear the neighbouring houses. No telling how many people will be indoors at this time of the evening. In short, if Pedersen doesn't come out, going in after him would be a total 'mare, sir."

"I hear you," Spicer said.

"On the other hand, if he does open the door, we'd have a clear shot. If Pedersen shows any sign of aggression, we could take him out easily enough."

Grace's frown deepened.

"There's a huge audience, sir," she said. "Loads of mobile phones taking videos. We'll be all over the TV news by now."

"Agreed," Spicer said, turning to stare at the shiny black door. "Take up your position, Rick. Be ready to move the moment he makes an appearance."

Jarret dipped his head to Spicer and Grace, and withdrew to his preferred vantage point behind the BMW as the seconds ticked by. Traffic in nearby streets rumbled slowly along, grinding through the gears, and going nowhere fast. Although it approached seven o'clock in the evening, England's capital city remained little more than one step away from gridlock.

Come on, Pedersen. Show yourself.

Another minute ticked past.

And another.

Spicer tried to swallow, but a chalk-dry throat wouldn't cooperate. Sweat dampened his armpits and ran in a line down the middle of his back. He tugged at the front of his vest, trying to pump some cooling air onto his skin. It didn't work.

Halfway down the sunlit side of Fleur De Lis Road, the black door to Number 8 opened inwards. Sunlight glinted on its shiny panels.

At last.

An elderly gent with neatly cropped grey hair, wearing a blood-stained white shirt, dark trousers, and shiny leather shoes, stepped out onto the stoop. He raised his left arm aloft, hand open, fingers splayed wide. The right, he held clamped against his narrow chest. He looked pale and distressed.

Pedersen stopped for a moment, searching both sides of the street. Left and right. He swayed, stretched a steadying left hand towards the doorjamb, and leant against it. Using his arm as a brace, he lowered himself to sit on the single step. His head dropped, his chin sank into his chest, and his shoulders sagged. Slowly, his left hand slid across to cradle the right.

The old man looked shattered, pitiful. Harmless. On the other hand, if his confession turned out to be something other than pure fantasy, that same old man would turn out to be a multiple murderer.

How deceptive looks could be.

Spicer turned to Grace.

"Doesn't look too dangerous, does he?"

Grace shook her head.

"The right hand's a mess, though. Bloodied and swollen to beggary. At least that much of his story's true."

A gunshot boomed, the echo rolling loud around the nearby tall buildings.

Pedersen jerked. His head lifted. Shock registered on his gaunt face. A new patch of red blossomed on his shirtfront—directly above his heart.

A second gunshot cracked. More echoes rolled.

Pedersen jerked again. His head dropped. Slowly, he toppled forwards from the stoop and out onto the pavement. He landed face first, in a crumpled heap.

God above!

A female onlooker screamed. Another howled. The crowd scattered. People ran for cover.

Outside Number 8 Fleur De Lis Road, an elderly man lay bent and still on the pavement. Blood ran from his chest and formed a shallow pool on the pavement around his head.

35

Thursday 1st June – Andrew Grantham

Elder Street, Shoreditch, London, UK

Two shots. Both clean through the heart. The old man couldn't have felt a thing.

Grinning like a fool and tingling with professional satisfaction, Grantham pulled away from the window. He gently lowered the bottom sash and closed the fastening.

"That's the way to do it," he whispered to the Ruger. "Good girl."

Grantham removed the magazine, slid open the Ruger's bolt, confirmed it as unloaded, and tugged on the recessed locking lever. He twisted the barrel anticlockwise a quarter turn and pulled it away from the action sub-assembly in a move he'd practised time and time again. Next, he dropped each half into its cutaway recess in the carry case and zipped the two halves together. With the strap over one shoulder and everything secure, he declared it as a done deal.

From start to finish—firing to takedown and pack away—it had taken less than twenty seconds. The cops outside wouldn't have had time to react, let alone located his sniper's nest and start searching.

Time to wander off. No need to rush. Rushing would only draw attention to himself.

After a quick eyeball to confirm the place as clean and clear, he crossed the room and opened the door a crack. Heart pounding loud in his ears, he held his breath and listened.

Silence.

Grantham pulled the door, popped his head through the wider opening, and checked left and right. Both sides clear. If it hadn't been, his Glock 17 would have dealt with any witnesses. It would have been a pity, he didn't particularly relish the idea of taking out innocent bystanders, but he'd be prepared to pay the price to secure his freedom.

Darwin called it right.

Survival of the fittest—or the better prepared.

Still smiling from the high, he stepped fully out onto the fourth-floor landing and strolled towards the staircase, removing his skin-tight Nitrile gloves along the way.

Whistling tunelessly and holding tight to the case's strap, he skipped down the eight flights of stairs without rushing. On the ground floor, he unlocked the front door and emerged into the cool evening sunlight. He paused in the covered doorway to wait for a gap in the foot traffic.

Outside in the sunshine, he turned left on Commercial Street, heading away from the blue lights, the sirens, and the panicked screams, and ambled along the pavement. No need to hurry. He only had a twenty-minute stroll into work, and he wasn't due in until midnight. It gave him plenty of time to shower, scrub off the gunshot residue, find something to eat, and catch up on some lost sleep.

Perfect.

36

Thursday 1st June – Anthony Simms

Elder Street, Shoreditch, London, UK

The door to Number 8 opened wide, and the old man stumbled through the opening, his left hand reaching for the sky. Slim smiled.
About time.
"Here he comes."
Larry stopped packing his Bergen and approached the window, standing far enough back to avoid being seen.
"Took his time," Larry said, sucking loudly on a boiled sweet that made his breath smell of pear drops. "The cops have been here ages."
"That's what I was thinking," Slim said, scanning the area around the plot.
The police had blocked off either end of Fleur De Lis Road and cleared it of pedestrians and traffic. Either side of their obbo point on Elder Street, windows overlooked the scene, some open, most closed.

"He doesn't exactly look sprightly, does he," Larry added.

He crunched the life out of the pear drop, smacked his lips, and dug a fingernail into his mouth to clear the sticky remains from his teeth. He grabbed a paper bag from the bed, snaffled another sweet, and held the bag up to Slim.

"And that hand looks a mess," Slim said, shaking his head to refuse the offer.

Pedersen slid down the doorjamb and slumped onto the stoop. His shoulders sagged and he looked ready to collapse. A most unhappy bunny.

Slim snorted in disgust. The murderous old man deserved all the pain he had coming. After what had happened to Molly Williams, the captain would have been justified if he'd terminated the bugger outright. Pedersen should think himself grateful to still be drawing breath.

Crack.

Pedersen jerked. A bullet ripped into his chest. He crumpled.

Crack.

A second bullet hole appeared next to the first—above the heart. Slowly, Pedersen toppled forwards and faceplanted onto the paving slabs.

The gunshots echoed around the buildings, muddying the origins.

"Bloody hell!" Slim snapped.

"Sounded like rifle shots."

"Where'd they come from?"

Slim leant closer to the window, tracing the shots' trajectory from the point of impact back to the possible origin. He worked his way left to the adjacent buildings.

Movement!

A window on the fourth floor, five buildings away, slid down. Behind the glass, a pale face and a black metal rod showed briefly. Other windows in the building opened, and people popped their heads through, trying to catch a better view of the show.

"Did you see that?" Slim said.

"What?"

"The window." Slim pointed to his left. "Fourth floor. Fifteen from the left."

"What about it?" Larry asked, drawing his Glock, and racking a bullet into the chamber—a reflex reaction.

"It just closed," Slim said, doing the same with his SIG. "I caught sight of a gun barrel. Looked like a carbine."

"What's the plan?"

"Dunno. What d'you reckon?"

Larry frowned. "I'd love to know who and why. Wouldn't you?"

Slim nodded. "How we gonna do that?"

Larry crunched his sweet. "If I were the sniper, I'd bugger off damn quick before the cops lock this area up tight as a drum and start a house to house."

"Makes sense."

"Let's go," Larry said, moving towards the door. "Leave the Bergens." He jammed the Glock into his shoulder holster and zipped up his jacket.

"Where to?" Slim asked.

"Out front."

"Why?" Slim asked, holstering his SIG and following Larry's lead.

"That building opens onto Commercial Street. Anyone leaving will have to pass us."

Slim smiled at his buddy. While Slim had been doing the majority of the watching, Larry had been scoping the scene not just feeding his face. They stepped out onto the landing and jogged down the stairs, side by side.

"What makes you think he'll pass us?" Slim asked, keeping his voice low.

"If he turns right," Larry said, just as quiet, "he'll be heading towards the police barrier. Why would he do that?" He shrugged. "Worth a go, right?"

They reached the grimy, litter-strewn ground floor, pushed through the main door, and stood on the porch. The single lane of Elder Street led directly onto Commercial Street, which stretched out to their right, running northwest to southeast. Across the road, Quaker Street broke off from the busy Commercial Street. Pedestrians, some running, others walking fast, many jabbering into mobile phones, flowed towards the High Street.

Larry pointed straight ahead.

"Cross the road and stake out Quaker Street in case he heads that way. I'll stay this side."

"Comms open?"

Larry tapped his earpiece three times. The corresponding clicks in Slim's ear confirmed the system's operation.

Slim strode out onto the pavement, dodging the flow of people. He reached the kerb and looked both ways. The near lane ran clear, but traffic on the far lane had ground to a standstill. The road curved around to the right, obscuring the junction with Fleur De Lis. He jogged across the road, sidestepped between two stationary cars, and reached the far side without incident.

Quaker Street curved around to the right, following the route of the railway line. Slim strode out until hidden from Commercial Street, made a three-sixty-degree turn, and retraced his steps, stopping short of the thoroughfare. The stationary traffic provided good cover.

On the other side of the main road, Larry leant against a brick wall. He had his mobile out and occasionally raised his head to look about him in apparent confusion, playing the lost tourist to perfection.

"Charlie One to Charlie Two," Slim said. "I'm in position. Over."

Larry shot him a surreptitious okay signal and kept reading his mobile.

Pedestrian traffic rushing away from the scene slowed to a trickle. People, believing themselves far enough away from the gunfire to be safe, coagulated into small groups, blocking the pavement. They turned to face the way they'd come and started chatting, some into mobiles, others to their neighbours. Distant sirens wailed, signalling the approach of police reinforcements.

"*Charlie Two to Charlie One. Is it time to call the captain? Over.*"

"It was next on my to-do list. Over." Slim tapped the earpiece once. "Charlie One to Alpha One. Come in please. Over."

"*Alpha One to Charlie One,*" the captain responded after a short delay. "*Reading you. Over.*"

"Where are you, sir? Over."

"*On the M1 heading north, to the farm. Why? Over.*"

"Have you been listening to the news, sir? Have you heard? Over."

"*That's a negative, Charlie One. What's happened? Over.*"

"The retired jeweller, sir. He's dead. A sniper got him. Over."

The comms fell silent for a few moments.

"*Are you still on scene? Over,*" the captain asked. It hadn't taken him long to digest the information.

"Yes, sir. I think I saw him. Charlie Two and I want to ... Hold on, sir. Over."

Off to Slim's left, a lone man caught his attention. He strolled along, dodging between the slower-moving pedestrians. A bag dangled from a strap across his shoulder. A rectangular bag large enough to carry a takedown carbine, and heavy, judging by the way it tugged at his clothing, and by the way the man clamped it in place with his left arm.

"Eyes up, Charlie Two. Potential target. Tall, short-cropped, sandy hair. Carrying a shoulder bag. He's passing you ... now. Over."

Part-hidden behind a brick wall, Slim pulled out his mobile, selected the camera app, and zoomed in tight. He took three head-and-shoulders shots of the man and pushed out onto Commercial Street, breaking cover.

"*Got him,*" Larry said, barely moving his lips. "*He's sus alright. Bugger's actually smiling. Ignoring the commotion, too. Not interested in finding out what's going on.*" Head down, Larry waited for the man to pass in front of him and for the gap to stretch out beyond twenty metres before bumping himself away from the wall and dropping in behind, matching Sandy's pace. "*I'll take the first lead. You follow on that side of the road. We'll swap places at the lights. Over.*"

"Copy that, Charlie Two," Slim said. "Alpha One, are you happy for us to follow him? We're on foot. Over."

"Yes, but do not engage. Repeat. Do not engage. Keep the comms open. I'm on my way back to you, and I'll want a running commentary. Over."

"Roger that, Alpha One. Over."

At the traffic lights, Sandy used the pelican crossing to reach Great Eastern Street and strode out, increasing his pace. The rectangular bag bounced against his left hip. Slim and Larry followed on either side of the road, keeping well back.

Half a mile into the tail, Sandy stopped at another crossing and swapped the bag from his left to his right shoulder. Poor man must have been weighed down by the mass of the rifle, if not the moral weight of the kill.

They followed at an appropriate distance, swapping places regularly and occasionally staying together to change their visual profiles. As the captain instructed, Slim kept up the commentary the whole way.

"Alpha One, we've reached Old Street. Sandy's entered a Burger Bar. Killing the retired jeweller must have given him an appetite. There's a pub next door. Charlie Two and I'll pop in for a swift half. Not many pedestrians around, we'll stand out if we stay in the open. We can keep eyes on through the pub windows. Over."

Slim and Larry ducked into the busy pub and stood in the crush waiting to be served until Sandy passed by the pub, chewing on a fat bun that dripped grease onto the front of his dark top. They allowed him a few seconds to wander off before exiting the bar, unserved, and dropped back onto the trail.

They crossed the street to join City Road and carried on, side-by-side. Slim made it look as though he was leading a one-sided conversation, Larry nodding occasionally to reinforce the impression. Ahead, Sandy finished his burger, crumpled the wrapper into a ball, and tossed it into the gutter.

"Naughty, naughty," Larry said, speaking for the first time since starting the tail.

"*What was that, Charlie Two? Over.*"

"Sorry, sir. Sandy's not only a killer, but he's a litter lout. He's just thrown his burger wrapper in the street. Walked right past a litter bin, too. There's no need for that. Over."

Slim grinned and shook his head.

"We've reached the junction with Baldwin Street, sir," Slim announced. "Won't be long now, I reckon. Over."

"How'd you work that out?" Larry asked, shooting Slim a sideways glance.

"*Yes, Charlie One. Do tell. Over.*"

Slim smiled at the audience. Although justifiably proud of it, he didn't often have the chance to show off his deductive reasoning.

"Well, look at it this way. Sandy hasn't hailed a cab, he's walked past a couple of dozen bus stops, and at least two underground stations. We've just passed Old Street Underground, sir. Unless he's got a car parked around here somewhere—and he's ignored two NCPs already—I reckon he's close to home. Certainly within easy walking distance. Over."

"*Sounds like a reasonable assumption to me. Over.*"

"Me too," Larry said, shooting him a wink. "Nice work, Sherlock. You should've been a detective."

"Nah," Slim said, smiling. "I applied to join the cops but failed the physical." He pointed to his walking boots. "Don't have flat enough feet."

"So," Larry said, "the Marines were your second choice?"

"Third," Slim piped up. "The fire service rejected me, too."

They carried on, two old mates enjoying the stroll.

"Alpha One," Slim said after a few moments' silence, "we're still on City Road, heading northwest. Sandy's waiting at the crossing at the junction with Bath Street, heading for … He's heading into Shepherdess Walk, sir. Hang on, he's turning around. Checking his six for the first time since we picked him up. We're going to carry on past. Over."

"See that café?" Larry said, pointing ahead and speaking up loud enough for Sandy to hear if he chose to. "All day breakfasts, it says. I'm starving, me. Let's go."

"Sounds like a plan," Slim answered, rubbing his hands together. "I'm with you, mate."

Without crossing the road, they carried on. Sandy didn't so much as glance at them, but turned right and marched along Shepherdess Walk.

Once out of sight, Slim and Larry crossed the road, dodging the slow-moving traffic. They doubled back on themselves and turned left into Shepherdess Walk in time to see Sandy pass The Eagle pub and climb a set of steps leading up to a five-storey building whose walls had once been white, but the passage of years and the accumulation of city grime had faded them to a dirty grey.

Protected by a set of blue railings, the steps led up to a flat landing area and beyond that, dipped down into a wheelchair-friendly ramp. Sandy stopped at the main doorway, took a plastic card from a back pocket of his jeans, and slotted it into a card-reader built into the brickwork. The metal-and-glass door popped open. Sandy stepped aside to allow a man wearing a dark blue uniform out first. They exchanged a few words of greeting before the uniform marched off and Sandy ducked inside.

"Bugger me!" Larry said.

"Report, please. What's happening? Over."

"It's Sandy, sir," Slim said, hardly able to believe his eyes. "He's just let himself into Shoreditch Police Station. He's a bloody cop!"

37

Thursday 1st June – Early Evening

Shepherdess Walk, Hoxton, London, UK

Packed nearly to the rafters with boisterous customers, *The Eagle* had all the charm and character of any city centre pub and tried hard to be all things to all people. It served half-decent pub grub and offered keg ale from a local micro-brewery along with the usual assortment of lagers, wines, and spirits. It didn't serve cocktails. Its red-and-gold flock wallpaper, polished oak bar, and ceiling supported by black, cast-iron columns, gave it an authentic atmosphere.

Kaine sat at one of the few empty tables with his back to the wall, facing out and giving himself the best view of the crowd. He left half his chips and the tail of his cod, pushed his plate away, and sipped his alcohol-free beer, waiting for Slim and Larry to finish. Larry had ordered an extra-large portion—fish, chips, and mushy peas—and packed it away with ease, while Slim vacuumed up his steak-and-ale pie and mash. They downed cutlery at the same time and leant back in unison. Thankfully, neither belched.

Kaine waited until their waiter had cleared their plates and taken their dessert orders—coffee for all three, and a Belgian chocolate brownie and vanilla ice cream for Larry—before continuing the debrief.

"So," he said, looking at Slim, "how sure are you that Sandy's the sniper?" He had to speak up to make himself heard.

"One hundred ... well, ninety-five percent."

"Why?"

Slim glanced at Larry before answering. "We didn't actually see him pull the trigger."

"No, I mean why are you so certain."

"Ah, I see." Slim looked up and his face creased as he searched his memory. "If you'd been there you'd know. His reaction was so different from everyone else's. I mean, people were running scared. Panicked from the shooting, but Sandy ignored everyone and simply walked off as though nothing was happening."

"And he was smiling, don't forget," Larry said, eyes roving in search of the waiter with his dessert.

"I didn't actually see him smile," Slim said. "Too far away. And he had the shoulder bag. Okay, he'd removed the badge, but it looked suspiciously like a Ruger takedown case to me. Heavy enough, too."

Kaine pursed his lips, still needing a convincer.

Slim leant further forwards, urgency written on his rugged face.

"And now we know he's a—"

Slim broke off when the coffees and Larry's dessert arrived and held off until the waiter left with Larry's heartfelt thanks. He tucked into his brownie as though he hadn't eaten in a week.

Where on earth does he put it?

"As I was saying," Slim continued. "Now we know Sandy's a rozzer, I'm even more certain. In fact, I'll revise my estimate up to ninety-eight percent."

"Again, why?" Kaine asked.

"Well, sir. Think about it. There's a load of cops blocking off a couple of streets. Blue lights are flashing. Sirens are wailing. Shots have been fired. A man's just been murdered, and there's blood pumping all over the pavement. Sandy might not have seen anything, but he'd have been aware of the people running, so what does he do?" His voice started to rise. "Does he go and investigate? Does he try to find out if any of his cop buddies have been hurt? Does he offer his help? Does he bollocks."

Kaine frowned and patted his hand in the air over the table.

Slim cast his eyes around the pub to make sure none of the nearby customers were listening. The crowd just kept on eating, drinking, and chatting. In the far corner a lone punter, beer in one hand, continually fed coins into a flickering slot machine. Stern-faced, he didn't seem to be enjoying the process.

"Sorry, sir," Slim said, lowering his voice. "Anyway, Sandy doesn't do any of those things. Instead, he heads off in the opposite direction like nothing's happened. That's right, isn't it, Larry?"

Larry pushed the final piece of ice-cream-covered brownie into his mouth and nodded.

"S'right," he said, after swallowing the mouthful. "I'm with Slim, sir. Sandy's the shooter alright. Little doubt about it."

Kaine was inclined to agree with Slim's interpretation of Sandy's actions. A decent cop would never turn his back on fellow officers. It worked the same way in all the tight-knit uniformed services. People had each other's backs. Without such support, people died and the whole system fell apart.

"It begs the question," Slim said.

"Just the one?" Larry asked, turning to face his mate.

"Okay," Slim said, "it begs a load of questions, then. But first is." He took a breath. "What are we going to do about it, sir?"

"Give me your thoughts," Kaine said, keen for input from men whose judgement he trusted.

Larry and Slim exchanged glances, but remained silent.

"C'mon guys. I want your opinion. Slim?"

Slim raised his powerful shoulders and let them fall.

"To be honest," he said, "I'm not sure I give a damn, sir. Does it matter that Pedersen's dead? I mean, the old man had it coming after all."

"But we've uncovered a dirty cop," Larry announced.

"So what?" Slim asked. "He won't be the only one, and it's not our job to clean up the Met. And anyway, Sandy won't have been working alone."

"What makes you say that?" Larry asked, a slow frown deepening the creases on his brow.

"Stands to reason. How could Sandy have known Pedersen was planning to fess up? Someone must have told him. Someone else must have been worried that Pedersen was going to drop them in the crapper."

Kaine nodded and held up a hand.

"Okay, points taken. Would you like my thoughts?"

Slim and Larry nodded, again working as a unit.

Kaine sipped his coffee. Nice and strong, it gave him an instant and pleasant buzz.

"I'd like to know who sent Sandy to Elder Street in the first place. He had to have been there before my visit. I'd also like to know *why* Sandy shot Pedersen."

"Isn't that obvious, sir?" Slim said, pulling a face that suggested Kaine had missed something simple. "Someone wanted to shut him up. Right?"

"Why?"

"Because Pedersen had information the dirty cops didn't want exposed?" Larry suggested.

"For example?" Kaine asked, hoping they'd see things the way he did.

"Their identities, of course. They couldn't risk exposure."

"Because?" Kaine rolled his hand forwards in encouragement.

"They were partners?" Larry suggested.

"Which means they were culpable in Molly Williams' murder," Slim announced. He nodded, finally getting the message. "Which means we have to take them down. Right? This comes down to protecting the 83. Retribution for Molly's death?"

"Not quite," Kaine said. He dug a thumb into his chest. "*I* have to take them down, not *we*. God knows where this is going to end up. I'll be facing an unknown number of corrupt police officers and I can't ask you to help. It's too dangerous."

Slim arched an eyebrow. "More dangerous than facing down a village full of heavily armed insurgents, sir? I don't think so."

"Nonetheless," Kaine said, making ready to pull rank, "I can't let you—"

His earpiece clicked and he broke off.

"*Whatcha, Mr K and Team Charlie. How's you all diddling?*" Corky said, as irrepressible as usual.

Slim and Larry shared another quick glance but said nothing.

"Evening, Control. What do you have? Over."

"*Corky's identified Sandy, Mr K. Would you like to know how?*"

Not really.

"Yes please, Control. Over." Humouring Corky usually worked well, and Kaine would never want to offend the volunteer genius.

"*Corky accessed the Met Police's HR files and compared the photo IDs with the slightly out of focus shots Mr S took. ... Sorry, Mr S, but it had to be said.*"

"I was working on the fly, Control," Slim said, clearly put out by the insult to his skills with a mobile phone camera. "Over."

"*Corky's just messing with you, Mr S,*" he chuckled. "*Kidding, he is. Anyway, Sandy's none other than Detective Sergeant Andrew Grantham of the Metropolitan Police Service. Just been promoted, too. Works out of the Shoreditch copshop. He's part of the Met's Serious Crime Unit. His immediate boss is Detective Inspector Grace Taylor. Grantham is divorced. No kids. Parents deceased. Lives on his own in Wanstead. Corky's got his home address if you want to pay him a visit.*"

"That's a distinct possibility, Control," Kaine said. "Can you text me the details, I'll pick it up later. Over."

"*On its way, Mr K. And, by the way, Grantham's currently working the graveyard shift—midnight to eight.*"

"Now," Kaine said, "that *is* interesting. Over."

"*Corky thought you'd see it that way. Cheery bye, folks.*"

The earpiece clicked inactive. Slim shot Kaine a wry grin and shook his head.

"It won't work."

"What won't?"

"You're not ditching us, sir. We're in this with you all the way. Aren't we, Larry?"

Larry nodded and the waiter returned with the bill and a saucer with half a dozen foil-wrapped chocolates. Kaine paid with Arnold Jeffries' platinum charge card and added a tenner in cash for the tip. Larry pointed to the chocolates and looked at each of them in turn. After Kaine and Slim shook their heads, he grabbed them all and dropped them into his jacket pocket.

"Might have the munchies later," he said by way of an unnecessary explanation.

"Gannet," Slim muttered, stating the obvious.

Kaine's mobile buzzed with Corky's incoming text. He opened it and scan-read the tightly packed message, which contained Grantham's home address and a copy of his police personnel file.

Kaine reached for his coffee and took another sip.

The main door opened, grabbing Kaine's attention. A tall, slim-built man with hair the colour of wet sand pushed into the pub ahead of two other men—one short and wide, the other of average height with a mop of fair hair badly in need of a trim. All three were dressed in suits that positively screamed "plain-clothes police officers". He led the way to the last empty table in the pub. A card sticking up from a tripod stand in the middle of the table bore the word, "Reserved".

"It's Sandy!" Slim whispered, hiding his mouth behind his raised coffee mug.

"Yep," Larry added, nodding. He picked up his coffee and sipped. "Definitely."

They turned their backs to the table, leaving Kaine to act as commentator.

"They look pleased with themselves. It's a celebration. The other two are backslapping Grantham. The tubby one's gone to the bar.

He's buying. If we're right about Grantham being the sniper, this might be his reward for a job well done."

"We *are* right, sir," Slim said. "I'd put money on it."

Larry nodded his agreement.

Tubby returned to the table carrying a tray with three pints of beer and four shot glasses of whisky—expensive whisky going by the label on the bottle the barman had poured from. Police officers drinking beer and whisky chasers? Could they have been more clichéd? Tubby placed the tray in the middle of the table and the others helped themselves. They left the fourth shot glass untouched.

"They're expecting company," Kaine said, trying not to stare and barely moving his lips.

Grantham downed his shot in one, raised his pint glass in a toast, and said something. The background hubbub drowned out what he said, but his words drew loud guffaws from Tubby and his mate, Shaggy.

"Brazen, isn't he?" Larry said, after shooting a covert glance over his shoulder.

"What do you mean?" Kaine asked.

"Sandy ... I mean, Grantham, just admitted to killing Pedersen."

"He did?"

Kaine had almost forgotten about Larry's ability to lipread.

Larry nodded. "That was the gist of it. What he actually said was, 'Here's to the old man. May he rot in hell.' Then he added, 'We dodged a bullet there—unlike the old bugger.' That's what had the other two in fits."

"Such a charmer," Slim said.

The entrance door opened again and a striking woman in a well-cut trouser suit entered. The three celebrating detectives fell quiet. The woman stood near the door and scanned the bar, checking her perimeter before approaching the table. She wore her long dark hair parted in the middle and didn't feel the need for makeup. She ignored the appreciative stares of half the male customers in the pub—the other half probably hadn't caught her dramatic entrance—and headed straight for the reserved table.

"That'll be DI Grace Taylor, then," Slim said. "Makes a bit of an entrance, doesn't she?"

"Fine-looking woman," Larry agreed. "Pity she's dirty."

Slim scratched his chin. "Can't be so sure about that. Did you see the way the Three Amigos reacted when she arrived? Maybe she's clean."

After a moment standing over the table, glowering at the men, Taylor lowered herself onto the empty part of the bench seat close to Grantham and grinned. She punched his arm, reached for her shot glass, and held it up. Her drinking companions relaxed and listened to a second toast. Tubby and Shaggy tilted their glasses to Grantham, shouted, "To Andy", and drank.

"What did she say?" Kaine asked Larry.

"Nothing much. She just said, 'To Andy and a job well done.'"

"I reckon that's a clincher, eh?" Slim said, draining his coffee and lowering the cup to its saucer. "She's the Queen Bee and those buggers are her drones." Slim shuddered.

"What's wrong?" Larry asked.

"You know what happens to drone bees who mate with their queen, yeah?"

"No," Larry said. "Do tell."

Slim shook his head. "Look it up, mate. It'll make your eyes water."

Kaine had to agree with Slim about the eye-watering part.

Still shooting surreptitious glances at Grantham's table, Larry pulled out his mobile and ran a search. A few moments later he took his turn to shudder.

"I see what you mean. Nasty."

Fifteen minutes and another round of drinks later, the front door opened again, and a man entered, this one older, tired-looking. He spotted the four at the table and nodded a greeting. Grace and the others nodded back. It seemed friendly enough, but the atmosphere at the table had cooled, and the smiles had disappeared.

"Eyes up," Kaine said. "Who's this?"

The latest arrival headed to the bar, ordered himself half an orange juice and lemonade, and carried it to the table in the corner. When his back had been turned, Grace slid away from Grantham, distancing herself from her subordinate. The older man took one of two empty chairs left at the table.

Grace said something and the new arrival replied.

"What are they saying?" Kaine asked Larry.

"She just greeted him. Called him 'guv', sir," Larry answered. "Couldn't see the older guy's response, but she said they were celebrating Grantham's promotion before he starts his night shift."

The older man nodded, sipped his soft drink, and lowered his glass to the table. He leant to one side, took out his wallet, and slapped a couple of twenties on the table in front of Grantham.

"He's side on to me, sir," Larry said. "I can't read what he's saying, but Grantham's just thanked him."

Grantham said something to the guv'nor. His nodded reply made Grantham's smile widen, and he knocked back the remains of his beer.

"Cheeky bugger," Larry said.

"Go on, Larry," Slim said, frowning to show his impatience. "Don't keep it to yourself."

Larry lowered his head and held up his hand to hide his face. "Grantham just asked the guv'nor if he could come off nights to help in the Pedersen investigation. He gave him the okay, but said he can't swap shifts tonight since it's too short notice. Grantham seems happy about it, doesn't he."

Grantham snatched the banknotes up from the table and pointed to the older man's drink. Guv'nor placed his hand over his glass and shook his head. Grantham nodded and made his way to the bar.

"Look at that," Slim said. "That'll be the bugger's third pint."

"Plus that whisky chaser," Larry added.

"Yeah," Slim said, nodding. "The sod doesn't mind being over the drink-drive limit at the start of his nightshift."

"Grantham's a killer," Larry said, peeling back his lips into a sneer. "Must think the rules don't apply to him."

"I'm surprised the old boy doesn't say something. I didn't think the Met put up with boozing at work anymore. I mean, this isn't the seventies." Slim snorted. "Hang on, my mistake. I take it all back."

Grantham returned to the table with a fresh tray of drinks—two beers, one small whisky, and a tall glass of lemonade with ice and a slice. He set the tray down, picked up his glass, and took a tiny sip. After swallowing, he twisted his lips and said something that elicited a howl of laughter from his buddies. Grace and Guv'nor kept quiet.

A few minutes later, Guv'nor pushed himself to his feet. He said his goodbyes to Grace, nodded to each man in turn, and shook Grantham's hand. They waited for him to leave before Grantham broke the silence.

Larry gave the translation. "Grantham said he thought the old bugger would never go, and Grace told him off for being so insubordinate."

The three men roared, and Grace granted them a thin smile. She lifted her glass to her lips and sipped while scanning the bar, her eyes wary, never still. Her scrutiny reached Kaine, and he met her gaze full on rather than look away. She held his stare for a moment, then returned her attention to her team. She said something to Grantham, who nodded, sighed, and pushed his glass away.

"She's just given him his marching orders, sir," Larry announced.

Grantham stood, gave the table a theatrical bow, and left. Shaggy and Tubby cheered his departure.

Kaine read the time from the clock over the bar, 22:30. Fifteen minutes ahead of last orders. He drank the last of his coffee and set the cup down on the saucer. "Finish up, lads. I've heard enough, and I have somewhere else to be."

"*You* have somewhere to be, sir? What about us?" Slim asked, pushing his empty coffee cup and saucer away.

"I'm standing you and Larry down," Kaine said. "I won't need you for the next phase."

"Are you sure, sir?" Slim asked. "We'll be happy to watch your six. Won't we, Larry."

"Yes, sir."

Kaine shook his head. "Too many cooks. You've done a great job, but it's time to put your feet up for a while. Book a hotel in town for the night. I'll call you if and when I need you."

"If you say so, sir," Slim said, showing some reluctance to leave.

Larry side-punched Slim's thigh and stood.

"C'mon, Slim. We've been dismissed."

Slim climbed to his feet and dipped his head to Kaine. "Good hunting, sir."

"Thanks," Kaine said. "Head out the back way, I'll give it a minute."

Kaine waved them off and sat back, fiddling with his mobile. A few minutes later, he grabbed his jacket from the back of his chair, and headed for the front doors. He passed close to the table full of dirty cops—close enough to catch Grace Taylor's eye again. He shot her a pleasant smile and added a wink. She didn't return either.

38

Friday 2nd June – Andrew Grantham

Gordon Lane, Wanstead, London, UK

Grantham yawned inside his motorbike helmet, eased off on the throttle, and thumbed the indicator. He took the slip road off the A12 and hugged the inside lane, following the signs to Woodford.

Cars raced past him on the outside lane, but he took his time, keeping well inside the speed limit. Just because he rode a powerful bike didn't mean he had to thrash the life out of it. Being caught speeding again wouldn't go down well with the boss. Without his driving licence, he'd be forced out of the unit, and that wouldn't do his retirement plan any good at all. Besides, he'd find it difficult to explain away the contents of his Ruger case to an inquisitive traffic cop.

He kept veering left until reaching the junction with Lonsdale Avenue and finally made it onto Cambridge Park Road.

Nearly there.

For once, he beat the lights at the junction and made an immediate left turn into Gordon Lane.

He'd finally get some proper sleep in his own king-sized bed with its wonderful memory foam mattress. Bliss. With Pedersen in the chiller, there'd be no more extra-curricular obbos for a while.

He cancelled the indicator and cruised straight onto his new driveway. Laid in a herringbone pattern, the pavers looked the business. His next-door neighbours, the actual Joneses, had been impressed enough to book the same team of builders for their own new drive. Not for the first time, Grantham snorted at the idea of the Joneses keeping up with their neighbour. He kicked out the side stand, leant the Kawasaki over, and climbed off.

Grantham arched the ache out of his lower back and settled the Ruger case more comfortably on his shoulder. He'd been rushed off his feet all night dealing with a double stabbing near Old Street underground station. As a result he hadn't been able to slope off home to clean the rifle. That wouldn't do. He didn't want the barrel to start pitting.

Grantham stamped some life into his legs. He'd only had the Kawasaki a few weeks. It would take a few more miles to get used to its more crunched-up ride. Still, with summer on the horizon, he'd have plenty of time for that.

Grantham opened the up-and-over garage door and wheeled the bike into the darkened interior. He heaved it onto its centre stand, removed his gloves and helmet, and locked them inside the top box. After wrapping the anchored, canvas-covered chain around the rear wheel twice and padlocking it in position, he finally felt happy enough to close and lock the garage door from the inside. He shrugged the case from his shoulder and locked it in the gun safe under his workbench, ready for later. Then he unzipped his armoured leather jacket and hung it on the designated hook next to the personnel door leading into the utility room—making sure to tug the folds out of his sleeves and hang it properly. Grantham hated it when things looked untidy. He unlocked the personnel door, stepped into his utility room, and dropped the keys into the designated key drawer.

His comfy bed beckoned, but he'd need a shower to wash off the work's grime. In his whole life, he'd never once had a decent sleep without first taking a shower.

He kicked off his boots, set them to one side, and walked into the kitchen in his socks—the ceramic tiled floor cooled his feet. The kettle's siren call made him stop. He couldn't ignore it.

Why not?

No amount of coffee was going to keep him awake after the day and night he'd been through, and he deserved a decent brew.

"Go for it, Andy."

He filled the kettle with just enough cold water for a single large mug. Couldn't waste electricity. The planet needed saving.

Five minutes later, raking his fingers through his helmet hair, he walked his sugar-free coffee through the kitchen and into the lounge. He set the mug down on its coaster, dropped into his favourite armchair in front of the TV, and reached for the remote.

"Drop the remote, Andy."

A man's quiet voice. Behind him.

Grantham shot to his feet. Spun. His heart lurched.

A bearded man stood in the open doorway, a semi-automatic pistol—a SIG—held steady in his right hand. A SIG pointed at Grantham's chest.

Shit! Oh fucking shit.

A slow smile stretched the man's thin lips.

"We don't need the TV," the bearded man said, speaking softly.

Grantham's heart lurched again, then started racing.

"Who the fuck are you?" he snarled.

"Shut up, Andy. I'll be asking the questions."

Christ! The fucker knows my name.

Grantham clamped his jaws together.

"That's better," the man said. "We don't need to make too much noise. Wouldn't want to disturb the neighbours, now, would we. Although the Joneses next door are both out at work, of course. She's a teacher at Wanstead High School, and he works in the city. A hedge fund manager. A real highflyer is Jeremy Jones."

Christ. He knows everything. Everything.

Grantham swallowed. Tried to hide his shock, but it must have shown on his face. He opened his hands and held them out from his side.

The smiling man with salt-and-pepper hair and white-flecked beard jerked the SIG's muzzle up. A signal. Grantham raised his hands and uncurled his fingers.

Sweat formed under his arms, rolled down his forehead, and stung his eyes. He breathed deep, trying to tamp down the anger and compress the fear. Adrenaline surged through his system, but he couldn't run, couldn't fight. To do either would be suicide. So, he stood still, hands raised in pitiful surrender, and he waited, desperate to empty his bladder.

The gunman stepped through the doorway and entered the front room.

"Sit," he barked. "Now."

Grantham hesitated, and the bearded man jerked the SIG towards his favourite chair.

"Do it, Andy. I don't want to kneecap you, but I will if I have to." He lowered his aim.

Grantham tensed his thigh and his right kneecap bounced involuntarily, ahead of the bullet's knee-shattering impact. He turned his back to the man and lowered himself into the chair. The soft upholstery engulfed him.

Oh God. I'm dead. I'm dead!

Grantham closed his eyes and waited for the bullet to the back of his head.

Metal scraped on cloth. The bastard was preparing to shoot!

Shit!

Something cold touched his neck. Multiple rapid clicks followed. Power surged. Every muscle in Grantham's body tensed. Fingers and toes clenched. His stomach cramped. Pain ripped through him.

Light faded.

39

Friday 2nd June – Morning

Gordon Lane, Wanstead, London, UK

Kaine pulled the trigger and held it down for three seconds. The stun gun clicked and drove thousands of volts of electricity into Grantham's neck. He flapped, grunted, strained. His legs shot straight out from the chair, his arms clenched tight into his chest, and his whole body tensed. Spittle flew, and the smell of burning flesh hit Kaine's nostrils. A dark patch spread across Grantham's lap.

He released the trigger and withdrew the gun.

Grantham flopped back into the chair, panting, groaning. Sweat glistened on his face and his bare arms.

Kaine allowed him thirty seconds to recover before speaking.

"That was a three-second count," he said.

"Bastard," Grantham gasped. "You fucking—"

Kaine leant in and repeated the cycle. This time, he counted to five before releasing the trigger.

Recovery took a little longer. Kaine allowed him another thirty seconds. Grantham gasped and gagged the whole time.

"That was a five-second burst," Kaine said, "but I imagine it felt much longer."

"Bastard," Grantham repeated, with less force.

The third burst lasted as long as the first—three endless seconds. Kaine granted the killer cop a full minute for the pain to ease before pressing the gun to Grantham's sweat-slicked neck.

"Stop," Grantham sobbed. "Please ... no ... no more."

Kaine pressed the electrodes harder into the soft flesh of the trembling man's neck. Grantham tried to pull away, but Kaine followed his movement and kept the pressure on.

"I can keep this up for ages," Kaine drawled. "Are you going to co-operate?"

Grantham nodded.

"Y-Yes," he cried. "God ... please stop."

Kaine yanked the gun away and stood up straight. He dropped a heavy-duty cable tie into the man's sodden lap.

"Tie your wrists together and pull it tight with your teeth. Properly tight. I'll check."

Grantham complied, but his fingers trembled so much it took him three attempts to feed the tail into the ratchet head, loop it around his wrists, and tug enough tension into the tie.

"Hold up your hands." Kaine tested the bindings. They held enough tension for the plastic to dig into the flesh around Grantham's wrists. "Well done, Andy. Now we're getting somewhere. Stand up."

Grantham shook his head.

"I-I don't think I can."

Kaine leant forwards and touched the electrodes to Grantham's shoulder. He yelped, shot to his feet, and stood, swaying, hands held low in front of his groin. His face carried a definite shade of green.

"Don't try playing me, Andy," Kaine said, raising the stun gun, and stretching out another smile. "There's plenty of charge left in this little beauty for me to have hours of fun. Of course, that all depends on how strong your heart is. I've read that multiple shocks can stop the heart. A few people have died under that much strain. Let's make sure it doesn't come to that, shall we?"

Chest still heaving, Grantham hung his head. Whether in defeat or shame, Kaine couldn't tell and didn't really care. Dirty cops were amongst the lowest of the low, and dirty killer cops were the lowest of all.

"Garage," Kaine barked.

Grantham's head snapped up and a questioning frown creased his forehead.

Kaine drew the SIG from its shoulder holster.

"In case you forget who's giving the orders. Go on, move."

The killer cop staggered forwards on weak and trembling legs and worked his way through the kitchen and utility room. By the time they reached the garage, his legs had recovered a little. Although stiff, they seemed to be working well enough.

Grantham stopped at the Kawasaki, but Kaine slammed the meat of his free hand between Grantham's shoulder blades and pushed him towards the back of the garage—the end with the very well-equipped machinist's workshop. Taking care to keep his back to the garage door, Kaine grabbed Grantham's shoulder and spun him around to face front.

"Sit," he ordered, deepening his voice.

Grantham looked around him.

"Where?"

"On the floor and scoot next to the leg of your workbench."

"What?"

By the time Kaine drew the stun gun from his pocket again, Grantham had hit the deck, squirmed to his left, and leant his back against the solid metal leg of his heavy-duty steel workbench. The bench's leg had been securely bolted into the concrete floor. It would take a socket wrench and unbound hands to free it. Kaine had confirmed its status during his overnight search of the house and garage.

"That's better," Kaine said. "Not particularly comfortable, I imagine, but it won't be for long." Kaine smiled through the lie. "You can ask questions if you like, but please keep your voice down. The neighbours don't need to know our business."

"Wh-Who are you?" Grantham asked. He spoke quietly and craned his neck to look up from the spotless concrete floor.

One thing in Grantham's favour. He did keep his billet and garage tidy. A place for everything and everything in its place. The workshop end of the garage contained all the equipment necessary to strip down and rebuild any number of small weapons.

"Don't you recognise me?" Kaine asked, opening a wall cupboard, and removing one of the six haulier's ratchet straps lined up neatly on the lower shelf.

Grantham frowned and shook his head.

"Sh-Should I?"

"Oh dear. I am disappointed. I imagined I'd have made more of an impression. Try to picture me wearing a blue baseball cap."

Slowly, recognition revealed itself on Grantham's expressive face.

"Pedersen's house," he spouted, eyes wide, staring. "The delivery man. It was you!"

Kaine gave a little half bow. "Got it in one. Well done."

The last lingering trace of doubt Kaine had regarding Grantham's guilt melted away with the recognition.

"You killed Bogdan," Grantham said, a statement, not a question.

"Nope. The valet was very much alive when I left the house. Not particularly happy with himself, but alive. Pedersen killed him. Kicked him to death. Haven't you heard the recorded confession?"

Grantham nodded.

"'Course I heard it, but didn't believe it. Not at the time. Wh-What do you want with me?"

Kaine tilted his head to one side and smiled. "Patience, Andy. I'll come to that."

He unfurled the ratchet strap and dropped it into Grantham's damp lap, which had dried a little with his body heat and had started to smell.

"Now," Kaine said, "here's how this is going to work. To save me the effort, you're going to wrap the strap around your chest and the bench leg. After that, you'll feed the tail into the ratchet head, and tighten it. And I'm going to give you a full thirty seconds to complete the task. Any longer and you receive a burst from the stun gun. Ready? On three."

"M-My hands are tied! I-I can't ..."

Kaine dropped his smile.

"You'll have to work it out. Consider it a test of your ingenuity and dexterity."

He stretched out his arm and dug the stun gun's electrodes into Grantham's hip bone. The killer cop needed his upper body—including his neck—free if he was going to complete the task.

"Three, two, one ... go!"

Grantham squealed. He grabbed the tail of the strap, twisted at the waist, and fed it around his back and behind the metal leg.

"Five seconds," Kaine said. "Well done so far."

The desperate man twisted around the other way and tugged the strap onto his lap.

"Ten seconds."

Gasping, Grantham held the ratchet section between his knees, handle pointing up, and tried to feed the tail into the narrow opening.

"Fifteen seconds. Keep going, Andy."

Grantham failed four times, but finally succeeded in threading the eye of the needle. Unfortunately, operating the ratchet and tugging on the tail at the same time with his wrists secured by the cable ties proved impossible.

"Twenty seconds. Time's nearly up, Andy," Kaine said, taking a malicious pleasure in goading his unfortunate captive.

Three seconds early, Kaine pressed the stun gun's trigger and held it down for a count of five. He didn't mind breaking his word to a corrupt police officer.

Again, Grantham stiffened, jerked, kicked, and grunted as the stun gun discharged its controlled bolt of lightning. After Kaine released the trigger, Grantham lay gasping, arms and legs flaccid, exhausted. Before he could recover, Kaine grabbed the ratchet and tugged it around to the side, out of Grantham's reach. He pulled the tail all the way through the mechanism and worked the ratchet lever until the strap had tightened enough to restrict Grantham's breathing. The strap had twisted at the front, but it didn't affect the action. To test the strap's tension, Kaine plucked it at the back where it stretched between Grantham's upper arm and the bench leg. It sounded a little flat, like an out of tune bass guitar, but it would hold the man in place well enough.

Kaine took another two cable ties from his pocket, looped one around Grantham's ankles, and pulled it tight enough to restrict the blood circulation to his bare feet. Then he pushed the feet towards the cop's bound wrists, bending his knees out wide to allow the movement, and used the second cable tie to secure the wrists and ankles together. The resulting cramped position would make Grantham's breathing even more difficult. It looked both uncomfortable and a tad comical.

Finally, keeping his back to the up-and-over door at all times, Kaine sat, crossed-legged, in front of his pitiful captive. He placed the stun gun on the floor between them and waited for Grantham to recover from his latest jolt.

Time to get serious.

40

Friday 2nd June – Morning

Gordon Lane, Wanstead, London, UK

"Let's talk about Abe Pedersen," Kaine said when he'd judged Grantham to be recovered enough to focus on something other than his pain.

The man's breathing had slowed to as near to normal as the tightened strap would allow. Pink spittle stained the corner of his mouth from where he'd either bitten his tongue or the inside of his cheek. He didn't look at all happy—or in the least bit comfortable.

Such a shame.

Head lowered, chin tucked in, Grantham looked up at Kaine through hooded eyes.

"Wh-What do you want to know?"

"Who ordered you to kill him?"

Grantham shook his head. About the only part of him he could move freely.

"I-I didn't kill anyone."

Kaine grabbed the stun gun and jabbed the electrodes into Grantham's exposed right ankle.

"No, please. No!" Grantham squealed, shaking his head. He tried to squirm away but the strap around his chest and the cable ties binding his ankles and wrists together kept him in place. Sweat leaked from him. Kaine tweaked the trigger and released it immediately.

Grantham spasmed and gagged.

"Okay, okay," he screamed. "I-I killed him. I killed Pedersen."

"I know that," Kaine said, "but who gave the order?"

"My b-boss," he said after a momentary delay.

"DCI Spicer?" Kaine asked as a test. The previous night's session in The Eagle had shown Spicer as being out of the loop.

"Y-Yes, Spicer," Grantham said, keen to drop the DCI's name into the mix. "Spicer ordered the hit."

Kaine twitched the stun gun once more.

"No! Don't," Grantham yelled. "Please don't."

"Keep your noise down!" Kaine hissed. "I won't tell you again. I repeat, who gave the order to kill Pedersen?"

Grantham's shoulders sagged as much as the strap would allow.

"My boss, DI Taylor," he blabbed. "Grace. Grace did it." His chin trembled and tears started rolling down his cheeks. A fresh damp patch stained his lap.

"Amazing Grace?"

Grantham continued nodding.

"Y-Yes. Grace."

"Why?"

"To stop him talking. To ... shut him up."

"Again, why?"

Grantham gasped, jerked his head up, and he stared at Kaine, pleading.

"I-I can't breathe."

"Yes you can. Stop panicking and try to relax." Kaine laughed at the absurdity of the advice. As though anyone could relax when contorted into such a position. "Why did you need to stop Pedersen talking?"

"B-Because we've been ... working together for the past two years."

Kaine nodded. They'd guessed it right.

"He's been paying you protection money?"

Grantham nodded again. "At first, yes. My team ... we're part of the ... the Met's organised crime task force. Intelligence pointed us to Pedersen. We investigated but couldn't find anything to charge him with. At least, not officially. Grace put the investigation on the back burner and approached Pedersen privately. She made him an offer he ... couldn't refuse."

Kaine kept silent and let the man talk. Once he'd started, the flood gates opened, and there was no stopping him.

"At first, we just took a couple of grand a month to turn a blind eye. Then, Grace saw an opportunity. She figured that with our knowledge of the London drugs scene, we could make use of Pedersen's Dutch connections. A natural business progression, she called it. Pedersen ran diamonds into Amsterdam, and we ran drugs into London using the same route and contacts. We split the profits down the middle. It worked brilliantly ... for a while."

"What went wrong?"

"The old man started getting greedy. Short-changed us on the diamond smuggling side. That's when we started watching Pedersen's house. A ... couple of weeks ago. An off the books stakeout. Then the shit hit the fan. Yesterday, when he called in and started confessing, he had to be silenced. But ..."

Grantham blinked. His tears dried.

"But what?"

"Why do you care so much about a shit like Pedersen? The old fucker was nothing but a diamond smuggler with a drugs side hustle. His death is meaningless."

Kaine scrunched up his mouth and shook his head.

"I don't care. Not really."

Grantham frowned.

"So wh-what's all this about? Why torture me?"

"I don't care that Pedersen's dead. But after what happened in France, I wanted him to suffer."

"France?" Grantham asked, frowning. "What's that about France?"

"It doesn't matter. Not to you." Kaine wriggled some life into his backside. Although immaculately clean, the floor didn't make the most comfortable of seats. Time to draw things to a conclusion. "Where did you put the Ruger?"

The remaining colour drained from Grantham's face, but he chose not to deny the takedown carbine's existence.

"In the gun safe, I suppose," Kaine added, almost as an afterthought, glancing at the gun safe beneath the workbench.

"I-I …"

"Oh come on," Kaine said, allowing exasperation to bleed into his voice. "I watched you arrive on your nice big Kawasaki. You had the case strapped to your back and you didn't bring it into the house. Therefore, it must be in the gun safe. Where are the keys?"

The dirty cop swallowed again.

"Utility room. First drawer on the left when you walk in," he said, nodding towards the personnel door leading into the house.

"I have to say, you showed some nerve carrying it through the streets. What would have happened if you'd been stopped and searched."

"If anyone had stopped me, I'd have shown my warrant card. No one's going to search a fellow police officer. Least of all a detective."

"Good point."

Kaine climbed to his feet. His knees and back creaked on the way up. At least his backside approved.

"I'm going to get the keys. If you make a sound, I won't bother with the stun gun, this time. I'll use the SIG, and then I'll disappear out the back garden and through the alley before anyone can raise the alarm. Understand?"

Teary-eyed, Grantham nodded and kept his mouth shut. A broken man.

Kaine found the keys easily and returned to the garage.

"Well done, Andy. Thank you for keeping quiet."

Kaine squatted beside Grantham, unlocked the black metal gun safe, and raised the lid. The Ruger case fitted inside so snugly, the safe could have been made for it. He left the lid open and the case inside, and stood back.

"That's it, Andy. We're all done. I have all I need."

"That's it?"

Kaine nodded.

"You're going to leave me here?"

Kaine ignored the question. He took a deep breath and tugged a rectangular package out of his jacket pocket. Wrapped in brown greaseproof paper and the size of a block of butter, it didn't look particularly dangerous, but it made Grantham shudder.

"What ... what are you doing?" he croaked.

Kaine raised a finger to his lips, bent, and placed the package on the floor in front of Grantham, who watched the process with growing terror and sweat bathing his face.

"This," Kaine said, his voice hushed, "is enough Semtex to blow you and this garage into orbit. But it's perfectly inert without this." He dug a hand into a different pocket and removed a small metal rod. It had a point at one end and a square block attached to the other. "Which, as you can see, is a detonator."

He stuck the pointed end of the rod into the block and stepped back.

"By the way," Kaine whispered, "the sensor on the end of the detonator is a comms receiver. Make too much noise when I'm gone and poof." He held up his hand and snapped open his fingers like a flower. "No more Andy, and no more garage."

"What's to stop me shouting now and taking you with me?" Grantham asked, his voice little more than a sigh.

"Good question. But the answer's simple," Kaine said, speaking up. "I haven't activated it yet. That's what this is for."

From the same pocket as the detonator, he pulled out a small burner phone and powered it up with his thumb. When the screen finally glowed into life, he placed the mobile alongside the bomb and backed away.

"And that's that. I'll prime the bomb remotely after I'm well clear of the garage. Oh, do you see this?" He turned his head and brushed his hair away from his ear. "This is an earpiece. If you shout, I'll hear you through the burner, send the signal, and you die. Neat, isn't it?"

"H-How long are you going to leave me here?" Grantham called, softly.

"That depends on how long your colleagues take to respond to my call."

"What!" Grantham shouted, then he blanched and stared at the bomb, shaking.

"That was your first and last chance, Andy, my man. The next time you shout will be the last thing you ever do." Kaine stared down at the pitiful excuse for a human being. "You know what I hate more than most things?"

Grantham shook his head.

"Dirty cops."

The dirty cop shuddered as though he'd been slapped in the face.

"You're supposed to protect the public, not line your pockets at their expense. Drug dealing, smuggling, murder. It ends here. It ends now. Goodbye, Andy. I doubt we'll be seeing each other again."

Kaine waved and left through the internal door.

Once in the kitchen, he tapped the earpiece once. Before he could say anything, Corky burst in with his customary greeting.

"*Whatcha, Mr K. How you diddling?*"

"Morning, Control. Did you catch all that? Over."

"*Yep. Sure did. Want old Corky to make the call?*"

"Yes please, Control. Alpha One, out."

* * *

STUCK in nose-to-tail traffic heading north on the Archway Road, Kaine couldn't hold off any longer. He pressed a button on his steering wheel and said, "Call Marie-Odile."

"Would you like me to call Marie-Odile's mobile phone?" the phone's virtual assistant asked, ever so politely.

"Yes, please," Kaine answered in a similar manner, not to be outdone by an app.

The call took a while to connect.

"*Capitaine, est-ce toi?*"

"*Oui, Marie-Odile. C'est moi.* How's the patient?"

"Oh dear, he is terrible." The poor woman sounded close to tears.

Worry stabbed at Kaine's chest.

"What's wrong?"

"He refuses to follow the instructions of the doctor. Will not stay in bed and rest his arm. He wishes to discharge himself from the hospital and return home. *L'homme est incorrigible.* Will you speak to him, *Capitaine*?"

Kaine relaxed and allowed a smile to form. Typical Rollo. With one very notable exception, he detested all medics. He'd been under doctor's orders only a few times in his life.

"Of course I will. Put him on."

"*Oui. Un instant s'il vous plaît.*"

The car ahead of him in the queue, a dark green Vauxhall Insignia, nudged forwards a few metres and then stopped again. Kaine allowed the gap between them to grow. Behind him, a white van driver blared an angry horn. Kaine glanced at him through the rear-view mirror. The driver, a red-faced man in his twenties with long dark hair and a scraggy beard, scowled, waved him forwards angrily, and mouthed something unacceptable and unrepeatable at him.

The phone line crackled and Rollo said, "Yes, sir?" He sounded a little abrupt. Snappy even.

"Morning, Rollo. How's the arm?"

"Hurts a little, sir. But at least I can move my fingers."

"Are you following doctor's orders, Colour Sergeant?"

"Of course I am," Rollo barked. "Why wouldn't I?"

Still mouthing obscenities, the white van driver leant on the horn again. Kaine relented and nudged his car, a seven-year-old BMW 3 Series, a few metres closer to the Vauxhall. Van-man rolled his dirty wagon to within a kiss of the BMW's rear bumper, scowling at the back of Kaine's head the whole time. His red face darkened to heart-attack purple.

"That's not what Marie-Odile says, Colour Sergeant. What's this I hear about you wanting to discharge yourself early and head back to Bordeaux?"

Rollo cleared his throat. "I'd be better off at home. More comfortable. You know what I'm like with hospitals. Horrible, germ-filled places." He paused a moment and added, "You know more people die in hospital than anywhere else, right?"

"Rollo," Kaine said, drawing out his old friend's name, "the ESAPP Med Centre is immaculate. The cleanest clinic I've ever seen. And you've only been there two days. At least stick it out for the weekend. Stay 'til Monday. For Marie-Odile's sake. She's worried about you. Don't forget, in France, doctors are gods. They must be obeyed."

The Vauxhall nudged forwards another two metres, its brake lights flared, and it stopped again. Behind, the purple-faced Van-man revved his engine, trying to intimidate Kaine into edging forwards another few centimetres. What was the point? Kaine ignored the impatient oaf.

"Monday? Do I have to?" Rollo asked, sounding like a spoiled child. He might well have been pushing out his lower lip.

Kaine grinned. "Yes, Colour Sergeant. You do. Suck it up, Marine."

"Aye aye, sir," Rollo said, resigned to obeying his latest orders. "What's that noise? Are you in traffic?"

"Just a bit. Behave yourself, Rollo. Don't rush the rehab, and follow your doctor's instructions to the letter. I need you in full working order. So does Marie-Odile. Do I make myself clear?"

"Yes, sir. Clear as crystal." He couldn't have sounded any more reluctant or resigned to his fate.

"Good. Give my best regards to Marie-Odile."

"Will do, sir. Same to the doc."

Kaine pressed the button on the steering wheel to disconnect the call and glanced in the rear-view mirror again. Revving his engine even harder, Van-man slammed his fist into the top of the steering wheel, one heartbeat away from total apoplexy. His foot slipped off the brake and his van jerked forwards, crunching into the back of Kaine's Beemer.

Give me strength!

The van's offside door creaked open, and Van-man jumped out. He slammed the door closed and stormed to the front of the van to inspect the damage.

"What the fuck's wrong with you, arsehole?" he roared.

Kaine activated the electronic parking brake, slid the selector into park, and climbed out of the Beemer. He strode to the back of the car and studied the man long enough to take his measure. A few centimetres taller than Kaine, the man's five-litre beer belly bulged out from a dirty T-shirt and hung over the top of a pair of oil-stained jeans.

"Your mistake, son," Kaine said, maintaining his distance at greater than arm's length.

"I'm not your fucking son."

Kaine grinned. "And nobody's more grateful for that than me."

"Huh?"

Van-man glared at Kaine, who met his eye without a quiver.

"You reversed into me!"

Kaine sighed.

"Look at the rear window of my Beemer," he said, pointing behind him without turning his head.

"What about it?" Van-man stretched his neck to peer over Kaine's shoulder.

"That black dot at the top is a rear-facing dashcam. The whole incident is being videoed and the film stored in the cloud," he lied. "The bump is your fault entirely." He paused to let the information sink in. "Now, calm down, get back in your van, and we'll say no more about it. Unless you really want to exchange insurance details."

In the queue behind, car horns sounded as drivers lost patience with the wait.

"Fuck you, arsehole."

Jaw clenched, lips peeled back in a snarl, Van-man curled his hands into fists.

"Don't do it, son," Kaine said, shaking his head slowly. "It really isn't a good idea."

Van-man hesitated, tottering on the brink of throwing the first punch.

Unblinking, staring Van-man right in the eye, Kaine held up his hands, palms open, left hand pressed slightly ahead of the right. First defensive position. Prepped for action without making it obvious. Goading Van-man would only force his hand.

Your move, son.

Doubt and fear blasted their way through the furious bluster. Van-man dropped his hands and backed away.

"Fuck you, arsehole," he shouted and returned to his dirt-encrusted van. As he climbed behind the wheel, he added, "You ain't worth it."

After crunching the gears, he found reverse and backed a few millimetres away. He raced the engine and scowled at Kaine the whole time.

Keeping one eye on Van-man for signs of an attack, Kaine examined the damage. The BMW had gained a couple of extra scratches and a small dent to the bumper, but both light clusters remained intact. Nothing major. The damage wasn't worth an insurance claim. With minimal risk of being stopped by a hawk-eyed traffic cop, he stared hard at Van-man for a moment before returning to his car to find that the Vauxhall had disappeared around a distant bend in an empty northbound lane.

He slid back inside the Beemer, shifted into drive, and shot away, leaving a cowed but uninjured Van-man and his heap of rubbish behind him in the dust.

41

Friday 2nd June – Andrew Grantham

Gordon Lane, Wanstead, London, UK

Grantham waited, hardly daring to breathe. Sweat trickled down his forehead and into his eyes, stinging like a bitch. He blinked. More sweat flowed. Tickled his nose. He tried to hold back the sneeze. Failed. Clenched his whole body in preparation for the bomb detonating. It didn't.

The torture continued.

Time dragged.

Seconds stretched into minutes.

Minutes took hours.

Every muscle in his body burned with cramp, and every joint screamed out for movement. A searing agony sliced into his shoulder blades. His restricted ribs grated against each other every time he breathed.

In the hall, the landline rang, muffled by the distance and the walls between it and the garage.

Grantham held his breath. Stared at the bomb.

The phone rang for ages, then stopped. Seconds later, it rang again, droning on, incessant.

At each moment, Grantham expected to hear the sirens wail, signing the end of his career. Signalling the end of life as he knew it. For an ex-cop, life in prison would be a living hell.

Shout, Andy. Scream. End it. End the pain.

Grantham thought about it, he seriously did, but couldn't bring himself to commit suicide. While he lived, he had hope, and he wasn't brave enough to choose the coward's way out.

Traffic on the nearby Cambridge Park Road raced past in both directions. At one time, a two-tone horn's blast nearly stopped his heart.

Grantham held his breath. He stared at the bomb and the mobile phone on the floor next to it. Again, nothing happened.

A hoax?

Was the bearded bastard messing with his head? Trying to break him? If so, why? He'd told the bastard everything. Answered all the bugger's questions.

He heaved and strained against the cable ties, trying to break the locks, but only succeeded in ripping the skin on his wrists, making them bleed. God, they hurt. Every movement a stinging, tearing, agony.

Still, he couldn't drag his eyes away from the bomb.

* * *

HOURS OF AGONY LATER, a double rap on the front door made him jump. Pain flared through his joints, and the plastic ties bit deeper into his wrists and ankles. He tried not to cry out. Failed.

The burner remained silent. The bomb didn't blow.

A fist banged on the front door. Its echo reverberated through the hallway and into the garage.

"Grantham!" Grace shouted, anger straining her voice.

Grace! Thank God. Thank God.

"Grace," he called quietly, not taking his eyes from the bomb. "I'm in the garage. Be quiet."

"Grantham," Grace yelled, slamming her fist into the door again. "We're coming in."

"Stay back," he said, straining his voice with a coarse whisper. "There's a bomb!"

The screen on the burner phone next to the block of Semtex glowed brighter.

Oh Jesus.

Heart racing, Grantham closed his eyes and waited to die.

The front door opened. His tormentor, the evil bastard, must have left it on the latch.

Footsteps clacked on the hall's tiled floor—Grace's high-heeled shoes. They drew closer. Behind them, another pair clumped and squeaked, these had rubber soles. One of the guys?

A shadow darkened the utility room. Grace, the most beautiful creature he'd ever seen, appeared in the open doorway. The fat lump, Herriot, stood behind her, peering over her shoulder. She stared down at him, fists planted on her hips, head shaking slowly. She took a breath and opened her mouth, preparing to speak.

"There's a bomb," Grantham whispered, nodding at the device on the floor close to his feet. "Keep quiet. It's sound activated."

Grace clamped her mouth shut, and the muscles in her jaw tensed. She stared at Grantham in disgust.

"You bloody idiot," she muttered.

She stomped into the garage, squatted in front of the bomb, and studied it closely.

"Don't," he begged quietly. "Don't touch it. Release the webbing strap and get me out of here."

Grace sighed and shook her head, her eyes filled with disgust.

She reached for the detonator ...

He winced and half-turned his head away, unable not to look.

... pulled it from the packet, and held it up to him.

Still nothing happened.

"Moron!" she growled, barely in control. "It's nothing but a propelling pencil with a metal sharpener stuck on the end!" She threw it at him like a dart.

The sharp point struck him in the neck. He yelped.

"Fuck off," he screamed, the tension released. "What was that for?"

She picked up the block of Semtex and threw it at the nearest wall. It broke open and a pale-yellow goo splattered over the brickwork, hung there for a moment, and slid to the concrete floor.

"Margarine!" she barked. "You've wet yourself over a block of margarine. Moron!"

Anger boiled over, topping relief.

"Stop calling me that."

"I will, the moment you stop being a moron."

Behind her, Herriot shook his head and tried to hide a smirk behind his raised fist.

Margarine! Bloody margarine?

The evil fucker with the beard had played him for a fool.

Shit.

Grantham ground his teeth and pushed his hands out as far as they would go, ignoring the painful scrapes and cuts.

"Free me," he growled at Herriot. "There's a pair of tin snips in that drawer."

Herriot drew closer but Grace stood and stepped between them.

"What did you tell him?" she asked.

"Who?"

"The man who did that to you." She waved a hand towards his bindings.

Shit.

Grantham swallowed.

"Nothing," he said, shaking his head. "I told him nothing."

"Liar! That's not what he said."

She strode forwards and drove the point of her shoe into his ribs. The air exploded from his lungs. Winded, he couldn't catch his breath. He gasped. His eyes teared, his vision darkened, and his nose started running.

Grace stepped back a pace and stood over him again.

"He called me at the station," she said, a cold calmness slowing her words. "That's why we're here. He said you confessed to killing Pedersen." She paused a moment as if gathering her thoughts. "That was bad enough. But then you told him I ordered the hit, which is unacceptable."

"I-I …" Grantham couldn't breathe, couldn't force out the words, and ended up shaking his head.

Grace turned to Herriot. "Kill him."

What? No. For God's sake, no.

Grantham gasped. Herriot straightened.

"Are you kidding?" the fat prick asked.

Grace relaxed her shoulders. "Yes. Of course I am. I wouldn't give you the pleasure. If I wanted the moron dead, I'd shoot him myself. And I'd use his precious Ruger to do it." She jabbed her finger at the open gun safe and the case it contained.

Grantham's chest finally relaxed enough for him to suck in a lungful of air. The bitch had turned on him. So much for their so-called special relationship, their bond. All the times they'd screwed each other's brains out had meant nothing to her. The bitch.

So be it.

"Well?" he said, looking at Herriot.

"What?"

"Release the fucking strap, you mug!"

Herriot glanced at Grace, seeking permission. She nodded and he crouched down to release the ratchet clamp. The blue strap slipped through the mechanism, the tension released, and the restriction in his chest eased. The utter joy of being able to breathe without constriction flooded his senses. He'd never take breathing for granted again.

Grantham filled his lungs, but a stab of pain in his side came as a sharp reminder of Grace's kick to the ribs. It didn't hurt that much, but the embarrassment struck deep. He wouldn't forget it in a hurry. The bitch kicked him while he was down. Kicked him like a dog.

No bloody way would he forget it.

Grantham eased his back away from the table leg, feeling the instant relief. The sharp metal edges would have cut deep creases in his skin, and his whole body would be one huge fucking bruise. The fucker would pay. Somehow, he would pay.

He looked up at Herriot.

"The cutters?" he said. "In the third drawer down." He nodded towards the cabinet.

Herriot tugged open the drawer and scrabbled about inside, making an unholy mess. Fuck, it would take forever to tidy up.

The tin snips made light work of the cable ties and the blood flowing into his hands and feet caused him as much agony as the stun gun and Grace's kick to the ribs.

"Help me up," Grantham said, thrusting his right elbow towards his so-called mate.

"Oh, right."

Herriot grabbed under his arm and pulled him to his pounding, thumping feet.

"They look nasty," Herriot said, looking at the slices cut into his bloodied wrists. "Painful?"

Stupid prick. Of course they're bloody painful.

Grantham nodded. "A little."

Grace sniffed the air around him and her perfect little nose winkled.

"You stink of sweat and worse. Go take a shower. We need to talk."

He narrowed his eyes and prowled closer to her, but she held her ground. Amazing Grace Taylor, the fearless bitch.

One day, woman. One day soon.

"The bastard kept belting me with a stun gun," Grantham said, trying not to sound pitiful. "It's no bloody wonder I smell. You'd smell, too."

"I wouldn't have let the sod sneak up on me," she countered, still sneering.

Yeah. Right.

Whatever warm feelings he'd ever felt for her had disappeared with the kick to the ribs. They'd been replaced by a cold, steel hatred.

He clenched his burning, stinging, pounding hands into loose fists. His wrists stung to buggery, but at least his hands had started working again.

"I'll be right down," he snarled. "Help yourselves to a coffee, and don't make a mess."

* * *

IT TOOK twenty-five minutes—fifteen of them spent standing under a pulsing hot shower—before Grantham felt good enough to pad downstairs in fresh clothes, to find the kitchen like a pigsty. How was it possible to spill so much coffee and sugar granules over the surface when making three mugs of coffee? As for splashing all that water over the drainer, what the bloody hell was all that about? It looked as though a troop of chimps had been let loose in the place.

Bloody Herriot. The ham-fisted clown.

It had to be him. Grace wouldn't deign to make drinks. She never had at the station and wouldn't start here.

"About time!" she called. "We're in the lounge."

As if I can't tell where you are from the direction of your voice.

"I made you a brew," Herriot said.

Made a shitload of mess, too.

"Thanks," Grantham said, walking from the kitchen into the front room.

Grace sat in his favourite armchair even though she knew it was *his* fucking chair. She did it on purpose to confirm her status as boss.

Fucking bitch.

He eased onto the sofa next to Herriot and let out a grateful sigh. Despite the hot shower, his body ached all over and would do for days. He yawned long and hard, and reached for his coffee.

"Are we keeping you up?" Grace said in full-blown sarcasm mode.

"Well, yeah," he snapped. "You bloody well are, actually. I've just got off a night shift, remember. And I've not exactly had a restful morning."

Herriot shuddered in apparent sympathy.

Grace snorted.

Grantham cast his eyes around the room. Apart from the fat lump, Herriot, nothing looked out of place. The intruder hadn't messed with anything.

"We've already searched the ground floor," she said.

"For what?"

"Bugs."

"Bugs?" Grantham frowned. He hadn't considered bugs.

"Listening devices," she said, talking slowly as though he was a child. "Your torturer might have been here all night. No telling what he might have planted. We searched, but found nothing. It's safe to talk."

"Good. Right. I was going to suggest we sweep the place," he lied. "I've got a scanner in the garage for just that very task."

"Yeah," Herriot said. "You would have."

"What does that mean?" Grantham snarled, in no mood to be jerked about."

"Keep your hair on, Andy," Herriot said, flapping a hand in the air as an apology. "I just meant that your garage is banging, mate. I've never seen a place so full of gear."

"Oh," Grantham said, nodding. "Right. And yeah, it is. Most of the kit's my dad's, but I've added bits. My dad ... he was an engineer. Taught me loads. Did I tell you?"

Herriot nodded and looked at his coffee. "Once or twice."

Grantham blew across the top of his drink and took a tentative sip. Despite all his faults, Herriot knew how to make a decent instant coffee. Strong with just enough milk and no sugar. On the other hand, was it really possible to screw up making instant?

"Where's Lee?" he asked.

"Back at the station," Grace answered. "Someone around here has to do some police work. He's leading the house-to-house on Fleur De Lis Road."

"We're part of the team searching for the evil scrote who shot Pedersen," Herriot added. "Didn't you know?" He shot Grantham a lopsided grin.

"Yes, I did know," Grantham said, the brief levity improving his mood a little. "Nasty piece of work. Hope we find him soon."

"Me too," Herriot said, taking his turn to snort.

Grace raised her hand to silence the hilarity.

"So," she said, "what are we going to do about Packard?"

"Packard?" Grantham asked, before taking another sip. His stomach grumbled, reminding him that he hadn't eaten for hours. He had a pack of bacon in the fridge. A bacon buttie would hit the spot as soon as he could get shot of these two and catch up on some lost sleep.

"He's the one who broke into your home, spanked your arse, and trussed you up like a Christmas turkey," Grace said, through a deep sneer. "At least, that's the name he gave when he called the switchboard and asked for me by name. Jim Packard."

Grantham leant forwards, tensing against the sore back and the ache in his side. The ache from her kick. "Did you run his name through the PNC?"

"Of course I did," Grace said, still sneering.

"He's the one who played the delivery man and broke into the Pedersen house."

"Yes, I know. He told me. He also told me he'd forced Pedersen to give himself up and confess to being a killer and a smuggler."

Bloody hell.

"What the fuck does he want?"

"What do you think?" she asked.

Grantham gritted his teeth. "I don't know. That's why I bloody well asked."

"He wants a cut," Grace said.

"What?"

"You heard. He wanted what he called hush money for letting us continue in business."

Grantham considered the irony of the situation. Dirty cops being squeezed didn't really bear thinking about.

"The greedy bastard," he said. "How much?"

"He hasn't said yet."

"Are we going to pay?"

"No, of course not. We're not giving him a penny," Grace said. "Not one."

Ignoring the discomfort in his ribs, Grantham leant towards the coffee table and set the mug down on its coaster. He stared into Grace's dark brown eyes, trying to read her thoughts.

"What's your plan?" he asked.

Her aggressive sneer turned into a sly smile. Beautiful as she was, it didn't look good on her.

"Easy," she said. "I'll agree to pay the bastard off, but on my terms. I'll set the time and location of the drop—somewhere isolated and out of London. We'll surround the place. Then, dear Andy, I'm going to let you have some payback. I'm going to let you shoot him in the face with your fancy rifle."

Grantham nodded and allowed his own smile to form. His face was just about the only part of his body that didn't hurt when he moved—apart from his tongue where he'd bitten it.

"I like the idea of payback, but Packard isn't stupid. You saw what he did to me. Is he going to fall for it? What happens if he brings back-up?"

She glanced at Herriot before turning her dark eyes on Grantham again. A cold shiver of excitement rippled through him. Fuck was she hot. Even the bruised ribs couldn't turn him off—not completely. Fuck, did he fancy her.

"As far as he's concerned, you and I are working alone. He doesn't know about Geoff or Lee. When he sees me, his guard's going to be down. Apparently, I have that effect on some people." She smiled and warmth returned to the room.

Christ, she's good.

So goddamned hot, and with a bod to die for. Maybe he *could* forgive her for the kicking. Consider it a love tap.

Yeah, right.

"And if he asks where I am?"

"I'll tell him you're in hospital, recovering from the heart attack you suffered during the arse-kicking."

Herriot snorted and didn't bother trying to hold it in.

Grantham shot him a withering glare that shut him up and made him look at his coffee again.

"And if he does bring back-up," Grace added, "Geoff and Lee will be there to take them out. Won't you, Geoff?"

Herriot broke out a grin and nodded.

"We will."

A mobile phone buzzed. All three of them stiffened. Grantham's heart jolted. It would take him ages to recover from the pasting Packard had handed out. And from the psychological torture of the fake bomb. The absolute bastard.

"It's mine," Grace said, leaning to one side and reaching into her trouser pocket.

Fuck she filled out her clothes so well.

She read the caller ID, and her right eyebrow arched.

"Packard," she said.

"Put it on speaker," Grantham hissed, receiving an angry glare for his pains.

All the same, she accepted the call and hit the speaker icon.

"Yes?" she said.

"Hello, Amazing," Packard answered, a smile lightening his tone. "How are you this fine afternoon?"

Grantham tried not to shudder at the sound of his tormentor's voice.

"What do you want?"

"How's Andy?"

"Do you care?"

"Not really, but how is he?"

She looked coldly at Grantham.

"On his way to hospital. You worked him over pretty well. Who knew he had an underlying heart condition?"

"Oh dear. I'm really sorry to hear that." Packard didn't sound the least bit upset. "Still, he's in good hands. The NHS is a wonderful organisation. A little stretched at times, but—"

"What do you want?" she repeated, speaking over him.

"You know what I want, Grace," he said, calm as anything. "Money."

"How much?"

"Fifty thousand pou—"

"How much!"

"Fifty thousand to start with. In cash. Used notes, new notes, it doesn't matter to me either way. And then, twenty grand a month, every month after that. You see? I'm not greedy, but don't try to stiff me, or I'll drop you so deep in the brown stuff you'll choke."

"Fifty," she said, jutting out her jaw and staring at Grantham as she answered. "I can't get hold of that much cash ... not until tomorrow."

Grantham held his breath. The silence in the room stretched out for a few seconds before Packard's smooth response.

"Okay, I'm a reasonable man. I'll give you until midday tomorrow."

"Tomorrow evening," she countered.

"Midday," he said. "I'll call you in the morning with a location."

"No. We'll set the drop—"

"You think I'm stupid? Say goodbye to your career, Grace. And goodbye to your freedom."

"Wait!"

The call clicked into silence.

"Shit," she said, staring at the mobile.

Herriot's right hand curled into a fist, and his knuckles cracked. "Do you think he's—"

The phone buzzed again. Grace almost dropped it in her hurry to accept the call.

"Hello?" she said, urgency in her normally cool voice. "Packard? Hello?"

Packard said something Grantham couldn't hear. He waved at her and pointed to his ear. She caught his meaning and hit the speaker icon again.

"...your last chance, Amazing," Packard said, cool as ice. "There's only one person in charge here, and it isn't you. Do we understand each other?"

"Yes," she said, sounding sullen, beaten.

"Good. I'll call you tomorrow morning with the drop location. Be prepared for a long drive. I need plenty of space to see you coming. And I'll want to see the money. Make sure it's in a clear plastic bag. You won't be surprised to learn that I don't trust you, Detective Inspector Taylor. Oh no. I don't trust you one little bit. But you have money, and I want some of it. Only my fair share, mind. I'm not greedy. Not really." He laughed. "Keep this phone fully charged, Amazing. Laters!"

Again, the mobile clicked, and again, Grace stared at it.

"Told you he was smart," Grantham announced. "So much for setting up an easy hit. We'll have to follow you to the drop and take him out on the fly."

She shrugged. "It was worth a try. Okay, this is how we'll play it. When he calls with the location, the three of you can go ahead. Hopefully, he won't be expecting anybody but me. I'll follow in the Škoda. Alone."

"And if he changes the drop point along the way?" Grantham asked.

"We'll use radio comms. I'll keep you in the loop. It's the best I can think of right now. Can either of you think of an alternative?"

They thrashed out the possibilities and variables for an hour and a half, and ended up going round in circles, getting nowhere. In the end, Grace called an end to the discussion and summed it up with, "It's Packard or us. We have to take him out or we'll be working for him for the rest of our lives. Whatever it takes, he has to die. Got it?"

Herriot nodded, falling into line as he always did.

Grantham said, "Yes, boss," yawned, and stood, hoping she'd take it as a signal to bugger off. He had a day's sleep to catch up on, but only after he'd tidied the house and cleaned the Ruger. Sitting in the lounge, jawing all day wouldn't get any of that done.

"Okay," Grace said, "I've got the message. Get some sleep. I need you on your A game tomorrow. And"—she held out her hand—"I'm sorry for kicking you. Shouldn't have lost control like that. Forgive me?" She smiled.

He lowered his head and grunted an acceptance.

Like fuck he forgave her. His ribs still hurt where the pointed toe of her shoe landed. One day soon, after they'd dealt with Packard, he'd get his own back. By Christ he would.

Grantham ushered them out of the house and headed into the garage, returning to the scene of his abject humiliation. First Packard, then Grace. He salivated at the sweetness of the payback.

Smiling, he took a recently washed and neatly folded boilersuit from the drawer below the one that needed tidying, shook it out, and climbed into it one stiff leg at a time.

42

Saturday 3rd June – DI Grace Taylor

Shepherdess Walk, Shoreditch, London, UK

While pretending to work on her computer, Grace Taylor kept glancing at the mobile on her desk, willing it to ring.

Grantham sat at his desk across from her, watching and waiting, and filling in forms. Herriot and Rathbone, the likely lads, keen but not too bright—the perfect foot soldiers—sat at their desks, working through the paperwork from the Pedersen door-to-door canvass. Thankfully, none of the locals had seen anything to raise their suspicions. At some stage, she'd have to task the team to widen the search area but not before they'd exhausted all the other avenues. She didn't want to appear too keen to move on. Their murder investigation had to be perfect. Beyond reproach. Textbook.

Using ballistic analysis, the specialists had identified the sniper's nest quickly enough, but the forensics team had found the fourth-floor bedsit on Elder Street spotless. Not a trace of anything useful. No prints, no fibres, not a thing. Say one thing for Andy Grantham, he might not be the best in the sack, but he did know how to keep a place clean and tidy. Thankfully for them all, the guy had to be way out on the OCD spectrum.

In the far corner of the office, one of Callum Hinds' unit said something and roared with laughter. Others joined in. Happy in their work. And why wouldn't they be? The buggers had been handed the easiest investigation ever—the ram raid. What a bloody stitch up. Being the most senior DI in the unit, Hinds had the pick of all the best jobs, and the ram raid investigation couldn't have been more of a peach. With three armed robbers already in the cells and only the hunt for three bikers left, the case was a total slam dunk—courtesy of an unknown, have-a-go hero who'd fled the scene out of what, modesty? Fear of the police?

Who knows?

Ordinarily, Grace would have kicked up a real stink for not being given the case, which would have done wonders for her clear-up record. She'd have killed to be given such a gift, but she'd kept quiet. Investigating the Pedersen murder as Spicer's second-in-command couldn't have worked out better. Spicer happened to be one of the good guys. Never one to micro-manage, the DCI allowed his teams to work their cases as they saw fit, as long as they kept him fully briefed. Perfect. It gave her and the guys the opportunity to bury evidence, muddy the waters, and make certain that no one would ever come within ten miles of the truth.

The perfect scenario.

No one would be arrested or charged for the Abe Pedersen killing. His "untimely" death would end up adding to the growing list of unsolved murders investigated by the overworked and under-resourced Metropolitan Police Service. A statistic that no one would shout about too much.

Of course, an unsolved murder case wouldn't look good on her record, but what did she care? Grace had long given up on the idea of further advancement. Not since the last promotion board had rejected her application out of hand. As DI, she'd reached her level of competence, at least according to the hatchet-faced Commander who delivered the pronouncement. The evil bitch.

At the time, Grace had thought about playing the race card, but ended up keeping her mouth shut. It suited her not to draw any adverse attention to herself or her team. Instead, she'd approached Abe Pedersen with a business proposal he couldn't afford to turn down, and brought Grantham and the likely lads along for the ride. Not that she'd had to drag the greedy pricks kicking and screaming. They jumped at the opportunity to earn a little untaxed income. And a little turned into a lot. They'd been creaming it in for more than two years. The most difficult part about the whole operation was how to launder the cash effectively.

Grace and her sister had invested in businesses—legitimate operations—such as hairdressers, beauty salons, and nail bars, which turned modest profits. Soon, she'd have enough set aside to hand in her notice, but not yet awhile. Being a detective had its perks, and plenty of them.

Turning rogue had been a fateful decision, the point of no return. A highly lucrative point of no return, but not without its challenges. Jim Packard, for example. She had no idea how he'd identified Grantham as the sniper. Maybe Pedersen had told him about their business arrangement for some reason. Either way, the grasping sod presented a challenge that needed to be dealt with immediately. She couldn't allow it to fester, or the added pressure would tear the team apart. Already, she'd allowed her lack of self-control to sour the team dynamic. She shouldn't have kicked Grantham in the ribs. An unforgiveable and dangerous mistake. She'd have to make it up to him soon or the resentment would gnaw away at the team she'd taken so long to build. Paying him some more personal attention might do the trick. Sex usually worked with action men like Andy Grantham. If not, she'd end him in the same way he had ended Pedersen. A double tap to the chest. Quick and easy. Almost painless.

Grace's gaze shifted from the mobile phone to the flight bag dangling from the hook under her desk. Fifty thousand pounds in used fifties didn't take up that much room. It weighed a little over one kilogram and filled less space than two house bricks. The stacks filled one large sandwich bag and fit into her flight bag perfectly. She'd considered using bundles of cut-up newspapers, but decided against it. With real cash she'd have a better chance of drawing Packard into her trap. The sight of so much money would work on his greed. Blind him.

She had the readies—and more—in her house safe and could have produced it immediately, but she'd put Packard off to find out how far she could push his buttons. Not very far, as it turned out. Still, the man had given her the extra day, which showed two things. He was deeply money orientated, and he could be swayed.

The mobile buzzed.

Her heartrate jumped.

Caller ID, Packard.

About time.

Grantham and the likely lads sat up straighter and paid close attention. No one on Callum Hinds' seven-man team so much as batted an eyelid, being too wrapped up in their check-box operation. Investigating by the numbers, the only way the numbskulls could work.

Grace controlled her breathing, picked up the phone, and hit the green icon, surprised to find her finger steady. Nerveless. She could handle this.

"Packard, about time," she said, nodding at Grantham. He and the others stood and hurried from the office. They'd head straight for the car park and wait for her text. "I thought you'd forgotten about me."

Packard laughed. "As though that would ever happen. Do you have my money?"

"Yes."

She peeked at the dark blue flight bag with the British Airways logo, which contained all the money as window dressing, and a small surprise—an unregistered SIG P365. One of the best concealed-carry handguns ever built, according to the sales brochures. Totally illegal in the UK, but readily accessible to anyone who knew where to ask and had enough cash. If Packard wandered close enough, the SIG would earn its five grand price tag.

"All fifty thousand?" Packard asked.

"Yes," she answered through a dry mouth.

"Good. How long will it take you to reach Chingford Golf Course?"

"No idea," she lied. A Londoner from birth, she knew how long it would take on a Saturday morning, especially when using blues and twos.

"I'll give you sixty minutes. Use your blue lights and the traffic will simply melt away," Packard said as though he could read her thoughts. "Park in the members car park and call me when you reach the club house. I'll give you further instructions from there."

The connection ended.

Grace took a moment to text the location to Grantham, who would relay the address to the others, and they'd all race ahead. Smiling, she stood, grabbed her jacket from the back of her chair, and unhooked the flight bag.

The excitement of the chase coursed through her system. Life was made for such moments. Moments when she took control of her own destiny.

She crossed the office, running the gauntlet of admiring glances, some furtive and sideways, others blatant. Still, she was used to the attention. She'd been plagued by it since puberty had given her the curves. Inwardly, she sneered at them. No doubt about it, she could have had her pick of any man in the room, but why bother? She had bigger targets to aim for than low-wage cops with their tongues hanging out, dribbling.

At the far end of the office, the double doors swung inwards, and Graham Spicer pushed into the room. She carried on towards him without missing a step. She'd always liked Spicer, mainly because he'd been one of the very few straight men in the station who'd never hit on her. Not even in jest. He searched the large office, peering over the acoustic panels, looking for someone. As she emerged from behind one of the columns supporting the ceiling, he caught her eye, smiled, and beckoned her towards him.

Hell. Why now?

She plastered a pleasant smile on her face and approached the man with silver hair and warm brown eyes who always smelled fresh and clean—unlike some of the men she came into close contact with.

"Morning, Grace. Can you spare me a moment?"

Something about the way Spicer tilted his head to study her didn't feel right. She'd never seen the look before, not on Spicer's face.

What's going on?

Tension twisted her guts. Nervous tension.

Grace tugged at the flight bag's strap, which threatened to slip from her shoulder. Warning bells rang in her head. Had she zipped it up properly? Visions of the money and the SIG spilling out over the office floor ran through her mind.

Stop it, Grace.

Of course she'd zipped the bloody thing up. The money and the SIG were secure.

Act naturally.

"Can it wait, sir?" she asked, throat parched, voice scratchy. "I'm going to meet a contact who claims to have information on the sniper." She blurted out the lie spontaneously and would have to remember to write it up in her logbook before the close of play. It wouldn't be a problem, though. There were plenty of people she could call on to play the part of informant.

Spicer's smile faded and his brown eyes darkened.

Her heart lurched and her stomach gurgled as the nerves ramped up.

Normally, she could read his thoughts, but this time ... Jesus, what was going on?

"Sorry, Grace," he said, shaking his head, "Commander Overton needs a sitrep for the press release. I'm due to see her in half an hour. Can you pop into my office for a moment? I won't keep you long."

Candice Overton calling a press conference on a Saturday? It didn't happen often, but with such a high-profile case, the idea didn't stretch the imagination too far. On the other hand ... it was an anomaly. Grace didn't feel comfortable with anomalies. The gurgle in her stomach grew into a churn, and she stretched the smile again.

"Mind if I pop to the loo first? I'm bursting."

She had to ditch the money and the SIG before this went any further.

"Can you hold it in, Grace? I promise not to keep you long."

God. He knows! He knows.

She gripped the strap of the flight bag harder. If push came to shove, she had the SIG.

"Not a problem, sir."

He held the door open, stepped back, and allowed her into the hallway first. A hallway filled with uniformed officers, all of whom stared at her as though she'd grown a second head.

Someone stepped up behind her, grabbed the flight bag, and tore it from her grasp. Someone else, a powerful brute of a woman, took hold of her upper arm and held it so tight the blood flow to her hand stopped.

"What are you doing?" Grace screamed. "Get off me!"

Spicer loomed close.

"Grace Taylor," he said, voice deep and booming, "I'm arresting you for the murder of Abraham Pedersen, corruption, and perverting the course of justice. You do not have to say anything, but it may harm your defence if you do not mention when questioned something which you later rely on in court. Anything you do say ..."

43

Saturday 3rd June – DCI Graham Spicer

Shepherdess Walk, Shoreditch, London, UK

Trying not to show his utter contempt, Graham Spicer watched the blood drain from Grace Taylor's face. She turned from calm, radiant beauty to snarling, vicious shrew in the blink of an eye. Curses spat from her mouth, and it took three officers—two females and a male—to wrestle her to the floor and circle the cuffs around her slim wrists. Only then did she calm down enough to let herself be taken away to the custody suite and the bare grey walls of the holding cell. He'd leave her to stew for a few hours before taking charge of the first interview. Anti-corruption officers would head the main investigation and lead the interviews with Grantham, Herriot, and Rathbone, but Spicer would take first crack at Grace Taylor. By God he would.

It had been an unwelcome first. He'd never arrested a fellow officer before, and it gave him absolutely no satisfaction. In fact, it hurt more than he could have explained to anyone. The betrayal he felt outweighed any sense of delight at solving a murder and putting a bunch of criminals behind bars. They were four of their own, for God's sake.

Standing in the hallway outside the detectives' open-plan office, he wanted to cry, but fought to hold the tears in. It wouldn't have looked good for a senior officer to bawl in front of his troops.

How had he missed the signs?

What a God-awful mess.

The horror show had begun late the previous night, initiated by an unexpected phone call. A phone call that led to the arrest of four long-serving detectives. Part of Spicer's chosen team. Officers he'd worked alongside for years. Officers he'd trusted. Corrupt officers who'd committed murder to cover their crimes. Corrupt officers who'd piled further disgrace on the Met Police, whose reputation already had been sullied by so much scandal, so much wrong-doing. An organisation accused of being institutionally corrupt, misogynistic, racist, and homophobic. An organisation that Spicer had spent the whole of his adult life working for. Supporting. And Grace Taylor's team had added to the list of police offenders.

Bugger it.

Spicer cast his mind back thirteen hours.

He'd just finished a late dinner and had settled down in front of the TV with Lila.

* * *

THE PHONE in the hall burst into life. Spicer groaned. The only people who used the landline these days were cold callers. He let it ring. Beside him on the sofa, Lila stirred.

"Aren't you going to answer it?" she asked.

"Nah, let it go to voicemail."

"It could be work."

He grunted. "They know better than to ring my landline. They'd call the mobile."

The ring continued for a while then stopped. Spicer settled back and reached for the remote.

"What do you fancy?" he asked. "Do we have anything recorded?"

"There's that US cop show. You know. The one with all the gunplay and the car chases with that butch female detective."

"Oh please." He groaned. "Don't we have an Attenborough, or a house renovations show?" He hit the button and scrolled through their saved shows, but the landline started ringing again. "It's a Friday evening for God's sake. Can't they take a bloody hint?"

Again, the phone rang for ages before cutting off.

After five seconds of silence, the bloody thing bleated for a third time. Lila sighed and made a move to stand.

"Okay, okay," Spicer said, holding up a hand to forestall her, "I'll get it."

He jumped up and stalked through to the hall where he snatched up the handset.

"Hello!" he snarled and waited for the sales patter.

"Good evening. Is that DCI Graham Spicer?" the caller asked. Male. Well spoken. No discernible accent.

"It is. Who's that?"

"My name's Packard, sir. Jim Packard."

Spicer searched his memory for the name and drew a blank.

"Do we know each other?"

"No, sir. Not yet."

"How did you get this number? It's ex-directory."

"I'm afraid I'm unable to answer that question, DCI Spicer."

"Okay, I'm hanging up. Do not call me again."

"I wouldn't do that, sir. Not if you want to know who shot Abraham Pedersen."

Spicer stiffened. A crank call. It had to be.

"Are you serious?"

"Yes, sir. Most definitely."

"Why don't you call Crimestoppers?"

Packard laughed. "Why go through an intermediary when I can talk directly to the man in charge of the investigation?"

Spicer took a breath.

"How do you know I'm the SIO? That information isn't in the public domain."

"I know a great deal, Mr Spicer, but we're wasting time, and I don't have all night. I have things to do. Places to be. Please go into your office—I assume you have a home office—and boot up your computer. I'll call you back in a few minutes." He paused for a beat before adding. "And please don't be tempted to call your work and try to trace the call. I'm using a burner phone and will be changing location the moment I hang up. ... Speak soon."

Packard rang off and the dial tone clicked in an intrigued Spicer's ear.

What in God's name ...?

"Who is it, love?" Lila called from the lounge.

Spicer made an instant decision. "Work. Sorry. I won't be long."

"Can't you have any time to yourself?"

"I really won't be long, love. Heading upstairs to the office. Why not watch that US cop show of yours?"

Spicer frowned at the handset for a moment before climbing the stairs to the third bedroom that doubled as a storeroom-cum-office. He took the phone with him. Once seated at his chair, he hit the power button on the laptop and waited for the machine to run through its start-up routine.

After an interminable delay, the password dialogue box appeared. A second after he typed in the eight-digit code, the phone rang. This time, he answered immediately.

"Packard?"

"It's me. Thanks for answering so promptly, and thanks for booting up your laptop."

"How do you know—"

"Do you see the green light on the screen? The one that indicates that the camera's active?"

Spicer frowned. The light shouldn't be glowing. He hadn't activated any of the programs.

"You shouldn't frown like that, Mr Spicer. It'll cause wrinkles."

Bloody hell!

"You can see me?"

"Well, yes. I can."

A window appeared in the middle of the laptop's screen, covering two thirds of the available desktop. Within it, smiled the bearded face of a man holding a mobile phone to his ear. He pulled the mobile away, and tapped a finger to its screen. The phone in Spicer's hand clicked and the dial tone returned. He pressed the red button, the phone fell silent, and he placed it on the desk alongside the laptop.

He had no idea where this was leading, but couldn't wait to find out. For some reason, Packard's approach struck him as intriguing rather than malicious.

"Good evening, DCI Spicer," the smiling man on the laptop screen said. "Don't know about you, sir, but I much prefer to see who I'm speaking to. A video chat is a far better option than a phone call, don't you think?"

Spicer ignored the question and took a moment to study the man on the screen. He had longish, wavy hair, greying at the temples, a full beard, neatly trimmed, and dark brown eyes. A rugged but honest face. Some might call him handsome. Certainly self-assured. The smile natural and not at all forced or threatening.

Spicer felt sure he'd seen the face before somewhere, but he'd be damned if he could place where.

"Who are you, and how did you gain access to my laptop?"

"As you've probably guessed, my name isn't really Jim Packard, but it's the one I'm using for the moment. The answer to your second question is irrelevant. But to put your mind at rest, your files are safe. I've not accessed any of your personal data. You have my word."

"For what that's worth," Spicer scoffed.

The minute Packard ended the video call, Spicer was going to pull the plug and have the laptop sanitised by the best digital forensics specialist he could find in the force.

"What do you want?" Spicer demanded.

Packard's smile faded and his expression became serious.

"I can understand your reluctance to trust a total stranger who cold calls so late on a Friday evening, but let's get down to business. I'm about to upload two MP4 files to your laptop. Video files. You will find them both highly entertaining—if a little upsetting in professional terms. I suggest you watch the shorter video first. In total, the viewing will take less than two hours."

"Videos?"

Packard nodded.

"Compromising videos?"

"For a small number of your officers, I'm afraid so, DCI Spicer."

"Are you serious? All this clandestine nonsense just to deliver a couple of videos? Why not email me the files and be done with it?"

Packard's smile returned.

"What would you have done if you'd received an unsolicited email containing two large video attachments, DCI Spicer?"

Spicer scratched an itch on his chin and thought for a second before nodding.

"Good point. I'd have deleted them out of hand."

"Exactly. Hence this direct, if somewhat unusual, approach."

"What do the files contain?"

Packard narrowed his eyes. "Watch them and find out. Call me on this number after you've watched them, and we'll talk again. I'll keep this burner for a short while. Goodbye for now."

He raised his hand and the window disappeared to be replaced by two more. The one on the left, *Video #1 – Garage*, lasted seventeen minutes. The one on the right, *Video #2 – Lounge*, lasted seventy-six minutes.

He worked the trackpad, hovered the cursor over the play button on the shorter video, and hesitated. What was he getting into here? If Packard had just uploaded a load of smut—or worse—onto his private laptop, Spicer could be facing some serious questions, but weirdly, Packard didn't give him any negative vibes.

"Do it, Graham," he muttered.

He hit the play button and the black window stuttered into life.

The timestamp on the upper right quadrant indicated that the video had been taken earlier that morning. The scene showed the inside of a double garage, shot from high up, looking down. On the right stood a gleaming yellow motorbike. A Kawasaki. Spicer recognised it instantly. He'd seen the damned thing in the station's car park for the past few months. It belonged to DS Andrew Grantham, who kept banging on about how nippy it was and how much time it saved during his daily commute.

As for Grantham, the man himself sat on the garage floor, a blue haulier's strap wrapped around his upper body, his hands and legs bound together with thick grey cable ties. Something that looked like a bomb sat on the floor between his legs. Grantham stared at the bomb, terrified, sweat rolling down his face.

"Bloody hell," Spicer said, reaching for the landline in readiness to call in the bomb squad.

Out of shot, a loud banging drowned out Grantham's heavy breathing. Someone shouted hiss name. With his eyes fixed on the bomb, Grantham called out, "Grace," his voice strained. "I'm in the garage. Be quiet."

"Grantham," Grace yelled, knocking again. "We're coming in."

"Stay back," Grantham gasped. "There's a bomb!"

Spicer watched the scene play out in front of his disbelieving eyes. He rewound and replayed the part where Grace pulled the "bomb" apart and threw what turned out to be a metal pencil at Grantham, who snarled in response. Spicer flinched again as he replayed the segment when she kicked him. He watched in disbelief and growing anger as Grace and Grantham, together with a near-silent DC Herriot, talked about killing Abraham Pedersen. The video ended immediately after Grace ordered Grantham to shower and change.

With much less reluctance, Spicer rolled the cursor over the second video and immediately hit play. This picture showed a low angle shot of a sunny and immaculately clean and tidy front room. Grace sat in the single armchair, while Grantham and Herriot filled the double sofa. A coffee table stood between them. The sofa and armchair pointed directly at the camera lens as though gathered around a TV.

Grantham, scrubbed clean and dressed in blue jeans and a light grey polo shirt, yawned. He reached for a mug on the coffee table in front of him and yawned again.

"Are we keeping you up?" Grace said, sarcasm weighing heavy in her words.

Halfway through the playback, Lila knocked on the door and entered the office without waiting. He paused the video, but before he could close the laptop, she caught sight of the screen.

"What's going on?" she asked, staring at the image, her brows knitting into a frown.

"Sorry, love. Can't tell you, I'm afraid. Work."

"Isn't that Grace Taylor?" she asked, nodding at the screen.

"It is. I didn't know you two had met."

"Last year at Riordan's retirement party. She came across as a little ... intense."

"Superior, you mean?"

"I was being polite, but 'superior' will do. Why are you watching a video of your subordinates? You don't fancy her, do you?" She smiled while asking the question, clearly confident in Spicer's fidelity after thirty-seven years of marriage—the vast majority of them happy.

"No," he said, definitively. "I do not."

"I was kidding, love."

"I know, but ..." he glanced at the door behind her.

"Okay, okay," she said, holding up her hands. "I get the message. I'll leave you to it. I've had enough TV for one night. I'm going to have my shower and turn in. Please keep the noise down when you leave."

"What makes you think—"

"That," she said, pointing at the screen, "looks serious. I imagine it's going to take you back into the office."

He opened his mouth to speak, but she leant close, pecked him on the lips, and left. She said, "Goodnight," as she closed the door quietly behind her.

Such a patient woman. A saint. A lump formed in Spicer's throat when he considered the difference between Lila and the other woman occupying his thoughts at that moment.

Spicer allowed the rest of the recording to play through without interruption. By the end, he felt even more sick to his stomach.

Damn it all to hell.

Spicer picked up the handset and dialled Packard. The call clicked off and a new window grew on the laptop screen, superimposing itself over the other two. Packard's head and shoulders filled the new window.

"How did you come by the videos?" Spicer asked without preamble.

"Illegally. I doubt they'll be admissible in a court of law, but that's not my problem. I can promise they are not doctored in any way."

"Actually," Spicer said, feeling on more solid ground, "evidence acquired through covertly obtained video recordings *is* admissible in criminal proceedings. Under Article 6 of the European Court of Human Rights, such evidence does not violate the accused's right to a fair trial."

Packard's eyebrows lifted a little. "That's good to know."

"Why?" Spicer asked.

"Why what?"

"Why did you send me the videos? You could have sold them to the media and earned yourself a small fortune."

"Money doesn't interest me. I'm looking for justice."

"Justice for whom? Abraham Pedersen?" Spicer asked, not quite believing him. Everyone had an interest in money.

"No," Packard said, shaking his head. "Justice for Molly and Micah Williams."

"Who?"

"Work the case all the way through. You'll find out. And don't forget to investigate Abraham Pedersen's confession. Overnight, I'll send you an email. It will contain names and contact details of people you and Europol might like to interview. That's all I have for you, DCI Spicer. We won't talk again. Goodbye."

"Wait! Let me say something."

Packard canted his head to one side and nodded. "Go on."

"Thank you." Spicer stretched out a sad smile to a man whose name was not Packard. A man whose face he'd finally recognised from a wanted poster. "Thank you for sending me this ... evidence. I appreciate it ... well, sort of."

"You're welcome, sir. Use it well."

"I will."

The window disappeared and with it so did the face of the UK's most wanted man. Although why Ryan Kaine would want to involve himself in a case of police corruption when he had so many troubles of his own defeated Spicer. That question would have to remain unanswered. Spicer had his own can of worms to contend with, and he'd be damned if he'd deal with it alone.

Spicer closed the laptop, unplugged its cable from the mains, and packed it away in its padded case, ready to take with him. The idea of watching the videos again twisted his guts into tighter knots, but he knew he'd have to sit through them at least one more time that night.

Sighing, he picked up the phone again and dialled a number from its contact list.

Commander Candice Overton took an age to answer and when she did, a stifled yawn rippled strongly through her words.

"Graham? Do you know what time it is?"

Spicer glanced at his wristwatch, shocked at how long he'd been sitting in the office chair.

"Yes, ma'am. I do. How long will it take you to reach the station?"

"What?" she asked, in a stage whisper. "You mean tonight?"

"Yes ma'am. Tonight."

"Are you serious?" Cloth rustled on the line as she presumably sat up in her bed.

"Yes, ma'am. Deadly serious."

"What's this about? If it's the Pedersen case, it can wait until the morning. It's not going anywhere."

Spicer set his jaw. If he was going to lose another night's bloody sleep to the job, so would she.

"It is related to the Pedersen case, but it most definitely will not wait until morning. How long, ma'am?"

She yawned again, clearly not minding that he heard this one.

"I'll need an hour."

"Thank you, ma'am. I'll see you at one o'clock."

Spicer left the house after kissing Lila a silent goodnight. No matter how many times he'd been called away in the middle of the night, he never left without giving her a kiss, even if she did sleep through most of them.

44

Saturday 3rd June – Early Afternoon

Mike's Farm, Long Buckby, Northants, UK

The sun burned through a bank of low cloud, shone through the gap in the curtains, and welcomed a bright new day.

Kaine woke to find Lara smiling down at him. The white gold pendant dangling from her neck caught the light and the little diamond shot multi-coloured daggers of refracted light into his eyes.

"Afternoon, sleepyhead," she said, smiling.

Lara leant closer, kissed him on the forehead, and backed away quickly before he had the chance to reach out and pull her into bed.

"Afternoon? What time is it?"

"Nearly three o'clock."

"What?" Bloody hell. He'd slept for thirteen hours straight.

Kaine pulled back the covers and sat up, then dropped them

again when he discovered he didn't have any clothes on. "I should have been up and out by now. How's Mike?"

She paused for a moment before answering.

"As comfortable as I can make him."

"I'll pop in to see him before I go."

"You're going out again? So soon. Why?"

"Will," he said, yawning and sucking in some much-needed air.

"What about Will?"

"He called when I was on my way here. He thinks he might have figured out a way through the Enderby conundrum."

"Why didn't you tell me last night? I'd have woken you earlier."

He winced and turned it into a grin.

"Last night, I had other things on my mind."

Her answering smile made his heart sing.

"Me too." She grabbed the pendant between finger and thumb and kissed it. "It's lovely. First real present you've ever given me."

"Rubbish," he said, raking his fingers through his overlong hair, brushing it away from his face. "What about that Glock I gave you in France?"

"That was hardly a present, Captain Kaine. So thank you. Again. I love the inscription." She backed further away and pointed to his bedside cabinet. "Drink your tea and turn on the radio. I think you'll find the news rather interesting."

"Tea?" Kaine turned and reached for the cup. By the time he'd taken his first sip and looked up, Lara had wafted silently from the room. He slapped the power button on the bedside alarm-radio.

"*...as I reported in the last bulletin,*" a reporter with an excited voice said, "*the Metropolitan Police have announced the arrest of four individuals in connection with the investigation into the death of retired jeweller, Abraham Pedersen.*

"*As you may remember, last Thursday afternoon, Mr Pedersen was shot twice through the chest while sitting on the front step of his house in Shoreditch, London. The shooting led to panic in the streets and fears of a terrorist incident. However, it has been confirmed that the three males and one female who are currently being questioned for the murder have no* known links to terrorism. As such, a terrorist motivation for the slaying has been discounted. In a shocking revelation, an unnamed police source told me that murder, conspiracy, and corruption charges are imminent. That word 'corruption' has led to speculation as to the identity of the suspects, but the police source would not be drawn on the matter.

"Interestingly, a second inside source has told me that despite their close proximity, the ram raid on Romilly Heart's Jewellery Emporium—which occurred earlier the same day—and Mr Pedersen's death are not related. Any association between Mr Pedersen's former career as a jeweller and the attempted violent robbery are understood to be purely coincidental.

"That being said, everyone wants to know the identity of the brave, have-a-go hero who single-handedly foiled the raid and saved hundreds of thousands of pounds worth of—"

Kaine slapped the power button on the radio. He'd heard more than enough hysterical hype for one day.

"Have-a-go hero, be damned."

At least DCI Spicer had turned out to be true to his word. As Kaine had hoped, he'd proved himself one of the good guys.

Kaine finished his tea, peeled back the covers again, and headed for the shower. Commander Gregory Enderby had languished on the back burner way too long.

The END.

THE DCI JONES SERIES

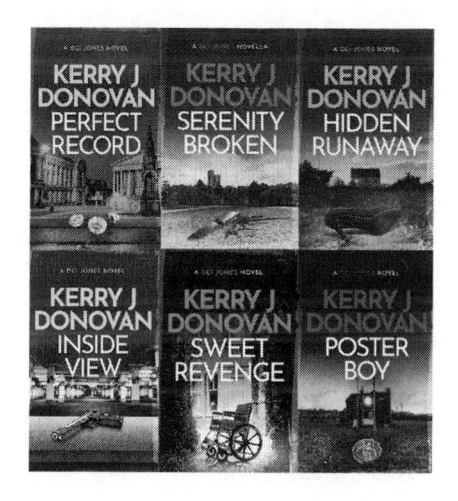

If you enjoyed Ryan Kaine, you may enjoy Kerry J. Donovan's fast paced detective series, DCI Jones.

fusebooks.com/dcijones

ABOUT KERRY J DONOVAN

#1 International Best-seller with *Ryan Kaine: On the Run*, Kerry was born in Dublin. He currently lives with Margaret in a bungalow in Nottinghamshire. He has three children and four grandchildren.

Kerry earned a first-class honours degree in Human Biology and has a PhD in Sport and Exercise Sciences. A former scientific advisor to The Office of the Deputy Prime Minister, he helped UK emergency first-responders prepare for chemical attacks in the wake of 9/11. He is also a former furniture designer/maker.

http://kerryjdonovan.com/

facebook X

Printed in Great Britain
by Amazon